William

Enjoy

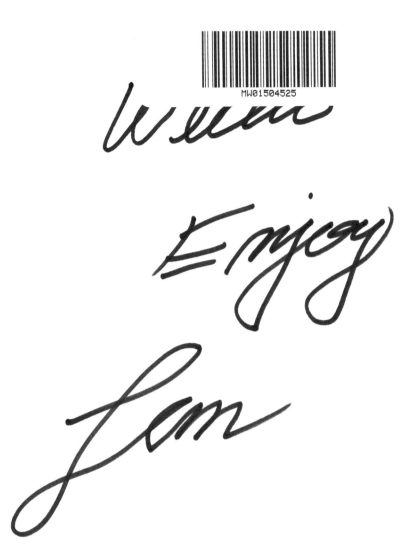

Sam

Other books by Lem Moyé

- *Statistical Reasoning in Medicine: The Intuitive P-Value Primer*
- *Difference Equations with Public Health Applications* (with Asha S. Kapadia)
- *Multiple Analyses in Clinical Trials: Fundamentals for Investigators*
- *Probability and Statistical Inference: Applications, Computations, and Solutions* (with Asha S. Kapadia and Wen Chan)
- *Statistical Monitoring of Clinical Trials: Fundamentals for Investigators*
- *Statistical Reasoning in Medicine: The Intuitive P-Value Primer—2nd Edition*
- *Face to Face with Katrina's Survivors: A First Responder's Tribute*
- *Elementary Bayesian Biostatistics*
- *Saving Grace—A Novel*
- *Weighing the Evidence: Duality, Set, and Measure Theory in Clinical Research*
- *Probability and Measure in Public Health*

# CATCHING COLD:
# VOL 1 - BREAKTHROUGH

Hearts must first break to strengthen
(A precovid-19 novel)

LEM MOYÉ

Order this book online at www.trafford.com
or email orders@trafford.com

Most Trafford titles are also available at major online book retailers.



CatchingCold@principalevidence.com

Print information available on the last page.

ISBN: 978-1-6987-0545-3 (sc)
ISBN: 978-1-6987-0547-7 (hc)
ISBN: 978-1-6987-0546-0 (e)

Library of Congress Control Number: 2021901316



*Trafford rev. 01/26/2021*

Trafford PUBLISHING www.trafford.com
**North America & international**
toll-free: 844-688-6899 (USA & Canada)
fax: 812 355 4082

# CONTENTS

To hold on to another, first hold on to yourself.

# A SINGLE SECOND

Scientists, isolated on their islands of intellect, blunder through the blinding fog of sex, affection, and acceptance.

On Monday, December 27, 2015, Dr. Jon DeLeon leapt into this haze for his Alora.

The thirty-nine-year-old ex-university scientist let the smartphone's display pull him into her picture, the one where her dark hair flowed like a river of redemption. He closed his eyes, smiling as she roamed through him, seeking out his dark passages—lighting them, cleansing them.

Forgiving him.

Two months after a six-year marriage crashed, he and Alora were still talking, still laughing, still teasing.

And here she was, calling him, their relationship flowing into new, deeper waters.

Tapping "Accept," he disconnected the reporter who'd been spewing empty queries about Jon's work into his ear like a hose sprays mist over baking summer pavement, the tiny question-droplets evaporating before they hit the hot surface.

"Alora," he said, his hands gripping the old Android tightly as if all at once, he was holding her the way that she loved, making her gasp, followed by that delicious double inhale. "I have an audience waiting out there for me, but I'd rather listen to you."

Her voice with its sweet hope landed, then glided up the abandoned road to the heart of the award-winning scientist.

"Well, guess what, Dr. DeLeon?" she asked, laughing into his ear. "Aaron and I were engaged today. And do you—"

"I—"

"Know what else? I'm having his baby. We are—"

The world went white hot.

At once, the professional in Jon took control. *That's my voice speaking,* he thought, *congratulating my ex-wife. Why, no,* his voice said, sounding more and more distant, *I had no idea you were close to anyone when is the date yes congratulations great news OK gotta go bye.*

Jon disconnected the call just as the swell of feelings knocked him off his mental feet. His mind, spinning both left and right at once, disoriented and subdued him, making him an easy target.

No time, the thin scientist thought as he dropped down onto the cold floor, jamming his back against the dirty wall of the dim church hallway. Head up, sandy brown hair drenched with sweat, he whimpered,

"Jesu—"

The second emotional blast wave slammed home.

Paroxysms of emotional pain surged. Eyes saw nothing. Jon's left ring and small fingers, instantly plugged into an electric-emotional circuit, went numb, the paralyzing voltage flying through them, severing the scientist from himself.

Adrift, the nationally recognized scientist writhed in emotional agony.

The disintegration took a single second.

# LIVING THE ROOM

"Jon? Jon? What's going on?"

The scientist's head snapped up to see Pastor Phil staring from across the hall.

Dressed in jeans, a white turtleneck, and a heavy black sweater open in the front, the short, fat man looked like a giant penguin, holding open the side door to the sanctuary for them both.

"What just happened to you? Are you OK?"

"Yeah, yeah. On the way, Phil."

Jon pushed himself off the wall. Grimacing, the scientist walked, one stiff leg after the other, across the darkened hallway into the sanctuary.

"You don't look good at all," Phil said, grabbing Jon's arm.

"I got a piece of bad news, s'all," Jon said, now holding his head up, looking at his friend.

"And that gave you this . . . this seizure or whatever that was?"

The scientist waved his right hand. "Yes, but it's passing."

"Look, I can pull the plug on this thing toni—"

"And if you do that, Phil, I will never be able to face lecturing again." Jon stood straighter, pulling his friend closer, heart racing. "It's my fight. Let me finish it." He looked in the minister's eyes. "Please, man."

Phil pulled back, and Jon took three short breaths, staring his friend in the face.

"I've not failed you yet, Pastor. And I won't tonight."

Phil stepped aside.

Jon was nowhere near ready.

He knew that, but the beast was out now. Either he or it would be destroyed. He was scared and determined, frightened and willful. He wanted, needed to sta—

"Good evening, everyone," Phil said from the stage, facing the audience. "We are thankful to have Dr. DeLeon talk with us tonight in our 2015 'Science Meets Religion' series."

Jon, standing a few feet from the pulpit to the left of the minister, jaw set, stared stiffly ahead.

His left hand and wrist began shaking. He moved them back around him.

"I have been to his talks before," Pastor continued, "and I can promise you it will be exciting."

Jon saw the pastor turn to him.

"Ready, Jon?"

Jon limped the few feet to the pulpit then looked up to face the crowd. Holding tight to the dusty, grainy pulpit with his right hand, the left now useless, Jon shivered, working to keep this head up.

The fear-bayonet slammed through his stomach, its hilt now jammed against his warm clammy skin.

The thought-attack assault was physical, his head quivering at the force of the emotional blows. Jon's concentration, a powerful presence just ten minutes before, was replaced by the roar of his racing pulse, rushing him to his breakdown.

"Good evening, ladies, and gentlemen . . ." he said, leaning over the pulpit, squinting as he searched his now slivered mind, fear-sliced beyond recognition, for the next sentence that should have been waiting for him.

*Just give up and sit down*, something inside him screamed, cleaving him from the common-cold lecture he'd planned to give to this Sunday evening.

What was he going to say? Sweat broke out on his forehead as he scanned the audience.

Muscles, now paralyzed, refused to exhale the stale gas in his lungs, forcing him to suck in a huge swallow of cold air.

In-in-in, he thought.

In, until his lungs threatened to break his chest open, bursting out into the room to proclaim their pain.

*You were never any good at lecturing*, his mind hurled.

*End this agony and go home,* smashed another thought. *Now!*

He swayed for a moment before the audience, the damning thoughts continuing their hammer blows.

"The cell, the human cell is defense . . . less," Jon's warbly voice uttered.

*Stop talking.*

He couldn't remember the sentence. How was he going to—

*Be the quitter you are and just quit!*

Show these people—

*Leave!*

What viruses did—

*Get out of here!*

To cells if he couldn't—

*Go. Leave. Now!*

Jon's chest muscles seized as the thoughts, like hard cold bricks, slammed into the scientist.

*And if you can't give this lecture to churchgoers,* the thoughts mocked, *how will you ever talk to scientists again about your work?*

A rivulet of sweat coursed down the small of his cold back.

He shook his head, clueless about the next sentence, and the near-weightless feeling of blood rushing out of his stomach to muscles that hung limp and unused told him relaxing was out of the question.

Closing his eyes, he exhaled hard.

How could he collapse like this, after so many years of solid presentations? The pulsing headache turned to beats of frustration.

Then indignation.

Anger.

He *would* face this reckoning, he thought.

Hot, merciless, ruthless rage.

He would not—could not—go to that defeat again.

He couldn't find the words. Fine.

They'd been stolen.

Make some more.

No.

Not words.

Actions.

Jon grunted, hoping it sounded like he was clearing his throat. Then raising an arm that appeared thick and alien, deformed by the heavy sweater encasing it, he pointed to the far corner of the church sanctuary behind the audience.

"Imagine," he said, "that this entire sanctuary is a single living cell, one among millions that live inside your nose."

Words.

Finally.

Way off the script, but not so far off the message.

He poured himself into his arm, keeping it up, like pointing to the distant, dirty ceiling was pointing the way to victory.

"Cells are very small," he said. "One needs a powerful microscope to see them. But let's pretend we're inside a living cell like we're inside this sanctuary, looking around."

He had no idea where this was going. A dark path for sure, but the only way out of Dodge.

The image came alive for him. He wanted to breathe but pushed the idea away, knowing the fear would race up for him like a confined fire that, once released, roars up into the open air like a living thing.

"Its membranes are the walls of this church, keeping the cell's contents inside, protecting them."

Don't stop, he thought. It didn't matter where this was going. His heart trip-hammered. He pursed his lips.

"Imagine that that's where we are now: inside the cell, floating in the cytoplasm, the cell's thick, liquid interior. We are observers immersed in the stuff of life. Surrounding us are the tiny structures that work to keep the cell alive so it can do its job—making protein, producing energy, repairing its membrane, ridding itself of waste."

Now.

He took a deep breath, sweet and cool. His chest tightened as his bronchial tree reacted to the cold air. Why couldn't I have pushed the attack off earlier? Why was it violent?

No time for that now.

"This is what the cell must do: absorb food, produce energy, communicate within itself in order . . ." Jon paused, then lowered and softened his voice, surprised at the words that tumbled out next.

"To live."

He saw a man to his right and then an older woman in a gray wool sweater front and center each stir as though each was finding room for themselves within the image Jon was painting for them.

The sweat was cold on his forehead. He took a chance, tried to speak again.

"You are in this cell. It's like a . . . a small community. Or a tiny home.

"And its function is to help take care of you, to warm the air you breathe through your nose, to make substances that protect the lining of your nose. It is the home of life, and it lives for you.

"But with all this activity of life going on, the cell doesn't realize that a stranger has come in, unannounced."

Keep it up.

"A very small stranger, to be sure."

One more.

"A particle consisting of a bit of weak acid surrounded by a smudge of protein."

Roll it, roll it, roll it.

"If the cell is this large room, then this protein speck is the size of a pebble. The cell didn't notice as the tiny invader punched though the living membrane to get inside. Why should it? The cell is so large, how can something so small be a threat? It's like a whale being threatened by a minnow."

Where the blazes did that sentence come from, Jon wondered, his love for the role of speaker starting to wash over him. He saw the cold and still audience staring back at him in the dim light. He wanted their imagination.

And he had it now.

He was breathing in rhythm now, feeling it, moving his ey—

No one focused on him. He whirled and saw Phil Larson standing. The minister, belly protruding over the top of his jeans, pointed to his watch.

"I'm sorry, folks," Pastor said. "I just learned that the National Weather Service has bumped the winter storm advisory to a storm warning, so I'm afraid we're going to have to end much earlier than we thought. Jon, I do apologize and thank you for your time tonight."

"I understand," Jon said, smiling as he shrugged his shoulders. Turning to the audience now twisting and turning at the news, he said "Thanks very much for coming out to hear a science talk in hard weather."

He acknowledged the applause with a wave of his hand as the people began milling about, talking with each other as they struggled back into their thick coats.

"Best science talk I ever started to hear," someone called to him in the front row.

"Thanks for that," Jon said, placing his warm hand on an unfamiliar coat-covered arm.

"It was short, but it was wonderful," Phil said, reaching a finger in between the buttons of his flannel shirt to scratch his belly. "I never liked biology, but then again, no one's ever made it come to life like you did."

"I enjoy the imagery too," Jon said, nodding with a smile as questions about his ex-wife and the lecture fragment, hot needles in cold butter, pierced his mind.

She was gone. Pregnant and—

"There's someone I'd like for you to meet," Phil said, moving his large body aside.

"Dr. DeLeon?"

An outstretched hand snaked from around Phil's right side, reaching for him. For a moment, Jon thought it was a third hand coming from Phil, birthed from the minister's large flank.

"Jess Emmit."

"Yes," Jon said, grabbing the hand, leading the short man around Phil out into the open. "How are you, sir?"

"I've been very interested in meeting you," Mr. Emmit said, coming into full view. "That was an amazing beginning to a talk that actually, I wasn't looking forward to." He scratched behind his right ear.

"It was the start of some fun," Jon said, still holding the shorter man's hand. "But I did make the virus out to be the bad guy."

"Yes," Jess said, standing a little straighter. "I'd say you pretty much demonized it."

"I shouldn't have," Jon said, letting his hand go. "The virus isn't trying to kill anything. In fact, it just wants to make more viruses. It has no interest in what eventually happens to the cell. But it disrupts too many of the cell's internal processes. It's the cell death that gets the virus into trouble."

Emmit squinted. "I don't get that."

"Suppose," Jon said, taking Emmitt's arm, pulling him closer while lowering his voice, "you want to sleep with another man's wife. She tells you he's gone for the day, so you go over, and she lets you in. When you're done, do you really turn around and burn their house down?"

The sentences had leapt out of Jon's mouth before he knew it. Holding his breath, he looked at Jess, studying his face for a reaction.

The short man looked at him, eyes wide open, not breathing for a moment, then roared with laughter.

"Great, I get it. The virus should have let the cell live."

"Not the best story for church—"

"I'll say. Still, it's a hoot."

Jon watched the investor look down. When he looked up again, it was with a new face—all business.

"OK, Dr. DeLeon," he said, drawing closer to the scientist. "What can I do for you?"

"Well," Jon said. "We're looking for donors for our organi—"

"Churches look for donors," Jess said, waving an arm at the parishioners heading for the doors. "Don't you mean investors?"

"CiliCold is doing well, but yes, we could use more financial support."

"What do we have in common?"

Jon felt like he was a bug being scrutinized, having its features catalogued and identified. His stomach jumped once.

*Cool it*, he told himself. *You've done this lots of times. Just finish it up.*

"I'm out on a frigid night, looking for support to wipe out an illness that afflicts us all but on which science has turned its back." Jon stopped talking, letting his eyes fix on those of his questioner.

*Be the hunter*, he thought.

Then Jon gave the name of the illness.

"Why?" Jess said, his head leaned back, his face tightened. "Most everyone else abandoned the search years ago."

"Not us."

Jess's smile stayed fixed, but Jon saw the investor's eyes harden. The temperature felt like it dropped ten degrees.

"Many people have tried what you are up to. And failed. Too many viruses, and they mutate at the drop of a hat."

"Not for CiliCold."

Jess cocked his head. "Why do you think that you can succeed?"

Jon took Jess by the arm and steered the shorter man away from the light and the crowd. "Because we've done it before."

Jess stopped in mid step, looking up at Jon as he pushed his glasses back up his nose.

"You mean—"

"Haven't you heard?" Jon said, filling his voice with incredulity. "Your reputation says that you follow the tech firms up here."

"Well, what—"

"Then you must come by."

"How about in two weeks?"

"How about in two hours?"

Jon saw light fill Jess's eyes. "I couldn't do that—"

Close him, Jon thought. "Tomorrow, then?"

"Sure. Early morning."

Jon steered them back to the crowd. "I think we can stay in business until then."

They shook hands.

"Tomorrow it is."

"You don't want to miss what we have discovered."

Jon let the shorter man leave first, Jess's long coat almost down to his ankles. Looks ridiculous, Jon thought, until the blast of frigid air from the open doors reminded him just how cold it was out there.

Jon turned and looked back into the room. The initial shock of the night as well as the numbness was now gone.

He knew though what was waiting for him once he left the church.

The heart hole. The abyss was wide open, pulling him, begging him, beseeching him to enter. Every place he put his mind, there it was. How do I not g—

"Going home now?"

Jon yanked himself back from the ledge at Phil's voice.

"Yeah. Yes, I think so."

"I was wondering how you were going to mix religion in with your talk on virology."

Jon smiled at his friend. "I planned to turn in over to you, Preach."

"Fat chance," the preacher responded, laughing. Then Jon noticed that the smile faded. "Listen, Jon. I hear things are over with you and Alora." At the mention of her name, the scientist's mouth stayed open. Frozen. Jon saw Phil's eyes soften, and he felt the minister's touch on his arm.

"Jon?"

"Yeah. Things are finished. She's, uh, traveling in a different orbit these days."

"Well—"

"Goodnight." Jon grabbed his heavy coat and turned to walk outside, all but knocking over a short girl in a thick gray coat and a huge warm-looking gray hat.

The hard wind's punch stole his breath as Jon opened the heavy metal door. He dropped his chin into the scarf wrapped tight about his neck.

An old enemy—so hated, but familiar—was back.

It was inside him, settled in like it had never left.

And as his feet crunched through the hardpack snow, now almost lavender in the fluorescent glow from the high parking lot lights, Jon realized that there was no place that he wanted to go.

# SHARDS

At 7:03 a.m., the early January wind tore at Breanna Vaughn, whipping her hair into a small anger-tornado that lashed her own face.

The thirty-year-old staggered, step by hard step through the crunching snow. Some steps were shallow, others deep, as she weaved along the apartment's outside wall to the circuit breaker box, the thin skin on her hands rubbed into coarse red flesh.

She cried out as a frozen sliver of dirty wood knifed into the palm of her right hand, an initial blood-jet hitting the freezing snow at her feet.

Squeezing her right hand into a ball and holding it up, Breanna aimed the flashlight with her left along the wall where she thought the breaker box would be, jabbed the flashlight's switch.

Nothing.

"Damn it," she said, hurling the plastic light to the ground. Wasn't Ethan supposed to remember to keep the batteries fresh for the winter?

He hadn't bothered—as usual.

Breanna tried to dismiss the thought about her husband, but it wouldn't move. It stuck there, an ugly, dirty fly caught in frozen sap, as her numb fingers pushed along the dark, snow-covered wall until they were stopped by what felt like a box.

Got it.

The wife shivered again, then squeezed the latch at the end of the box, not feeling the pressure on her fingers, just praying that her fingers did as she begged them to.

Nothing.

The latch, coated with thick dirty ice, wouldn't budge.

Should've brought a match, she thought.

Suddenly, her fist, fast and hard, crashed down on the stuck latch. It sprang open; ice shards launched through the air and onto her face.

Hurry now.

She felt for the breaker that wasn't aligned with the others.

Got it.

Breanna flipped it hard to the right, where it stayed.

Closing the door to retrace her steps, back up the alley to the front door, a roaring wind gust from behind hit her like a plank of wood, knocking her forward and down. Her left arm reflexively stretched out, its hand first hitting then breaking the thin crusty surface. Her body fell through into the sparkly, soft, cold powder underneath until her face smacked the dirty top layer of ice-snow.

Lying there for a moment, she took some breaths then pushed and staggered her way out of the drift. She pulled her coat tighter around her, then took one high step after the other, a child's giant-stepping game in the snow, until she had groped her way to the end of the alley and the front walkway.

Slipping on the bottom of three steps heading up to her front door, the wife pulled her way up the banister, barely feeling her frigid feet through the running shoes.

Opening the door, a quick icy wind ripped the handle out of her hands, swinging the door all the way around to slam into the outside wall behind it.

"Damn it, Breanna, you need to be more careful with that door," Ethan called down from the bathroom that was right up the inside stairs. "I can feel that blast of air from here." His pale face under light brown hair, the bottom of it white with shaving cream, appeared at the top of the stairs.

She turned to lock the door behind her, then heard the crying from the dining room.

"You've gone and woke Jackie now," Ethan said. "Don't you think that you'd better see to her?"

"Ethan, why the h—"

She choked it back. Better to get ready for the job interview than to get into another fight with him. Besides, the whimpering from the dining room told her that he had left Jackie, their two-year-old, alone.

Again.

She rushed to be with her baby, shoving all else out of her mind.

# A LITTLE FRUMP

An hour later, the wind-buffeted Toyota shimmied, and Breanna lifted her foot from the gas. The Corolla moved for a sickening two-second slide to the left, the tires finally yielding to gravity and dropping into the hard ice rut made by the long row of cars in front of her as she inched along Route 26 heading west toward West Lafayette.

She checked her watch: 8:10 a.m. 1/4/2016.

Breanna looked right as she crept by the Shenandoah Street entrance, passing a car stuck in a lane with its hood propped open. A knot of people stared down, examining the engine, their combined rising, frozen breaths looking like a hard-freeze cigarette fest.

Nausea. Out of nowhere.

She opened the door of the stopped car, vomiting into the frozen snow. She couldn't help but look down at the yellow, steaming remains of breakfast, its noxious odor drifting up as though it wasn't finished with her yet.

Pulling her head back in, Breanna slammed the door shut, closing her eyes to get her breathing under control. In a few seconds, the wave passed, and she shifted the car down into neutral, leaving her foot gently on the brake. Her head, now relaxed, leaned back as far as it would go on the headrest.

Her mind wandered as she sat through two light cycles of nonmoving traffic.

Suppose she got home tonight, and he wasn't there?

Where did that thought come from?

From nowhere. From everywhere.

Her right, gloved hand swept a strand of hair from her eye as she said, "Sis."

The phone rang three times.

"You hadn't called for a while."

"I know, Rita. I'm—"

"A bad morning?"

"Could've been worse." Breanna relaxed her hands' death grip on the steering wheel and closed her eyes, taking deep breaths.

"But bad enough," Rita said. "What did he do today?"

"Nothing to help, as usual. But more of nothing than usual."

Breanna heard her older sister laugh. "Is he still working?"

"Barely."

"How are you doing?"

"On the way for a job interview now."

"Another? How many interviews is this?"

*Who needs the third degree now?* she asked herself. Breanna tightened up, her breaths more shallow. "I don't know, Rita. Five? Seven? Three times? Who cares?"

She took a deep breath and held it for a bit. "Sorry. Anyway, this firm is desperate for an accountant."

"You need cheering up," Rita said with a laugh. "Want to reminisce some? I have the topic: old college days."

"Guess what I was doing this morning?" Breanna asked. She knew she had to fess up.

"What's that?"

Breanna opened her mouth but hesitated. Keeping her lips tight, she savored the sarcastic zeal they enjoyed so much, letting it envelop her like a thick, warm quilt. Rita was so upbeat this morning.

She knew that her next words would change that.

"Still there, Breanna?"

"Yeah. Counting lines this morning."

"And?"

Breanna sat quietly.

"Shit, Brea. Did you do the test right?"

"Yep. Plus I'm nauseous. That almost never happens unless—"

"You're preggers. OK . . . OK . . . all right, then. Between the two of us, you're the analytical one. But seriously, lose him."

"Well, now that—"

She jumped at the horn blaring behind her. Jerking her head up, she saw nothing but empty, icy road in the haze illuminated by the headlights. The traffic light was stale green.

"Sorry, Rita. Gotta go."

"Tell me soon."

"First I have to nail this job."

With bile on her breath and a makeup touchup required, Breanna parked behind a McDonald's just across the street from her destination.

Walking through the door from the frigid air into the warm restaurant, she slipped on a puddle of dirty water. At once, her right hand extended down to the floor, barely keeping her on her feet.

Another nauseous wave fluttered by, this one not landing. In a moment, she was upright, striding past the heavily bundled commuters waiting in line for scalding coffee.

She saw that the restroom was empty.

Thank goodness.

Standing in front of the mirror, the thirty-year-old took her thick wool coat off and stood with both arms outstretched on the narrow sink, head down, willing and praying that the urge to throw up would pass.

After a minute, she washed her mouth out with Listermint from the last small green bottle she carried in her purse, then studied herself carefully in the mirror.

Her loose below-the-knee dress didn't give away a single curve.

Frumpy, but a little frump isn't so bad for an accountant, she thought.

Breanna stared in the mirror, then hiccupped so hard it hurt.

Have to keep it tight for this interview.

She blinked twice then studied her face in the mirror.

The face staring back at her was a little on the pale side, but a touch of makeup could fix that. She went to work.

A minute later, stepping back, she studied the result.

Her hair, as always, was the star of the show.

Parted high above her left eyebrow, the thick hair fell in two slow cascades, shorter on the left than on the right. More spectrum than color, the broad strands, while white at the forehead, streaked themselves into gray close to her ears, than black as they extended, ending just above her shoulders.

This rainbow of white, black, and grays cradled her face, a face that was pale and perfect, with the brownest of eyes, angular jaw, and high cheekbones. An ex-lover had said that hers was a face created to be adored.

Had been nice with him, she remembered, until it wasn't.

Placing her coat over her arm in front of her, Breanna walked with small rapid steps through the cold noise of the serving area out onto the street.

The snow had stopped, and finally, sunlight was breaking through the thick clouds blanketing northern Indiana. Breanna stepped around the larger snow piles, then having made it to the street, dashed across, pausing every few steps to keep from falling in the snow-ice-salt mix.

Finally.

Shielding her eyes from the bright white sky and the snow whipped up by the hard north wind, she took a deep breath and walked through the door with the company name that was cut white and deep into the thick glass.

CiliCold

"Incoming!" announced a mechanical voice.

She whirled.

No one.

"Ms. Vaughn?"

# CILICOLD

To her left was an Asian woman about an inch taller than Breanna, with black hair cut just below her ears.

"Yes, I am Breanna Vaughn," she said.

The woman, wearing a white coat that extended down and beyond her knees walked closer to her, then closer still. The accountant was ready to step backward when suddenly the Asian woman stopped, looked Breanna squarely in her face, then after a slight bow of her head, held her right hand out.

"Nice to meet you," the greeter said in a soft voice. "I'll be interviewing you today. My name is Rayiko Snow."

Breanna missed her name, noticing instead the slight left lip droop.

Not too obvious, but not avoidable. Must be old, she thought. No evidence of embarrassment. Birth de—

Focus and speak.

"Hello. I thought I would be interviewed by Dr. DeLeon."

Breanna was talking too fast, and she knew it. She took a deep, slow and quiet breath, noting that this woman's gaze didn't waver from her face.

She wasn't waiting for the interview anymore, she realized.

It had just started.

"He'd planned to, but he thinks it's important that he be with the scientists as they design their next experiment."

Experiments? What kind of place was this, Breanna wondered. A new throbbing in her head came alive. "I'm sorry to ask you this, but how do you pronounce your name?"

"Ry-ee-ko."

"Thank you, Rayiko. Please call me Breanna." She smiled, both arms holding her purse that was dangling by its chain in front of her. "I would welcome a conversation with you, but will I need to come back to see Dr. DeLeon?"

Breanna noted Rayiko's silence as she guided her to an office to the left of the entryway. "I am hopeful that our discussion will be enough, Breanna. Plus," she saw Rayiko glance out of the window, "I'd hate to have you come back in this kind of weather. It's difficult getting around this time of the year."

"I'm not from Indiana," Breanna said, following her. "I wonder if I'll ever get used to these winters."

"I am not from here either," Rayiko said, smiling, "but the spring is gorgeous."

"You are so right, Rayiko. It's"—Breanna paused for a second—"metanoia."

Breanna saw Rayiko stop walking, then turn around. "What is that?"

"It's like, uh, spiritual rebirth," Breanna said, walking up to her.

Rayiko smiled, then pointed. "That, and more. Please have a seat."

"Thanks," Breanna said, sitting in the comfortable chair. Relieved to be off her feet, she looked around.

This didn't feel like an office, she thought.

Actually, it felt more like a hunting lodge without the stuffed animals.

Beyond Rayiko were two other huge chairs, one blue, the other brown, a few feet from each other, in front of a massive bookcase. A red-and-gold rug lay over a hard wood floor between the chairs. Breanna sat, noting that Rayiko took the other chair.

*She makes no noise when she moves,* Breanna thought. If there were no lights, nobody would know that Rayiko was even in the room.

"This looks like an old-style living area," Breanna said, sitting on the edge of the chair facing Rayiko.

"This used to be a three-story building full of apartments, plus a basement. We have high water needs here. It fits the bill."

"I bet the landlady was glad to get tenants," Breanna said, her eyes settling back on the interviewer.

Rayiko cocked her head, then smiled, nodding. "My compliments, Breanna. You did some checking."

Breanna nodded, concentrating on Rayiko's voice. No accent, but that wasn't uncommon in the Midwest. Yet it wasn't flat or rough or twangy. Clear. Airy.

"It took a little bit to get used to all of the rooms being scattered over the three floors," the delicate Asian woman said, opening her hands toward her, "but then again, how many bosses can offer each of their employees an office with a bathroom?"

Breanna smiled. "Of course. I didn't think of that." She leaned closer to her interviewer. "I knew that Dr. DeLeon was a scientist, but I don't know much more. In fact, I couldn't find very much on the Web about CiliCold. You make vaccines here, right?"

"Well," Rayiko said, putting her hands back in the lab coat's pockets, a new worry line appearing on her brow, "we produce vaccines here for some pharmaceutical companies, but"—she paused for a moment—"I think I'll let Dr. DeLeon tell you what else we do."

The smile was back and the worry line gone.

"What we could really use is some help with the books, now that Solana had to leave."

"Solana?"

"Yes. She was our accountant before she became ill." Rayiko paused for a moment. "Solana was great, but her rehabilitation has taken longer than any of us thought."

"An accident?"

"No." Rayiko looked down. "A very tough illness. Nobody anticipated it."

The worry line was there again.

"Would you like me to turn the heat up?"

"Thanks. I'll be fine in a moment," Breanna said. "Why did you ask me?"

Rayiko pointed down to Breanna's fingers tightly clasped in her lap.

"It's cold out there," Rayiko said.

Worry line disappeared.

"Would you like some coffee with me?"

Breanna's stomach rolled over.

"Maybe just some water?"

"Tea?"

"Perfect."

"Give me a couple of minutes, and we can both have a cup."

As Rayiko left, Breanna stood, took off her coat, and walked to the bookcase. Ignoring the books, she ran her left hand over a long empty spot on one of the shelves, right hand covering her stomach. The wood was brown with red. Maple? Smooth and textured, yet it didn't have the feel of hardwood. Could it just be pin—

"That was Dr. DeLeon's idea."

She turned, and there stood Rayiko holding one of two cups out to her.

"Thanks." Breanna accepted one, holding the steaming mug with both hands. "What was his idea?"

"The books," Rayiko walked over to the case, crossing the streaming sunlight. For a moment, Breanna thought she could see right through this diaphanous woman.

"He wanted everyone to bring their favorite book here to work. Not really to store, but to share."

Breanna looked back at the books, pursing her lips, then at Rayiko. "Kind of a comradery of readership?"

"Yes. To let one colleague read a cherished thing of another—very different, bordering on intimate. Another example was last month. Then, he asked that each of us contribute music to a playlist that plays in the background here."

Breanna wanted to ask why he did it, but let the thought pass. If she was hired, she might find out. If not, it wouldn't matter.

That last thought pricked some sadness.

She wanted to work here, regardless of what they did.

She bit back the impulse just to blurt that out.

"Rayiko," she turned, "I do like this place."

"Tell me, Breanna," Rayiko said, eyes fixed on her face again, "what book would you bring for us to learn about you?"

Breanna turned back to Rayiko and smiled. "Great interview question."

Rayiko smiled back.

"I have to warn you, Rayiko. It's nonfiction. You have any room for one of those?"

Rayiko nodded to the bookcase, and Breanna saw that she left her hands deep inside the lab coat's pockets.

"You may be surprised. There are a few nonfiction books up there. There's also a virology text and one on probability."

Breanna laughed, and she was pleased to see Rayiko join in. "Well, I won't be spending any time with those. Anyway," Breanna continued, moving a strand of hair from her right eye, "mine is *Alexander Hamilton*. It's by Ron Chernov."

"Biography?"

Feeling Rayiko's gaze, Breanna felt she was being searched for secrets by this delicate creature using quiet interest as her gentle interrogation tool.

"And why is that your favorite?"

"Hire me, and I may tell you."

They laughed, Breanna reaching out to touch Rayiko's arm for a moment.

"I can tell you, Rayiko, that his life was one of relentless struggle," Breanna said. "And he endured until close to the end. Then, he lost himself." After a moment, she added, "When he was no longer needed."

Breanna turned back to the bookcase, running her hands along the smooth wood. "Where did the company get this, Rayiko? It's magnificent."

"He did it. Took him five months of evenings."

"Five months of eve—"

"Three years ago. Dr. DeLeon worked from November through March on this wood. Each night, plus most weekends." Rayiko paused for a moment, and Breanna noted that the worry line was back.

"Jon explained that woodworking helped him keep his wits about him during the winters."

Breanna simply nodded, working to absorb this odd place

"Well," Rayiko said, motioning back to the chairs, the line gone. "Let's cont—"

They both turned to the new commotion behind them.

# WHALES

Jon whooshed through the CiliCold entrance, pushed by a stomach on acidic overdrive.

"Who was that, Robbie?" he asked, hustling by the desk of his exec sec while pointing to the two women in the small living room to the left.

"The applicant for accounting," she replied, standing as he approached. Trim, light brown hair to her shoulders, perfect skin, and dressed in a smart gray suit and pink blouse.

He stopped, pursing his lips. As the owner of CiliCold, he'd need to sign off on any new employee. Should he meet the applicant now?

Forget it. No time. He inhaled deeply.

"Rayiko will find me when it's time to talk the hiring talk," he said, smiling. He stepped closer to Robbie. "How was your holiday?"

"It was OK."

Smile that was too big under eyes that were too soft. Robbie could not hide her feelings.

"If you want to tell me, I'll listen to you. But whatever happened, Robbie, this is a new year. We get to forget the old ex—"

"What is that supposed to be?" The voice, thick with a nasal Latino accent, came from the kitchen. "I asked for sunny side. I can't tell if this is an egg or snot."

Ah, Jon thought. That would be Luiz.

Breakfast is served.

"Robbie, let's you and I talk later,"

"OK. Oh."

She reached for the ringing office phone with her left hand, sitting back down, but not before Jon tenderly squeezed her right. She looked up, flashing a smile his way.

Jon walked on to kitchen in the back—smallest in the apartment building.

No wonder Luiz and Dale get worked up in here.

But he also knew that space didn't matter to them. They cared for little else except viruses and immunity.

And not having money to conduct additional experiments, Jon thought.

That made them a little restless too, the owner remembered.

"Simple," Dale answered, potbelly bigger than ever. "If there's a napkin next to it, it's an egg. If there's a Kleenex, then it's snot."

Jon laughed and walked over to the table. "Hey, guys, welcome back from the New Year."

"El jefe, greetings." Luiz shoved the breakfast plate over to him, almost tipping it. "Ready to eat?" the short immunologist asked.

"Uh," Jon said, pushing the plate away. "I—and I'm sure that I speak for all *Homo sapiens*—will take a pass." He smiled at the short immunologist with his long hair.

Luiz chuckled and put the plate down on the small wooden table that rocked on its unequal aluminum legs. "See, Dale, I told you. You could be arrested for even calling this food, much less taking responsibility for it."

Dale pushed Luiz away, then sat with his head down, thick glasses close to the plate's contents. "Looks OK to me, stumpy."

"What it looks like is manslaughter." Luiz rested his hand on Dale's back, peering over his shoulder. "Maybe it's alive?"

"The question is whether we're alive," Dale said, turning around. "Hopefully, Jon, you have graced us with your presence to tell us that you landed a whale."

"Whale?" Luiz looked at Jon. "How could there be whales in Indiana? It's landlocked."

"Financial investor with serious ducats to throw our way," Dale said, putting the plate down and starting to stand.

Jon watched his colleague's belly, which had been resting on the tabletop, now stretch and sag to its full upright girth.

"Why don't you learn to speak American, Luiz?" Dale said, twisting his face into a sneer.

"I have a better idea. Why don't you name that gut?" Luiz said.

Dale patted his girth. "People would pay to see this baby."

Luiz threw his hands up. "This is what I work with every day."

Jon leaned against the refrigerator, laughing with his two scientists. "Looks like no whales in Indiana this week," he said, shaking his head.

"There aren't any whales," Dale said, wiping his nose with a dirty handkerchief, "because folks with serious coin know a few things, and one of them—"

"Here we go."

"Is that what we are attempting is impossible."

"You know," Luiz pointed a finger across the kitchen table at Dale, "half the time I don't think that you believe in what we're doing here."

Jon saw Dale's wrinkled hand pause in its habitual mop of his bald pate. "Don't tell me I don't believe in this project. I was working with EM micrographs when you were toddling around barefoot in Tijuana."

"Ease up, old-timer." Luiz smiled, peering down at the Android he'd been fooling with on the table. "The other half of the time, I don't believe that it's possible either."

"It's nothing to me." Jon pushed himself off the wall and away from the two virologists. "I don't believe anything you guys tell me anyway."

"Well, there you go," Dale laughed. "We can all go home."

"Sure we can," Luiz chimed in. "Broke. Here." He tossed the phone to Jon.

"You fixed it?" Jon caught it with his left hand, then twisted it around in the air, trying to catch a signal. "I really like this phone."

"Nope." Luiz tossed the headlight/magnifier he'd been wearing to look at the phone on the table. "Jon, this is 2016, and you have a circa-2010 phone."

"I love my S4."

"So do the antique electronics collectors."

"What you really need is an iPhone," Dale said, taking his out for his boss to see, "the phone of professionals. Oops."

Dale's iPhone fell, clattering on the yellow tile.

"Exhibit number 1," Luiz said, shaking his head as he pointed to the iPhone on the floor. "The unprofessional perspective from a nonexpert."

Jon picked the iPhone up, turning it over in his hands. "Looks like you cracked the screen protector."

Dale shrugged. "No prob. I get a new one every week."

"And I'll get a state-of-the-art iPhone," Jon said, slipping the broken S4 into his shirt pocket. "After you guys make us rich." Standing behind them, he patted each on their backs.

"If we had some ducats to run some experiments, we could—"

"I got money." Jon loved these moments.

Dale looked up, his chest flying forward like he'd just been shot in the back. Luiz turned toward Jon with open mouth.

"Don't get too excited." Jon scratched his neck. "Not a whale, just a big fish."

"Wonderful." Luiz rolled his eyes. "Now our boss is quoting Old Testament Jonah."

Dale stroked his chin. "The Book of Jonah actually says 'a great fish.'"

"What is this, virology or Sunday school?"

"You'd better hope that it's both, my young friend." Dale smacked the back of Luiz's head.

"And when you two wannabe scientists finish, uh, breakfast, maybe we can get back to work." Jon sat at the table. "Ready for one more rep, guys?"

Dale smacked his forehead. "Hot damn. Now you're talking. Luiz, can you set the stage for this next replication?"

The younger scientist pulled his lab coat on over his narrow shoulders. "No problem. Wanna go with a rhino?"

"Let's go with what we know." Jon looked from Dale to Luiz. "The adeno."

Both virologists looked at Jon.

Dale tilted his head. "The same one?"

"Yeah," Jon said, turning his back for a second, "and the same vaccine prep, OK?"

Jon turned seeing Dale look at Luiz, who silently nodded his head. "Look, Jon, this would be the fourth—"

"Uh, I need a moment with you."

Jon turned to see Rayiko standing in the hall just behind him. "I had no clue you were back there," he said, shaking his head. "How do you do that?"

"I work for an absent-minded scientist," she said, stepping toward him. "When you have a moment, Jon, you and I should probably discuss . . . things, including the new applicant."

When he nodded, Jon saw her turn and wave hello to the virologists.

"Hey, Rayiko."

"We have a job opening?" Dale asked, looking from Luiz to Jon to Rayiko. "Already we're hiring new people? How can we do that?"

"Sure we can," Jon said. "Don't you guys know that we need somebody to help us count the money we don't have?" Jon turned back to Rayiko. "Did we find someone?"

Jon saw only sensitive neutrality in her smile.

Sweet, but no answer. He enjoyed her presence but almost never wanted to talk about what she needed to discuss.

"Go ahead, Jon." Dale dried his hands. We'll hold off on rep discussion until you're done. Besides, I need a cigarette." He picked up his coat and headed down the hallway.

"You're gonna freakin' freeze out there, man," Luiz called after him.

"With a cigarette in my hand, I don't care."

Jon and Rayiko walked out of the kitchen, taking slow steps down the darker hallway, its narrow walls forcing them together.

All at once, Rayiko turned. "Interesting presentation at the church last month, wouldn't you say?"

# LABELLE 'EM

What she had heard? How could she have heard? Jon's pulse picked up. Of course.

He inhaled, then spoke slowly, trying to keep an even voice. "So you were there, huh?"

"I go to your lectures when they're nearby."

Rayiko looked up at him. "I'd never seen you present that way. It unnerved me, and just looking at the people sitting nearby, I wasn't the only one affected."

He said nothing, comforted as he always was by her presence, but still anxious to get away from a hard conversation.

She leaned in, eyes narrow. "You frightened people, Jon, especially just before you started talking about putting them inside the cell."

That Sunday's shock was alive and stirring inside him now. He bit his lower lip. Then he had an idea.

"I LaBelle'd them," he said.

"La what?" She tuned up her face.

"Ever hear of Patti LaBelle?"

Rayiko leaned back against the dark-green wall on the other side of the hall, arms folded. "Well, sure. She does those diabetes commercials."

Relieved at this conversation's new direction, Jon laughed, letting some of the tension flow out of him.

"Well, yes, but before that, she was a soul singer."

"She sang in church?"

"Maybe, but not what I'm talking about. She was an R-and-B performer—part of a group." He was relaxed now, immersed in the conversation that was flowing farther from that Sunday. "Her background singers were the Bluebelles."

Jon watched as she moved her left foot to the left while shifting her weight to the right, cocking her head to the right as well.

He laughed, now at ease with his program admin. "How you manage that stance is beyond me, but just hear me out, OK? Patti was the star of the show, but she was, uh, kind of a free spirit."

"Lots of rock stars are—"

"Not like this. In one performance she was late for the show—her own show that had already started without her—then burst onto the stage in mid song, throwing the timing of the other performers off. Other times she would start a song with the Bluebelles then stop in mid chorus and savage them for being off key."

"In front of the audience?" He watched her soften some, arms at her sides.

He nodded. "There were instances when she would rake the background band over the coals for not keeping up with her."

"Wha—"

"She'd even raged at the audience for not paying attention, all in the most outlandish clothing. She was—"

"Insane?"

"No, not insane." Jon leaned toward her. "Unpredictable. But she kept the audience involved. Gave them a real show, and in the end, everyone, emotionally spent, felt like they were part of the act as well."

Jon took a small step closer to her. "The fright was part of the act."

Watching new hardness pour into her face, he sank backward, sighing.

"Well, you weren't performing in some rock show, looking for someone to yell at," she said, arms crossed in front of her. "You were giving a talk to churchgoers in their sanctuary. They came to learn something about science, not be emotionally drained." She took a deep breath. "I've never seen you like that. It was disturbing, Jon."

She would not be deflected, he realized, exhaling. "Yeah. I got a phone call just before," he said, biting his lower lip. "It really threw me, and I had to find something, anything to jumpstart the lecture."

There.

The truth was out. He'd been a desperate man that night, lost and grappling. He sagged against the old wall, holding his breath, preparing his heart for the sad, sharp pain that she would deliver.

"Alora?"

He nodded.

"Of course it was. Nobody takes a can opener to you like she does."

"Yeah." He rubbed his left thumb and index finger together. Back and forth. Back and forth.

She reached up, placing a hand on his shoulder. "Your feelings aren't like icicles in the spring, melting away on their own. You have to face them. And I'm not going to lie—"

"I—" he said, his voice almost a whisper.

"About it. It's going to hurt you." After a moment, he added, "More than it has so far. You have to face them. Feel them. Maybe in the end, em—"

"You're right." He came off the wall. "Yes, right. But I need to concentrate now, especially when we are designing a new experiment." He checked his watch. "Hey, I'm late for Dale and Luiz. How about you and I catch up later at lunch?"

Jon watched her neutral reaction to his invitation, wondering what went through her mind. Why were things so complex with her? But he knew he was always better off with her nearby—light, airborne, out from under himself.

But maybe she was really upset about the LaBelle thing.

"Listen, Ray—"

"We have some things to go over. Sure."

He was pleased to see a smile flash across her face, brief but engaging, like the first warm sun in March, when you knew that winter was at long last on the run.

"Good deal."

"Back from your cancer break?"

"I'm good," Dale said. "Let's assume our positions." He and Luiz walked down to the basement, where the experiments were run.

Walking through the animal area to get the viral sample, Dale watched as the rhesus monkeys, each in their own special cage, rushed forward, little faces pressed against the tightly wired mesh, small paws outstretched as far as they could go. He loved their warm, moist, and musky smell. He knew the monkeys, smelling him and Luiz, were reacting expectantly.

"I know, I know, Bessie. But you've already eaten." Turning to his friend, he said, "Luiz. You measure the aliquot, and I'll isolate Gertie."

"Got it."

"You know," Luiz said, adjusting the setting on the auto pipette as Dale put the monkey in her isolation cage, "in this series of tests, the vaccine only worked one time, and that was the first time we tried it."

Dale thought carefully about his next words as they donned masks and gloves. He knew that they would churn his own already dangerously active stomach.

They blurted out on their own.

"You know what this is, don't you, Luiz?"

"Sure I do." Luiz was quiet for a moment as he finished adding the aliquot. "I've known all along. We are simply trying to replicate the one positive finding we ever had. And we are failing at that."

"And Jon is desperate to see that that single success we had is reproducible," he said, watching Luiz check the dilution.

"Haven't done it yet."

Dale locked the rhesus into the smaller cage by herself. "This is our fourth attempt. Every time, we give the proto-vaccine. Every time, we wait for three days. Every time, we give the virus."

"And every time, forty-eight hours later, viral particle loads go through the shingles and the monkey sickens. Another failure for Jon. And us."

"Roof. They go through the roof. Damn it, Luiz. How long you been in this country?"

"Not long enough to get a gut like that. You know, if you cut that big thing off, if would probably live on its own. We could call it Dale 2.0."

"Whatever." Dale took the inhaler and walked over to the rhesus, who turned her pink and curious face to him.

"She sure looks happy to me," Dale said, preparing the aerosolizer.

"You two would make a great pair. You know," Luiz said, after a deep breath, "I think the first experiment was a fluke."

Dale turned to look at him. "You don't think that result was real?"

Luiz drew the strings, tightening his own mask. "There was no doubt that once the vaccine was given, and then the virus was loaded two days later, the rhesus' viral particle count stayed near zero. Something good happened. I'm just saying it wasn't the vaccine."

"We need to find out why that one worked." Dale turned to the rhesus in the case right in front of him. "Hey, Gertie. I just need you to take a sniff of ADN-102A."

The young female responded to Dale's voice, and with a happy, short twitter, put her face up against the wire. Dale seized the back of her head, squeezing hard on the aerosolizer, jetting a fine virus-laden mist up the monkey's nose.

Gertie yelped, then scooted to the far end of the cage where she sneezed twice then looked up at him.

No anger in those eyes, Dale thought, just a mixture of question and pain.

What betrayal first feels like, he thought, putting his face close to the cage.

"Oh, c'mon, Gertie. You know I don't mean you no harm." Dale reached into the right pocket of his coat and pulled out a large marshmallow, holding it with two fingers, moving the white fluffy mound back and forth against the cage.

In a flash, the young rhesus was back. Gertie held her paws below his hands, and when she was set, Dale let the meal fall into them. She stayed there, burying her face in the delicious treat.

"When did she get the vaccine?" Dale asked, rubbing the monkey's head as she enjoyed her reward.

"Five days ago, *ese*. Per protocol."

"First blood draw for antibodies?"

"Baseline draw is today."

"Well," Dale said, giving her head a final scratch, "let's see if my girl comes down with the sniffles."

# SELF-SMILES

"We didn't have to meet for lunch, Jon. It would have been OK for us to meet at the office," Rayiko said, fighting to keep her face neutral. She really did enjoy this restaurant. It was quiet, open, and the minimal overhead incandescence didn't intrude on the natural light streaming in through the tall windows. It left nothing to shadow, illuminating all in silvers and grays.

But why did he have to be so extravagant, she wondered, pushing her hands down hard into her lap. She knew that the company wasn't paying for it—the lunch was on his dime. But this was for work, and when it came to CiliCold, she was more comfortable working in the background than being at Christos New City Grill with her boss.

"Sure, we could have," he said, "but we don't get out much with the weather and my schedule. Plus, you are my project administrator, my right arm at CiliCold. The only way I know to show my appreciation"—he looked down for a minute, then back up—"is to, well, show it."

"Besides," he continued, now smiling, "we need to catch up on things in a place where we won't be so interrupt driven." He scooted his chair closer to their table. "OK, what do you need to tell me about Bre—"

"And what would you like to start with?" the waitress, who looked to Rayiko like she was fourteen, asked.

Rayiko smiled, watching Jon, hands up in the air, laugh.

So very odd, she thought, that this man who wrapped his arms and legs around self—

"Well, OK," he said shaking his head, "almost no interruptions."

They gave their drink orders.

"So you think Breanna is a winner?" He placed the napkin in his lap.

"Breanna's got self-confidence backed by real competence."

"References?"

"From reputable groups and solid."

"But you know . . ." Jon said, looking away for a moment, then leaning across the table. "CiliCold can be a, well, a quirky place to work."

"How do you mean?"

"We follow the rules most times, but we do go off-road some too. I think it really started to push Solana's buttons, right up until her attack. Well, you know the rest." He paused for a moment then said, "You think Breanna can manage it? Oops."

He swept his hand across the front of his sweater, completely missing the beads of Coke that he spilled.

"Solana's stroke wasn't due to CiliCold work," she said, sipping her Sprite. "I hear the whole thing is tied up in court. But Breanna is different."

"How so?" Jon cocked his head.

"Not only does she not mind quirk, I think she likes it."

"Well, there's an oxymoron for you," he said. "Anything else?"

"She told me she was pregnant."

He shrugged. "Probably doesn't matter. We'll be lucky to be in business nine months from now."

She smiled to herself, keeping her face neutral—a self-smile. "You have to sign off on her, but I think she'll be a good fit."

Rayiko watched him as he rocked his head gently left then right, then she sat back as the waitress placed their menus in front of them.

"OK, let's go with her. Oh," he said, looking up at the waitress. "How about the rigatoni with sausage and peppers?" He looked up. "You?"

"One slice of the house special pizza."

"Great choice," Jon and the waitress said together. Rayiko smiled as they laughed.

The waitress took the menus and left, leaving them with their drinks.

"I've been too busy and haven't kept up with you," he said." He paused for a second. "That's my fault. How are things?"

"I am fine."

"Ah," he said, leaning closer, "my laconic project admin. I would ask 'What would I do without you?' but we both know the answer to that, don't we? Tell me, how are Richard and Gary? Oh, thank you," he said, the waitress placing their entrées in front of them.

"Richard is doing fine." She swallowed her first bite of thin crust. "He just got a second promotion in database architecture. Now he is interviewing at the new Subaru plant out on 52." Not so sure about

Richard, she thought. His ambition was growing. So far there was still enough room in the house for it, but—

"Wow. I admire his drive. And your son?"

She smiled despite herself. "Gary is a three-year-old mess."

"I'm not sure the world will be ready for Gary, but he'll sure be ready for it." He paused, then lowered his voice for a moment. "Your brother?"

She said nothing, hoping they could eat in silence for a few minutes as she collected her thoughts. She cared for her brother, cared for that smart man dearly. Her only sibling, he snatched up the family computing skill gene set—PhD in computer sciences at Stanford, then advanced systems design at Cisco. But . . .

After another moment, she put her fork down, then said, "He is struggling some." She took a deep breath, trying hard to find words that seemed strewn like belongings across a turbulent sea. "He was doing well since his first rehab, but now . . ." She shook her head. "He's missing work again, not taking care of himself. Disheveled. Unshaven. Makes all the money in the world—"

"Yet never has any."

She saw Jon looking closely at her, sucking his lower lip. Then he said, "Even the best rehab programs have dismal track records. I know he means a lot to you. What do you want to do?"

"Well," she said, letting the waitress take their plates, "he won't listen when I talk to him about it. Actually," she said, tapping her fingers on the table, "I can't talk much at all about it." She looked down, then felt his hand on her right arm.

"Then we won't," he said in soft tones. "How are your parents?"

"Still divorced."

"Yesssss," he said, smiling as he removed his hand and leaned back. "I think that you told me a couple of years ago that your mom was from Korea—no. Japan, right?"

He remembered. A self-smile. "Yes, and my dad, Beom, is Korean."

"Where are they?"

"She is in LA with my brother. That's where my information comes from about him. My dad's on the east coast, maybe New York."

"Well . . ." he trailed off.

She was pleased. Most people said, "Your parents couldn't get any farther apart on this continent, could they?" or some such insipid joke. She was sick of that. And although Jon couldn't have known how she felt about it, still, he chose to be quiet.

"Divorce is always a sad thing," he said after a bit, nodding, "but you know, they created someone wonderful in you. That I should benefit from that overwhelms me."

She watched him take a deep breath.

"OK. So where are we with CiliCold money, now that you are turning the financial reins over to our 'quirky' accountant?"

She smiled. "We haven't crashed and burned, but . . . well, we have leaves on our wings," she said, brushing at a crumb on the table in front of her. "I need you to look at a spreadsheet tomorrow though. By the way, didn't you talk with someone after Sunday's lecture?"

"Sure did, his name was . . . was . . ."

She watched him think for a minute, He closed his eyes tight as he wiped his hand across his right eye over and over. She knew after all of this time that he wasn't in pain. He was just trying to coax the memory back as if he could rub—

"Jess," he said. "Yes, Jess." Suddenly, he looked relaxed like he was relieved that his memory hadn't failed him. "I followed up with him for a visit, but he couldn't come by. Must have been impressed though. His foundation dropped five K on us. Here." He reached behind him in his coat to pull out the check.

"Maybe he liked the LaBelle thing?" she said, taking the money. She studied it for a moment, then placed it in her small purse.

He shrugged. "Begging for money is easy. Getting them to actually sign on the line that is dotted is tough."

"You work hard, Jon."

"And I won't stop."

"I know you won't. But you should let our group know why you won't, especially Robbie."

"Saw her this morning," he said, nodding slowly. "She looked on edge. I'll talk with her soon."

"Soon?" She shook her head. "You should talk with her sooner than that."

"OK. Oh," he said, looking at his watch. "We need to skin out." He waved for the check and put cash down.

"I have one final question for you," he said, smiling as they stood up and picked up their coats.

She was curious. He wasn't playful much anymore—probably tired. She looked up at him.

"What can I do for you, Rayiko? I can't ensure your comfort at CiliCold if I don't know what you need."

"Such a silly question," she said, pulling her coat over her shoulders.

She started to laugh, then pulled it back. She knew that to most people, laughs were easy, throwaway things. But to her, a laugh was opening a secret, revealing a corner of her soul.

"Seriously," he said, touching her sleeve. "What do I need to know about you?"

She turned and looked up into his face. "That you'll never figure me out."

"Of course I won't." He leaned closer. "All special women have their secrets."

"Let's head back," she said, self-smiling.

# CONNECTED

"I can do, uh, 8:30 a.m. Would that be all right?"

Jon held his breath after his question. So much of the future rode on this. Without secondhand equipment, CiliCold had no chance of meeting its goals.

"We can have the equipment out for you to inspect by then. Today's Tuesday, right?"

Jon closed his eyes and exhaled. "Yep. The 5th."

"OK, come by this morning. Hope you can find what you need."

"Your department is a godsend for us," Jon said, shaking his fist in triumph. "Thanks for taking my call."

He hung up and, for the first time since he arrived at work at 5:00 a.m., savored the taste of victory. If Purdue could provide mint-condition equipment in the collection of surplus machines from the university today, he reflected, CiliCold could update on the cheap.

That would make Dale and Luiz very happy, he thought, turning back to his desktop, using the mouse to sweep aside the whining and whistling apps from the display. Burrowing down through the electronic layers that fought back as each new email pushed its client to the forefront, he finally ferreted out the Excel budget workbook Rayiko sent him yesterday.

Jon zoned in, letting himself be pulled into the logic of the budget. The markings in the worksheet transformed from black pixels on a grid to numbers, and then into friends. He listened to what they told him about the budget issue, absorbing their love language. After a few more moments of careful attention, probing, and pleadings, the solution to the budget problem willingly surrendered itself to him. He only needed to make—

"Dr. DeLeon? I . . . I knocked but you didn't look up."

Robbie stood at the door.

Trim, dark jacket covering a bright white blouse over a dark-gray skirt, cut stylishly just above her knees, the thirty-two-year-old blonde looked like she just walked in from a board meeting.

Yet irritation seized him. Her entry was the first disruption in a day—like all days—that would be chock full of interruptions, fracturing his concentration, keeping him from his real work. He breathed slowly and evenly, careful not to betray how angry, how resentful he was of a universe that gave him requisite skills, but denied him the requisite time to wield them. Whose idea of an existence was t—

But as she came closer, he saw that her brave smile and wide eyes transmitted not concern, but fright.

Jon took a moment to clear his throat, losing the swallow of irritation that his attitude had brewed up for him. Swinging the monitor with its budget display out of his way, he stood.

"Come on over, Robbie," he said, waving her to a chair on the opposite side of the scratched-up desk. He walked around the desk to take the hard wooden chair next to her. "You warm enough?"

"Sure."

He noticed that her legs were wrapped around each other, her hands pressed down tight and hard in her lap.

"I know that you sometimes come in before most everyone else," Jon said, "but this is early even for you. So, Exec Sec, what's up?" He saw that the new worry lines around her green eyes were immune to his smile.

"Dr. DeLeon, I wouldn't have bothered you," she said, shifting in her seat, looking down in her lap, "but, well, I wanted to talk about my job."

"OK," Jon said, taking a deep breath. Why was she so concerned about her job performance, he wondered. She'd had them before, and they were never a problem. He leaned his head down to try to catch her eyes, but they were glued to her lap.

Strange.

"Robbie, I haven't yet reviewed your performance assessment with Rayi—"

"No," she said, turning to look at him now, eyes red. "Not my performance evaluation. My job. Whether I get to keep it."

There it was. Robbie hadn't finished college, he knew, but she was no dummy.

She understood there was trouble with money at the company.

He kept his gaze off those eyes as he considered just mollifying her.

No.

There was real fear in her.

He decided.

"Robbie, let's you and I just talk this through. What have you heard?"

"Well," she said, eyes in her lap again, fingers pulling at some hidden tissue, "Dale was talking down in, I guess, the main kitchen, about . . . well, you know the kind of things that he says. 'One failure after another,' 'This is going nowhere,' things like that."

He smiled at her. "Sure sounds like him, Robbie. But wh—"

She twisted toward him, placing both hands on the right arm of her chair. "Dr. DeLeon, if this company fails and I lose my job, then in this market, it's over for me." She moved both hands to her eyes that were overflowing with tears. "You know that I'm divorced. I'm barely holding on with my baby now, and if this comp—"

"Robbie." He stood, and she followed, now standing, facing him. He stepped toward her, holding his arms out, looking into her eyes. She took a step to him, and he gently embraced her.

She cried it out on his shoulders for a few moments. Then she said, "Dr. DeLeon, I am just so afraid. I don't want to go on welfare."

"Robbie, Robbie," he whispered into her right ear, her head on his shoulder. "How long have you worked with me? Don't you know that I wouldn't let that happen to you? You have been so loyal to me. I would give my salary for you. Don't you know that, sweetheart? I will not let you down."

They held on to each other for a moment more, then released.

"You and I will solve this now," he said, guiding her back to her chair. "But first, how old is Shannon?"

"Oh." She wiped her eyes with the ragged tissue. "She just turned three."

He kept his eyes on her. "Not a bad age to be."

"Maybe not for her, but it's hell on me." She laughed, then coughed into her Kleenex.

He shook his head. "Maybe, but don't forget that I've seen you with her." He cradled his chin in his hand, still looking at her. "Remember the July $4^{th}$ party?"

"Yeah. I brought her then." She dropped her eyes.

"And other times too, right?"

"Yep."

"Tell me something, please?" he asked, noticing that her sniffling had ceased.

She looked at him, the tears now stopped. "If I can."

"Today's not the first time that you've been concerned about CiliCold, is it?"

"No."

"I don't know what babies know about worry," he said. "But Shannon seems to have none of it when she's with you. You never let your concerns get in the way of your relationship with her." He sat up straighter, wagging his finger at her with a smile. "Lots of moms can't do that."

"I hadn't heard that from anyone, Dr. DeLeon." Robbie said, putting her wet Kleenex away.

"Well, it's true. I know she's a blessing for you. I see that in your eyes every day. But—"

"Yes, Dr. DeLeon?"

"You are a blessing for her as well."

They let the moment pass in silence. Jon was tempted to hold her hand but put the thought aside.

"Robbie, Dale's pretty brusque," he said. "Listening to him talk sometimes makes me wonder if I will lose my own job, but"—he held her eyes with his—"I know better. About my job. And about yours."

She turned from him to put her elbows on the desk, placing her hands on her eyes, the tears now flowing again.

"Robbie." He put his hand on her right wrist. "It's OK for you to be concerned. That's why you're here now.

But also be assured. The company is in good shape. You will keep your job. And you'll get paid."

He paused for a moment, then continued, "I am not going to fire you or furlough you or lay you off. Let's you and I just take a moment to think about that. You are going to continue to be paid here. You will be fine."

She sobbed for a few moments more. He let his hand rest on her wrist.

"Better now?" he asked.

"I am. Yes. Thank you."

"You have a job, and so do I."

She looked up, and he saw that her eye shadow was smeared. "Then why does Dale talk that way?" she asked.

"Dale is Dale." Jon removed his hand, stood up, and walked back around the desk to his chair. "He's good at this technical work, but sometimes acts like he knows everything about the company. I really like him, but he can be an irritant. Here."

"He's a pest, all right." Robbie laughed, taking his handkerchief, wiping her eyes again.

"I won't tell you not to listen to him, but if he ever makes you doubtful about your job, you come see me, and we'll fix it."

"OK," she said. He saw a real smile break through and cross her face.

"OK. Enough about him." He rubbed his hands back and forth across each other. "Robbie, let me tell you something. What we are doing here requires that we fail."

She crossed her legs and put her hands in her lap. "How's that?"

He turned in his chair to face her. "We're on a good path here. But paths to success are built from the broken concrete of failure. They have to be, right?" He paused for a second, holding his hands out to her. "The best way forward is not clear, so we stumble as we try to find it. If everything was already worked out, then—"

"We'd have the answer," she added, her knee jumping as she tapped her foot against the floor.

"And the cure would be clear to us all."

She cocked her head. "Then how do you know that we'll find it?"

"Great question, Robbie."

He turned to face her, his heart quickening. When he had first interviewed her for a job four years before, she had exclaimed, "I'm not a scientist, Dr. DeLeon, but nobody will work harder for you than me." He took a chance, and he was bowled over by her energy, her will to be excellent.

The other department secretaries put their hours in. Robbie put her life in.

When she had nothing to do, he'd spied her retyping papers of his that were already published, just to get the used to the special word processing character set.

They had worked together now for four years, one at the university, then after staying behind when he left to start CiliCold, she rejoined him six months later.

That was before Shannon, and before Robbie's divorce.

He tapped his upper lip with his finger a few times. "Let me ask you, do you believe you will always be a good mom to Shannon?"

New determination rushed into her eyes, filling her voice. "I think so."

"How do you know?"

"I'll make mistakes," she said, head high. "I already have. But they were honest mistakes, and I learn from them." Robbie paused for a moment, licking her lips. Then, "My Shannon will learn from them as well. We will make it because . . ." She stopped and looked at the ceiling, then turned to him. "Because we have to. We need to. There's no other choice."

Jon saw her lip tighten. Eyes dry. Fierce.

During that bitter divorce time, he discovered that she was an open book to him. Genuine, asking him primal questions about her life, she trusted him for guidance, for companionship, and for solace. And while he felt a heated rush sometimes, her perfume in his head, blood rushing through his ears, he never caressed or held her in a hot embrace.

That fire would destroy their relationship, he knew. So while he commonly felt its heat, he refused to hold on to it.

Jealousy's blush had burned off months earlier, and he doted on her now, listening to her stories as men (and one woman) entered and left her life. She came in on weekends, to keep up with the unending correspondence and email and database work, entering information, generating reports. To keep babysitting costs down, she sometimes brought Shannon in tow.

Everyone at CiliCold knew her struggles and cared about her.

She was family.

"I know that about you, Robbie. I think there is nothing that you feel stronger about than that." He leaned across the desk to her. "That's what I believe about CiliCold. We will find a way to make it work."

She looked at him, and he absorbed the fight in her, the determination that had convinced him three years before that she was the exec sec he need—

The solution jumped at him.

"You and I are pledged to each other, Robbie," he said, still leaning over the desk. "You will make it work with Shannon. I will do the same with CiliCold. C'mon. Stand up with me, now."

He stood and came around the desk to face her. She stood about a foot from him—no touching, eyes burning into eyes.

"So, Robbie, I'll do two things now to express my commitment to you. The first is to give you a 400-dollar-a-month raise, beginning now."

She put her hand up to him at once. "No. Dr. DeLeon, I didn't come here to ask for more money. I just wanted to know—"

"You wanted to know if this company could make it through this tough time." He took her hands in his. "This is a commitment this company makes to you, Robbie. Do you accept it?"

"Yes, I do, Dr. DeLeon."

"Second," he said, still holding her hands, "you have my pledge that, should I see trouble coming that we can't survive, I will come to you directly. You and I will talk as we are talking now. You'll know what I know, and you will have the maximum time to plan."

"Uh-huh." She was breathing faster now.

"So unless you hear from me, Robbie, don't worry about CiliCold money. Every check that you receive will be a new sign of the company's and my commitment to you."

"Deal." She took a deep breath and exhaled slowly. Jon could feel the tension drain away from her. He let go.

"Does this mean we're engaged?' he asked with a smile.

"Dr. DeLeon," she said, blushing.

"Get scootin'," he said, smiling. "See you in the lobby in twenty minutes."

His phone rang and she turned to leave, whirling away from him, her long blond hair created a swooshing golden arc behind her. Robbie was nothing but class. Such a dresser. He imagined the delight of not having the dress in the way, but pushed the thought aside.

Robbie dedicated herself to CiliCold, he reminded himself. She now needed reassurance that the company would be there for her. She needed to rely on him with no qualifications, to be able to rest on his promises.

That he would give her. That was all that mattered.

He picked up the phone, then stopped, the phone halfway to his ear. "Robbie."

She turned to face him.

"Our experiments will fail. But we won't."

"Do you know that?"

"I know it, Robbie."

"Then answer your phone, boss." She gave him a smile that stayed with him after she left his office, the smile that only younger women own and bestow.

He looked down at the S4.

Disconnected.

I'm going to have to get this fixed.

But like so many other things that needed fixing (cars, teeth, shoes, home computer, his baby birds screeching for worms nibblets), he knew they would need to wait for the right time.

And time was going by. He jumped up, then headed toward and out of his office door, coat half on.

He stampeded into Rayiko.

"Oh! Sorry. I shouldn't always be in a mad dash," he said, holding her arm to make sure she didn't fall backward from their collision.

"Oh," was all that she said. Rayiko's poise amazed him. She looked perfectly unperturbed, even when startled. "Where are you dashing to so early?"

"Over to Purdue, where they're auctioning some surplus equipment of theirs." He removed his hand from her arm and finished putting his coat on.

"What a thoughtful idea for gifts, Jon, with Valentine's Day just a month away."

They smiled at each other.

"I'll look for a surplus gas chromatography machine for you to give to Richard," he said, smiling. "No man should be without one."

"Thanks much, but I've already taken care of my husband for Valentine's Day."

"Well then, Rayiko," he said, with a serious face and laughing eyes, "I guess the intriguing question is what did he ask me to get for you from the auction?"

She shook her head. "Hmm, I know him better than that. You'll be gone all day?"

"The morning for sure. Don't know about the afternoon yet."

Rayiko leaned toward him. "You talk to Robbie this morning?"

"Yes. She's going with me." He drew closer to his program admin. "She's afraid that we'll fold."

"I thought so," she said, also drawing closer. "I encouraged her to come in a little early to speak with you."

Of course Rayiko did, he thought. She always knew. He marveled for a second over this ability of hers. Like the sky, seeing all, but itself invisible.

"I think she's better now," Jon said. "For a while, anyway."

He knew that she knew better than to ask what he had told Robbie.

"Jon." She cocked her head. "She's not the only one who's concerned."

They looked at each other. "Time for a town hall?"

She shrugged. "It could make a difference."

"OK. I'll ask Robbie to set it up for later this week. Wednesday?"

"Sounds good." She stepped out of his way.

"I'm outta here."

"You should meet Breanna later."

"I will. Promise. First, Robbie and I will snatch some free equipment."

"Make it count."

# FULL-BLOWN ILLNESS

"Dale, Luiz," Jon called down to the basement as he and Robbie placed the equipment on the kitchen table ninety minutes later.

A moment later, the two scientists trudged up from the basement in dead silence. No banter. Trouble was brewing. Jon blinked, fighting sleep's imperative to keep his eyes closed.

"Let me know what you think," Jon started, "about this donation from the univer—"

"Say, that's a SKU T720C-TP." Dale pushed past Luiz to approach the instrument. "Compound microscope with LCD screen."

"Not just that," Luiz said, standing opposite Dale on the other side of the new equipment. "It's got an illuminator and a 2500× magnification. Say, Jon, this isn't bad."

"Keepers, Jon?"

"Robbie brought us good luck," Jon said, unbuttoning his coat, "and yes, Dale, it's ours now."

"You mean mine," Luiz said, reaching for the plug.

"Get in line, amigo," Dale answered, depositing himself on the seat in front of the microscope.

"Well, Robbie, let's get back to work and let these boys have at their new toy."

"OK, Dr. DeLeon."

Jon let Robbie walk past him to her office, and Jon turned to the right, under the staircase to get to his office.

"Uh, Jon?"

He whirled.

Luiz.

"Thought you might want to hear about the last experiment."

Jon looked at him, frozen feet forgotten, his dripping coat halfway down his sleeves. "Tell me."

"Like the other four reps. The rhesus has the full-blown illness."

"Thanks, Luiz," Jon exhaled, then closed his eyes. They weren't even close to a solution. "Guess we'd better come up with a new plan."

"You're the boss. Also . . ." Luiz looked down, then back up at him.

"Yeah?" With no reproducibility, Jon knew they had nothing.

"Alora. Well, we heard about her taking up with—"

Jon put his hand on Luiz's shoulder, patting it twice, then after a pause, once more. He turned from the immunologist and walked into his office, closing the door behind him, biting his right hand to control his sobs.

# STOP BY FROM TIME TO TIME

Next morning, Breanna peered through the cigarette smoke, eyes wide open, hands on her hips.

"Did you hear me, Ethan?"

She heard a sneeze, saw his arm move up, pause, then elbow swing back and forth across his body. She didn't have to see to know what her husband had done: picked his nose, studied the dig, then wiped it on his T-shirt.

Suddenly, her stomach rolled over, ready to heave. Jumping up, she ran from the breakfast table, just making it to the small downstairs bathroom in time.

Five minutes later, she walked back to see the newspaper still there, Ethan still behind it.

"What's going on with you and that vomiting shit?" he said, flipping the page.

She thought hard. Did he have a right to know? But life was terrible with him. Maybe she should have an abor—

"Well," he said, turning the page, "you just gonna sit there?"

"Must have been breakfast. I'm fine now."

"Good."

The hell with him, she thought. "Are you going to tell me what happened at work?"

"Nothing to tell," the voice from behind the paper said. "Not my fault at all."

Breanna ignored the breakfast before her, sitting at the kitchen table in her slacks and bra, letting the flakes wilt in the skim milk. Inside, she quaked. Fear, rage—they mixed and swilled inside, threatening to take her voice, to drive her actions.

She closed her eyes, calming herself. Just get through the morning, she thought.

"Ethan," she said slowly, picking up a spoon to navigate the seaweed-like flakes through the thin milk-fluid, "we moved here from Terre Haute for this position for you," she said, staring across her cereal. "My dad set the job up for you. You've only been at it for six months."

"Well, what do you want me to do?" the newspaper voice said. "It's, you know, cutbacks. Student enrollment's down, and they have to slice into the faculty. Guess it's just temporary."

Then after a pause, he said, "Not really sure."

"Well, Ethan, since we need your money, how about a conversation? For example, how much longer will you be working?" She knew money would be OK with them both working. The rent was fair. Her car was paid. But now . . .

Ethan put the paper down for a second. She saw that he hadn't shaved. In fact, he hadn't shaved for a few days.

"Couple of weeks."

"Are you going to the college today?"

"Well, I got some sick time coming, and I'm not feeling all that hot, so I thought I'd just, you know, sit it out at home today."

Breanna turned her head. What a sluggard. She bit her lower lip, then said, "You watch the baby." The statement just shot out of her mouth like a rock right to and through the newspaper.

He turned the page of the paper. "Why don't you just take her to a child care place? I'm not into watching her today. Besides, we wouldn't want Jackie to catch anything."

Like your damn laziness, she thought. Her head pounded.

Move on, she commanded herself. "Well, did the university let David go?"

"Ramirez? Davey? No. Guess they didn't. Hmmm," he said, moving the newspaper back into place in front of his face.

"Well, he was hired after you, so why do you think they kept him?"

"Hispanic." The newspaper shrugged. "That's all I can think of."

"If they knew you were this stupid, Ethan, they would never have hired you."

And I wouldn't have married you, she thought.

She watched the newspaper come down.

Good. Bring it.

"What did—"

"David works hard. You don't. He teaches the large service classes, over seventy students in one of them—at least that's what you told me. Plus, he teaches during the summer. You never offered to do that, did you?"

"Well, it wasn't part of my contract, was it?" He was back behind the paper.

She lifted her right hand, ready to heave the hot coffee cup and its steaming contents right into the middle of his paper. Instead, she balled her small hand into a tight fist and placed it in her lap.

"When's your last check?"

"'Bout three weeks from now, I guess."

"When are you going to start looking for another job?"

Breanna jumped at the sudden hard crunch of the newspaper as he crumpled it. "When you stop bugging me, woman—that's when. Damn. I gotta sit here and listen to this?"

"No," she said, leaning forward. "Heaven forbid that you actually have to do something you don't want to do. But you know what? Now you gotta figure out how we're going to pay for this apartment, our cars, and take care of Jackie while you're out of a job."

"Just relax, Breanna. You're always so uptight about money. I can go to my parents for some money, and you can go to yours. We'll get by until things settle down."

"They're already settling down, right into the toilet. And you can forget about me going to my parents. The point is—"

"The point is, I don't want to hear from you.

The paper suddenly shifted at the new noise. "Hear that, Breanna? Now you've gone and woke Jackie."

Brenna stood up to go upstairs. The baby stopped for a moment, and with the shred of control that still held her together, she turned and faced him. "Ethan, get it together."

He whirled in the chair to face her. "Oh, so now you're my boss. Well, I'll tell you what, girl. You go to your boss and get a raise out of him. Then you can come back and tell me about what a lousy worker I am."

He slammed his fist on the table, sending the milk carton flying up into the air to splat against the wall. "I've brought money home, Breanna, every single week. And if I need to stop for a bit, well, there's worse things than us having to do without for a little while. Like I told you, we'll get by."

Ethan's look was hard, wild, touching on hatred. No way the baby was staying here, she thought.

"I'll get the baby," she said, turning from him and walking to the living room.

"You do that," he called after her. "And then get your ass to work. We need to rely on you for a while now."

The force of the conversation plus the rage in his voice scared her. She dressed the baby, then herself, and took the baby outside. After placing Jackie in the car seat, she sat behind the steering wheel, her body twisted to the left, feet in the snow.

And she cried.

She could fight Ethan, she could fight her morning sickness, she could fight the budget. But she couldn't fight the universe. Not alone. She cried until the tears along with her energy were sapped. All that remained was her nausea.

And Jackie.

She was wrong, she thought. She wasn't by herself.

"Thanks for the help, God," she said, as she stroked Jackie's cheek, then turned around to start her drive out. "Feel free to stop by from time to time."

# A NEW SHERIFF

Two hours later, Breanna stood up from her desk at CiliCold, ceaselessly rubbing at the hard knot in her neck.

One week at this job and she was pissed off already.

*What is it with these folks?* she wondered for the fifth time that morning, pushing away from the display with its dizzying array of Excel workbooks. She took the legal pad that rested in her lap and threw it on the floor.

Breanna looked down at it for a moment, then picked it back up and threw it on the desk. Pregnancy was really getting to her, she thought.

That, and Ethan the Asshole.

She shook her head. The accounting here really was a mess. For example, why did they need so many supplies? She didn't recognize the names of half of this equipment, and from what she saw on the Net, you didn't need it to manufacture standard vaccines.

Exhaling, she walked across the creaky floor to the windows looking out on nothing but an old frozen brick wall ten feet away. The wind whipped the snow through the narrow alley, in tight swirls resembling baby white tornadoes. Putting both hands to her head, she tried to think this place through again.

Everybody was so busy here. Dr. DeLeon, whom she hadn't even met yet, was pulled in a million directions—meetings, fundraisers. Whenever she got a glance of him, in a hallway, he seemed so earnest, no-nonsense.

Except with Rayiko, who was busy with her own work managing—what?

Vaccine management? Unlikely. Breanna shook her head, clueless.

And the other scientists, Luiz and Dale. Not only did they stay in the lab most of the day, but there wasn't an evening when one or the other wasn't working after she left.

But working on what?

Even Robbie was busy. Rarely did Breanna hear her on the phone in a private conversation. There were always calls to catch or make, emails to manage, or data to enter.

Or bills to bring her.

Bills.

Sighing, Breanna walked back to her desk.

A lease for a DNA sequencing machine. Oh sure, she thought. You really need one of those to make a vaccine. They had two. And how about the analyzer?

These costs ran into the tens of thousands of dollars per year.

Breanna closed her eyes and stood still, believing she could actually feel the old house shake as the gray sky's winds whipped around it.

And the animal bills. Why did they need monkeys?

In fact, the CiliCold vaccine production rate was paltry—enough to let the company meet its payday obligations, but little more.

So, she asked herself, squelching a belch, what was the one-sentence description of the problem?

Biomolecular equipment and animal expenses were threatening the CiliCold bank.

OK.

It was time she learned just where the company that she worked for was putting its main effort.

She turned around, moving a wisp of hair out of her eye. Rayiko had told her that she needed to construct a financial plan, but Breanna knew that if you don't know the business, well . . .

She pursed her lips for a second, trying to remember who'd told her that. Long time ago. Her first real job after school? No. Earlier, sometime in col—

Marshall.

It had been Marshall.

She tap-tapped her brow as if she could thump the thought away. But it fought back, and the advice had been good, so she let it have its way with her for a few seconds. Then she strode back to the desk, scooped up her laptop, and headed down to the first-floor kitchen where the action was.

She arrived and saw only Luiz sitting there.

Good.

Luiz always seemed civil, and everybody said he knew his stuff—whatever that was.

She entered and he looked up.

"We don't see you in our neck of the woods often," Luiz said, sitting at the beat-up, stained kitchen table, as he peered into a notebook that, to Breanna, bulged with scribbled pages.

She sat across from him on one of the rickety wooden chairs. It scraped hard against the old tile floor as she scooted it closer to the table.

"Hi, Luiz. I actually have some questions that I hope you might answer for me."

"No hablo inglés, señora bonita," he said, his voice light with a new singsong lilt.

She laughed. He was a kid in a forty-year-old body, she thought, on the short side, hair down to his shoulders. Dale, on the other hand, could be formidable—like playing chess against someone who was both good and didn't like you. She would really need to bear down to deal with that guy.

"I just want to ask you about your work with viruses."

"Don't ask me. That's Dale's bag. Mine's the B cell."

No way I'm letting him off that easy, she thought, putting her laptop on the table. "But you're both involved in the virology that goes on here, right? At least, that's what Rayiko told me."

"It's complicated." He shrugged. "We're both working on the same thing though."

"Well, that's great, because," she thought for a moment, pushing away her main question. She would just nibble around the edges for starts. "I have a few questions about some invoices."

"Happy to oblige if I can." She watched him stroll to the coffee pot. "How about some coffee on yet one more frozen day? You're in luck. Dale made this brew."

"All the mornings are frozen here. Thanks, I'll take one." She didn't drink coffee much, but this frigid morning, she would take a chance on anything hot, despite her nausea.

"What can I do for you?" he said, returning with a cup for each of them.

"Well," Breanna began, scooting the chair around so he could view the HP's display when he sat back down, She navigated through the PDF invoices. "Here. Look at this one."

Luiz sat down, then put the pencil he'd been using behind his ear. His notebook rested on the table. He picked it up, closed it, then took the biggest rubber band she had ever seen and wrapped it around the bulging composition book. He did this carefully, she thought, almost tenderly, like he was saying "au revoir" to an old friend. Then he turned his attention to the laptop display, following her finger with his eyes to the line item.

"Yep, this is a machine that we needed."

"Really? It's a lease for a microarray analyzer."

"Well, we sure use it." Luiz turned to her.

"Why do you need that for making vaccines?"

"OK, OK." He smiled, pushing back from the table. "Vaccine production is how we pay our bills, but it's not where Dale's and my major effort go."

Progress, she thought. She leaned forward. "And what exactly is it that you do?"

The high-pitched voice from behind her said, "I could tell you, but I'd have to kill you."

Breanna jumped.

"Well, look who's here," Luiz said, smiling and clapping his hands. "When did you get in, Wild Bill?"

"Snow in Indy delayed our arrival by thirty minutes. Once we landed and I got north of 465, I made decent time." Breanna twisted around to see, bumping her HP close to the edge of the table. She reached to keep it from falling to the floor.

"Man, it's always colder up here. Good catch, whoever you are," the stranger said to her, the snow on his pants melting onto the floor.

"Let me make introductions," Luiz said, waving his hand in the newcomer's direction. "Breanna, meet William Cantrell, known to the civilized world as Wild Bill, the only funky regulator on the planet."

"Regulator?" Breanna asked. Who the heck was this freakin' guy, she wondered. She looked up into a slender face with brown eyes, clear complexion, and a small mouth. Thinning, straight, jet-black hair swept down across his forehead to thick black sideburns that extended all the way down to his jawbones.

Wearing a long-sleeved white shirt, thin black tie no thicker than a razor, black pants, and slip-on shoes, he looked like he was right out of a 1950s engineering school, even though she pegged his age at about thirty-five. She thought that he had everything but a pocket protector.

"I said 'funky regulator,'" Luiz corrected her. "Most of the regulators are tight-lipped and full of themselves—half bankers, half lawyers, acting like the essential grease that runs the research world. But not ole Wild Bill. Say, man, where do you keep your slide rule in that outfit?"

"That's classified," he said, pushing a stick of gum into his mouth.

Breanna smiled despite herself, doing what she could to sit on a giggle.

"Breanna's our accountant," Luis said, walking over to the sink. "Guess Jon thought we needed somebody to help keep us honest. Sharp as a tack. She was about to corner me on what we really do. So—"

"Which is?" She turned to Luiz, who poured the cold coffee down the drain.

"How was DC, Wild Bill?" Luiz asked.

"Great. You could actually look down and see pavement. Not just dirty ice."

"Wild Bill," Luiz said, turning to Breanna, "keeps us in good with the feds."

Breanna wrinkled her forehead. "I don't understand. Why does the FBI care what we do?"

Wild Bill laughed. To Breanna, it sounded like a soft, high-pitched yelp. "Not the FBI—the FDA." He yelp-laughed again, shoulders loose, both hands forward spinning imaginary six shooters. "There's a new sheriff in town, little lady."

Breanna laughed with him.

"Seriously," he said, "neither the FBI nor the FDA are paying much attention to us these days. My main work is to deal with the animal people."

"And just who are they?" Breanna asked. "Do we pay them too?"

"The federales that monitor animal experiments," Wild Bill said, sitting down, shoving another piece of gum into his mouth. "And no, ma'am, we don't pay them."

Breanna looked up, making a face at the white ceiling with its incandescent bulbs. She really enjoyed these folks, but their insiders' language was maddening. She looked over to Luiz. "But we're just making vaccines, right? Why do we need to experiment with animals—"

"Expensive animals too," Luiz said, hand cupping his chin as he shook his head. Then in a quieter voice, he added, "And not always good results."

"Hello? Guys?" Breanna looked to Luiz, then Wild Bill. "Will someone tell me what we are talking about?"

Wild Bill looked at Luiz, who tuned away.

"What's wrong, Luiz?" Wild Bill said, pointing to the scientist. "Did Dale get to you too?"

"Of course Dale did."

Breanna watched all heads turn as Dale strolled into the kitchen. Legal pad in his left hand that hung down by his side, right hand in his lab pocket, belly protruding.

Thank God men don't get pregnant, she thought. They're way too ugly.

He threw the pad onto the table, where it skidded, stopping when it hit Breanna's laptop.

"Dale got to him because Dale's argument is right," the fat scientist intoned.

"O ye of little faith," Wild Bill said, smiling, scooted his chair around to face him.

"Faith my hairy ass. Oh," Dale looked over to Breanna, shrugging a brief apology her way. "Sorry."

"Ah, yes. Breanna," Wild Bill said, leaning over to her, pointing to the bald scientist, "that was one of the many solemn quotes from the Book of Dale." He laughed then looked back at Dale. "All eminently ignoble and ignorable."

Dale, waving a hand in Wild Bill's direction, sat down across from Luiz. "Did you tell Jon, ese?"

"Yep."

"Another negative test?" Bill asked.

Breanna saw that Wild Bill was no longer laughing.

"How many does this make?"

"Four," both Dale and Luiz said at once.

Breanna looked from one to the other. "Negative for what?"

Dale pulled a cigarette from his shirt pocket and matches from his jeans. He paused, absorbing the looks from the three of them. "OK, OK. Damn it, I can't help it if I love these sticks."

He passed the cigarette under his nose, inhaling deeply, then put it back in his pocket. "I've been up all night, so you'll have to forgive my pushiness." He exhaled. "The first finding was a fluke. Maybe it was the reagent mix or the wrong viral dilution, but whatever it was, it wasn't a durable finding."

"But it did happen," Luiz said, now looking intently at Dale. "We don't know why, but we know we inactivated the virus. That monkey was given the vaccine, then the virus. Forty-eight hours later, no viral load. That, my friend, is a fact."

"So this is just about vaccines?" Breanna asked. She put her questions aside, now wanting to just be part of the conversation. "You're saying that what we make doesn't wo—"

"It's also a fact," Dale said, eyes narrowing, "that we cannot reproduce that result. What good is it if we can't repeat it?"

"Guys," Wild Bill said, walking over to, then lazily leaning against the wall under the fluorescent light, "we have the money and we have a finding. Seems like it's worth puzzling through this some more before we call it quits."

"Well," Dale said, putting his hand on Luiz's shoulder, "the economics haven't changed."

"I'll say," Wild Bill added, scratching his hair with rapid back-and-forth motions so fast that Breanna thought he was trying to set it on fire. "Infections are an expensive problem. We drop almost three billion dollars per year on over-the-counter medications, plus another four hundred million on prescription meds. And that's just this country."

Luiz peered into his coffee cup. "Where the hell do you get these figs, WB?"

"Just my job, baby."

Luiz laughed as Breanna's stomach rolled over on itself and she looked away.

"Anyway, does Jon know about this failure?" the regular asked.

"Yep," Luiz said, adding some creamer to his cup. He turned to Wild Bill. "Have you heard that—"

"Yeah," Bill said.

Breanna noticed the sudden change in his voice: lower, the humor gone.

"Alora's got the Web on fire with the news," the regulator said, then made a harsh sound that Breanna swore was a horse snort.

"Everybody knows?" Dale said, turning to look at all the faces in the room. "Jeez."

"Is that real sympathy coming from you, Dale?" Luiz asked, turning to face Dale, back against the sink.

"Actually, yeah. I damn sure have never been where he is."

"Well, he's going to need your help, Bill," Luiz said, lowering his voice.

"Yeah," Dale looking over at Bill, who was fingering his tie. "You gotta go talk to him, Wild Bill. I go head to head with Jon on science, but this shit . . . goodness."

"You know how he is on this," Luiz added, Breanna barely able to hear him.

Breanna watched Wild Bill open his mouth to say something, then close it. He studied the tabletop, then answered, "Yeah, yeah, yeah. I'll go see him."

Dale and Luiz got up to leave. To Breanna, the pair could not leave the kitchen fast enough.

"Where are you guys going?"

"Back to work."

"And my questions?"

Breanna watched Dale look at Luiz, who walked back over to her. Dale turned and left.

"We're actually not the best ones to answer them." Luiz said. She could barely hear him.

"Then who?"

"Better speak to the boss," he said. "But . . ." They both turned to watch Wild Bill saunter out of the kitchen, making the right turn under the stairs, heading for Jon's office.

"Let's give him some time first, OK?" Luiz patted Breanna's shoulder, then left her alone in the kitchen.

# HIGH MARKS

"Home again, sailor?" Jon asked. "Home from the seas?"

Bill had heard more oomph from a dead South Carolina dog than from his friend's voice. "The one and only." WB had just entered his friend's office. No lights. The only illumination available came through the windows, the gray hues lighting his troubled friend's left side.

The regulator walked up on one of the two chairs on the opposite side of the desk, and pulled a Wild Bill, lifting his leg over the back of one to sit.

Jon smiled. "And how are the good folks at the FDA treating us?"

Bill paused, halfway down to the seat. "They're ignoring us."

Jon was silent. Then he said, "And that's because . . ."

"We're not making much progress, so they're not showing must interest, but, Jon . . ." Wild Bill said, getting up. He strolled over to the door to close it completely, then returned to do another Wild Bill on the chair. "That's not why I'm here."

"You know?" Jon said.

"Yeah," Bill replied a moment later. "Pretty much everybody on the planet does. Damn Facebook and Instagram."

"She called me just before my Sunday night lecture, and well . . ." Jon began moving his right index finger in figure eights on the battered wooden desktop.

Wild Bill froze, a new stick of gum halfway to his mouth. "Just before the lecture?"

"Yeah."

"Did you give the talk?" Then, after only a moment, Bill said, "Yeah, of course you did." Bill shifted in the seat, his pulse quickening. "What'd she say?"

"Well, she was pretty pleased. Wanted me to congratulate her. You know . . . to be happy for her."

"Are you?"

"I think so."

Bill noticed Jon was staring hard at his desk.

"You've been divorced for, what, six months, Jon? And during that time, you've shown her that you wanted to rekindle, right? To get back together with her?"

"Well, I don't know—"

"I'm a kidder, remember, Jon? Don't kid me. You give her extra money. You talk to her two or three times a week. You're available when she's having a bad time."

"Sure, I di—"

"You lent her your car when hers was broken. Jeez, Jon, you're playing husband. What are you going to do next, Romeo, sing of your enduring love under her balcony?" Bill rubbed his forehead like he was trying to eradicate a stain.

"I wouldn't put it that—"

Bill's pulse raced. *Have to push him through it,* he thought.

"I get how tender this is for you, Jon. But we have to get you on the other side of this. So tell me," he continued, "Did Alora appreciate this post-divorce attention you've been giving her?"

"You know, Bill," Jon said, looking toward the window, "I think sometimes that she—"

"Well, let's look at this." Bill brought his leg down off the chair arm. "She showed her appreciation by going out with a colleague of yours, boffing him until she was pregnant, and then bragging to you about it, saying that you should be glad. Am I hearing this right? And didn't you know this guy Aaron? From the university?"

Bill's jaws tightened as he said that, and he pulled out another stick of gum.

"Yeah, yeah, yeah. OK, Bill, I hear you, but she has the right—"

"Yep. Sure she does. Just like a man has the right to walk into a DC crowded subway car, and shout, "Damn. Look at all these skanks."

They stared at each other. Then burst out laughing.

"Where do you come up with this stuff, Bill?"

"Dunno, man. But, I'm not talking about *right,* Jon. I'm talking about *smart.* Let me ask you." Bill took a deep breath, then lowered his voice. "Would you ever do what she did to you to anybody?"

"Don't know what you mean?"

Bill drew his fist into a ball. "Jon, do I need to spell it out? Would you break up with a girlfriend you were very close to, then drift back together with her while you were fucking someone else, getting them pregnant, and then tell your ex-girlfriend that she should be happy for you?"

"No."

"Why not?"

"I'd care about her feelings."

"Hey, Jon." Wild Bill leaned forward. "You haven't been keeping up with current events, man. People don't give a damn for others' feelings. They think inconsideration's just fine." He shrugged. "In fact, they always have."

He saw that Jon was about to speak and put his own hands up. "You expect others to be the way that you are and that, my friend, brings on a world of hurt, just like what you've got now. By the way," Bill said, pointing to Jon's left arm, "what's going on with that?"

Jon looked at his wrist. "Don't know. Whenever I get, you know, emotional, my two fingers go numb. It's an ulnar nerve thing. Small and ring finger. Bad days, it goes up my arm."

Bill sat up. "Any chest pressure or pain? Nausea or vomiting? Pain in your neck or jaw? How about sw—"

Jon put his hands out. "No, Bill. I read the same things you do. No sweating either. And it's not brought on by exertion."

"Just emotional gymnastics, huh?" Bill pushed his glasses back up his nose. "Not cardiac?"

"Just feelings."

"The mind suffers, and the body cries out."

Jon looked up at Bill. "Yeah, I suppose something like that. Who said that?"

"Cardinal Lamberto. *Godfather III.*"

Jon rolled his eyes. "Goodness, Bill."

"That was about diabetes, I think," Bill said, scooting the chair back, "but I think I'd rather have diabetes than what you've got. At least there's treatment for that. Patti LaBelle told me last night on a commercial."

He saw his boss start to get up, then slouch back into the deep chair.

"You always struggle when somebody doesn't rise to your marks. Jon, your standards are the problem."

"I should lower them?"

Bill puffed his mouth out, blowing his breath in a huff. "Lower them, hell. Get rid of them. Disconnect."

"I don't know how."

Bill leaned back in his chair, arms wrapped behind his head, and closed his eyes. "Jon, that's the first thing you said to me that I understand." He leaned forward, hands out, and in a soft voice, said. "Expect nothing from people, Jon."

"Well, I—"

Bill snapped his fingers. "Let's do something tonight. It's been too long."

"No, thanks. I've got—"

"Not anymore you don't." Rising from the chair, Bill dismissed his friend's agenda with a wave of his hand. "We're going out with some real women."

"I know you like—"

Bill turned to face him. "Damn straight I do. And so will you."

# PASSING BETWEEN WORLDS

By 12:50 p.m., Jon knew he should eat lunch but wasn't hungry. Hunger had walked out on him, he thought, like a lover who was past anger and had simply given up.

He turned right, hustling down the short hall with the single incandescent lamp, then right again to bound into his office.

His left foot lifted then landed on the first step and looking straight ahead, he saw through the black iron bars between the steps the door to the far apartment rooms.

It was open.

Accounting.

Jon paused in mid step. He hadn't been down that way since the new accountant arrived.

Rayiko would be on my case about this lapse, he thought. Plus, he knew he needed to tell someone about his adjustment to Robbie's salary.

He winced. The usual culprits of his headache, dehydration and insomnia, were coming out to play, and they just weren't fooling around today. He blinked a few times, but no luck.

Turning around, he walked back down the hall to accounting, entering what used to be a bedroom. The bedroom furniture was gone, replaced with a huge beat-up wooden desk, well beyond needing refinishing, and two matching, scarred-up chairs. Pushing the large creaky brown door open fully, he turned to the left, where the room expanded about twenty feet over to two windows that opened out onto a dirty red-brick building on the other side of the small alley.

Seeing nobody, he turned to leave, then paused.

I always liked this room, he thought.

Maybe it was the odd mix of overhead incandescent lights combined with the fluorescent desk lighting that gave the room with its beige walls a warm glow. Walking through, he felt less like he was entering a room, and more like he was passing between worlds. It felt electrifying, kind of magnetic.

Turning to walk out, he saw a woman who could not have been over five foot three inches tall walk in and drop a thick pile of folders on the desk about six feet in front of him. She coughed. Through his fatigue, Jon saw that this short woman in a black pantsuit had a clear, pale complexion and . . .

Hair.

Hair that swept right and forward from the back of her head down across her forehead, just over her right eye, continuing down in rolling synchronous crescents to splash onto her ear. His weariness retreated at the sight of hair that was not salt and pepper, but a living rainbow in shades of gray.

"Hi."

She was looking up at him, talking to him. He squared his shoulders, trying to clear his head.

"Yes. Hello. We haven't met. I'm J—Dr. DeLeon. Rayiko told me that you'd be here, and I needed to meet you. Also," he dropped his eyes for a moment, "I have a situation that I would like your help with." It was a struggle to keep his eyes focused on her face and away from her hair, alive with streams of color that flowed as she tilted her head to him.

"Hi, I'm Breanna. Breanna Vaughn."

They shook hands, Breanna looking up at him. How tiny her hand is, Jon thought. It fit so nicely within his. His head throbbed for a minute.

He hesitated, and the professional's rectitude rushed in to fill the gap.

"It's nice to meet you, Breanna, but I've gotten myself into a bind." He swallowed. "And I'm afraid that it will cause more work for you." He laid out the new arrangement he had made with Robbie.

"That's another forty eight hundred dollars a year that we need to find," she said, taking a seat behind her desk.

Her manner had changed, he thought. It was a little clipped. He cleared this throat. "Do you think we can—"

"Bet you also didn't consider the fringe, did you?"

"No," he said, unsure of what to do with his hands. "You're right."

"Well, that's what I'm here to do." A hint of a smile appeared at the corners of her lips.

"It couldn't come at a worse time, I know," Jon said, moving over to sit in a chair to the left of the desk. "The company's pretty strapped for cash."

"Don't I know it." She looked full into his face, eyes narrowing. "So why did you agree to this?"

Jon shrank back a bit.

"We need Robbie," he said. He thought for a moment, pursing his lips. "And she needs us."

"Well, I have to tell you, Jon," she said, her right index finger rubbing her angular jaw, "I've been all over these sheets and I don't see how this is going to happen. I can go over it with you if you like, but . . ." Her voice trailed off as her head leaned closer to the display and she began typing.

At once, a solution, swept through his mind. "I know how we can do this," he said, drumming his fingers on the desk.

"Get the money? From where?" she said, focused on the large monitor. The experiments are—"

"From me."

"What?" He saw her fingers lift from the keyboard.

"We'll take it from my salary."

He watched her sit up straight while turning to look at him, eyes full of questions. "You—"

"Dock me the same amount, including, er, fringe. That makes the entire transaction revenue-neutral. There." He exhaled. "What do I need to sign?"

"Actually," Breanna said, sucking her lower lip. "I don't really know. I've never faced this before."

"Well, you're our accountant," he said, smiling. "I bet you'll find some paper somewhere in here for me to sign."

"Jon?" Her mouth opened and closed a couple of times. He knew she was looking for some awkward words.

He leaned forward. "No, Breanna. My relationship with Robbie is not illicit, but we do go back a ways. Robbie has been loyal to me and this company, and I am devoted to her well-being. She needs to know the company will stand with her."

"And your word that the company would stand with her was not enough?" she asked, scratching her forehead. "You have to pay her?"

"Would it be enough for you, if money was super-tight?" he asked, cocking his head, lifting his hands to her.

She exhaled. "I guess not." She turned back to the display. "What reason should I note in my documentation?"

He paused, then replied, "Jon's honor and commitment."

"That's a new one."

"Happens to be true."

"The same kind of commitment that it takes to work wood all winter?" she asked, smiling as she keyboarded the information.

He leaned back, laughing. "No. That's one hundred proof desperation. The winters are deep and dark here. Woodworking pulls me through them."

They both laughed.

Breanna picked up a pencil and began writing on a legal pad. "Did you talk to Robbie about all of this?"

"Woodworking?"

"No, Jon," Breanna said, laughing again. "The raise."

"Yes. We talked about it last week."

Her eyes narrowed. "Well, Jon, you should have told me about this earlier—an email, anything. I should have known the day of, not the week after."

He knew she was right. "Yes, Breanna. I deserve that. And I apologize."

"Maybe talk to me before you make the decision, ok? It will be easier for the both of us."

"You're a hundred percent correct, Breanna. I'll be sure to do that. Thanks for the time today."

"Of course. Like I say, that's what I'm here for."

He got up and turned to leave.

"You know—"

Jon turned back around. "Yes?"

"I bet Robbie thinks you're a miracle worker." She smiled.

"Miracle worker?" He ran his hand through his hair. "That's yet to come," he said, turning back to leave. "But we'll get there. Well, nice to meet you, Breanna."

She just nodded, then turned away.

For a moment, he thought she had started to cr—

The S4 rang, and feeling new fatigue pressing down as if from on high, he turned and left.

An Alora thought tried to cut at him, but for a few sweet moments, it didn't find his deep, aching place.

# COUP DE GRACE

The huge man brought his giant fist down on the hotel radio-alarm clock, shattering the blaring digital instrument in two blows. In seconds, the cheery voice of the vapid weather reporter collapsed to a warbly hiss.

She must be ugly, he thought. That was why they put her on the radio.

The broken clock died at 2:55 p.m.

Now, awake and energized, his hate hymn, the daily waking-up recitation that galvanized his day, rolled into his thoughts, raring to go. Right on time, it was waiting for him to climb aboard.

But first, Jasper Giles, VP-Legal of SSS Pharmaceuticals, had himself a little email to send.

He pulled his massive frame up in the hotel bed, grabbed his iPhone, and stabbed out the message with his fat fingers, keeping his painful toe from rubbing up against the sheets.

◆

"Objection."

"Counsel, please approach," the judge said, motioning with tiny hands for both plaintiff and defense counsel to approach the bench. "Bailiff, let's keep the jury here this time."

Al Sanus, attorney for SSS defense, prepared to stand, but stopped, frozen in a half crouch, as his co-counsel whispered, "You have to get the judge to overrule plaintiff's objection."

Al shrugged. "You know how independent—"

"The firm and SSS don't give a damn about that, and you know it. Here, read." Larry thrust his iPhone into Al's hands, its screen displaying the single email.

Jan. 14, 2016

To: LarryWallipson@JGilesLLP.com
From: Jasper@JGilesLLP.com
Re: Today

Just spoke with SSS leadership. Our client fears that yur trial will lead to a finding of guilty with punitives nrth of a billion dollars. I also beleve such a holding by the jury will lead to a derivtive action by the shareholders. This wll upst the Tanner takeovr. Use any means necsary to block this reslt. Gut ther experts.

It is your responsiblity. Get it done.

Jasper

Al studied the message, dropped the cell in Larry's lap, then strode straight to the bench. *I have a job to do*, he thought. That damn email changed nothing.

He turned his attention from the jury, who looked bored out of their gourds with yet one more objection-driven delay. He let his hands fidget with his thin blue-and-white tie, the one that signaled, "Whoever's wearing me doesn't care about how he looks," to the jury.

*You guys in the box just keep thinking that*, he thought. *Not about my money, just my cheap tie and sharp argument. I've actually gotten on with the jury pretty well in this second week of the trial. Sure, there are a couple of jurors who like the plaintiffs, but we're doing—no, I'm doing fine for Triple S.*

He turned his attention to the judge. She really looked angry, he thought. She was probably pissed because the day was dragging. Witnesses were taking forever, what with all of the objections and sidebar conferences.

He shrugged. Let the judge be anxious to move this trial along. The more nervous she was, the less patient she would be with the plaintiffs' stupid objections.

His palms were sweating. But he knew it wasn't due to the building's old heater, itself in a losing battle with the three-degree Chicago outdoor temperature. Sweat was pouring down his back. He looked back at his co-counsel, then to the bank of stiff plaintiff lawyers on the other side of the aisle.

Yeah, everybody was sweating. They knew how critical this case was. SSS Pharmaceuticals was a whale, and plaintiffs were looking to harpoon her.

The only thing standing in the way was him.

It was high-voltage, glorious, and dangerous.

Now at the bench, he turned his head, just a quick look at the gallery of attendees. He wondered if—

"Are you with us, Mr. Sanus?"

He snapped his head back, front and center. The judge, he saw, was now down and in front of the bench, standing with the attorneys.

And staring at him.

She was angry.

Actually, she's pretty short. Grey hair all coifed up, exposing what looked like the largest forehead on the planet.

Settle down now, he reminded himself. Cool, calm, confident.

"Yes, Your Honor," Al said, ignoring the sweat beads popping out on his head like chickenpox.

"You hot, Al?"

He turned to plaintiff's counsel.

Of course.

Like Hank Petson, the lead plaintiff counsel, really cared. Not two feet away. Three inches taller, trim, wearing an elegant suit—simplicity itself, dark blue. White shirt.

Too clean. The jury hates clean. They like regular.

And a bow tie, for heaven's sake.

Always the bow tie with this guy.

"This is the fifth sidebar we have had this afternoon, and the eleventh so far today," the judge said. "Neither of you is paying attention to the jury, whom you each must convince. If I had my way, both of you would lose."

Al watched as Bow Tie started his speech.

"Your Honor, I can't help but object when—"

"Mr. Petson, we are out of both the jury's and the witness's earshot, so let's dispense with the linguistic dramatics," she said, turning to face the taller man.

How do you like that, Bow Tie? Al dropped his head, working to hide his enjoyment of the moment. Pompous ass thinks he invented the law.

"Mr. Petson, let's get on with it," the judge said, hands crossed over her robe.

"Defense counsel," Petson started, "is attempting to impeach our witness during cross-examination using the witness's own notes."

"An entirely proper procedure," Al stated. "Why has the doctor changed his mind? His article says one thing. His notes say another. We have an obligation to get to the heart of this staggering contradiction."

"Please, Mr. Sanus," the judge said, raising a tiny hand to within a foot of his face. "Let Mr. Petson finish."

"Thank you, Your Honor," Petson said, shifting his weight. "The witness's notes are old and irrelevant since they were followed by his published treatise."

Al saw that Bow Tie was standing straighter and straighter, as if he could grow into his own argument. The defense attorney was going to enjoy taking this guy down.

"The final version of that paper," Bow Tie continued, "has since been published. It is that final version that contains Doctor's opinions, not the early musing on a manuscript draft that itself has never seen the light of day."

Bow Tie looked like he should be coronated for his argument.

"Mr. Sanus? Your response?"

Al, unable to keep his eyes from narrowing, believed he could actually feel his adrenal glands squeeze as he delivered his argument, a sharp sword through the belly of his opponent.

"Your Honor," Al said, "these earlier notes reflect the witness's prior state of mind. Clearly, those writings provide a very different opinion than the one that plaintiffs explored with him during the direct examination. I should be allowed to examine in detail how and why Doctor's position changed, since that position is central to his testimony."

Al nodded to the judge. "That is all I ask: Why did the witness change his mind?"

"Your Honor," plaintiff's counsel said. Al noted Bow Tie's hands were behind his back. The man is still confident—so much the better.

"You just can't allow Mr. Sanus to go on a fishing expedition for poorly formed opinions, opinions that had been updated outside of and well before this litigation."

Al struggled not to smile at Bow Tie's fatal mistake.

Never tell this judge what she could not do. All Al had to do was sit back now and enjoy the show.

"Mr. Petson," the judge said, walking over to Bow Tie. "It is in my purview to either sustain or overrule your objection. Do you agree?"

Petson stepped back so fast he tripped and almost fell. "Your Honor, I only meant—"

Here comes the coup de grâce. Al leaned forward on the balls of his feet.

"Then, Mr. Petson, I am prepared to overrule your objec—"

"Your Honor, defense has no objection to withdrawing the witness' notes and ending this line of inquiry."

What the hell? Who was that? Al swung to his left, noting that both the judge and Petson's heads also turned to this new voice.

Al's mouth dropped.

Jesus, no.

# VESPULA GERMANICA

She had arrived.

Al was speechless and cheap-dress-shirt-wet-with-sweat scared.

The case was going so well too, he thought, grinding his teeth.

Sure, Dr. Franklin, professor of endocrinology, seated right there on the witness stand, was sharp and experienced, but Al was set to take him down, especially on this old note issue.

All he needed was for the Court to overrule plaintiffs' objection, a ruling that was in his hand, but clearly impossible now.

*What do I do?*

He thought for a moment. *Is she going to serve as a consult for me?* he thought. *Offer advice on this cross-examination?*

His face hardened.

No. She could not be here for that.

She was taking the case from him.

His hands were jammed so hard down into his pockets, they tore the slacks' inside fabric.

Then he looked at plaintiff's counsel.

Petson was rubbing his own chin so fast Al thought plaintiff's counsel would tear it off.

So Bow Tie was nervous too.

Well, so he should be. Nobody wanted to go toe to stiletto toe with Cassie Rhodes, who, having announced her presence, stepped into the judge-attorney conference.

Al was at a complete loss, standing deathly still in open court.

Choices? He knew the answer before he finished the question.

Cassie Rhodes was lead council for SSS on this case, and when she walked to the mound to see you, you had only one choice.

Give up the ball and head for the showers.

"Your Honor, please accept my apologies for this interruption," Cassie said, her deep voice living on the brink of sensuality, disarming them all. "Mr. Sanus has an emergency that he must see to at once. It is my client's wish that I proceed with the cross-examination of this witness and, in fact, inject myself more directly into this case."

"Is this true, Mr. Sanus?" the judge looked at him, noting the new softness in her eyes.

Tell her no, a voice in Al's head screamed. Tell her that you are prepared to proceed.

This is your case.

Your cross.

You are ready.

You prepped, and with the court's permission, you will proceed with the examination of this witness.

Damn it to hell. Tell her. Tell them all.

He looked in Cassie's direction. She flashed her eyes at him and gave the smallest shake of her head.

All at once, he was weightless. Of little substance.

Of no matter.

And now, no importance.

"Yes, that's true, Your Honor," Al said.

The attorney deflated as the judge turned from him.

"Any objections, Mr. Petson? Ms. Rhodes has made an unusual request in my courtroom today."

Al saw Petson's eyebrows shoot up and down one, two, three, then four times. He knew plaintiff's counsel was struggling to get a grip on this greased pig. But he also knew the judge was impatient and Petson could not play for time.

In the end, Petson waved his hands side to side, shrugged, and nodded.

"Our recorder will need a verbal response, sir," the court said, the snap in her voice back.

"No objections, Your Honor," Petson said.

"OK. Ms. Rhodes, would you like a brief recess to confer with co-counsel?"

"No, Your Honor," she said, ignoring Al. "In the interest of time, the busy schedule of the court, as well as this witness, I am prepared to move forward with the cross-examination."

Al watched.

Perfect posture. Olive skin, dark hair down her back. Not a single molecule out of place.

Choked by the epithets that were ready to come blasting out of his mind, he felt his pulse hammering.

In his ten years in the courtroom and forty years of life, he had not known hate until this moment.

"All right, then," the judge said. "Mr. Sanus, you are excused, sir."

Al watched the judge return to the bench and plaintiffs' counsel and Cassie go to their respective tables. The judge introduced the new counsel, then said, "Ms. Rhodes, please proceed with the cross-examination of this witness."

As Al worked his way by her and through the narrow center aisle, she rested a perfect hand on his shoulder. When her lips approached, he inhaled her gentle fragrance, a waft of her soft peppermint breath flowing across his face.

His anger melted like snow in the warm sun as she first hovered just above his left ear then whispered the first words she had ever said to him.

"You're fired."

# NOTHING BUT NET

He was in the catbird seat, and Dr. J. T. Franklin, expert witness for the plaintiffs, knew it.

The center of the action.

On the witness stand, he let his eyes wander from the floor, then over to the feet of the jurors, then to the shelf of the witness stand itself, which held the stack of papers on which he had been fielding questions all damn day.

He knew better than to make eye contact with the jury. Defense counsel might think he was trying to communicate with them using eyebrow signals, mind melding, or some such Jedi nonsense, and object. So he just let his eyes roam, hiding his intent: to hear what counsel was discussing.

He strained so hard that he thought he felt his ears wiggle. The conversers were just to the left, but he learned nothing from their hushed voices.

So he settled back down, scrubbing any vestige of disappointment from his face. Of course, he'd seen many of these conversations before. He'd been an expert witness now for over three years and had testified against SSS Pharmaceuticals and their anti-diabetic drug, Palmesia, in eight cases. This did not include his work as an expert in five or six other cases over the years for both sides. He was used to these legal antics and maneuvers.

*They're probably arguing about that note I placed in the margin of that early paper draft,* he thought. *Defense will likely have a chance to come after me on that.*

He shrugged. How was he supposed to know that one of his notes (and he'd made hundreds of them on many, many manuscript drafts) would appear on an exhibit in this trial? The note was an old idea, on an old draft of an old paper that never got published—nothing nefarious about that.

He brushed his jacket sleeve with a quick wrist flick. It was a long day.

Of all of the days to bring his wife to court.

She'd always wanted to know what he did during these trips and what the courtroom was really like. Janet was sitting in the row right behind plaintiffs' counsel, prim as ever, proper as always.

And admiring eyes on him.

His stomach twisted some, but he pushed it aside. Well, now she knows what court is like: chilly and full up to the gills with waiting around.

Suddenly, he was tired. He closed his eyes. Maybe—

His eyes snapped open immediately at the new voice.

He looked at the gathering of attorneys and noticed a new arrival. Well, either that or Ms. Europe 2016 found her way into the courtroom by mistake. No need for him to be embarrassed checking her out. Everyone was.

So many tall women appeared ungainly, a little wobbly, and definitely uncomfortable with their height.

But not this one.

Goodness.

Just over six feet. Black skirt and cream blouse. No rings on her fingers. No earrings and no necklace either. Absolutely nothing to detract from her stunning beauty.

*Wonder what her background is.* Eastern European descent? No. Cheekbones were too high, and that perfect skin was a touch too dark. He couldn't quite make out her eyes without staring, but he thought they'd be dark as well. Maybe black-olive dark like—

Suddenly, the gathering broke up, the quarterback-judge sending players to their assigned spots on the court-field—time to get back to work.

Well, that was a nice break, he thought, regardless of the reason. Better sit up.

He turned to face the smaller man who had been questioning him so far, but that attorney was gathering his things.

Strange.

Just as he noticed the tall dark woman standing and turning to him, he heard the judge say, "Ms. Rhodes, please continue with the examination of this witness."

What was this, some kind of midcourse correction?

She walked across his visual field, placing herself in the center aisle, looking down to the left at some papers on the defense table.

*I bet she won a Nobel Prize nomination for those legs. I wonder what she's—*

"Dr. Franklin, I am Cassie Rhodes. I will be continuing your cross-examination today."

*Well, let's get to work*, he thought. He adjusted his own paper pile so that he had an unobstructed view of the jury and they of him.

The jury was everything.

"Yes. Nice to meet you, Ms. Rhodes."

"I only have a few questions to ask you."

"Really?" he replied. He knew that was a gambit to get him to think that they were near the end and that, anticipating an early ending, he would let his guard down.

A rookie move on her part.

But he decided just for grins that he would play along and start out by being solicitous.

"Ms. Rhodes," he said, voice gravelly with the concern of a distinguished physician. "I hope that Mr. Sanus is all right."

She continued studying the document, showing her Nobel Prizes, saying nothing, then, "Are you OK, Doctor?"

Still not looking at him, just studying the papers.

From deep inside him, a warning light started flashing.

He ignored it, but shifted in his seat. He'd tried to be nice, but she dismissed the overture. Well, OK.

"I am fine, thank you."

If that's how she's going to be, he thought, then hell, let's go to war.

"Dr. Franklin, the jury has been told that you have a considerable background in endocrinology, correct?"

"That is right." A harmless enough start.

"I assume that you are compensated well by the university?"

There it was.

The money. Nothing but the money with these people. He was tempted to ask how much money she made, but that would be a cheap move on his part. Even though the retort would feel good, the jury would look at that response as sarcastic and surly, and he would lose them.

He decided to play it straight.

"I am compensated fairly for my services, yes."

"And you are paid to be here today?"

She was asking the questions but she wasn't looking at him, or the jury, for that matter.

This was odd.

But it was another routine question. He chalked it up to a weird day. The warning light blinked off.

"I am."

"And what are you paid per hour for being here today?"

"$700 an hour." He knew that she already had the answer to that. She just wants the jury to know and wants to see me squirm. Cut me down to size.

But not today, not for her.

He turned away from her and toward the jury. It was their attention that he needed, and them that he had to persuade. "This case required substantial effort, and I worked hard on it."

"Tell us, Dr. Franklin, how much money have you made testifying like this over the years?"

Still the money. The number she asked for would set the jury back on their heels. He shifted a little, resting on the balls of his feet like a prizefighter. He had to take the sting out of his answer.

"Over a million dollars over five years," he said, then added, "but actually," he chucked to let the jury know something humorous was coming. "I don't really control what happens to it."

"Oh?" She looked up. "I didn't ask about control. But since you brought it up, who does?"

"My wife."

Relishing the moment as the jury members laughed, he didn't worry about the information that he had just volunteered. Look, he thought, picking up on the hint of a smile from the judge, even the court liked it.

Score one for the home team. And this was just the finances. Wait until we get to the science part of this. That was his high ground. He would bury her.

But she still looked away from him, appearing now to be focused on a single sheet of paper. It was not the usual 8"-by-11" document. Much smaller. And yellow.

"Does your wife ask you to buy jewelry, Dr. Franklin?"

He shot a glance to his wife as the blood suddenly fled from his stomach, leaving him with a weightless feeling. What would cause the defense attorney to ask that question? What does she know? This devastating question was like a punch headed right at his face.

Needed to slip it.

"She does not, but I buy it anyway."

Some of the jury members were still chuckling, but he was focused on Ms. Rhodes now. This was going someplace that—

"Did you buy a $30,000 earrings, bracelet, and necklace combination for her?"

To Dr. Franklin, the courtroom was dead silent, a grave.

Then Petson said, "Objection. Your Honor, this goes beyond the scope of cross-examination. Doctor answered Ms. Rhodes' question about how much he made. What he does with this money is not the concern of her or the court."

Doctor's head was hot with sweat. Damn it, how could she know what he bought?

"Your Honor," Ms. Rhodes said, looking at the judge, voice full, nonthreatening. "Doctor volunteered what happens with his money. I didn't ask him that. I'm just following his answer."

"Just a moment," said the court.

As the judge took time to review the transcript, Doctor scrambled. If Rhodes knew about the bracelet, did she also know why he bought it? How could—

Then it hit him.

She knew of the purchase. Anybody who knew someone at the credit card companies could get that. Rhodes knew the what, not the why.

What was the countermove?

"Overruled," the judge was saying. "You may proceed, Ms. Rhodes. Ask your question again, but let's move it along, shall we?"

"Thank you, Your Honor." Doctor watched her turn to him like a shark turning to the blood in the water. "Dr. Franklin, did you buy a $30,000 earring, bracelet, and necklace combination for your wife?"

Deflect, he thought. The move was to deflect,

Franklin sat back in the seat, deliberately breathing deeply, getting his pulse to slow. He knew that he had this now.

Sighing, dropping his head, and rubbing his brow, he said "Well, you spoiled my surprise, counselor. I was going to give it to her." He stole a glance at his wife, who wore that "I'm puzzled but not unhappy yet" look. He would have to buy another one for her, but that was OK. Like the mouse said, "Keep the cheese. Just let me out of the trap," he thought.

"Oh. You were going to give it your wife? Is she here?"

"Your Honor," Mr. Petson stated, rising, "I really must object. We continue to extend well beyond the scope of proper cross examination95."

Franklin saw Ms. Rhodes look up. "If the court pleases," she said, standing before the bench. "The witness himself brought the issue of money control up and how he uses it. I believe I have the right to pursue a matter that the witness himself volunteered. However, I am mindful of the time and am almost done, Your Honor."

"Objection overruled. Continue, please," the court said.

"I will answer," Doctor said, seeing his light at the end of the tunnel. He had to keep himself from standing up. Pointing her out, he said, "Janet, my wife, is right there." Then, for good measure, he added, "You just ruined my surprise for her." He was giving his wife a chance to help him out of a jam. Janet looked surprised, but pleased.

Win-win.

Swish. Nothing but net.

He looked back at Ms. Rhodes, who stood quietly, now looking at him.

Nailed her cold, he thought. Bitch.

"Well, Dr. Franklin," Ms. Rhodes said, walking toward him. Her voice was mountain-lake even, her posture perfect. "'Janet' is not the name on the bracelet." She held the bracelet out to him.

There.

In front of his face. He didn't have to see it to be reminded that the bracelet had "Eva" etched into it.

Time slowed down.

Several gasps reached him from the jury box.

He closed his eyes tight. Teeth together.

When he opened his eyes, he saw Janet leaning forward, staring at him. He watched as her eyes, first wide open, slowly narrowed, then became unfocused as they filled with tears.

Then he looked to Ms. Rhodes' eyes.

Coal-black, morbid eyes. Frightening eyes. Not lifeless, but he believed that if he stared at them long enough, they would suck the life out of him.

His world collapsed.

"How did you—" he started.

"Doctor, I will continue to ask the questions. Is Eva a pet name for your wife?"

"No. I—"

"The fact is that you were not planning to give this jewelry to your wife. You had already given it to someone else. Eva. Correct?

"Yes."

Rhodes pressed in on him, like a snake, relishing every delicious contraction as it squeezed the life out of its victim. "But you did not say that this jewelry was for, what is her name, Eva when I asked you before. You said that you gave them to your wife. Who is Eva? Is she a family member?"

"No."

"Your Honor." Doctor saw Petson fly up from his chair. "I object to this entire line of questioning. Nothing Ms. Rhodes has said has anything to do with this witness's testimony and is improper cross-examination."

Franklin felt the condemnation like a downpour, washing away any future expert work, as well as what was left of his career.

"Your Honor," Ms. Rhodes said, "this witness has lied today, under oath. He is a perjurer. He has lied about who manages his money, lied about purchases made with that money, and even lied to his own wife, who is in this very courtroom. He has chosen to dishonor himself, lying about money, lying for lust, lying for a living."

"Thank you, Ms. Rhodes. I am going to sustain plaintiff counsel's objection."

Doctor's head snapped up. Sustain? Then, maybe—

"Of course, Your Honor," Ms. Rhodes said, keeping her eyes on him.

What was the point? Franklin knew that it no longer mattered. The damage was done.

As he watched Rhodes walk to him, he actually shriveled back into the chair, now hard and unforgiving. And he didn't dare look at the jury.

Or at Janet, although he could feel her eyes burn through him. He hiccupped.

"Dr. Franklin, are you going to answer any more questions today?" Ms. Rhodes asked him.

Watching his life evaporate before him, he said, "No."

"Your Honor," he heard her say, "this witness, as the court has seen, is an unreliable liar. Now we learn that he is unable to complete his testimony. The court must therefore strike his entire appearance today. He cannot be relied on for anything."

Hiding his face in his hands, he felt the jury soaking up his humiliation.

Suddenly, he heard Petson say, "Your Honor, may I ask for a brief recess to confer with my client so—"

That was it.

He exploded from the witness chair, shouting at the court, the jury, the attorneys, Janet—anyone who would listen.

"No. No recess, no conference. I am sick to death with this process, and done with all of it."

The judge sat quiet for a moment, then said, "Doctor, you are excused from the witness chair. Please retake your seat for us in the galley, if you don't mind."

She then turned to the jury. "I sustain defense counsel's motion," she said. "The jury is to ignore all of Dr. Franklin's testimony. It will be stricken from the record. And"—she looked toward the brown wall clock on the faded back wall of the court—"I think we have heard enough for one day. We are adjourned. Please return at 9:00 a.m. tomorrow."

"If I may, Your Honor," Ms. Rhodes said. "Just one other thing. I would like to have this witness sanctioned for perjury."

The final nail in the coffin, a sanction would follow him like the scarlet letter.

He could never testify again.

"We will discuss it in the morning out of the presence of the jury, Ms. Rhodes. You and defense counsel suggest a time, preferably around 8:00 a.m."

The judge then gaveled the day's proceedings to a close and left the court after the jury was excused.

As the courtroom emptied, Janet Franklin, shaking with rage, humiliation, and despair, stood up and walked toward her husband.

"Ms. Franklin?"

She turned, almost losing her balance as the high heel buckled under her.

Cassie Rhodes towered above her.

Janet, her heart pounding, her head throbbing with rage, said simply, "Yes."

"Ms. Franklin, I can put you in contact with a very good attorney skilled in navigating through divorce proceedings if you are interested."

Such cold eyes, Janet thought. She turned to look at her husband, who had staggered down from the witness stand and, with both hands extended and resting on the jury box, was hanging his head. To her, he looked worse than worn. He looked like he had lost the fight of his life.

And she noted with a gasp that he now looked like an old man.

She spun. "Go to hell, Ms. Rhodes. That was my husband whose career you just assassinated, whose reputation you just destroyed. He and I have been married for forty-five years. We have inflicted more pain on each other than that stupid brain of yours, full of legal stunts and meaningless minutia, could ever imagine.

"We would have worked this out," she said, stamping her foot. "Now"—she drew back from the attorney to gaze at her broken man—"you have ruined him."

Janet saw the coal eyes just stare back at her.

"Don't be such a mouse, Ms. Franklin."

Janet, leaning into the taller woman, her wrinkled face barely reaching Cassie's smooth and flawless chin, said, "Do you have a son?"

"No."

"Good, because if you did, he would eat dog food."

Janet didn't yelp, nor did she cry when she felt the smack of the attorney's hand across her face. She did hear the gasps of those who were still left in the courtroom, then heard nothing as the courtroom fell silent.

"You're an animal," Janet said as she pushed her way past Ms. Rhodes, heading to her husband. "A wild animal. And wild animals get put down."

# I AM THE STORM

Cleveland "Cory" Meriwether squinted in the conference room's harsh light, studying his notes for this January 15th interview that would send him back to the top of the newscaster heap.

Just a few minutes more now, he thought. He flipped the pages back and forth, testing his memory of the provocative subject.

"Just be patient," he whispered to himself.

*Nobody, I mean nobody, has been able to land this interview.*

And it was Giles, the man himself, who had called.

*He called me.*

Corey shook his head at this turn of fortune. After a few years of self-imposed exile, fortune in the form of Jasper Giles, lead counsel of SSS Pharmaceuticals, was shining high and hot on him now.

Shame it couldn't be live on TV, he thought, but that was small potatoes. Meriwether had been selected, and it would be a choice that would breathe new life into a dying career.

His own.

Since his retirement from cable news, he thought, yanking a page from the yellow pad so hard he tore it, he'd done the obligatory things: written a book, done some traveling, played with the grandbabies as they coughed and shit and threw up on the floor, watched the cancer eat away at Hanah, his beloved wife.

If all this was the reward, then to hell with it. It felt like what it was—punishment.

Three years earlier, he thought he'd seen the yellow caution light to slow his career down, and obliged. Instead, it was the red light signaling the end of his productivity. He missed the compressed days, the week-after-week grind of relentless deadlines, terse engineers, screaming producers.

And here he was, on the brink of the dive back into the good deep water. The very idea—

"Meriwether?"

Corey snapped his head up and found himself staring up into the face of Jasper Giles.

Damn, he was fat. And ugly.

Not just ugly, Meriwether thought, God-awful hideous.

"Mr. Giles?"

Large hook of a nose jutting out from under small eyes that could not hide under the thin, damn-near-hairless eyebrows. From below, it looked like his hairline had caught the train for the coast years ago. Blinking for perspective, he saw that the head sat atop an expensive suit, itself pushed to bursting by a barrel chest and a huge belly. He felt sorry for the clothes that were just on the verge of exploding.

"Who were you expecting, Sharon fucking Stone?"

"H-hello." Corey rose to shake his hand. "It's so good to meet you, Mr. Gi—"

"I thought that we might have a few minutes of conversation before you start the interview, to give us, well, a chance to get to know each other."

The ex-anchor paused half standing. "Oh, OK. I appreciate that."

"Mind if I sit down?"

"Please." He pointed to as chair about five feet away.

The huge man limped over to the wooden chair with its thick upholstery, turned around, swore, than getting behind the chair, pushed it over close to Corey's seat.

Meriwether watched helplessly as Giles plopped down, farted, then leaned over until his face was just inches from his own.

The interviewer pushed back a little, despite himself, the sweat popping out of his forehead

"You know, people say I intimidate them," Giles started. "I hope that I'm not doing that to you."

"Well, that's your reputation." The waft of mint on Giles' breath couldn't begin to cover its repugnant odor. *What is that?* he wondered as his stomach squeezed down on him. Oil? Paint? No. But maybe—

Turpentine.

The recognition rolled his stomach.

"So what do you want to know about me?"

Corey wanted to inhale, but there was no way he was letting any more of that stink inside him. "Well, uh, for starters, why the law? You have a BS in biology from Hopkins. Then an MBA from, uh—"

"University of Illinois."

Meriwether watched his eyes narrow. His own chest hurt, and that new airy feeling on his neck announced that his hair was standing on end.

He wondered if this was how prey felt.

"Why law school?" *Gotta get control back*, he thought.

"All about injustice," Giles answered, staring back at him.

"And you have a crack team working with you," Meriwether added. "From what I hear, Sanus and Tholson are up-and-comers, and Cassie Rhodes, well, she is a force t—"

The interviewer swore that he could see the hostility leaping out from the lawyer. "Forget them," Giles said. He felt the sharp jab of Giles' index finger on his thigh. "Remember, I am the storm."

"OK, I guess," Meriwether said, clearing his throat. "Let's look at your first successful case. The Appalachian mine companies in the early nineties."

"In '92–'95."

"You fought for the Appalachian coal companies against the miners."

"Of course I did. The miners were the injustice."

The miners? He really said that, Corey thought, shaking his head. "The miners had to work in unsafe, despicable conditions while the companies made huge profits."

"The owners weren't in it to get poor, were they?"

The miners weren't in it to die either, Corey thought, choking the idea back. "But they could have supported their own employees."

"The miners didn't have to do anything. They could have thrown down their tool belts down on the ground and walk away. Quit. That would have taken real courage. Guess they'd be astrophysicists somewhere now, right, Meriwether?"

Giles showed his yellowing teeth. Corey thought it was an attempt at a smile.

"Plus," the lawyer continued, mid-belch, "there would always be others to take their place."

Meriwether fixed a collar that didn't need adjusting at all. "So are you saying that the miners were wrong to sue for better conditions?"

"I'm saying they got what was coming to them."

"Well, didn't many miners die because of conditions your client didn't want to improve?"

"They die all the time, right? And no hope of any other job with their backgrounds, so . . ." Giles shrugged.

The room spun dangerously for a second. "No. Yes. But these deaths were due to the terrible conditions down in the shafts."

"And if that hadn't killed them, then it would have been the spinney boo or the alcohol or the oxy. Why should a company be forced at great expense to change conditions that will not have any real tangible effect on the outcome?"

Let's get off this, Corey thought, looking at his notes. "And the California coast oil spills?"

"It was an honor to fight on behalf of the oil companies. They do a tremendous service to their country."

"Maybe so, but they also polluted several thousand square miles of pristine coastal water."

"So do volcanoes, but we don't sue them, right?"

Corey thought the great litigator was going to spit.

"Well, we can't stop volcanoes, but we can stop oil companies."

"Not when they are operating legally and are not negligent."

"The State of California disagreed."

"The State of California lost. We beat them and their penchant to punish people who work hard to make a profit. Now look here, Meribedwetter—"

"Meriwether—"

"Lucrative enterprise comes only at the end of great work. But your viewers should know that that work is disruptive. It's intrusive, relentless, unremitting, and destructive. People like you, as well as government, want the benefit of the profit but want to avoid the cost. That's not progress—that's not even life. Instead it's the mantra of professors—"

He said "professor" like it was a curse, Corey thought.

"Who never did a hard day's work in their life."

"You used the word *mantra*. Some say your mantra is that you like corporations and not people."

"Not true."

"But your record is—"

"My mantra is that I love corporations and despise people."

Corey shivered at the new chill in the air.

"Corporations turn the disorganized slop of thousands of individuals into a concerted effort that makes an impact, provides a service."

"Well, so does religion?"

"Wow," the attorney said, leaning in closer. "And what a great track record they have. Shining examples of the best mankind has to offer. Like the Third and Fourth Crusades? Slaughter for nothing but booty and land and women. Know who the Huguenots were?

Corey shook his head. "Well, I think—"

"I bet you think they were some family in an insipid TV soap opera," Giles snorted. "They were French Calvinists who were murdered by Catholics. Thirty thousand men, women, and children butchered on what is known by knowledgeable people as the Saint Bartholomew's Day Massacre. That was toward the end of the seventeenth century. Know the only person who killed more since?

"I . . . no, I don—"

"Hitler."

What the hell? "You think Hitler was right?"

He saw Giles had to think about that one.

"No."

Corey exhaled. "Well, at least we see eye—"

"He didn't go far enough."

His pulse jumped. "What?"

"He should have killed all the Jews, Muslims, Hindus, born-agains, Catholic holy men that he could find. All those who believed in the redemption of humanity deserved an oven."

"Now wai—"

"They deserved to die because they stupidly and stubbornly think that, now having experienced 5,000 years of 'the blessing of religion' and its terrible trail of slaughter, humanity will ascend to some greater civilization. Well, you know what, Meriwether? The sooner they die, the sooner we'll have our chance. Corporations are our best chance and love of the company the individual's best hope."

"How about devotion to family?"

"If you define it as lust for women, it's perfectly natural and a hell of lot more fun. But what do I know?" he said, winking. "I never married."

What a surprise, Meriwether thought.

"What do you think you are, some corporate Dr. Strangelove, Giles?"

"Make fun of me all you want." He scratched his nose. Meriwether held his breath, afraid the man was actually going to pick it. "I support corporations because they are the only effective remaining force in the world. They are the best hope of a destructive species living on a dying planet." He belched.

"Commodities are getting scarce, consumable energy is running low, armies are unreliable, real estate fluctuates wildly, and people, well . . ." The lawyer shrugged. "People are no damn good."

Maybe people like you, Corey thought.

"Do you deny, Meriwether, that unions and universities, countries, and churches can no longer deal with our problems? The question of our survival is too adult a puzzle for them to solve."

Corey stared at him, ignoring the stink, like he was facing down an animal.

Suddenly, Giles smiled. "You think I'm ruthless?"

The hell with the interview. "I think you should be jailed at Riker's."

Giles smiled. "Time for me to feel some pain, huh?"

Meriwether just stared

"My ruthlessness only hastens the day when companies will take their proper place in this world," Giles said, sitting back in his chair.

"For the benefit of misanthropes?"

"I accept your definition if that's what it takes to face facts and just say what we all think—the time of the individual is finally, mercifully, at an end."

"When did your morals take a vacation?" Corey said, gathering his notes.

The attorney twisted in the chair, grimacing. "When I realized that people with their ideas and dreams and visions are no more than temporary disgusting blips on the clean corporate radar scope."

"What about ethicists?"

"Ethicists die by the hundreds every day. Exxon is eternal."

"You know, Mr. Giles," the interviewer said, now standing, "the people who actually work for these companies may disagree with you. They leave, burnt out and spent, by the thousands."

Giles shrugged. "Just human goo clogging the well-oiled corporate machinery."

"So you hate people."

"I hate the government. Its feeble attempts to control companies make it look like a pitiful old man struggling to control a young, truculent dog. I have nothing but ridicule for those do-good consumer groups with their consultants who, like ticks, grow fat off the sick blood of a dying leftist culture. I rage at that anachronism of the twentieth century, the environmentalists."

"Well, you have yourself quite a mantra there."

Giles smiled. "It's my hosanna of hate."

"Well, it's about time for the interview."

"Sure, let's go."

Corey sat back down, blood flying through his blood vessels. Giles' hatred had set him back on his heels. But he was ready now, feeling it strong. "This worldview of yours will make a great story for my viewers."

"No, it won't because they won't know it."

Meriwether sat back in the chair. "But we just talked about—"

"I know that. I said it. But you won't go into it. Giles leaned forward, his face almost over Corey's chair. "In fact, you will never say anything about what we just discussed."

Meriwether, standing, balled his fist. "I will ask you any god—"

"I will deny it all, getting word out that you poisoned the interview. Your career will die again. This time, permanently. Get that, and get it good."

Meriwether sat back down, arms flapping onto his thighs.

"That's better. Now, let's get started," Giles said, squeezing his mass back into the chair. "Call the cameramen back in. Hey, want to see pictures of my parents?"

# PAIN SNAKE

With the pointless interview over thirty minutes ago, Giles limped out of the ornate room into the hallway, knocking over the table of fruit that had gone uneaten.

*It's bad today.*

He couldn't stop here, needed some place secluded. The sweat broke out all across his pale forehead.

Yes.

He remembered a small waiting area by a set of blue elevators in the back, well away from the hotel's grand front entrance.

Once there, he fell into one of the two black chairs, hoping it would hold his huge frame. It didn't matter that the pain leaped up at him when he plopped into the deep upholstery. After the wood's loud groan of protest, it decided to withstand his weight, and he stretched his feet out, right one over left.

He'd take his right shoe off, but he knew it wouldn't matter. Nothing he could scratch.

How long had it been?

One year.

Yeah. One.

Started like a tickle.

Just across the top of his right foot. Toe level. No swelling. No redness. No nothing. Well, maybe if he was pushed (*and no one pushes me*, he thought), he'd say it was like the tiny toe hairs were being brushed back and forth across the skin.

Of course, he was way too big to actually inspect his feet. The fact was that he hadn't seen his own toes in years. Occasionally, he'd try to get down there and reintroduce himself to them, contorting his flaccid, sweaty nakedness into ridiculous positions to get just a glimmer of a toe. Hoping to see—what?

A bump? Redness? Pus?

Just looking for anything odd, to convince himself that there was in fact a reason for these eerie toe sensations, maybe sparking a hope that the sensation would go away.

But he never got close enough to see the small, smelly things, the obscene body-twisting attempts just making him sore in the morning. So he quit trying, just trusting and knowing that, like his paralegals, his toes would be where he needed them and then just do his bidding.

Meanwhile, nothing stopped the tickle.

Not steroid cream.

Not antibiotic ointment.

Not antifungal salve.

Not scratching with an unraveled hanger.

Nothing. Nada! Doctors were useless—couldn't even stop an itch. He sneered. A small itch! No wonder the clods got sued all the time.

He shifted in the chair, twisting his right foot, hopefully away from the pain.

In three months, the itch transformed itself: less of a tingle, more of a burning sting just below the laces of his size 13 wingtips—like a small hornet was trapped under his skin, trying to sting its little way out. In desperation, he gave up his beloved shoes, going to size 14 slip-ons.

The pain hornet was unappeased.

Like today.

The dirty, angry insect, or whatever it was, was doing a number on his foot from the inside out. Tick . . . tick . . . tick. *Sting.* Tick . . . tick. *Sting . . . sting . . . sting.*

But he had been around the block with this. He knew the pain would pass on its own, so he sat there as minutes turned into a quarter hour. Then, when his foot went numb as it always did, he called for the Uber, wondering how long it would take him to walk on the slick, waxed floor to the hotel's front entrance.

# NEED TO KNOW

"What?" Breanna said, shaking her head in the CiliCold conference room. "Why work on the common cold? I mean, I guess I know why, but nobody's working on that, right?"

She'd thought these folks were smart. Now, after Jon's financial disclosure two days ago and this revelation, well, she just didn't know.

"Nobody with any sense," Dale said, moving his chair back, lifting his clogs onto the tabletop. "Ah, much better."

"Theoretically, it's possible," Luis said.

"Sure, and theoretically it's possible to have angels fly out of your ass."

Luiz looked across the table at Dale. "Temper, temper, mon capitán"

"Sorry," he said.

Breanna said nothing, staring at Dale like he was a seventh-grade truant.

"I didn't sleep last night." He shrugged.

Always the excuses with this guy, she thought.

"Then why isn't anybody else working on this?" Breanna asked. "Look, guys," she said, holding her hands out, "The reason that this company is barely afloat is not because we make flu vaccine, but because we use this expensive equipment and these animals. Now I learn that these," she bit her upper lip, slowing down some, "these extra expenses are to try to cure the common cold—something that no one has done and that many have given up on. What gives?

"And," she added, turning to Wild Bill, "why can't we just cure it with a vaccine, like we do with the flu? Isn't that the one thing we do produce here?"

"Cure it? Good question," the regulator said, pulling a Wild Bill on the chair while looking over at Luiz. "Tell the little lady," he said in his best Southern drawl.

"Well, the cold's caused by viruses," Luiz said, taking out his notebook, and turning to a blank page, head down. "By well-known viruses, actually, and of course, since we make vaccines for other viral diseases, then it stands to reason—"

She shook her head. "Wait a second, Luiz. Before you go there, tell me why we don't build up immunity to the viruses that cause the common cold without a vaccine, like we do to other diseases?"

"We do?" Dale said, leaning forward. "Name one."

"Stop messing with her," Luiz said, pointing a finger at Dale.

"Well, how about measles, Dale?" She wrinkled her brow for a moment, drawing on old memories. "Maybe mumps too?"

The room was silent.

"Well, well, well," Dale said, with a wide smile, leaning back, closing his notebook. "Looks like our new accountant knows more than just accounting."

"Are you an asshole every damn day of the year, Dale?" Breanna tried to stand, but gave in to the nausea and sat back down.

Absolute quiet in the room, then after a few moments, Wild Bill asked, "Are you OK, Breanna?"

She ignored him. "I'm pregnant now, and I had good high school teachers then."

"Didn't know," Will Bill offered, scooting forward into the backward seat. "About either one of those—"

Breanna put her had up to Bill, while staring at Dale. "I also get tired of smarmy smart-asses who believe that they know everything but can't explain anything." She leaned over toward the virologist. "Just in case you're unclear, it's my job to save this company financially and—"

She tapped her foot on the table leg a few times. Then in a hushed voice, she said, "Well, please just answer straight questions with straight answers, OK?"

"Well, you're right," Dale said after a moment, running both hands back over his bald head. "Our bodies have a great knack for remembering infections. In fact, we have special cells called memory cells that help with that."

"And," Luiz said, "their memory can last a long time. In some cases, like measles and mumps, these memory cells remember the infections for the rest of our lives. If the virus sneaks into your system—"

"And they do. Probably every year or so," Dale added.

"Ready to stir up more trouble," Luis continued, "then the memory cells recognize them and produce substances—"

"Antibodies, right?" Breanna said, remembering another high school remnant. Some of what they were saying was so familiar, other parts new. She leaned forward, irritation vanishing, eager to learn.

"That destroy the virus."

"So the memory cells are like watchdogs," she said, pursing her lips, "and when you are re-exposed to the virus, they sound the alarm."

"Not really sound, though," the regulator said, doing a Wild Bill with another chair. "It's more chemical."

"Right," Breanna said. "They produce chemicals that other cells detect and react to. Then the other cells go after the viruses?"

"Yes, but the memory cells make their own, as you say, antibodies."

"Quite a system," Breanna said, looking at each of them.

"It took billions of years to develop it," Dale said, shrugging his shoulders.

"So," Breanna said, shifting in her seat, pushing the folders with their invoices aside, "memory cells protect us from prior infections. So why doesn't that work with the common cold? We do we get colds over and over, Luiz?"

"Actually," Luiz started, taking a sip of coffee. Breanna watched the muscles in his face tighten into a hard grimace. "Ugh. This is awful," he said, putting the cup down and pushing it to the edge of the workbench. "I'd rather be cold than drink this."

"Well, you made it," Dale said.

"Not saying I didn't." Luiz put the cup down and turned to Breanna. "What I meant to say was that the system does work against the common cold."

"Not for me it doesn't," Breanna said. "I must get three or four each year."

"We all pretty much do," Luiz said. "The problem is, they are different colds."

"Different colds?"

"Sure. Colds caused by different viruses. So your cold last summer may have been caused by, say, a picorna, but—"

"A picorna?"

"Yeah, like the *Star Trek* captain," Dale said.

Breanna stared at him, pleased that Luiz and Bill were doing the same.

"OK, OK. Sorry," Dale said, holding his hands up to shield himself.

"Pretty funny actually," Breanna said, smiling at Dale. "Sorry I popped off a minute ago. I'm not feeling so good, and I was getting only attitude from you, not answers."

Dale nodded.

"A picornavirus is a type of virus," Luiz said. "Anyway, say the picornavirus infected you four months ago, making you sick. Your immune system remembers that, and now that it has recovered, is watching for another of the same picornavirus. But then an adenovirus comes along. This is a new one for your immune system, and boom, you're sick again."

"OK," Breanna said, with a nod of her head. "Like the flu."

"Influenza is different," Dale said, taking a big swig of the coffee that he made himself. "Ah, now that's refreshing." He smiled at Luiz.

"You're better with coffee. I'm better with B cells," Luiz said.

"The reason influenza is different," Wild Bill said, waving off both virologists, "is because there are only a small number of viruses that cause the flu in any given year. We can keep up with them and make a vaccine that protects against them."

"Yeah," Dale snorted. "And sometimes the experts don't get them right, and the flu vaccine fails for many people. Even with a just a few flu viruses, we almost missed the curve with H1N1," Dale said, pat-pat-patting both hands on the table.

"Your respect for scientific effort knows no bounds," Luiz said with a smile.

"Don't get me started."

"Too late."

The two scientists laughed, Wild Bill yelp-yelping.

"Well," Breanna asked, "how many viruses cause the common cold?"

"Hundreds?"

Her hand jumped to her mouth. "Hundreds?"

"Worse than that, because they're always changing." Luiz shook his head. "This year's anti-rhinovirus vaccine wouldn't work against next year's rhinovirus because the virus changes. We can keep up with three or four viruses changing, but not hundreds all the time."

"You'd think the damn viruses don't want to be stopped," Dale said, looking back at the coffee pot.

"They just do what they do, Dale," Luiz said, turning to Breanna. "It's not just people. Plants also get viral infections. Animals too, like dogs who get distemper. That's a virus. Mosquitoes get them. So do birds, even—"

"Serves mosquitoes right," Dale said.

Breanna smiled at him. He was an irritant, but also a laugh.

"Bacteria," Luiz finished. "They have their own set of viral infections. You know," Luiz said, rubbing hands together, "if aliens came to this planet and surveyed all that is happening here—"

"They'd run like hell and put up warning beacons for the rest of the galaxy to heed," Dale said. Wild Bill yelp-yelp-yelped.

"Maybe," Luiz continued, "but not before they declared Earth the world of the viruses. These things are here by the millions of trillions, and they infect everything."

"Gee, Luiz, that's real sweet," Dale said snarkily. "Maybe we should rename this planet Virusepia."

"OK," Breanna said, feeling the tug of her office, her anger replaced by hollowness. "OK. So the attacking viruses are always changing, and scientists can't keep up, right?" She watched Wild Bill and Dale nod, and thought she'd been a real bitch to Dale. She couldn't afford to get fired.

"The B cells can only make antibodies to what they were exposed to before," Breanna said, standing. "I need to go, but what if—"

She bumped against the table, knocking her laptop off. Dale lurched, catching it before it hit the cold wooden floor.

"Thanks, Dale. That would have been a disaster."

"Sure thing."

"What were you saying?" Bill asked.

"Just that— Oh, hi, Robbie. Don't you look nice."

"Thanks. You have a call, Breanna," Robbie said. "Sounds pretty serious."

# ICE PICK

Ten minutes later Jon, heading to Robbie's office to confirm his next fundraising appointment for the day, walked by the kitchen, where he saw Dale sat working.

Jon shook his head. Only Dale would work through his calculations in the kitchen.

"Hi, Dale." He stopped and entered, joining Dale at the small table. "How are things in Virus City?"

Dale shrugged. "We got trouble in Virus City, my friend." He scratched the arms of both exposed elbows, lab coat sleeves rolled up well above them.

"Something with the experi—"

"No way," Dale said, cutting him off. "But from what I hear, Breanna just screwed up an order of our equipment. Well," he continued, blinking twice, "should've known no one's perfect." Jon watched Dale bury his head back in the notebook.

"First I heard of it," Jon said, thinking that things had gone so well with her. "Let me see what's going on."

He reversed direction and headed to accounting, where he found Breanna hunched over her desk, Dell notebook perched on the desk corner, desktop monitor open to a spreadsheet.

"Hi," Jon said, hands in his pockets, "I just saw Da—"

"I don't know what the hell you people think you're doing," a new strident voice shouted, "but you'd better get us that check for the equipment that we had delivered to you."

Jon turned at once to the speakerphone that was barking at Breanna. He watched her hand tremble as she sat, not taking notes, not asking questions, just frozen.

"I said we need the money for this equipment," the voice screamed as Breanna now started to shake.

Damn, Jon thought. She was rattled.

"Anybody still on the line over there?" the dry voice said on the phone. A pause, then it said, "Damn deadbeats."

"One second, please," Jon announced in a loud voice, then reached over the top of the desk display and put the phone on mute.

"Goodness, Breanna," he said, taking a seat next to her desk. "I'll manage this. But who is it?"

She sat, hands trembling. Not a word.

"Breanna?"

Nothing.

"Breanna," he said softly. "Look at me." After a moment, he added, "Please."

She turned her head slightly, looking down between the monitor and Jon, away from the phone. Jon reached over, pushing the phone away.

"You don't have to take abuse while you're here with us."

She looked at him now.

"No abuse while you are here, OK?" Jon pointed to the phone. "What company is on the phone?"

"F-Fielding."

"Phosphoimager and gel scanner," Jon said in a soft voice, nodding.

"They say that we owe another five thousand dollars for the Storm 485."

Jon shook his head. There was something familiar about this. Maybe last year? He wondered. Breanna shifted, and he caught a hint of a knee moving back from the desk. He blinked his eyes twice, than once more. There was a meeting last summer offsite.

No.

The power of the thought stole his vision for just a moment.

The meeting had not been offsite.

It had been here.

Right here.

Fielding himself had come over, taken the tour, and offered a discount on his machine.

"Hey," he said, touching her arm. "I just need a second, Breanna, and I think I can help to resolve—"

His voice trailed off as he searched the S4. He navigated to the email search screen, then taking a deep breath, he carefully typed in "Fielding" and hit Search.

There.

From A. Earl Fielding.

The email offering the discount.

"Take us off mute," he said, voice rising.

She hit the button, and he saw her look at him curiously through red-rimmed eyes.

"Please explain the issue," Jon said. "Precisely."

The reedy voice went through the concern again, then, rising to a higher pitch, said, "So, we're going to take our equipment back unless you pay what you owe, and pay it now. I don't get you peop—"

"You're confused," Jon cut in.

"It's not confusing at all, Einstein," the nasal voice on the phone sniffed. "You owe us $5,000 for Storm, and we are not in the habit of giving away our machines."

"You are misinformed," Jon said. "Mr. Fielding requires no additional money from us for this purpose."

"Excuse me?" the nasal voice jumped up another octave.

"Are you having trouble with English today?" Jon retorted, leaning closer over the phone.

The phone was dead still.

"Do you want me to ask Mr. Fielding to join us on the phone?" Jon asked. "Maybe he can help with your language difficulty."

"What does Field—I mean, Mr. Fielding have to do with this?" the voice, now less grating, asked.

"He offered us a discount for exactly the amount that you claim that we owe. Can you accept an email?"

"Well, uh, sure."

Breanna put the email address in front of Jon. In ten seconds, Jon forwarded the email over. Probably going to the bowels of that place, he thought, where this knuckle dragger must work.

"Do you have the message?" Jon asked.

"Uh, yes. Yes. I'm looking at it now."

"I don't believe you," Jon said, as he drew closer to the phone, his stomach now a hard knot. "Why don't you read it out loud so we can all hear? For the record."

"I . . . I don't really want to do that, but I think this resolves it."

Jon waved his hand like he was backhanding a bug. "I will tell Mr. Fielding that we spoke."

"Uh . . . What . . . what will you say?"

"That if you and I meet, I'll do your eye exam with an ice pick."

Stone silence.

"Are you threatening me?" the voice responded, full of astonishment, tinged with fear.

"Still struggling with English over there?" Jon asked. "Well, know this." His lips were almost touching the phone as they moved. "Don't you ever talk to my accountant or any of my people here as you did today."

"Listen, I was on—"

Jon hung up, his pulse racing, back coated with sweat. He wasn't just angry.

He was caught up in fury. He wanted the dweeb to push back on the email, to put his hands up so Jon could knock his sorry ass to the ground. For a few delicious moments, he let anger own him, rule him.

Then after a couple of blinks and a sigh, he was back. He saw that Breanna was looking at the email then back to him.

"You saved me," she said.

He smiled, and leaned forward, quiet for a moment, then replied, "Shucks, ma'am. T'weren't nothin'."

They both laughed, good and long. Jon felt the tension flow over and off him like sweet spring rain.

"I ran into Dale downstairs," he said, slouching a little in the chair, "and he told me a little about this mess."

"I could see what this guy was saying," she said, "but he was rude and demanding and I . . . I—"

John had lots of questions. She was an experienced accountant. Surely she'd dealt with pissed-off clients before. *What was different about today?* he wondered.

He looked at her. Not the time for the third degree.

It was a time to hold her, comfort her.

No.

He moved his chair away, heart and arms aching to reach out to her.

"Actually," he said, suddenly wondering what to do with his hands, "we should have told you about the discount arrangement. Could have saved you all this trouble."

"Don't handle that as well as I used to," she said, voice shaking again.

He shrugged, arms still fighting to hold her. "No sweat," he said, starting to stand. "I think there are several more discounts that we get from various manufacturers. How about if we find some time and I'll work you through them?"

She looked up, reaching her hand partway to him. "How about now?"

Jon looked down, now certain of his purpose. "You sure?"

"All yours."

He sat back down. Then pulling up his list from the note app in his S4, he spoke softly and slowly, reviewing the details of the special arrangements with several of their suppliers. She drew close, writing all that he said.

"Who's texting me?" Jon asked hours later in his own chair.

The empty office didn't respond.

His phone said 6:27 p.m.

"You made my day."

He stared at the small display, looked around, then stared again.

Sixteen characters filled him with wonder, incredulity, and delight.

He read it again, a new message being pounded home with each powerful beat of his heart.

# LIGHTNING

The video clip was not high-def, but Abigail Johansson, court reporter for the deposition *Solana Sherman v. SSS Pharmaceuticals*, saw that all fifteen attorneys sitting around the polished maple table were glued to the images of Don and Solana Sherman sitting at their breakfast table.

Abigail's heart pounded, her head aching with each beat, her palms moist.

But she stared too. She couldn't help herself.

Strange, because there was not a single movement on the video.

Not one sound coming from the functioning audio track.

Yet here she sat, like everyone else, transfixed by Solana's eyes, or what little that they could see of them, whites barely visible through the narrowed, rigid slits of her thin lids.

At once, the beast uncoiled and struck.

Sixty seconds before, the video started with the couple sitting at the small kitchen table in their apartment for breakfast, just small-talking their way through another early morning. All of it boring fare to the attorneys, Abigail saw. But they did boring for a living, so really, who cared?

Actually, she silently confessed to herself, she was bored too, except when the husband pulled his wayward tie, dripping with milk, out of his cereal bowl. Twice. She stifled a giggle.

*My husband would never do that*, she thought. *If I had one.*

Suddenly, she saw Solana sit up straight, her head snapping back so hard that her sunglasses, delicately perched across the top of her head, flew right to the ceiling and out of view of the camera. Everyone jumped at the crash the lens made on the ceiling, shards flying everywhere.

"Whoooah!" her husband exclaimed. Actually, to Abigail, his voice didn't sound upset, just surprised, even jovial. Solana, he had said in his own earlier deposition, reacted terribly to kitchen messes (at least that was what she remembered him saying). Yet here his wife was, making one. You could read the quizzical look on his narrow face, and Abigail wondered along with him what had gotten into her.

"Solana?" he said.

Now, the reporter noticed, everyone sat forward.

Abigail's stomach tightened as the camera revealed only the whites of Solana's eyes were visible, the rest (iris? pupil? She didn't know or care) moved so far left in their sockets that she swore that they disappeared. Meanwhile, her head (quite a pretty head) started a slow, quiet, sinister twist to the left—toward her husband and the camera.

"Solana!" he now cried out, leaning over the table with its plates of cereal, fruit, and toast to gently touch her left shoulder with his right hand.

Her head continued its leftward turn, turning so far left that Abigail knew that there was no way that his wife could see Don. Left, left, left—stretching Solana's neck and facial muscles so taut that they were visibly twitching in agony. Left, left, left—the long black hair swishing first against, and then away from her neck as the combination of gravity and position controlled its response. Left, left, left. At its physical limits, unable to twist any further, her head started to tilt over on itself, still to the left.

Just watching this made her own neck hurt.

On the tape, Abigail saw Don gawk with helpless horror at his delicate wife's upper body tilting up and leftward, following her head, lifting her chair onto its left two legs in an ungainly wobble.

Then, a new, soft voice on the video. Nobody could hear, but his depo transcript showed that he thought that she said to him, "Don, it hurts. What's . . . going . . . on? Don . . . Don."

Abigail saw the young wife grimace, fighting against a new, terrible force that with each passing, degrading moment, took control of her body. She gaped as the new beast stol—

The movement stopped at once.

The chair quickly righted itself on all four legs with a sharp thud. Don and his twisted Solana sat quietly.

Abigail and all the viewers around her sighed in relief. One or two of the attorneys loosened their ties, while others looked around, pleased that it was all over.

The time feed on the video said August 25, 2015, 8:54:27 a.m.

Everybody jumped at the sickening crunch Solana's head made as it slammed into the breakfast table. The forceful impact split her forehead and demolished the breakfast plate, spitting food and glass in all directions, the broken fragments skittering across the cheaply tiled floor of the small kitchen.

Abigail's hands shot to her mouth, heart pounding in pure terror as Don jumped toward Solana. His awkward grab missed, his own chair clattering over near hers. Solana said nothing, the blood from her lacerated face streaming across the top of the table, making its thick way to where Don had been seated.

Abigail heard someone vomit their breakfast onto the polished wooden table.

Heard Mr. Giles shout, "Clean that crap up and keep the video going. We don't want to be here all day."

But she didn't dare turn from the screen.

Don was up now, behind his wife, grabbing her shoulders, trying to pull Solana's head out of the food.

But Solana wouldn't budge.

To Abigail, Don looked like a crazy man gesticulating and grabbing one of his wife's arms, then the other, then the shoulders, then a full Nelson. But his wife stayed fixed and unmovable. She looked like a demented karate expert who kept pushing hard against the block that she expected and failed to break with one determined blow.

*Sheooooushhh.* Solana suddenly exhaled as she slid off the side of the chair. Plunging forward, Don shot his right arm out to catch her but failed as, with a *thap*, his wife fell to the linoleum floor, rolling to the right until she pinned her right arm and leg underneath her.

Don swore, kicking his wife's chair out of the way with a savage thrust of his foot, the chair slamming against what sounded like a pole light that crashed to the floor.

Abigail watched as Solana's left side shook violently. Her left arm flailed, banging over and over onto the floor, her left leg banging its shoeless foot against the hot radiator, scalding its flesh and breaking its bones as the wild electricity raced through her.

White cotton balls filled Abigail's vision, lightheadedness taking over, the stink of vomit filling the room. She turned from her recorder then jumped off the chair as a paralegal shot up and bolted from the room, followed by two others.

"There go your careers, sweethearts," she heard Mr. Giles call after them.

Suddenly, the lightning left, and the seizures released their control.

Slumped in her chair, Abigail cried, her breaths coming in soft ragged gasps as she watched Don Sherman, sitting in urine and feces, holding the broken body of his young wife in his arms. "Sweetheart, mía," she heard him say. "I'll get you through this. We'll be OK. OK . . . OK . . ."

The image froze.

# WHIPPED

"Turn the lights up," Jasper yelled, ensuring that his anger owned the room, "and get somebody in here to clean this damn mess up."

"Maybe we should recess?" he heard Leland Runland, plaintiff's counsel, suggest.

"No. Bring the witness in." He turned to Runland, the opposing counsel sitting across the table. 'Why haven't we—" He stopped, putting his pudgy left hand out to opposing council while turning toward the reporter. "Are we— What's your name?"

"Abigail Jo—"

"Are we still on the record, Abigail?"

"We are."

He twisted back to Runland, hand still out. "I asked you why you haven't shown this to us until now."

"It . . . it was just produced to us."

What a worm, Giles thought. Pale, short, heavyset, more pink than white, Runland looked like he was ready to be basted for Thanksgiving dinner. With horn-rims, no less.

The door to the conference room opened, and he saw Cassie stride in.

"I don't believe you," Giles said, turning back to Runland. "I'm lodging an objection on the record here today to exclude this entire video. It's bad enough that you interrupted my examination of my witness by showing this so-called evidence."

"You stated that you wanted to see it as soon as possible," Runland replied with tight voice.

Giles smelled his fear and jumped up. "Not only is it prejudicial, but I don't believe that it's free of doctoring or electronic manipulation. Plus, you didn't follow proper procedures in turning it over to us. You read me, Runland?"

There.

Defense counsel surveyed the room.

Nicely quaffed.

Giles had established authority and asserted control. Now for an unanticipated magnanimous act.

*Oh, I just love this shit*, he thought.

Giles smiled, stretching out his right leg under the table. “Defense is willing to stipulate that the plaintiff had a nervous attack of some kind.”

He could almost feel the Runland sphincter relax.

“May I finish examining my witness, Mr. Runland?”

“Of course,” Runland said, motioning to the door for his paralegal, just outside the room to wheel Solana in. “I’m going to provide running objections as you proc—”

“Yes, yes, yes. Of course you are,” Giles said, rotating around so that he faced Solana Sherman seated at the short end of the maple table just to his left. The court reporter sat across from him, and Runland to the reporter’s left.

Jasper let a cold eye rove over the young witness, She didn’t look an ounce over 115 pounds to him, and he couldn’t believe that she was twenty-three. Looked more like seventeen.

A special delight, this one. Her head hung low, but not low enough for her shoulder-length black hair to hide what he knew were dark eyes and perfect olive skin. Her only mar was her savagely twisted right cheek and neck muscles, a residual of the so-called stroke she accused his client’s medication of producing.

And of course, her useless left arm and leg, all of which that sleaze Runland argued was SSS’s fault.

They dared accuse SSS Pharmaceuticals—his client for years—of causing her stroke. This accusation, this rank obscenity was like stabbing his love-labor, his America, through the gut, he thought. His anger swelled as he hissed air into his mouth, sending it on its way to tight, bronchitic lungs.

And he was here to stop it.

“Objection as to form.”

Giles ignored the hapless plaintiff’s attorney, shifting his own massive 6⊠5⊠ 390-pound frame so that it blocked the sun’s warm rays from reaching the small witness through the large windows. The towering effect excited him, and his penis swelled. Smirking, he cocked his head to the right, closing in.

"That was quite a performance on that video, Ms. Sherman," Giles said.

"Objection as to form." Runland said, barely audible.

Giles ignored the comment and leaned across the table toward Solana.

"Can you please remind us where you worked?

"CiliCold, sir."

"And what is that?"

"It's a company that makes vaccines."

"Vaccines? For what, exactly?"

"I'm not a . . . a doctor, but I think the flu, colds. That kind of thing."

"Colds?" he pushed his chair back. "What is that, some kind of joke?"

"No. No, sir."

"Can you please speak up?" Giles thundered, pointing to the rest of the room. "Nobody can hear you."

"I . . . I will try to speak up. My voice is not the same since my stroke."

"How convenient for you," he said,

"Objection as to form," he heard Runland utter.

"So maybe CiliCold gave you this so-called stroke with their testing," Giles said, turning back to the witness. "Did you ever consider that before you leveled this wild accusation at my client's drug?"

"Objection as to form."

Out of the corner of his eye, Giles watched Cassie take some notes. Don't know why she's here today. I don't need a second-seater to depose this cripped-up Latina.

*Be nice,* he thought, *if only for a few more minutes.* He sighed, then said, "OK. I withdraw the question."

He noticed opposing counsel relax as if he'd won the legal victory of the month.

"Now before the video," he started, "I asked you a question, which you did not answer. In fact, you took more of the medication than you were told to."

She said nothing.

"Isn't that *right*?" he yelled.

"Objection as to form," Runland whispered.

He heard no breathing from anyone.

Swiveling his head on top of its fat neck back around, he saw that the slight, breast-less thing of a woman recording the deposition's proceedings had stopped her tap-tapping. All was still, few daring to breathe the air that he nicely poisoned with his venomous questions.

*She thinks my client hurt her?* he asked himself. *You hurt yourself, little mamacita.*

Giles' twisting acidic stomach squeezed down, forcing a bile jet into his throat, blocking for a moment the hot pain that twisted through his right leg today.

His internal speed brakes kicked in again.

Sure, he could bring this deposition to an end with a series of quick, devastating questions, but not yet. *What's the rush?* he thought. *We have a tasty morsel here. Let's take our time.*

Like a rapist in an alley with an eye on his prey, he paused to savor the moments that he knew would lead to the psychological ravishment of this woman-child.

"I'll ask again," he said to her, closing his eyes, working to keep a low tone. "Didn't you take more medicine than the recommended dose before you had your . . ." He hesitated for just a moment, not wanting to say the word *stroke*, to keep it off the record. That was for plaintiff to do. He wouldn't even acknowledge the possibility. "Your physical problems?"

"Why don't you understand?" she asked, raising her head just an inch. "I was following my doct—"

"What I don't understand is why you won't answer my question," he said, pushing his huge face closer to hers. "Isn't it true that you took more pills than the label recommended? You did not comply with the instructions that were there, plain as day for anyone to see, on the label, did you?"

Solana looked around. Giles knew she was desperate for help. "Pero, mí médico—"

"Maybe you have forgotten what country you are in," he said, raising both arms in what he knew to be a show of mock frustration.

"Yes, yes, sir. I'm sorry. My, my doctor told me—"

"I know you're sorry, but I don't care what your insipid doctor told you," Giles said, dropping his voice even lower, so the recorder, sitting on the left side of the witness, had to lean closer to him to hear his question. He raised his right hand until it was a foot off the table.

"I am asking you what you chose to *do*," he roared, hand slamming down on the table like a thunderclap, its explosive decompression shooting across the table.

He delighted as both the witness and mouse court reporter jumped at the impact. Solana whimpered, pulling in her narrow shoulders, causing the front of her dress to open some. Giles tilted his head up for a moment, allowing him a delicious peek down its front, almost licking his lips in enjoyment at the sweat that now glistened on her light skin.

Satisfied for the moment, Giles filled his huge lungs with air while permitting himself a look to his right at the jumble of junior lawyers stretching from just beyond the reach of his right hand on down the table, busily scribbling notes.

Picking up the cheap pen sitting on the unused yellow pad in front of him, he turned back to his left then sat up straight for a moment. Then he leaned forward to take another delectable bite out of the helpless witness with her full, quivering lips.

"Objection as to form." Then a moment later, he added, "And argumentative."

Giles' head pivoted to the right, bringing Runland into sharp focus on the other side of the smooth wood conference table

"What did you say?" Giles asked, looking across at the frumpy opposing counsel, who sat hunched in his chair, sweeping heavy locks of grey-infested brown hair out of his eyes. *He's not even wearing a tie and jacket*, Giles snarkily said to himself. The rumpled clown was out of his depth.

"Just . . . you are badgering—"

Giles threw his pen against the wooden table, where it skipped across the smooth surface and all but fell into the lap of Runland, who, making an attempt to catch it, missed completely.

"Ms. Sherman," Giles said, turning away from her inept counsel, "you are here under oath. You sit here because you filed a lawsuit against my client. My . . . client." Giles almost rose from his seat at his own words, letting himself get caught up in his own intonation. "You are not a child, so cut the crap and answer my questions right now."

He shot his right arm in Solana's direction, pointing a long index finger at her, a finger that ended in a splintered and dirty nail, its tip flexing, reaching to hook her soul. His eyes glaring, he said, "The fact that you have a lawyer here with you doesn't give you the right to sit there like a petulant child."

"Objection," Runland offered, in a voice so low that the mouse court reporter had to lean her thin head toward him to hear. "Objection as to form. And you are badgering."

That was it.

"You get to say 'object to form.' That's it," Giles shouted across the table to the quivering Runland.

"And you are interrupting my questioning of this witness," he said as his eyes shot daggers across the table toward opposing counsel. "Again."

"Uh, no—well, yes."

Giles smelled the fear. "This is my deposition of this witness, and I will ask my own questions in my own way." His thick spittle landed on the table between him and Runland. "Object all you like," Giles replied. "I have a right to ask this witness questions and to demand answers. The question was simple. Your witness should be capable of answering. I'll ask again."

He watched Runland inhale.

"You, Mr. Giles, are bullying my—"

Giles jumped to his feet, trying to ignore the right ankle that gave no relief, demolishing Runland's gaze with a stare that he'd knew hurt like a hammer. "She's old enough to sue, she's old enough to answer my questions. It you don't like that, you can leave."

He leaned his large form over the table, and the huge black shadow of his form reached the full way to plaintiff's counsel. "I'm telling you that we will stay here all day until we get answers to my questions. And if we cannot complete this deposition, the case does not go forward. You got that, counselor?"

He saw Runland did not back down, and he almost smiled at the plaintiff attorney's false courage.

"If you persist in addressing my witness like this, sir," Runland replied, "I'll . . . well, I'll have to call the judge to see what she thinks."

"Oh," Giles said, feigning fear, letting his voice rise to a full falsetto of mischief, "the judge. You want to call the judge? Well then." Giles stood straighter and straighter. "Is that what you want to do?" He unlimbered his huge frame. He towered over the table, his shadow stretching across the table as if it alone could smash Runland. Giles' left hand moved down then into his pants pocket.

"Don't want to interfere with your right to call the judge," he said. "No, sir." His left hand pulled out a black-and-silver device. He saw that Runland couldn't resist squinting over the table to see what it was.

A cell phone. Giles hit a button to cycle it up.

"Go ahead. Call her," Giles said at the top of his voice. His left arm raced first up, then forward, then down hard like a fielder firing the ball to home plate.

But this time, the destination was Runland's head, six feet away.

Everyone gasped. Giles sneered as his own team of lawyers jumped out of their seats, necks frozen in stiff consternation. The mouse reporter leaped from her chair and struggled to take a step away from Runland. Ms. Sherman dropped her head to the desk and covered it with both arms. He saw Runland jam his feet hard into the carpet then shove his wheeled chair back from the table, scooting away from the assault. Somewhere on his path of retreat, Runland lost his balance as the chair, not designed for escape, tipped over, spilling its occupant onto the floor.

Jumping up, Giles stormed over to Runland, as Runland, still in the chair, flapped around to extricate himself, eyes full of fright.

Giles towered over him. Runland, trying to twist out of the now-broken chair, was a helpless goldfish knocked out of his bowl, flopping around on the floor. Giles leaned in for the kill, glaring at plaintiff's counsel as he filled his mind with hate.

Then, Giles smiled, opening his right hand to reveal the phone he never released.

The huge defense attorney stood straight up, turned and laughed out loud, heading back to his side of the table. Sitting, he placed the phone on the table and with his left hand, snapshotted it across the smooth surface toward Runland. The phone, airborne for just a moment, hit the floor in front of Runland, where it bounced hard off the waxed wooden surface, battery going in one direction, the rest of its contents spilling in others.

"What are you waiting for? Call the judge," Giles said. "Get up off the floor, counselor, and call the court. By all means, tell her what has happened here and see what she'll say. You really think she's going to stop this deposition? We won't stop"—he turned, twisting his big head to fully face Solana, looking at her like a wild beast looks at fresh kill—"until I get my questions answered."

Runland sat up and coughed. "You continue to act this way, and I'll ask for—"

"Maybe we should take a break," a chubby attorney with thin blonde hair, in a suit two sizes too tight, said.

Giles never broke his stare-down with Runland. "Not until I get my question answered. I want my questions answered first. Then we can quit for the day. I don't think we can get much more out of this . . . this witness." He dismissed Solana into meaninglessness with a hand wave.

"Let's, let's just finish this," Runland said, looking around for another chair to sit in, like a child who had wandered without his parents into a room of strange adults.

Giles also knew that opposing counsel wasn't the only one who wanted to call it a day. He saw in the eyes of his junior associates that they all thought he had gone too far. He sighed, jotting a brief note to Cassie: "Cassie, maybe we should go after CiliCold?"

He started to push it down the table, but stopped in mid shove. Pulling back, he added "Good luck at the Tanner beat down tomorrow." Grimacing at the pain that snapped and crackled in his right foot, he shoved the note down the table in her direction.

"Let's proceed for just another minute." He lied. Giles wasn't done, not by a long shot. The spiritual whipping of Solana Sherman took another ninety aching minutes, the sun having long since fled from the winter sky.

# BOUNCE

"Don't be a hero tonight," Kevin said after he pulled the Audi in front of Brisé's for the last time in his wife's life.

"Heroine," Dana answered, waking up from her nap in the comfortable passenger seat.

Kevin Wells, VP-Marketing of Tanner Pharmaceuticals, rushed around the back of the car, trying not to slip in the snow. The flakes were huge. If they fell faster, they would probably knock people over.

He cursed himself for this idea. She was far too sick now to bring outside in weather like this. But this was their anniversary, their last one.

What did they call her clear cell carcinoma?

It just took a moment to remember. The great masquerader. Yes. Neither he nor she knew the reason for her initial weight loss. Always struggling with her weight, his wife used to brag to Cristen, her younger friend, that whatever it was, she could live with the weight-loss part of it.

That was the easy part, he thought. Maybe the end would be too. At this point, he didn't know anything anymore.

Getting to the passenger door, already held open by the valet, he picked up his 100-pound wife in his arms, turned, then carried her inside the restaurant and to their seats. There he gently put her down and helped her out of her coat.

"My hero," she said.

"Always, lover."

The docs gave her six months, her husband remembered, studying her face crowned by thinning brown tightly curled hair. On her good days, he could see her living for six years. But on nights like tonight when she had to chase her breath just sitting, he thought it would end in six days.

Death train was on its way.

Kevin knew that he had done all that he could. They had seen all the specialists, eschewing surgery but working through the shock-horror of chemo. They had ridden the medical roller coaster, rising and falling on the lab test results.

That over, he and Dana made all the arrangements, updating the wills, loving on their children, who, adults themselves, pretended to be strong through it all. Kevin was tapped out. They had hoped together, raged together, cried together, and suffered together. What else could they do?

We can enjoy tonight, he thought. Together. Loving their unpromised moments.

◆

"That was nice, Kev," Dana offered when Kevin sat her down in her chair and walked to his own seat.

"How many years have we done this, Dana?"

"Don't be a tease," she said, reaching for some French bread.

He leaned over to assist. "How many foreign ones?"

"Over thirty-five of them."

"Thirty-six restaurants, to be exact, Dr. Wells, and I really had to scratch for some of them."

"Well, Kev," she said, letting her eyes rove, taking in the deep-piled red-carpeted floors and luxuriant wallpaper that kept the noise of the room down, "you scored tonight."

He laughed. "Now you're the one being a tease."

The waiter came and, after a warm greeting, took their orders and left.

"We needed a good choice tonight," Kevin replied, his voice turning serious.

"I'll say," Dana said. "I'm scared stiff about what Triple S will do to my department."

He nodded. "The axes will start flying soon."

She looked at him. The candlelight deepened his facial expressions, darkening his brown skin. She always loved the effect.

"Asher heard he was out," he said.

"The executive vice president?" Her heart pounded for just a bit, then she felt it fall back into its usual irregular rhythm.

"Yes, but it won't be officially announced until tomorrow."

"I don't understand," Dana said. "I get corporate takeovers, but how do they expect Tanner to continue producing if they decapitate us?"

"They 'recapitate', this time with Triple S heads." Their corporate model is 'Buy 'em and fry 'em'."

"If I had any rage left, I'd hurl it at Meredith Douchette and her damn SSS."

"Save some for Giles and Rhodes. They spearheaded this."

"Ugh," Dana said. "When they get in the water, the sharks hightail it."

She watched him open his mouth, then close it.

"Thank you, honey, for letting me mix my metaphors in peace."

"Anytime, Doctor." After a moment, he said, "You know I'll be handed my hat too, right?"

Nodding, head down, she said nothing, letting them both enjoy their hors d'oeuvres, then entrées in silence. Then pursing her lips, she said, "Kev, I could never see you working for SSS."

"I'll start my own company before that happens."

She looked up at him, trying to squelch her laughter. His prior attempts to start companies had been disasters. Then she looked up.

He was laughing too.

"Don't worry. I won't try that."

"If you do, I will personally come back from heaven and sit on your chest until you change your mind."

He looked at her quizzically for a second or two. "You know I might like that."

"Dirty old man." She found his leg under the table with her foot and rubbed it. "You know,' she said, sitting straighter, "I'm concerned about my safety department."

He pursed his lips, giving her the same look she'd seen him give the chess board.

"I'm not a chess piece, honey," she said, starting her dessert.

"Oh yes, you are, my queen, and I'm just trying to protect you."

She watched him lean toward her. "We have to face the fact that one way or the other, you are out of safety," he said, swallowing some water. "If strength of heart were the metric, you'd be there for years, but it's not. We will need to transition you out, because you won't be healthy enough to stay. Triple S will ruin you."

She shifted in her seat, knowing that she couldn't abandon her team. "Cristen's not ready to take over."

"You have done all that you can. What she doesn't know, she will learn."

"I really enjoyed my times with her," she said. "So smart, so capable. We could have been friends since birth."

"She is an example of . . ." He paused. "What is that Swahili expression that you like?"

"Marafiki huzaliwa, si kutengenezwa."

"Yes." He nodded. "'Friends are born, not made.' We need to plan for you to get out and give Cristen the time she needs to adjust while you are still available to help." He swirled his ice cream in its thin saucer with his spoon. "The sooner the better would be good for the both of you."

She smiled at her husband. She knew that he thought her wish to stay at Tanner Safety was impossible, But he would still work to make as much of it as he could happen. "And what about you, Kevin?"

He leaned back and studied his wife. "Seriously?"

She smiled, reaching over to touch his hand. "*Serious* is on the table. Out with it, VP-Marketing,"

"Well, I'm not too old for new things and new people. Olivia has helped me these last few months. As for the rest, well . . ." He paused, then said, "Sipimi mafanikio ya mtu kwa umbali anayokwea, mbali kwa umbali anayoduta anapogonga chini."

"Well then," she said, laughing, "not bad, Kev. And what you expect is now what I demand of you. When I am gone, you hit bottom, but you bounce high."

# STAFF MEETING

Two days later, Breanna, face flushed and heart beating madly, hurried down the staircase heading to the first floor conference room. Hitting the first-floor landing, Rayiko suddenly appeared from her own small office to the accountant's right. Breanna pulled up short, almost spilling her coffee.

"Sorry, I'm just headed to the staff meeting, Rayiko."

"After you," she said, stepping back. "I'll be there in a minute."

The accountant's own hormonal surges were making her crazy as she passed in front of Rayiko, walking through a doorway with a white swinging door into a rectangular room.

The tangerine walls and white ceiling with its small chandelier hanging above a beat-up oval wooden table surrounded by six wooden chairs reminded her of a dining room. On the wall to her left was a large mirror, making the entire room appear longer than it actually was. The opposite wall wasn't a wall at all but an entryway to the living room.

The folding wooden doors that could divide the two rooms were open, and she saw through to its entryway blocked by a rolling blackboard, the kind that could spin on its horizontal axis.

Only Luiz was in the room, and seeing him reminded Breanna of her new, expanded role on the agenda. The accountant shuddered, putting the steaming mug of coffee down, hearing the steady beat of the cold rain against the old apartment building's walls.

Breanna refocused, looking around. "I haven't been in this room before," she said, sitting down. "Who found this building?"

Luiz took his lab coat off and hung it over the back of his chair. "Beats me. CiliCold was already here when I started working two years ago."

"Rayiko and Jon found it. We were in a real dive before," Robbie said as she walked in, waving at Breanna. She put her hand on Luiz's shoulder for a moment before she walked to a worn wooden chair on the other side of the table, ever-present pen and pad in hand.

"We're going to have to get you to go digital," Luiz said with a smile.

"Well, you never know," Robbie replied, winking.

Luiz and Breanna looked at each other. Robbie's aversion to electronics was legend. She'd prefer candles to incandescence. But to Breanna, sitting across from her, there was something else. Everyone knew that Robbie was full of life every day, but today she was vibrant, new energy rolling off of her in waves.

She got it at once.

When Luiz looked away, Breanna leaned forward and whispered, "Something up?"

Robbie looked around for a moment then mouthed the words "A date."

She winked.

Breanna smiled and mouthed "Way to go." She knew Robbie was struggling. Everybody did. It was great to see her excited and not worried about life.

"So this is where you've been hiding." It was Dale. Lab coat sleeves rolled up almost to the edge of the short-sleeve shirt he wore under it. "Breanna, I heard you were pregnant. How's the bun going?"

An irritant even while trying to be nice, she thought. "Really sweet of you to a—"

"How's yours going, Dale?" Luiz asked, slapping his friend's gut.

Robby, Breanna, and Luiz laughed. Dale shrugged and plopped down in the seat next to Luiz.

"Whatcha got there?" he said, pointing to a series of drawings in Luiz's notebook, open on the table.

The two huddled, whispering together.

They seemed like two halves of the same person, Breanna thought, smiling.

"Aren't you looking good, Robbie," Wild Bill said, walking in.

Breanna turned to see the lean regulator Wild Bill his way into a seat. She looked down to hide her smile.

"Good to see you, WB."

"Did no one have anything better to do than to come to work today?"

Everyone looked up.

"Hey, Jon."

"How are you?"

"What's shakin'?"

Jon sat down at the end of the table, then leaning across the empty chair to his left, got Robbie's attention. Breanna watched him whisper something to her.

"Oh," Robbie said, "I forgot." She bounced up at once and took off.

"Breanna?"

Startled, she looked across the table at Dale.

"How do you like paying the bills around here?"

"Easiest thing in the world when there's money in the bank. You just keep on making that flu vaccine."

"Got that right," Luiz said with a nod. "Oh, hi, Rayiko. How's life in H/R and management?"

Rayiko sat down next to Jon, waved with a smile, and said nothing.

"Hey, new accountant?"

Breanna jumped at Jon's voice.

"Let's see when we can schedule your first review."

"Oh." Her stomach flipped again. She'd forgotten, totally consumed by this being the first time she would give the staff meeting financial report. "OK. Anytime is fine with me." Her back was wet with new sweat. She saw Robbie come back, all smiles still.

"I think the afternoons would be—"

"Here it is, Dr. DeLeon," Robbie said, holding the envelope out for him.

"Will you please just hold that for me? And don't you go anywhere. I rely on you."

"OK," she said with a smile.

"How's Shannon?" Rayiko asked.

"Raising hell in the world, as always," Robbie said, putting the envelope down and then looking at Rayiko. "But it's good, and things could be worse."

"Maybe we can have this company in better shape by the time Shannon grows up," Jon said, smiling at everyone around the table.

"If not, Shannon'll be running it," Dale added.

Robbie applauded while everyone laughed.

Oh boy, Breanna thought, clapping lightly. Dale the Snarky is back.

"Well, that brings us to the first agenda item." Jon looked over at Breanna. "You know—" he sneezed. "Excuse me."

"When will you stop getting those colds, huh?" Dale asked.

Full up on smart-mouthing today, Breanna thought. At once, anger welled up in her.

Cool it, girl, she thought. Everybody around this table has known each other for longer than I've been here. She looked down at her papers.

"It's viral revenge," Wild Bill said, rocking the chair forward.

Jon put both arms out in mock surrender. "Yeah well, usually I'm the one who gives the financial report, and as you all know, your questions are usually a lot more detailed than my answers. With Breanna here, I'm happy to say those days are over. Breanna, why don't you let us know where we stand." He looked at Robbie, who was staring down at the folder she had brought in.

"Sure," Breanna said. "I'll get right to it. We need to clear fifteen thousand every two weeks to stay above water. Well, we've been doing twenty K—"

"Whoa," Luiz said. Breanna noticed that Wild Bill just grinned.

"Yes. This is how it breaks out," she said, passing hard copies of Excel sheets around.

She provided all the details: number of vaccine batches delivered, receipts received, bills paid so far this month, remaining invoices to be received, encumbered balances. Ten minutes later, she stopped. "Are you all OK with this?"

"Well," Wild Bill said, smiling as he stroked his chin then pushed his glasses back up his nose, "that depends on what you mean. I'm kind of overwhelmed, first by the good news and by the details. Everybody's clearly been working hard."

"Just keep those feds off our backs," Dale said. "We'll look out after ourselves."

"What I'm paid to do, man."

"There's better news." Breanna looked back at Jon, nodding.

"I found a don-, a donor who will give us twenty-five thousand dollars," Jon said.

Robbie's hands flew to her mouth. "That's incredible."

"Outstanding," Wild Bill said, saluting Jon. "Man, you can talk paint off the wall."

Luiz and Dale looked at each other for a moment, then Dale dropped his head. "Guess the donor doesn't know our recent experimental track record."

Jon was suddenly serious. "Dale, I shared everything with her. She knows we've been on the wrong track. So do I. But before we talk about that, Robbie has something for you all." He looked at her, and she stood and walked around the table, distributing what Breanna thought looked like—

Checks.

Breanna got hers.

$250.

"I know it's not much, but I wanted to thank each of you for your continued support for this work of ours. It's been hard go—"

"What?" Dale said, looking up from his check. "Does our accountant know about this, Jon?"

"Well," Jon started. "I—"

"Of course I know, Dale,' Breanna said. "Jon and I discussed this idea in detail, and I signed off on it."

"Can I see those details?"

She was within an inch of backhanding that sardonic face. "You come by my office after the meeting, Dale, and we'll review the bonuses' implications in all the specificity you want," she said. "However, if you would suspend your sarcasm for only a moment while you examine the spreadsheet in front of you, you'd see that the relevant computations are available, beginning on row"—she looked at hers for a moment—"43."

"What column?" he asked, glasses on, studying the spreadsheet.

"Just read it, man," Luiz said, pointing a finger to the correct location on the sheet. "See? It's right there."

Breanna and Jon smiled at each other. She remembered that they both recognized there might be some questions. It was her idea to bring the spreadsheet copies.

"OK," Dale said, looking up, taking his glasses down. "What else can I say?"

"Well, Dale," Luiz said, "you could say 'Thank you.'"

"Yeah," Dale said. "Thanks."

"Thanks, Jon," Luiz said, looking at Dale, then Jon. "This means a lot."

"Well," Jon said with a laugh, "don't thank me too much. You deserve more. You all do."

Everybody laughed.

"But, Dale, you were right about the other thing," Jon said. "I've driven us off the road."

The room was still again.

“Because of me, we’ve been trying to repeat an experiment whose results we—” He paused for a second. “No. That I misinterpreted. We have to go another way.”

“Well,” Dale said, leaning forward across the table, whose uneven legs made it rock as weight on it shifted, “what’s that?”

“Listen,” Luiz said.

“I was just asking Jon here—”

“Silencio.” Luiz stood up.

They all went quiet.

Wild Bill stood up.

“I don’t hear it,” Rayiko said.

“That’s because it stopped,” Wild Bill said, raising his hands to within six inches of the vents.

Breanna looked at everyone as they all looked up at the ceiling vent.

The furnace had quit running.

# JANUARY THAW

"Hey, Dana, I really have to go now," Cristen Sandbridge said, phone in her left hand, the right one wheeling the eighteen-speed through the garage to its closed door. Her heart raced as she meticulously steered the bike's tires around the syrupy oil patches spread out over the empty garage's dirty floor.

"I'm sorry to be a pain, Cristen, but SSS is buying out Tanner."

"I heard that," Cristen said. "Rumors are rampant that we are ripe to fall."

"Not rumors anymore," Dana said, coughing. "Anyway, it becomes public in twenty-four. I've been asked to meet their attorneys tomorrow and escort them through our building, for heaven's sake."

Cristen and the bike stopped. "Seriously, Dana, are you up to that? Sometimes you don't have good days, and this nonsense is not worth your running yourself down. Let somebody in corporate walk her around. They got us into this mess."

"Corporate folks are all afraid that they'll get the ax come the morning. Plus, I do my walking exercises most every day now."

"OK, I guess," Cristen said. Dana could still have good days at work, but there were times w—

She heard Dana laughing.

"Cristen, remember Carly Simon, 'I haven't got time for the pain'?"

"Yeah, we white girls sure can sing," Cristen said.

Dana laughed. "Some of you can. Anyway, after forty-five years, that song's starting to grow on me."

Cristen hadn't heard her friend relaxed enough to laugh for a while.

"It's good to hear you this way, Dana. You and I are pawns in this chess game."

"Pawns die early."

They strike early too, Cristen thought but kept that morsel to herself.

And sometimes they promote into queens. And then—

"We'll see first, then we'll know."

"See you tomorrow."

"Count on it."

Cristen disconnected, then jammed the phone into one of her jacket's tight pockets, zipping the acrylic pouch closed. She hit the door button, watching the old wooden door creak its way up, revealing the houses across the street and then the sky. The SSS safety monitor stubbornly fought the sharp reflex to guard her eyes from the glorious white sunshine now streaming through the garage's open entryway.

Three consecutive Indiana days in the fifty-plus range.

Pupils dilated in the dark now shrank in the presence of the bright sun as the still, cold stink of the garage was dispatched by the clean, crisp outside air. Cristen realized that she was actually present, actually existing in a moment that no self-respecting meteorologist ever admitted occurred, but that every self-respecting Indy resident accepted.

January thaw.

The snow would be back—oh yes, it would. February was godforsaken—short, dark days elongating as slowly as cold molasses, increasing only by the seconds, punctuated by heavy snows and savage winds.

But this was now, the bright sunshine of today.

That was what her dad used to tell her.

Before he left.

And died.

Years ago.

Years ago was done. Anybody who looked back should have their eyes torn out.

He used to say that too.

"Get going," she said to herself, as the electric garage door squealed like dying *Ratus ratus* rats, rolling itself down to the cold floor.

For the first time since Thanksgiving, she climbed on the bike and took off.

Not a single wobble on the start-up. A straight and true shot right down the driveway.

She turned right onto Fenmore, then headed south then east to Kessler Drive, the wind changing as her direction did, always attacking her.

She didn't care. She was dueling with nature, fighting the universe.

That had been her dad too.

But he'd lost that fight.

Enough, she thought, scooting her butt back on the seat as she squeezed both brakes.

Cristen looked both ways and smiled with triumph, knowing before she was there that there would be no traffic on Kessler.

South to 65 or north to Fifty-sixth Street?

The Sequoia 9 by 2 slowed to a crawl as she shifted down through the gears, the bike finally stopping on the ice-mush-covered pavement, awaiting her command.

First time out, she reminded herself. Let's do a systems check.

The bike was in great shape—of course, she'd seen to that herself. Racked it up, then pulled the tires from the frame. Fully degreased the gears. Made sure the crank set was perfectly calibrated, then fussing over the double chain ring, ensuring both were free of dirt. Aligned the jockey and idler pulleys. Carefully inspected and re-lubed the gears. Doted over the cassette. Degreased the derailleur. Meticulously checked its movement with the rear wheel relocked into the frame. Cleaned the disc brakes. Lubed up the chain.

There was no question of it. The bike was ready. Either up or down the hill, the direction did not matter.

The 9 by 2—her baby—was spoiling for a brawl.

Up to me, she thought.

Fifty-sixth Street was the safest bet. A half mile north on Kessler got her there, then west to Fenmore, south to her home. All totaled, about a two-mile outing.

Piece of cake.

She looked to the right.

Kessler south could be a bitch. Four miles down to I-65, then four miles uphill back to Forty-eighth Street and a quarter mile home. And once committed, there was no turning back.

That wasn't really true. There were side streets she could dump into to nip back home.

But you never did that. You committed then followed through.

Kessler meant a nine-mile haul. Period.

She turned the front wheel north to Fifty-sixth Street. Then reversed and headed south on Kessler to I-65. It would be hard going, she thought, for the first ride of the year, but it least it wasn't the pussy move.

The downhill ride was fun enough. Sure, the wind gusts ripped and tore at her, but her short and tight down jacket held them at bay. The wool mask kept some of the wind out of her nose and mouth, but at least it wasn't summer. Then, you inhaled bugs if you breathed through your mouth.

It was exhilarating. Desperate loneliness is not so bad, she thought as she squeezed into a tougher gear, slowing her pedaling, thighs pumping. The SSS safety monitor relished the speed as the houses with their partly snow-covered brown and yellow grass whizzed by.

OK. The divorce was difficult, but Brad's gone to who knows who for who knows why. Who cares? And I don't cry at night anymore, she thought. Dana was right. My getting to a counselor was a great idea. Four years after the divorce and I'm great.

Zero G and I feel fine.

That was her dad's too—his and John Glenn's.

She thought about her friend at Tanner Pharmaceuticals as she scooched and squeezed, coasting around a curve. Her heart raced, but she kept her mouth closed, moving air more slowly through her nose. Her lungs filled her chest with gaseous protest, but she knew that if she opened her mouth to breath, her heart would fly out, she felt so light.

So pleased to be away from herself in the house, to be part of the air, part of the thaw.

She thought of Dana. How long had she been at Triple S with her? Four years? The two of them oversaw the day-to-day safety operation. With Dana's MD and her own MS, plus their years of experience together, they managed the department.

They shared its burdens, shared some laughs.

The safety monitor laughed out loud as she thought of her boss's clothes. Cristen had her over for dinner to have a fashion session one night. Dana peered through Cristen's wardrobe, tried clothes on.

Dana had seen her Sequoia baby.

Dana, as it turned out, still bicycled some with a group then, and suggested that Cristen join them. The safety monitor shook her head as the 9 by 2 flew through another Kessler curve. No can do. Not just because she enjoyed riding alone. She just didn't want to spend two hours staring at somebody's ass.

All that ends now, she remembered. Dana was sicker. Her friend wouldn't make it to Easter. And Dana was right. Lots of new people hanging around Tanner these d—

I-65.

The highway interchange rose up out of the twilight to meet her.

Scooch and squeeze, squeeze, squeeze. The bike slowed to a crawl as Cristen slid down to and through the lower gears. Turning her head to assess up, down, east, and west, she pedaled across the street, then turned left to head back up Kessler.

She moved up the gears, even as Kessler's incline increased, surprised at how well she could pedal. But why be surprised? She worked her quads and calves all winter, spent hours on AD-AB exercises, working her vasti and collaterals. They were trained, taut, and tight.

Cristen broke into a sweat halfway up the hill, driving thoughts of her dad, her ex, and Dana from her mind.

She focused on alignment, on motion, on passing traffic. Loving it.

Tanner was on the chopping block.

The thought threw her cadence, and she shifted down to an easier gear.

By the time she got home, she was tired, quads bulging with pain.

Tomorrow would be a mean day at Tanner.

But as she put her baby away, the safety monitor knew she'd be prepared.

Trained, taut, tight.

# DECAPITATION

Opening her legs the precise distance under the skirt that was just a cut above the knee, she extended her shaped leg to the curb, planting the stiletto-heeled foot at just the right distance from the concrete's edge, exposing the perfect calves and a glimmer of thigh for the world to admire.

One, two, three, and lift.

She glided out of the limo in a smooth motion, like clear water flowing over smooth ice, then stood ramrod straight for two moments before striding toward the low Tanner Pharmaceuticals' entryway. In five seconds, she was through it and into the huge atrium with its high ceilings, filling the capacious lobby with light.

Covering her eyes, Cassie walked to the greeter that she knew would be waiting for her just a few feet ahead.

This is my eighth decapitation, she thought. They all go the same.

Starting with the official greeter.

Same broad smile that ended at the cheekbone. This one was different though, she thought. Black, and a little on the gaunt side. Looked haggard around the eyes and mouth too.

But like all of them, Cassie saw that this greeter could not hide the rapid breathing and wide-open pupils of fear.

She'd had them once, the lawyer remembered. Now, she recognized the look in others.

"Hello, Ms. Rhodes, I am Dana Wells, and I'll be escorting you to Dr. Tanner's executive office."

"Of course you are," Cassie said, walking by her.

She heard Wells ask, "Mr. Giles is not with you?"

"He has other things that he had to deal with," Cassie said, watching with amusement as the short scientist tried to catch up.

"Well, I hope he gets to enjoy Chica—"

"Does a group named CiliCold make vaccine for Tanner?" Cassie asked as they turned left to walk through a corridor of tall silver elevators, stopping at the last one.

"I don't know," Dana said, out of breath. "But I've heard of them. Let me see what I can lea—"

"I need the file by 10:00 a.m. Thanks, Ms. Wells. I know where I'm going. You get back to your work."

"I really—"

"I'll take it from here. Just get me that file, please." Cassis turned her back on the surprised scientist to press the elevator button. A moment later, she was being whisked to the fifteenth floor, relishing the coming day's interlude.

She would not be doing the talking today.

Today, Tanner Pharmaceuticals would take itself apart. She would simply observe. *Like the surgeon, my slicing work is over,* she thought. *Nothing else to do but to observe the patient carefully as they die.*

The elevator door opened silently on 15 as if to a tomb.

Cassie stepped out and her phone rang.

"Speak."

She listened, then said, "For CiliCold? Why?"

Walking to the left, she listened some more.

Kevin Wells' stomach jumped as he turned his head from the next marketing campaign displayed on his monitor.

"Who? Where?"

"Where else?" Marc Harper, senior vice president of Tanner replied, only his head visible from the hall at the office's entrance. "Dr. Tanner's office. Pronto. See you there." His head was gone in a flash.

Kevin pushed his hands hard against his desk, driving his smooth-rolling black leather chair back. Up at once, the sixty-four-year-old executive walked around the desk of his large office and out into the bright foyer.

"Seka," Kevin said. "I'll be in Mr. Tanner's office. Looks like everyone's been called to a—"

"I know," she interrupted, just hanging up the phone, swiveling around in her wheelchair to face her boss. "Don't forget that you're greeting that new marketing group at eleven this morning. Plus lunch with Roy Elps at twelve thirty."

Stopping in mid stride, the VP-Marketing stared into space. Then smiling, he said, "Please tell my good friend and competitor Roy that I won't be lunching today. Also, I was hoping to try that holo-marketing booth that I hear just arrived."

"No chance. You know how the new marketing groups love to see the VP in action! Work with them first, then you can play." She smiled, looking at him then pantomiming patting the sides and top of her head.

"Yep," he said. "I left my pick at home. I'll stop by the men's room—"

She rummaged around in her drawer and pulled one out.

He laughed, taking it from her. "Seka, when the aliens come, I will make sure that your name is on the list of the protected so no harm comes to you."

"Aliens won't help you today." Seka lowered her voice and leaned forward in the chair. "Word has it that this urgent meeting is a big deal. Any idea how long you'll be?"

"Not a clue," he replied. Then with a smile, he added, "Who knows? I may never come back."

"Be careful what you wish for, Mr. Wells," the sixty-year-old admonished. He noticed that some of the twinkle had vanished from her green eyes.

"Sorry. Well, we shouldn't be too long. Don't forget to tell Roy for me."

"No worries." Smiling, the secretary shooed him on his way.

Hurrying out, the marketing VP shunned the elevator, turning to the right, throwing the first door open, and bounding up the steps to the office of the president and CEO. He had just enough time for a men's room fly-by.

Cassie walked into the reception area for the CEO and president. It was all business: old linoleum floor tile, with chairs and file cabinets right off the Staples website.

The executive secretary jumped up. To Cassie, it seemed like she just flew out of her chair.

"Ms. Rhodes, we were expecting you. Would you like to see—"

"Thank you, but no. Please just take me to Mr. Tanner's conference room."

Dana entered the ornate videoconference center on the company's south campus, a quadrangle away from the CEO's office. The elegant room, with its plush deep-blue carpet and high-backed chairs, was configured to hold twenty people.

She was having a good health week. Plus, her makeup and clothing were spot on, thanks to her appearance-conscious Cristen. *I'm masquerading good health well so far,* she thought.

And she wouldn't need to do it much longer.

Now she counted over fifty, with people sitting on the floor, pushed up against the thick oblong table that dominated the room's center, or just standing in the doorway. She remembered a time when she would have been the only black person, man or woman, in a meeting like this. Now, no one color stood out. *Watu mrembo.*

She survived to see that. Whatever happened today, much had changed.

She eyed her safety group, squeezed against the wall, leaning against the long black bookcase lined with books that she never saw anyone read.

Dana began to push her way through the space between the long conference table and the wall, occasionally stepping over people.

"Hey, Dana."

Turning, Dana saw her senior monitor. "Hi, Cristen."

"Looks like the announcement's coming down," her monitor said, pushing the curly brown hair out of her eyes.

"What was the attorney walk-in like?"

"She was dead to me, Cristen. Barked out an order for me to get details on a company I knew little about."

"What was its name?"

"CiliCold. Ever hear of it?"

"Not me, but I don't swim in those corporate waters. Anyway, glad you're here. The team's pretty anxious with the secrecy and everything."

"I couldn't imagine not being here. Besides, I don't know what's happening either." She heard the nervous laughter all around her and noticed that most people were staring into the two large displays hissing with static.

"You know why we're here, Dana," Cristen said, flat gaze turning from her friend to the blank monitor. "We all do."

Kevin walked into the CEO's office, looking at the floor to hide the patina of sweat on his brow. He scanned the room and saw that he was the only coatless male.

Damn.

"Hey, Kevin."

"Hi, Olivia, this must be important if they want you here."

Olivia Steadman nodded. To Kevin, she looked tired and anguished. "If it's important," she said, "then Reg needs to be here."

"No, Olivia, if it's important, you need to be here." Tall, silver hair in perfect swirls down to her neck, just a touch of makeup required for a soft face with high cheekbones. To Kevin, she looked just like what a woman president would. Her knowledge about the FDA was legendary, her even tones and good judgment earning her the respect of that organization.

He saw her looking at him. Always such kind eyes, he thought.

"How's Dana doing?"

He dropped his head to get closer. "Much nearer to the end, Olivia." He looked left to see who was nearby. "We went out for dinner recently," he continued in hushed tones. "It's clear that she wants to spend her last few working days working," he finished, exhaling hard.

He saw her lift her left hand up to him. He held it as she, with the softest of touches, rested it against his cheek.

Holding it there with his, he said, "My dear friend, I could not go through this without you."

"Thanks, Kevin," she said, letting his hand keep hers on his face for a moment before moving it. "A strange day awaits us." She stepped back. "But Oscar will handle this. Dr. Tanner has been through so much in his career. We'll survive in whatever form needed with him."

Kevin looked past Olivia to the tall woman in black, sitting quietly at the ornate table by herself. "Who's our friend over by the table?"

"No clue, but she's not ours."

"Yeah. Well, we can't be here to be bawled out. You never deserve that."

"Anybody know who dragon lady is?" Seth asked.

"We were just wondering," Kevin replied, carefully controlling his voice, hair standing on end as it always did in the presence of the senior VP of drug development.

"Well, don't look at me," Seth said, turning to face Ivy Sandman, Tanner's executive vice president, who had placed a thin, tanned hand on Kevin's arm.

"Well, I was on the cell to one of my assistants," the exec VP said, "who just spoke with one of the assistants to Oscar's executive secretary, who was part of the conference call that he just finished."

"What did you learn?"

"Our new friend over there is an attorney."

"Sheesh," Asher Penland, chief financial officer, exclaimed with mock severity. "This room is full of deep brain pans, but we're reduced to hearing about our company's future from office staff?" Then, after a moment, he asked, "Well, what else did they say?"

"That we're go—"

"Hello, everyone."

Across campus, Dana settled into the back of the video conference room. The five safety monitors who worked for her stood, huddled together in the back. Dana thought they looked like children waiting for their angry parents to come home and beat them.

*What am I going to do?* Dana wondered. *Their careers here are ending, and I have nothing, can do nothing to defend them.*

Maybe they would all keep their jobs though, she thought. They were safety, and they stuck together so well. Look at Amber, who had brought work to the meeting and, with head down, deep brown hair falling across her face, pored through the reports she had placed before her on the floor. Melanie sat behind her, eyes closed.

Dana glanced at Devin and Jake sitting on either side of Amber, both quietly lost in their own thoughts. Jake was rocking back and forth just a bit, and Devin had now started in on her nails, gnawing them to nubbins.

No surprise, Dana thought. They were the two newest team members. Of course they're scared.

At that moment, Dana saw Melanie look up at her. The middle-aged safety officer brushed the thinning red hair from her brow, revealing a sweat-covered forehead.

*She's been here twenty years, and she's frightened*, Dana thought. *They can't let her go.* Dana placed her open hand on Melanie's back to help calm her.

Meanwhile, the technicians who had been playing with the settings on the flat-screen wall monitors stood, scooped up their tools, and headed out of the room, talking.

Dana thought they were talking about football. For a moment, she thought of Kevin. What must h—

"About time," Cristen said, flicking her hand toward the screens. "Those monitors always take too—"

In a flash, both screens filled with an image. Dana saw that it was the CEO. The lights dimmed, and the room was graveyard quiet.

Dana reached over and tapped Amber's arm. Amber looked up from her work.

Cassie watched from the front table as the CEO of Tanner Pharmaceuticals, Oscar Tanner, strode into the large office with its comfortable chairs. Tall, trim, and completely bald, he turned toward her and mouthed a hello.

She looked back, slowly nodding once. Get on with your script, Oscar, she thought.

He became all business. He was usually avuncular, she observed, but today he walked in like a corps commander. She knew his record. He'd been a physician for fifteen years before starting this company twenty years ago.

She watched as all eyes turned to him. She could feel their backbones stiffen as the CEO walked to the center of the room. Cassie remained seated alone at the table to his left, facing his corporate people, each of whom had a head on the corporate chopping block. His executive assistant closed the heavy wooden doors to the huge office behind her.

She looked around at the group that had spent their entire careers working toward, then becoming part of Tanner Pharmaceuticals.

Born to die, she thought.

"I'll be brief," Tanner started, "so it's probably best that you all remain standing." Tanner turned to Cassie, who gave him a single piece of paper off the top. He opened it and read in a loud voice:

> To: Board of Directors, Tanner Pharmaceuticals, LLP
> I hereby tender my resignation as chief executive officer of Tanner Pharmaceuticals.

Let the axes swing, Cassie thought, eyeing her shoe that moved ever so slightly left then right, left then right.

# GOOD GIRL

For a moment, Kevin forgot how to breathe. Dr. Tanner was the founder. He'd built this company up from nothing but his own funds, drawing no salary for the first eighteen months. And he'd mastered the important details of each major area: development, research, marketing, regulatory, even personnel. He wasn't afraid of knowledge, wasn't afraid of anything. He was the only man Kevin had ever known who was fearless.

The blow was physical. Kevin fought the urge to double over, forcing air into his lungs and letting his eyes rove around him. Seth had removed his jacket, and his shirt was soaked. Kevin wanted to glance at the floor around the man to see if he'd pissed himself, then wondered about the floor around his own feet.

Olivia's long slender hands had jumped to her face to cover her nose and mouth. Even the unflappable Ivy was breathing deeply.

Dr. Tanner removed the pen from his shirt pocket and leaning on the conference table quickly signed the letter he had read, ending his twenty-year-long tenure as the head of his own company.

The CEO looked up from the paper. "That's not all," he said.

Kevin watched Dr. Tanner turn to and reach out toward the solitary lady—this elegant, stoic creature—at the table. She shook her head, pointing to Tanner's exec sec.

For a second, Kevin saw irritation flutter across his hero's face, followed at once by the stiff, fixed stare of resignation.

Standing tall again, Tanner directed his exec sec to the audience, where she began handing out individual white envelopes. The room was dead silent.

"Ms. Rhodes, this just arrived."

Cassie looked up into the face of a secretary who, with tears in her eyes, offered a manila envelope to her.

"Yes," Cassie said, taking the envelope as Tanner began to speak.

"People," he declared, a new severity filling his voice, "it's over. Just read your individual letters, sign them, and let's get on with this day."

Placing the envelope on the table, Cassie watched the secretary walk over to the one named Seth.

This is the good part, she thought, wishing Jasper could watch this.

She saw the thin man snatch and rip the envelope open. The contents fell to the floor. He swooped down and actually read the letter in a crouch. As he looked up to the one named Kevin, Cassie thought she had never seen a colorless face until that moment. She'd heard about Seth's ambition in the meet with Jasper and Oscar, the pre-death autopsy. Seth was a top-riser and didn't care who knew it, with one day hoping to be CEO of a company—maybe this one.

Well, she thought as she watched Seth scan the room with unfocused, wild eyes, today would not be that day.

He suddenly rushed past the secretary and toward the door. He fumbled with the heavy doorknob and then fled from the huge room.

Very un-CEO-like, she thought, slowly scanning the room for other victims, like a hawk surveys the yellow-white winter desert floor for mice.

"When will the rest of our people know?" the one named Olivia asked, holding her opened letter by her side.

Somebody on the other side of the room sobbed.

"Playing the tape now," Tanner answered, now sitting. She noticed that the CEO's eyes were on his secretary, who was reading her own letter, watching as her career was rubbed out, Cassie thought.

"You mean you are not going to talk to them?"

It was Olivia again.

"No. Advice from counsel was to provide a videotape. That way everyone hears the exact same words."

"You should have told them yourself, sir."

Cassie turned to face Olivia, whom she saw was staring right at her.

Cassie simply stared back until the older matronly lady muttered what sounded like "Probably won't matter" and looked down at the floor.

That's a good girl, Cassie thought, turning to the envelope. She carefully removed its contents, examining each, setting aside the routing slip steering the contents to her.

CiliCold, she saw, was a small company run by a Dr. DeLeon, an outcast from a university. They subsisted on manufacturing influenza vaccine on consignment for several drug companies, including Tanner.

Not anymore, she thought. They'd be working for SSS now.

She looked up momentarily as two women cried in each other's arms, then returned to her reading. There in front of her was a statement of CiliCold's five-year goal:

> To identify and manufacture substance(s) demonstrated to prevent or cure the common cold.

Well, she thought, that was in their bailiwick, but not really plausible. Most relevant scientists had given up on that holy grail. But there was the answer, wasn't it? These folks weren't relevant.

But people were donating. And CiliCold was small, digestible.

CiliCold might not meet their goal, but they could—

The power of the thought made Cassie lean forward.

But how?

"Friends and colleagues," Cristen heard Dr. Tanner begin, his strong voice commanding the crowded conference room.

"We have played a central role in producing pharmaceutical products for decades. During this time, it has been my pleasure to contour this company, and together, you and I have shaped this industry.

"Our products have made major contributions in public health, and we have not had one, not one single product, withdrawn. That's a stellar record of accomplishment in these difficult times for our industry. I look back and marvel at our track record.

"These accomplishments were well beyond my dreams, but not beyond your abilities. They can never be taken from us.

"Yet we work in a dynamic and sometimes unforgiving industry," the voice of the CEO continued. Cristen marveled at the effect that his voice had on her. It radiated from the screen, entering her, empowering her.

For a moment, a vision of her dad filled her mind.

"We are not free of economic forces that we have worked hard to shape. That's how it should be. As you know, the rumor mill has been buzzing for weeks about the possibility of our purchase. Those rumors are fact. We have been purchased."

Cristen saw Dana turn to her, nodding. Cristen whispered in her ear, "Just like we thought."

As the CEO continued with his preliminary comments, Cristen saw heads nodding and people in conversation with each other.

"I guess the Wall Street wienies were right after all," she whispered. "We weren't competitive enough."

"Yep," Dana agreed, "and now the shareholders are saying the same thing."

Cristen remembered that for months, stockholders had been selling their Tanner stock, looking for better deals and higher returns for their investments. Since more people were selling the stock than buying it, Tanner shares, no longer in great demand, plummeted in cost, and the financial value of the company nosedived, following the declining stock value.

"Now," the Tanner CEO continued, appearing to Cristen to be more her dad than ever, "an acquisition isn't a bad thing, and we shouldn't be afraid of it. We cannot fear change, any more than we should fear our next good product idea. We are a courageous family, and courageous families stand shoulder to shoulder to face uncertainty."

She barely heard the next words.

Cassie watched as one by one, the remaining Tanner executives opened their letters, learning, every man and woman of them, that they had resigned, effective at once.

Cassie got up to leave, checking her watch. It had only taken ten minutes for Tanner Pharmaceuticals to cease to exist.

"We have been purchased by SSS Pharmaceuticals, and—" the CEO's recorded voice declared from the monitor.

Dana gaped at Cristen, whose right hand, balled into a fist, smacked into her own chest over and over as she stared at the monitor.

"No," someone exclaimed.

"How could that be?" another worker demanded.

"Son of a bitch."

"Not Triple S," someone else in the room loudly asserted.

"No, no, no . . ."

"Impossible."

"How could they?"

"As of today, your senior management has resigned to make room for a new leadership team. Meredith Doucette, along with Jasper Giles—"

Dana could hear nothing else over the loud cries, the swearing, the cursing. Expletives exploded from Melanie's mouth. Dana couldn't remember the quiet woman ever swearing about anything before.

Someone threw a laptop at the monitor. It missed, slamming against the wall.

"They'll fire you for that," a voice counseled.

"Yeah? Well, I should be so damn lucky."

"You will be."

Collecting herself, Dana motioned to Cristen. They both rose, telling their team to stay behind to finish hearing the death pronouncement. Within thirty seconds, the two of them had pushed their way out of the hate-filled room.

"Where can we go?" Dana asked.

"I have an idea."

"The usual show," Cassie said, as she closed the limo door behind her, the waves of welcome warm air from the limo's multiple vents washing over her.

"Any pushback?"

"Just the occasional eyeballing, but in the end, the sheep all headed to the slaughter."

"Would love to get the details."

"Of course you would. The usual?"

"I'll make reservations."

"Will give you the full autopsy summary tonight. Oh, by the way, I followed up on CiliCold from the depo." Cassie hesitated, reflecting upon the small company's possible transformative effect on SSS. It wasn't all in place yet, but . . . "Just a vaccine producer."

The line was quiet. Then he asked, "No bogie for us?"

*Until you think the thing all the way through, say nothing*, she thought.

"They make flu vaccine for us now, as well as for a couple of other firms."

"Who?"

"One is Ajax. Can't recall the other."

"You're slipping, Cassie. You used to have an iron memory."

"Jasper, it's been a long day."

"Cassie?"

She felt rather than heard the disgusting new thickness in his voice. "I have some company coming by tonight. Interested? I'm in a sharing mood, and we—"

She clicked off and pulled out the CiliCold folder again.

What a pig, she thought. *I'm surprised the whores don't pay him to stop contacting them.*

# TRIPLE S BITCHES

"Yes, Sandra," Dana said into her cell phone twenty minutes later. "I think you're right. Tomorrow's too late. Let's set the meeting up for an hour from now." The safety chief nodded, stiffening as she listened to the stammering voice of her nervous AA on the other end of the phone.

"Everybody means everybody. Of course you can be at the meeting. I want to give everyone a chance to react to what we just heard at the video conference, especially you, Sandra. I'd be lost without your help. Listen, I'll be with Cristen for a while. See you in 393BA at 11:30 a.m. Thanks."

Dana looked around at the far wall of the dining room that could swallow up all 300 Tanner employees, relieved to see that she and Cristen were the only two seated in the cavernous cafeteria.

She watched her safety monitor sit back in the hard aluminum chair, shaking her head. "Dana, why are you even here? What are the doctors telling you?"

"Not to be here," the safety leader said, exhaling. "What do they know?"

"But—"

Dana suddenly flushed. "I'm not dead yet, Cristen, despite what folks around here think. I'm going to finish the game with my people. Here. Not in a hospice bed."

She fell silent for a moment, relieved that no one else was around. "Anyway," Dana put her cell phone on the table in front of her, twirling it around for a moment, "poor Sandra's out of her mind with fear."

"What else would we expect?" Cristen asked, her voice rising. "She's only a kid. And," she continued, pushing her paper coffee cup aside, "you can bet that she's not the only frightened one around here today. Our people were scared before the announcement and petrified after. Good thing we let them stay."

"Why?" Dana asked.

"So they could feel anger rather than fear," Cristen said, her right hand in a fist rubbing back and forth across the table in brisk short movements.

"Well," Dana replied, "SSS will run this company into the ground."

"If we let them."

"How can we stop them?" the team leader asked, right hand rubbing her short hair back and forth. "They've already fired our leadership. Olivia's gone. So is the rest of senior management."

"We're left, for the moment," Cristen said, sitting up.

"Tanner said nothing about cutting safety," the department chief said. "He would have assur—"

Dana looked up to see Cristen's piercing stare directed at her.

"Well, maybe you haven't been keeping up with current events, but Dr. Tanner doesn't work here anymore. Listen, Dana, you said you want to stay. What do you want to stay as? A sheep chewing grass while they gut your herd, or something else?"

Dana closed her eyes, fighting a new wave of nausea. When she opened her eyes, she saw clear-eyed determination staring back across the table.

"What do you suggest, Cristen?"

"Well, for one thing, not slinking quietly into the night. Let's finish this fight. Be the Triple S bitches they don't expect."

"Offering?"

"Resistance."

"But how?" Dana asked, staring first into her friend's hard face, then down to the 8⊠ by 10⊠ manila envelope that Cristen had laid on the table between them. The envelope seemed about two inches thick. The safety team leader could barely make out the Magic Marker scribble across its surface, but thought it said "Baseball scores." She looked up at her friend in time to watch her say, "By any means necessary."

# HOWEVER WE CAN

Kevin was the first on what would soon be a crowded elevator, his thoughts whirling, with Olivia just behind him.

Not today, he thought. He stepped in, hit the Close button, then spun around, extending his arm across the open door just after Olivia entered.

"Hey, hey, hey," a heavyset man in a three-piece called out.

"Sorry, but this one's taken," Kevin said, his face a scowl. The suit walked off as the door closed, and he saw that he and Olivia were alone. Quiet, head down, she was clearly lost in thought.

With the elevator started, she looked up and said, "We have about a minute until the elevator starts to hit express floors." She looked at the ceiling, then sighed. "My office is going to be a zoo."

"Mine as well." He pulled his iPhone out of his shirt pocket. "My email is going cra—"

"Oscar didn't even inform his own employees," Olivia said, rubbed her forehead with her hand in staccato back-and-forth motions. "They trusted him. And he didn't even look them in the eye. He did it by video."

"He was advised to."

"By witchy woman, no doubt."

"Olivia?"

She looked up at him. Kevin saw that she was clear-eyed, but her lips trembled.

She took a step toward him and he extended his arms, drawing her to him, holding her close for a moment. Then he leaned back, still holding her arms, and said, "Our people now know that they have lost their jobs. Oscar Tanner is far from their minds. But they will need us."

He watched the VP-Reg drop her head in silence.

"You OK down there?"

"I know, Kev. I know." She looked up, then to her left toward the front of the silver elevator. "A sale was no surprise. Good drug companies get sold all the time. Marion became Marion–Merrell Dow, which became Hoechst Marion Roussel, which became . . . became . . ." Silence as she chased a memory fragment.

"Aventis," he said, letting her go.

"That's right. Which became Sanofi-Aventis, and on and on," Olivia finished, new determination filling her voice. "Life goes on under all of these different names, if you bother to keep track of them as they go by. But"—she shook her head—"I'd have thought that some other group would have picked us up. You know, like Solomon or Ajax, or even JRJ. But not Triple S. They're cannibals. They'll gut us."

She looked up. "So, what do we do?"

The elevator abruptly stopped at its first express floor. Through the open doors, stunned employees rushed in, forcing Olivia to stand closer to him, face to face.

"Olivia," he whispered into her left ear, "we endure. However we can."

The hand squeezing his was hers. He squeezed back.

# TOUCHED

What did I just do?

The breath of Meredith Doucette, CEO for SSS Pharmaceuticals, came in short-fire bursts as she rose from her knees, then turned right and took step after careful step to her office desk on the thirtieth floor of the Sovereign Building. A quick glance to the right revealed the low hills of eastern Delaware, their features still hiding in the predawn mist.

Her pulse was up, and the sixty-year-old scientist didn't have to pull out her mirror to know that that new warmth on her face was a blush, the first in years, pink to meet the sunrise. She felt like a teenager waiting for great news that she knew was on the way. Like when her folks were headed home with the new 1972 Buick. Or when the boy that she crushed on was waiting there at her front door for their first date.

*What on earth have I just done?* she asked herself.

*I am an accountant, lawyer, and (yes, yes, yes, I know) almost a nun*, she reflected.

She had just spent the last five minutes in prayer, the first time in years. But that wasn't the issue. She had tried to pray before, got nowhere. The door was closed for whatever reason.

But this. It wasn't like breaking through.

It was more like being pulled.

Yes, yes, yes.

And it was glorious. She loved it.

She felt vitalized, empowered. She was a drought-stressed tree that had subsisted on chlorine hose water for weeks then received a rainwater soaking.

It was just another Tuesday, another day in another week in another month of being CEO—the usual scut.

Acquisitions, arguments, depositions, filings, firings, add-ons, reshufflings, over and over, again and again, the same, the same, *the same.*

*Why did I ever stop praying?* she wondered.

She knew.

Of course she remembered when she stopped. In fact, she remembered the exact day. The world remembered.

The Tuesday, September 11, 2001.

It was his company's Take Your Daughter to Work day, and Walter took their two daughters, thirteen and ten, to his office at the New York towers.

That was that.

The last time that she saw them.

And the last day she acknowledged God.

Straight-up Catholicism had always been good till then, the Virgin Mary meeting all her needs right up until The Day That Ended Days.

Then, too much suddenness.

Too much horror.

Too much ghastly pain that lasted too long.

The bank had been broken, the water run out from the tub.

So after months of grieving, finding no answer to the ever-present one-word question, she returned to work, taking a vacation from religion. Time to exit from the existential, leave God in the rearview mirror for a little while.

And that was where He'd been for fifteen years.

And she'd gotten by just fine. Yes, just fine. And as she rose in the ranks of the pharmaceutical industry, she discovered that she could be as vindictive, as jealous, as greedy, as dishonest, as vengeful, yes, yes, yes, as hateful as any man.

Yet here she was, up from her knees and a loving experience.

One thing was clear this bright, good morning.

She'd been touched.

God was here, with her again.

And if He was back, well then, damn it, she'd meet Him where He was.

# FIFTEEN THOUSAND LEFT TO GO

"How bad?" Rayiko asked.

"Toast."

"Well, if that's the case, then it's the only warm thing in here."

He smiled, looking at her red cheeks. "It's got to be in the fifties already."

"Should we get everyone together?"

It was Tuesday morning, and Jon had just finished escorting the HVAC technician out CiliCold's office door, closing it as soon as the older man in thick gray coveralls and dirty collar was clear so as to keep as much of the precious heat inside as possible. He and Rayiko sat on the couch together.

"Not yet." He leaned forward, motioning for her to do the same, her ear close, her eyes staring at the hands folded tight in her lap.

She was either scared or cold, he thought. Maybe both.

He whispered his plan to her, seeing that although she pulled her head back for a moment when the hard part came, she still listened. When he was done, they both rose.

"Guess I'll start down here and work my way up," she said. Jon patted her shoulder, then turned and walked up the long stairs to the second floor to meet with Breanna, whose help he'd need to pull this off.

Forty minutes later, Jon returned to the first-floor living room. Rayiko wasn't there yet, but he knew she would join him for the announcement and discussion. He was leaning against the wall when she arrived a minute later.

"This is what I learned," he said when she crossed the room and stood with him. He showed her his notes and they spoke quietly as, one by one, all CiliCold employees, each wearing their heavy coats, joined them in the cold living room.

"Hey, Dale," Jon said, pointing at his multicolored coat. "Why are you wearing that jacket inside out?" Everybody laughed. Rayiko crossed the living room to take a place on the couch with the suede covering.

"Why do you think?" he said, flapping his arms across himself again and again. "It's cold."

"Forties all ready, I bet," Wild Bill said, sitting on his hands.

Jon saw Breanna sat next to Rayiko on the dark couch. The two began a muffled discussion. Wild Bill sat on the floor, Robbie behind him in an overstuffed chair, with her feet folded under her. Luiz and Dale sat in two adjacent upholstered chairs just six feet away in the small converted living room.

"When's the heat coming back on?" somebody called out.

"May."

"That soon, huh?"

Jon smiled at the easy jokes flowing around the room. They were at ease, and why not? They expected him to solve it. He still didn't know exactly what to say, but he knew the words were on the way. He could feel them, like you can feel a sunrise coming.

"Seriously, what's happening?" Dale again.

Jon placed his hands in the pockets of his thick cords, dropped his head to clear his throat, and then looking up, seeing all faces turned to him, began.

"I spent part of this morning with our HVAC engineers. The heat exchanger is out, and the electronics are fried. Plus the unit is old. He—"

"A new motherboard and exchanger?" Dale cut in. "Why isn't he working on it now? I saw him leave."

"Hey, Dale?" Wild Bill said, eyes down, voice level. "I'd like to listen to Jon for a minute if you don't mind. He's the only one here who has the information we need. What do you say?"

"Yeah," Dale looked down into his lap. "Fair enough."

Jon walked over to Dale, putting his hand on his shoulder. "Dale's observation's a good one," he said. "We're all thinking what he's saying." Jon looked around the room. "We don't have the money for the replacement unit. If we get the coin, they'll do the work, but, well, we're coming up short."

"How much do they need?" Luiz asked, blowing warm air into his fist.

"Just over eighteen thou," he continued, letting his eyes sweep across Breanna and Robbie. "Now, we have the money in our bank account. That, and a little bit more."

"Payday's tomorrow," Wild Bill said.

"Yeah," Jon said, looking at his regulator, "and we can't meet both obligations."

"How about using the grant money you mentioned at our staff meeting?" Luiz asked.

"Don't get it for a month," Breanna said in a quiet voice.

Robbie looked away. Luiz looked out of the window. Dale raised his hand, and Jon nodded to him. "No need for formality here, Dale. Thanks for being patient with me. Take your shot."

"You know, I can afford to do without new cash for a few days, I guess, with as much as Luiz and I make," he took a halfhearted slap at Luiz, who rolled his eyes. "I mean, I'll be OK, but some here make less and have more obligations than me. I can skip a check."

"Thanks. That's a big sacrifice on your part, but the bill is much bigger," Jon said, taking a step toward Dale. "We need something different."

"Like money," the regulator said, scratching the side of his head.

"Or an idea, Wild Bill," Jon said, standing in the center of the room. "Here it is. I've been talking to our folks at Tanner. It turns out that this flu season is lasting longer than anyone thought. A lot longer. Their best guess is that they'll be seeing new cases into July—"

"July?" both Luiz and Dale said at once. Wild Bill whistled.

"Yeah. Anyway, there's need for more vaccine. A lot more. And that means more of our killed virus product."

"You mean AV, don't you?" Dale asked in a low voice.

"Uh, right. Attenuated virus. Thanks. And they're willing to pay us $15,000 for three times our usual consignment."

Jon watched as all heads at once turned to the virologists.

"That's quite a bit of product." Dale said, rubbing his head. "We're," he looked around with outstretched arms, "Well, we're kind of a mom-and-pop operation, Jon. We typically do that in about a week. And that's with prep time. Plus, we haven't produced anything like that amount in about eight weeks. When exactly do they want it?"

"Forty-eight hours, at the latest." Jon said, smiling for the first time that afternoon.

"What?" Luis said. He looked around the room as if the answer to his question was within view, then looked back at Jon. "Thursday? This is Tuesday."

"They'll pay when they get it, not before," Jon said. "But they were quite clear. We can't be late."

"And we won't get the furnace until we get paid," Robbie said. Jon saw her shiver a little.

"That's the ticket."

"Hey, Jon." Dale was bouncing his right leg hard and fast. "Seriously, we just can't do that. You might as well ask us to have it ready in forty-eight minutes."

"Well," Luiz said, "we haven't done it."

"And we never will, Luiz," Dale said, looking over at him. "The staff req—"

"Uh, Jon, so that gets us the fifteen K," Wild Bill said, feet crossed and stretched out in front of him. Jon thought he looked so comfortable, like someone stretching out in front of a roaring fire, "we're still three K shy of the mark."

"I'll kick that in," Jon said.

He saw Rayiko's sharp look.

"Wait a second," Dale said, turning from Luiz to face Jon. "You said no one will forgo their pay."

"I won't," Jon said with a shrug. "I'll just fork it over from my savings. When you make us all rich, Breanna here can cut me a check." Jon watched Breanna smile as Rayiko now studied the floor.

"So," Wild Bill asked, "when can you virologists get us the juice we need?"

Dale shook his head. "Jeez, I don't know if t—"

"Give us a minute." Luiz moved his chair close to Dale's. Jon saw that all were quiet, watching the two virologists work out the details.

Luiz picked his head up, saying, "Can do."

"So, Thursday a.m.?" Jon said.

"But we're going to need help," Dale said, looking around. "The newest equipment available is fully automated. That we don't have."

"Is the help something that we can provide?" Wild Bill asked, looking over at the two. Rayiko stood up and walked to the wall to turn on the light. To Jon, she seemed almost spirit-like, bathed in the yellow incandescence.

Luiz shrugged. "Sure."

"So if we start in the a.m.," Dale said, scratching his head, "we can be done Thursday morning."

"We need to rethink at least some of this."

Everyone turned to look at Rayiko, who, hands folded in her lap, was looking straight ahead. "The furnace has been off for three hours. We usually keep the thermostat set at sixty-five degrees. It's one thirty in the afternoon, and the temperature in here is forty-eight. Anybody want to guess what it will be tomorrow morning when we come in?"

Not a word.

"She's right," Jon said, rubbing his chin. "And the forecast is nothing but deep cold for the rest of the week."

"Which means this is as warm as it's going to get," Robby said. "Excuse me," she said, stifling a belch with her hand.

"Which means," Wild Bill said, "that we have a long night ahead of us."

Jon shifted on his feet. "The earlier we start, the earlier we finish."

"It also means," Breanna said, "that by starting tonight, we can be finished earlier."

"If I can have the check by midmorning on Thursday, we'll have a new furnace blowing hot air before end of business same day. Rayiko," he said, turning to her, "how about if we let everyone go home when we're done Thursday morning? I can deliver the consignment, get the check, stay with the repair folks on Thursday, and close up."

"Jon, it could work that way, but—"

"OK," Jon said, turning back to the group. "Let's see what kind of shifts we can run."

Dale and Luiz looked at each other and shrugged.

"Both of us will need to be here the entire time anyway."

"Including this afternoon?"

"Especially this afternoon," Dale said. "Somebody's gotta plan this shindig."

"Shindig?" Luiz asked, looking at Dale.

"Jeez, Luiz, do not get me started."

"Won't we need to control the temperature in baths?" Wild Bill asked.

"Baths are electric, reg guy," Rayiko said.

"Duh," Wild Bill said, rolling his eyes

"And the utilities are paid up," Breanna added, nodding her head.

"Not at my crib," Dale said. "Why do you think I'm willing to stay here all night with this guy?" He gave Luiz a gentle push.

"OK," Jon said. He took out a checkbook and scribbled for a second, tore it, and walked over to Breanna, handing her a three-thousand-dollar check. "Only fifteen thousand left to go."

"Let's meet back here at, say, 5:00 p.m.?" Luiz said, standing up. "That OK with everyone?"

"I'll be back early myself," Jon said. "I have an errand that won't take long."

He ignored Wild Bill's questioning look and headed out the door, wrapping his coat around him as the wind tore at it. This call he wanted to make from his car. No witnesses.

"Alora?" he said into his phone, watching the $CO_2$ of his breath crystallize.

"Jon, thanks for calling."

"I need—"

"Oh, Jon, you won't believe it." And so she was off and running in his ear. Wedding excitement. Aaron was The One. Should they learn the sex of their baby or not?

Jon waited to tell her that he would not be providing additional money to her this month. As he waited, he remembered how this Aaron-marriage-baby thing had torn him up just a few weeks ago. That seemed like another person then.

When he finally said it, he was pleased that he had finally figured out how to dam up her word river.

"Weeell," she started, a new sharp edge cutting her voice, "I thought you could contribute more this month than usual. Actually more than the usual addition. We're really strapped with the wedding coming up and all."

"I only do the alimony from now on." Then after a moment. "That's the way it will be."

The phone was dead silent. Then she asked, "Somebody else?"

He shook his head to himself. *Keep it tight.* "Just work."

"Robbie," she said.

To Jon, her pronunciation ended with a hiss.

"I just knew you were fucking her. Tell me, Jon, is she worth the money you pay her?"

Jon's pulse kicked up, and he gripped the S4 tighter. His voice steady, he said, "No, I am not, and it's not your business, Alora. The only thing that matters is that I can no longer contribute above and beyond. Why that is remains my concern, not yours."

He bit back the rest.

"Jon, I don't see why you continue to work with those throwaways—"

*As opposed to what?* he wondered. *Spend all my time being your doting ex-husband?*

"They are dragging what is left of your career down. Aaron says—"

"I have a solid group now," Jon said, lowering his voice. "Once we get past this week's setback—"

"What you have is a ragged group of has-beens and wannabes trying to do what no large consortium has ever been able to pull off," she said. "Jon, the experts at NIH, CDC, SSS didn't quit on this common-cold quest because they were stupid. They stopped because they were smart. Maybe it's time that you do the same."

He kept his teeth together as his anger swelled, the air from his nose fogging up the windshield.

"I sometimes don't know who I'm talking to," she said.

"Well, let me help you." Jon gripped the steering wheel until his knuckles whitened. "You're talking to your ex-husband, who has met his obligation to you and will continue to do that, but no more."

"Did you speak to Aaron?"

"Why should I? I'm not marrying him. You are."

"That doesn't sound like you."

"I've had enough of you, Alora, and far too much of this conversation. Get married. Stay with your plan. It's a good one. I'll stay with mine. Goodbye."

He hung up, ready for a wall of pain that didn't arrive. Wild Bill was right. She was her own woman (God bless her and God help her). He, for better and for worse, was his own man.

# SCRAMBLING

Antigen checks to be sure the vaccine had the right virus. Double checking to be sure that they had enough substrate. And quality control checks, always quality control.

Jon was heading back into CiliCold, letting the thoughts about the upcoming all-nighter push his ex out and over his mental horizon.

Already halfway out of his jacket, he strode past the entry room into and down the short hall, toward the basement steps where the action would be these next forty-eight hours—

"Dr. DeLeon?"

He turned to see Robbie. She was bundled up tight in her jacket that stopped at her hips. He knew what she was going to—what she had to—say.

"Robbie, I hope you don't think we expected you to stay tonight. After all," he said, wagging his finger at her with a smile, "somebody's got to take care of Shannon, right?"

"That'd be me," she said, lighting up at the mention of her daughter's name.

"No question of it. How long will your sitter wait for you to get home?"

Robbie pulled up the sleeve of her fleece-lined jacket, checking the time on her watch. "Not for a while. I can stay till five, but I need to leave then. I really would like to stay here with everybody, but—"

All at once, tears spilled over her eyelids onto smooth cheeks.

Nodding, Jon tapped her shoulder twice, then whispered, "Stay as long as you can, but no more, Robbie. Shannon comes first, right?"

"OK."

She hugged him, then turned and hurried back to her office.

He watched her go, letting the moment first fill him, then pass. He then turned and headed down the wooden steps with the low overhead, to the basement.

There he saw Luiz, Dale, Wild Bill, Rayiko, and Breanna.

"Is this us?"

"I need to leave by eleven," Rayiko said, her voice even.

"Then we're glad to have you until then." He smiled at her, then turned to Breanna. "Can you give us any time?"

"I scrambled around and was able to find a sleep-in babysitter." She paused to wipe her runny nose. "I'll need to leave tomorrow morning about eight or so for a few hours, but I can give you all night tonight."

Jon saw Luiz and Dale, both of their heads down over a work table. "Well, Breanna, your presence will brighten things up around this dingy place tonight. How long do we have you for, Wild Bill?" he said, turning to his friend.

"You have me all night," the regulator said, leaning back against the wood-paneled wall, "although my girlfriends aren't happy with you."

"Oh yeah?" Jon said, laughing, "I just hung up from talking with them. They offered to pay me to make you stay one night, and triple for two."

Everybody laughed.

"Well, Dale, where do you want us?"

"Give us a minute, would ya? Luis and I are working out the profit-sharing arrangement."

They cracked up again.

# LIFE ON THE FARM

Ninety minutes later, Breanna walked up to the second floor, away from Dale, who was braying out orders to everyone. "Robbie, get these supplies. Rayiko, come downstairs and don't drop those syringes. Wild Bill, get out of my way."

Quieter here, she thought. She remembered, back in Tennessee years ago, she had worked for a home designer. He would put on demonstrations that required hours of what was always called last-minute preparation. Back then, she had all of the energy in the world, not minding the abuse the head designer hurled at his artists, draftsmen, and craft specialists as they stayed up to finish preparations for the sh—

"Do you agree with how I sketched the finances out?" Jon asked her as she passed.

"Oh."

"I startled you," he said, coming out from his office. "Sorry. I just needed a Dale break."

She smiled. "Me too. What a battle-ax."

Jon looked at her, then busted out laughing. Breanna put her hand to her mouth. She hadn't seen him this open, this out of control before. She started to giggle.

"Jon," she asked, "what's so funny?"

Jon, still laughing, said, "When I was a kid, maybe eleven or so, I went to a friend's party. It was OK, but his mother was all over the place, in everybody's face, making sure that we all behaved.

"Next day, my mom and dad called me into the living room. They said they had just gotten a call from his mother, who told them that I called her a battle-ax. 'Did you do that?' they asked me."

"Well?" Breanna asked. "Did you do it? What did you say?"

"I told them 'No, but only because I hadn't thought of the word. That woman was a real pain.'" He smiled again.

She shook her head. *What's so hilarious here?* she wondered. Finally, she asked, "That means a lot to you, doesn't it?"

Jon kept smiling. "Yeah, it's not really funny, but it was the first time that I remember being actually, completely, and openly honest with my folks. And they knew it and appreciated it. For a magnificent second, everybody's guard was down. They couldn't laugh, but it was a good moment."

She knew without asking that he didn't share this story with just anybody, maybe with no one else. She opened her heart to this new connection with her boss, the possibility thrilling her.

"Uh," Breanna said after a moment, "so what did you ask me?"

"Yeah. Right. Are you OK with my financial math on all this?" he said, waving his hand toward the hall where the steps led to the basement.

"Yes," she said, pausing as a shiver passed through her. "This entire effort should be tax neutral because the furnace is a business expense, even though we have to—"

Her phone buzzed. She knew who it was without looking.

Ethan.

She snapped it shut, shoving it back into her jeans' right hip pocket. "Never thought that I would be up all night helping to look after viruses," she said, looking around.

"I know," Jon said, bringing the zipper of his jacket down some. "Well, one way or the other, it's viruses that keep us up at night."

She smiled, pointing at the pocket of his jacket. "I haven't seen a members-only jacket for years."

He looked down at his jacket with a smile. "Actually, I bought one years ago. Liked it so much I went out and bought two more. Wore the first couple out over the years, so I'm down to my last one."

"My dad used to have one."

"Well then," he said with a smile, "he had good tastes." He sneezed. "I'm glad you could stay. I knew that the scientists would st—"

"When you're done with the high finance and fashion discussions, we could use some help, if you please," Dale yelled from down the hall.

"In a minute, Dale," Jon said.

Breanna watched him turn his attention back to her. "It's hard for Rayiko with her son," Jon said. "And of course, Robbie has no help at home, so she had to leave. But you have children too, right? I didn't expect that you would be able to work with us all night. I want to thank you."

"Well, it would be hard to turn this down." She shifted her stance just a little. "In any other job that I've had, the boss would have been laughed out of the office if he'd made this request of his employees." She looked him squarely in the face and saw neither evasion nor bashfulness in his eyes. "Yet there was no resentment. Robbie couldn't stay overnight, and she was actually apologetic."

Jon took a deep breath. "They feel what we do here strongly."

"As do you."

"Yes," he said, blinking twice, "but before we get to that, we first have to pull the fingernails from a few trillion viruses."

Breanna laughed. "Well, I'm no virologist, but I'm pretty sure they don't have fingernails."

"We have to weaken them. It's called attenuation."

"You mentioned that earlier."

"Ready for an immunologic quickie?" he said with a smile.

"As long as we can walk some. It's really cold."

"OK. Let's head down to the basement," Jon said, letting her pass. "That's where all the action will be anyway."

"I heard that you talked a little about immunity with Dale and Luiz," Jon said as she passed him in the hallway.

"And Wild Bill," she added. "Can't leave him out. Where did he get that name?"

"There was this bar, a knife, and a cattle prod. It's a long story."

"Did it involve jail time?"

"No," Jon said, laughing, "but it should have."

"OK. Go on."

"Anyway, we pick up immunity as babies from our mothers. I also heard that you came up with a few examples of our acquired immunity in some earlier discussions."

Breanna smiled, knowing he couldn't see her.

"What we—and not just us, but every vaccine maker—want to do is," he continued, "to give the person immunity without giving them the disease. One way is to kill the virus. We grow the virus in tissue cultures, then chemically alter it."

"You can't kill it, because it's not really alive, right?" She stopped when she came to the first set of steps, allowing Jon to catch up.

"Well," he said, touching her arm, "it looks like I have a philosopher on my hands. Right, we denat— oh."

He stumbled, and she caught his arm.

He looked down then looked at her, and for the first time, she realized how tired he was. Not a hair was out of place, and his clothes were unwrinkled, but still. For a second, she wanted to hold him, but shoved the thought aside, listening instead.

"The viral agent has an outer coat of what is primarily protein mixed with some lipopolysacchar—well, I mean fat and protein. It has to have just the right chemical composition so that it can twist itself into the shape it needs to slip into the cell. If we change the virus configuration a little bit, then the viral particle can't get in. It still is driven to enter the cell, but it no longer has the right shape, and shape is the key."

"So," Breanna said, "when this changed virus is injected into people, it doesn't cause the disease." She reached the bottom of the first set of steps and waited for him before walking around the short hallway to the second.

"Well, for the most part. Occasionally, very rarely actually, someone will get the full flu. But most all of us get just a hint of it. Our arm may be tender after the shot for a few hours."

"I get a little achy." She held on to the cold bannister.

"There you go, Kind of feels like the flu is coming on, but it never really arrives. Fortunately."

"And then the immune system reacts to the fake flu virus?"

"Well," he said, stepping from the last stair onto the first floor, "your immune system first reacts to the damage caused to your cells. When our cells are dying, they send out chemical signals. Other cells in our immune system pick up on them and take them—uh-oh."

Jon reached out to steady Breanna on the steps.

"Thanks."

"Turnabout's fair play. Anyway," Jon continued, letting her go, "these cells carry viral fragments back to what I call the antibody farm."

"What?" She turned and stared at him.

"Really. It's fields and fields of cells that are in the antibody-producing business. Think of them as living in an antibody farm. Hundreds of millions of B cells in this farm, and each one makes a unique antibody."

"B, like *bumblebee*?"

"No, B like the letter B. And each one of these cells can only make one type of a specific type of antibody. And we have many, many millions of them."

"How many different possible antibodies are there?" she said, sure to keep a tight hold on the bannister.

"Know what a google is?"

"Who doesn't?" she said, shrugging. "It's a search engine."

"Yeah. But it's also a number. It's a one followed by 100 zeros."

"And you are telling me that because . . ."

"You can have more different types of antibodies than that."

She stopped. "How is that poss—"

"Coming by, guys."

Breanna leaned one way and Jon the other as Luiz twisted by with a box under each arm.

"It's just the math. There are about 120 positions, and each can hold one of twenty amino acids. But the implications are enormous."

He put a hand on hers. "Breanna?"

"Yes."

"There are more possible antibodies that your body can make than there are stars in our universe."

She would have instantly dismissed this as a stupid verbal prank from Dale or anybody else. But this was Jon. She loved talking to him like this. It was the only time she ever saw him relaxed. Open. Free.

She ran with it.

"So each B cell makes one and only one of these antibodies."

"Right. And unlike red cells that only live for 120 days, they and their progeny can live for years."

He leaned close. So did she.

"Breanna, can you play a game with me? It's a good game," he whispered.

She smiled. 'Maybe just once."

"Imagine that you are one of these B cells. Your entire life is spent in the B cell farm. Do you like the dark?"

"Depends on who I'm in it with."

He smiled. "Well, you're in it with millions of companion cells. You're surrounded your entire life by other B cells that make other antibodies. All around you. Above and below you as well."

She saw that he was fully into it and wanted to get there with him. "OK," she whispered.

"And your mission, B-cell Breanna—"

"Should I choose to accept it."

"Yes, my *Mission Impossible* aficionado," he said, laughing, "is to make one and only one type of antibody. You with me?"

"Yep. Life in the B cell farm."

"Right. If the body is never exposed to something that you can react to, you never make your antibody. You go through life unstimulated. Your entire life was spent in waiting."

"Always a bridesmaid, huh?"

# BABY B'S

Jon laughed, shaking his head. "But if the body is exposed to the virus whose antibody you make, you get excited. You're turned on. You produce your antibodies by the hundreds, then by the thousands. And then, you proliferate. You divide. And your progeny—"

"My baby B's?"

"Yep, your baby B's start making antibodies themselves. And then they proliferate, all toward the goal of making antibodies to fight the infection that is underway."

She paused on the step. "It sounds complicated, haphazard, scary, and wonderful all at the same time, Jon."

"It keeps us, by and large, safe for our entire lives," Jon said, a step behind her. "We get in trouble when the B cell farm is presented with a viral particle fragment that none of them can match."

She turned to him. "Millions upon millions of these B cells, and none can match it? What happened to 'all the stars in the universe'?"

"It's possible to make that many, but we don't. We have a collection that serves us well, and this is the problem with the common cold," he said, leaning forward, getting closer to her ear. "Because we don't make all possible antibodies all the time, the virus can change just enough every year to confront our immune system with a viral particle it can't recognize."

"So one sneaks through that nobody—I mean, no B cell recognizes. What then?"

"Plan B. In our B cell farm, there are cells that are not committed to making any one antibody. These undifferentiated cells go to work, each testing whether an antibody that they can come up is the one that will fit the viral particle."

"Sounds kind of desperate."

"Think of it like, uh—" He paused on the step for a moment. "Like a combination safe with over a billion craftsmen nearby, each one thinking that he or she knows the combination. They will eventually crack it, but, Breanna, this is a desperate time for the body."

"Why?"

"Because while the B cells are working to find the right antibody fit, the virus is going to town on us. It's killing our cells and making us sick."

"We just have to wait for the antibodies?"

"Our body does other things to help: increases temperature, makes general types of substances that can attack the viruses. But that's only station keeping."

"Buying time."

"Yep. Then when an undifferentiated cell figures out the combination, it gets turned on like you were."

"OK."

"And if it's not too late and the body survives, then this new antibody-making B cell takes its rightful place in the B cell farm, waiting for the day that it is needed again."

"So when the virus appears aga—"

"That special B cell's waiting to zap 'em."

They stepped off the last step onto the basement floor. She looked up at him and, for the first time, saw no fatigue in him.

She smiled.

Walking the fifteen feet from the steps to the long series of work tables bathed in bright fluorescent light, Jon was struck by how warm he was in his jacket and sweater.

"Did the heat come back on?" Breanna asked her question betraying new hope.

"Nope," Jon said, turning to face her. "Basements are always warmer in the winter."

"Warmer in the winter, nice and cool in the summer," Luiz said. He was already monitoring temperatures in one of the many baths. Each of several tables had a series of wide, deep plates.

"It'll get cold down here soon enough."

"What can we do for you, Dale?" Wild Bill asked.

"We have tissue cultures that have to be incubated, and there are just too many for Luiz and me to do."

"I can help with that," Jon offered, sliding next to one of the flow units.

"We have three workstations," Dale said, rubbing his eyes. "Each of these tissue cultures has to be inoculated with this virus. See?" Dale said, with Wild Bill right next to him.

"Seems easy enough," Wild Bill said. "Don't you have to be certified to do this? Maybe a virus driver's license or something?"

"Not really," Luiz answered, moving some equipment to a corner. "We're using an approved viral strain whose successful attenuation has been authenticated. All we have to do is place the virus on the culture and let it do what it does. Nature takes care of the rest."

Breanna slipped next to Jon. "No eggs?"

Jon shook his head, looking down at her. "Definitely not chick embryos." He pointed to Luiz. "What's the virus having for dinner tonight? Retina?"

"No," Luiz said as he set up the second laminar airflow unit. "Kidney. African green monkey."

Breanna's face twisted involuntarily.

"Umm, umm . . . good," Wild Bill said, smacking his lips.

"And here comes the virus," Dale said as he inoculated tissue culture number one.

"Guess who's coming to dinner," said Luiz. He stepped back. "The second flow unit is all set up now," he said, moving over to the third.

"How long do we need to do this?" Jon asked, reaching for a white coat hanging on a gold hook jutting from the wooden wall.

"Well, the yield's not as great with these cultures as with eggs. But the eggs for live, attenuated virus have to be special—"

"Spelled *expensive*," Rayiko said.

"Right. I'm guessing, three flow units, five of us, the two not inoculating are moving the cultures to the inoculation stations, bringing new ones over, checking temp gauges. Probably . . ." He was quiet, his lips moving. "Carry the three."

Everybody stared.

"Thirty hours."

"Closer to thirty-six hours," Luiz said. "I don't know about you all, but I'm not at peak efficiency when I'm cold and tired."

"It's Tuesday evening," Wild Bill said in a low voice.

"Thursday," Rayiko said, nodding her head. "We're done Thursday afternoon, with a short break for sleep tomorrow morning."

"Well," Jon moving into position in front of flow unit 1 to the far left. "Harvest won't cut itself. Good time's wasting."

# GIVE IT TO HIM STRAIGHT

Being reared to believe that her fears would be used against her, she was more comfortable in silence. But for the very first time, Rayiko was ready to abandon CiliCold.

Angry with Jon and upset with herself for enabling his weaknesses, she kept her head down, trudging back to her workstation.

Well, enough coddling. She'd stop the support for a bit. Give it to him straight tonight.

Having made up her mind, Rayiko pushed the thoughts away, now losing herself in the evening's work. She was just tall enough to stand comfortably before the large laminar flow unit, drawing the weakened but potent virus into the syringe, then inoculating one tissue bay after the next.

It brought back the best part of biology for her. She always enjoyed the lab work then. Whether it was chem lab in which the right combinations of esters, aldehydes, and ketones produced crystal from liquid, or cell biology where spectroscopy would uncover the hidden tracks of proteins, it was always the same—you followed the instructions with care, plus a little bit more, to get the result that you needed.

Keeping track of an SOP with ten instructions wasn't enough, she remembered, smiling to herself. You needed an extra touch, an unwritten special attention to detail to get the magic to work, for nature to reveal herself.

"I always liked lab work," she said during a break. "I didn't realize how much I missed it."

"Not me," Jon mumbled with a mouthful of Wendy's hamburger, one of the several menu items that Robbie had dropped off for them all. "For me, lab was like the kitchen from hell. The right ingredients produced nothing but a mess, plus a bill for broken instruments. The theory was fine for me. That's why I chose epi over medicine."

"Well," he said, standing and stretching, "back to work. Whose turn to man or woman the hoods?"

"Me, Luiz, and Breanna," Rayiko announced, walking over to the sink. She braced herself, then turned the faucet on, and laughed when, bracing for ice water, hot water flowed out of the faucets.

"Guess the hot water heater is electric," Luiz said, throwing out the dinner debris. "I forgot that as well."

When eleven o'clock rolled around, Rayiko backed away from the hood. "Oh," she said as she felt herself falling backward.

"Gotcha."

It was Jon, catching her in the crook of each arm.

"Thanks," she said, moving fast to get her feet under her and stand up straight.

He was always there.

"Time for you to go home, isn't it?" he said, his voice low.

"I know. Will you come upstairs with me for a minute?"

"Sure," he said, turning to his right. "Dale, you ready to step in?"

"You bet. No better place for me to be than with my hands in a hood."

"And your head up your ass," Luiz added.

"G'night, Rayiko."

"Bye."

"See you tomorrow."

Rayiko thought she was wearing ankle weights as she trudged up the long flight of stairs to the first floor. It was already eleven thirty. It had been months since she'd been on her feet this long.

Just one more thing to do, she thought as she walked to the front door, Jon right behind her.

And she hated to do it. But . . .

She turned.

"You weren't honest with me about this arrangement," she said, facing Jon in the living room. The air between them was white with their merged breath.

"After we spoke, things changed," he said. "I didn't know what else to do."

She noticed he was rubbing his left hand. It had already started, she thought.

"You told me the company needed eighteen thousand dollars' worth of vaccine," Rayiko said. "If we completed that consignment, you wouldn't have had to contribute three thousands of your own dollars."

Jon nodded. "That's right." He was now rubbing his left arm. "But we couldn't have made that much vaccine by Thursday. We'll barely make the $15,000 consignment as it is. Asking our people to work through Friday, maybe into Saturday and Sunday in the freezing cold, to churn out the eighteen K worth of product was . . . well, too long and too much for them."

She looked up at this man whose project she had been running for four years. She was causing him pain, and she knew it. But he needed to know.

"Putting your own money up is a bad idea, Jon," she continued. "It wasn't right to do it with Robbie either."

She watched Jon avert his eyes, seeming to look around the room for a moment, not really focusing on anything.

Suddenly, they were back on her.

"Rayiko, I get that. But what was the alternative? If I hadn't provided money for Robbie, she'd be working for someone else."

"People do that all the time, Jon." Then, in a softer voice, she said, "The world doesn't fall apart."

To her surprise, Jon stepped back and snorted.

"The world? Rayiko, I'm not responsible for the world."

She watched him exhale, a long one, like he was expelling some emotional poison.

"I am responsible for those people downstairs, including you," he said. "To do as you say would have broken my commitment to Robbie. That would have damaged her, and I wasn't willing to do that."

His arms were now outstretched, pleading eyes on her. "Rayiko, in all my prior jobs, folks said, 'Good people are worth fighting for,' but when it's their own turn to do the fighting, many walk away. When push comes to shove, they don't sacrifice for good people. They let them go, shrug, and say, 'Gee, maybe we could have done better. How do we get someone else?'"

A moment passed. Then in a tougher voice, he said, "I did the same thing. Years ago."

She hadn't heard this before. "It was probably smart for you to let them go then, Jon. Don't you really think they are OK now, not anguishing over the inactions of their old boss Jon DeLeon?"

"Nevertheless, it was a personal act of cowardice not to intervene, and I have hated myself for it."

"But," she said, placing her open left hand gently on his chest, "isn't that the heart of your trouble now? You're worried about repeating the same mistake, but really, you've learned the right lesson too well. I know that you don't want them to hurt, to feel pain, if you can spare them."

She removed her hand. "Don't you see that by helping them, you are also in their way? Let them accept who they are so that they can get stronger."

Her heart caught, but she had to keep trying, to help bring an end to this never-ending suffering that he inflicted on himself. "Jon, you are intuitive about many things, but you do not know your people the way that you think you might. You don't have—and don't have to have—all the answers."

"Well, Rayiko," he said, "if not me, then who? It's always the same question, over and over. If not me, then who?"

He sighed. "Good people are worth giving up something of ourselves for, worth sacrificing for. That's what I did for Robbie. It's what I always do for her, and for my team members. For you as well, Rayiko, especially for you. You know that. If I'm damned for being this way, then so be it. But I am who I am."

"Maybe it's better to let them hurt and help them grow through it," she said, removing her hand.

"You mean 'Don't worry, they'll figure it out on their own'? How about the other side of the coin? They really are beyond their depth and would benefit from a hand, but the hand is not forthcoming because others believe 'Well, they'll just muddle through it on their own.' Things spiral to the bottom when we don't step in to help others."

He shook his head. "To me, that sounds like the excuse for inaction that comes from those who don't care enough to intervene."

Jon shook his read rapidly as if trying to clear it. "Rayiko, I'm tired. But," he said, putting his hand on her arm, "I'm not so tired that I am unaware of the strengths and weaknesses of those folks downstairs—my team. They work for me, respect me, and are here for me tonight. How can I let them down by pushing them unnecessarily through the weekend?"

She hoped that it wouldn't come to this. She took a deep breath, then, "How did that work with Alora, for whom you took an oath for life?"

Jon froze, then moved a half step backward. He bit his lower lip, then looked at her. She kept his gaze.

Then he said, "I . . . I should never have married someone whose needs I neither knew nor could satisfy."

She stepped toward him. "If you paid as much attention to yourself as you do others, you would find life's not just bearable, but enjoyable. In the meantime, you have to find a way to get yourself through this, once again. Why do you? How will you?"

He inhaled. "The same way I always do." He reached both of his hands over to her, tenderly fastening one button of her coat. "I carry on."

She kept her eyes on his while she buttoned the rest.

"Don't worry. I'll last a little longer," he said, voice stronger, "especially if my program administrator is by my side here at work. Is that where you'll be, Rayiko?"

She lifted her head, looking up at him, his need for connection palpable, beating inside her. "Where else, Jon?"

"Then we'll start again tomorrow."

They held each other for just a moment, then she turned to the door and the cold night.

On the slow drive home through the hard snow ruts, she played out in her mind all the signs pointing to Jon's instability: the blind optimism that he felt that they would make the scientific discovery that all credible scientists had abandoned, his inability to keep his ex out of his mind, the need to solve business financial issues with his own money, his fatigue.

She also knew that while logically, he saw what she was saying, emotionally, he was committed.

He lived on emotional commitment. Without that, he believed he had—that he was—nothing.

Yet he listened to her, always had an ear for her. That was something—maybe something good.

But it was late now, and the closer she got to her home, the stronger the pull of her own family, so she pushed Jon and his work out of her mind to spend a short time with her husband and son tonight.

# DEVOTION

The basement grew colder that night, but Jon noticed that Breanna, Luiz, and Dale didn't really care. One batch after another of cultures was sown with the weakened virus. They stayed up with no sleep, as the long dark predawn hours rolled by, injecting fatigue through each of them as straight and as true as they injected the cultures. It was easier for the stackers to stay awake, the physical work of moving and carrying the cultures to the huge incubators at least forcing more tired blood faster through tired brains and muscles. They slipped into a routine, surprised at the arrival of the first light through the old, narrow basement window.

Robbie arrived about 6:30 a.m., bringing fresh bagels and steaming Starbucks coffee. She said nothing about their red watery eyes; neither did she tell them the temperature in the upstairs offices that, more exposed to the buffeting winds, was now in the mid-thirties. She offered, and they agreed to be driven to their homes. So like zombies, she sleepwalked them out and into her huge Excursion for the drive to their homes. With the heat going full blast, they were each asleep within a few minutes, as she carefully navigated the snow-crusted roads to each of their homes.

Watching Jon, his back against the passenger window, head down on his chest, hair drifting down across his forehead, the exec sec said to herself, "I love these people. God help me, I do love them so."

# GET USED TO THE SMELL

"Glad you could hustle up here, Rhodes," Giles said, making a face as he scooted over on the short sofa in United's President's Club.

"If there's one airport I hate more than SeaTac, Jasper, it's Liberty."

She'd been pursuing her due diligence on CiliCold. Sure, it was already January 20 and she was taking her time to gather the information, but she enjoyed it—neither as taxing nor as boring as litigation prep with its endless exhibit preparations, strategic planning, preparing and responding to motions, and of course, knowing the deps.

Plus, this odd group had some novel ideas. She'd just been hitting her stride with CiliCold when she was summoned east.

"Jersey's not so bad, once you get used to the smell," he said, touching her arm.

"Then you get used to it, Jasper," she said, pulling away. "Meanwhile, I'm getting some breakfast." He touched her less these days, she knew, but she hated it more.

"If it's OK with you, I'll sit for a minute or two." Giles said.

Jasper didn't even watch her body walk-sway the way that he used to love to. Now, he just collapsed backward on the sofa, stretching his legs out.

In the three weeks since the interview, the VP-legal watched helplessly as the pain crawled up from his foot, the sharp torment-vines now surrounding his ankle. He looked down at it—fat, pale, and vulnerable beneath the sock.

He knew what was coming.

"Hurting today?" Cassie asked, standing over him with a plate of toast and some fruit.

She noticed. Damn.

"I'm fine."

"Why not see some specialists?"

"Why don't you get out of my business?"

Seen specialists, he remembered. The best, who stupidly poked, prodded, and probed. One of those educated fools used a tuning fork. A tuning fork, for the love of God. Like his leg was a friggin' piano.

Meanwhile, the pain spread.

Nerve conduction studies. Pain spread.

EMGs. Pain spread.

CT scans. Guess what, sports fans? Here comes the pain.

Giles swore that the pain tendrils fed on the tests and his anxiety, delighting in the fear that they sensed from him. Like a serpent with sharp spikes, the pain crawled on its belly up into his ankle.

Then suddenly, it stopped for a week, teasing him.

Until today, when the pain snake bit deep into his mottled ankle flesh.

"Interesting Sherman depo," Cassie said, sitting next to him, balancing a cup of tea with one hand and a roll with the other.

"Him or her?"

"Her, of course."

"I heard Runland wanted sanctions against me," Giles said. He burped.

He saw Cassie lean back and away. "He ever petition the court for them?" she asked.

"I gave Jim an offer he couldn't refuse."

"What was that?"

He leaned toward her. "Jim Runland's taken himself off as lead plaintiff attorney. It just took $75,000."

Scowling, she put the plate of food down on the brown corner table. "I didn't hear that from you, Jasper. You'll get disbarred."

"What are you getting tight on me about? It's just a deal between attorneys. Plus, it's tax deductible."

"Stop being your own worst enemy," she said, waving him off. "Do you mind explaining to me why I flew from Chicago to meet with you in a Newark airline club?"

"To fly to BWI," he replied, reaching inside his pocket. He pulled out her seating assignment for the Baltimore flight.

"Washington?" Cassie responded, eyes wide open. "I could have flown there directly from O'Hare." She left him holding the boarding pass out to her. "You still haven't answered my question."

"I said BWI, didn't I? Not DC." He twisted his leg in the chair. "Anyway, Triple S wants us to play a role in the Tanner takeover in Indianapolis. You and I need some face time to work out our . . . uh, our approach. Damn," Giles said, rotating his right foot in a vain effort to control the pain.

"I assume that you met with the SSS leadership in Maryland, then?"

"Of course," Giles said, wrinkling his huge brow in irritation. "Just finished with them and came up here to m—" He paused for a moment as his cellphone vibrated. He twisted it out of the lapel pocket of his expansive suit jacket, quickly scanning the text message.

"Our flight's boarding in forty. Let's get out of here," he muttered, grimacing as he placed weight on his right foot to stand. Instantly, a thin coat of sweat broke out across his immense oily forehead.

"You don't look so good—"

"Neither do you. Just get out of my way." He pushed by her, almost stumbling over a small animal carrier. "Let's go. We have an air tram ride plus a walk."

Now that he was walking, the pain subsided, and he was able to speed up to his brisk gait. He ignored the *wif-wif* of his fat thighs wearing his slacks' fabric thinner with each step as they rubbed across each other. Well, he thought, at least I'm walking now. He noticed Rhodes followed him as they stepped on the moving walkway headed in the direction of the AirTran signs.

"You were telling me you had the meeting," Cassie asked.

"Yeah. Triple S isn't sure that the Tanner purchase is going to cut it," Giles responded, huffing a little as he stepped off the walkway, beginning their walk to the train.

A moment after the train arrived, the two of them entered one of its many small cars built for eight passengers.

Giles noticed the two first were empty. He let Cassie in first, entered behind her, then turned.

A young talkative couple rushed up behind them to share the spacious car.

Giles instantly place a huge hand squarely on the young man's shoulder, stopping him in his tracks.

"Hey—" the man, bringing his body with its baby fat remnants to an abrupt halt, protested.

"Sorry for the inconvenience . . . friend," Giles said, driving his huge face so quickly into that of his new adversary that the young man involuntarily stepped back. "My colleague and I need the privacy. I know you won't mind," he added, finishing the sudden conversation by pushing the man backward while showing a full spread of malignant yellow teeth.

"C'mon," Giles heard baby fat say to his mousy-looking girlfriend. "Let's go to the next car."

"Yeah, you do that," Giles said to their backs as they left, then struggled to enter another car, already crammed full with other riders.

Giles observed with pleasure that the remaining passengers, having observed the incident, chose to push their way into other cars.

Or wait for the next train.

*Who cares?* He shrugged.

"So what's the problem with the Tanner sale?" Cassie asked, as the airport train slowly pulled out of the station, heading to the United terminal, two stops away.

"What?" Giles called, falling into the hard seat, leaving one between them.

"The sale, Jasper. The Tanner sale."

"Likely won't lead to an increase in dividends," he said, leaning over.

He watched Cassie shrug. "That happens sometimes," she said, looking at him. "Just don't delay the dividends or announce a decrease. They'll take a just a little haircut is all."

"Well, there are haircuts, and then there are scalpings. Plus, litigation could be doing better. I shouldn't have to tell you that." He started to cross his legs below the knee but thought better of it.

Cassie was not having trouble crossing her legs, he noticed.

He smiled. Good thought. Lust is healthy. At least I'm not in that much pain.

"They're going to yank your license if you keep going like you are," she said, placing her right hand up to grasp the brass pole as the car jolted forward on its electric tracks.

"Only if someone brings it to the judge's attention, which Runland will never do now that he's off."

He watched Cassie shift in her seat, then looked away. Didn't matter if she believed him or not, he thought.

"Don't know if you know that we also lost the Daubert hearings," he said. "Cases are going forward in California, and now in Georgia."

She leaned forward. "That's not surprising. There were plaintiff-oriented judges in those venues, plus they had decent science." After a moment, she added, "For a change."

"And lousy experts on our side," he added, working to sit up straight. "Their reports were shit. We may be looking at some heavy losses in the bellwether cases."

She turned to face him. "Certainly not all of them."

"Well, enough of them to up the price per case in any class action settlement."

"We model that?"

Giles looked down at his foot. He wanted to rub it so bad, just to touch it. But that he knew that would only make it worse.

"Yep. Close to a bil in losses."

Cassie puffed her cheeks out while tightening her lips. He thought she was going to spit tobacco juice.

"Take it easy, Rhodes. That's nothing. SSS'll get that back in a year. Lots of people think the major threat to drug corporations are the lawsuits brought by damaged plaintiffs."

"You mean 'allegedly damaged.'"

"Of course." Good girl, he thought.

"Well," she said, "some of the damages from those cases are outrageous."

"Give me an example." Giles applied his twisted smart-aleck grin all over his huge face. He was going to love this. A mind fuck was the closest he'd get to the real thing with her.

"That's not so hard, Jasper. One judgment against Kirog was well over $100,000,000. A few years before that, several plaintiffs won a $350,000,000 suit against Tycell."

Giles listened. Then, belching loudly, he simply shrugged. "I'll go you one better than that. Tycell paid over $21 billion in legal fees and settlement costs for their diet drugs."

"Making my point for me."

"Yet the company never folded."

"Not what I heard," Cassie said, turning from him and stretching out one leg on the seat. "At one point, they claimed to be teetering on the verge of bankruptcy."

"Just a head-fake," Giles said, not looking at her, watching to make sure no one entered the car as its doors opened at the next stop.

"What?"

He turned on her. "Oh, c'mon, Rhodes. Head-fake. Companies put that false rumor out there to scare off the trial lawyers. You know. It was a signal to the plaintiff attorneys that they'd better back off on the suits, or else the company would go belly up, and they'd never get any money. It was a company fake-out. The company's existence was never really at risk."

"Care to tell me why not?"

"Because, Rhodes, they never got kicked where it hurts." *I bet you know how to kick that way, sweetheart,* Giles thought, his eyes temporary losing their focus in another lust haze.

"I'm not f—"

"I know, I know," he said, shaking his head. "You're not following me. This is our stop." He twisted in his seat, grimacing for a moment, then pulled himself up to a standing position.

The two exited the train, slowly walking to their departure gate.

"Consumer lawsuits aren't really what the company worries about," Giles continued as they walked through the large open concourse with its shopping kiosks. "The shareholders are. They typically hold the keys to the company's survival—oh," he answered, stepping off of another moving walkway, his right ankle shooting a pain jolt up his leg as he placed it onto the hard, motionless floor.

"I know this story, Jasper," Cassie said, slowing down to stay in earshot. "By investing in the corporation, the shareholder loans the company money, billions of dollars."

"And the corporation uses that money to convince the banks to loan them billions more. Wait." He stopped. "Here's a restroom."

"There's the gate," she said. "That's where I'll be."

Cassie sat down at the gate in a chair with its back to the wall, dropped her head while rubbing her forehead.

She was so sick of this Jasper game, pretending to not know what she knew so well. How could she be a lead litigator and not know what the company needed to survive?

But to do anything else, to detonate her intellect on him, would just piss him off. He'd pushed promising litigators out the door just because they challenged him.

And the beast was out today. *Just look at him*, she thought. *Twisted. Evil. Just like Da–*

She crucified the thought, picking her head up, refocusing.

It was time to lose Jasper. She knew it in her bones.

But not just yet.

He turned left and slammed the door open to the men's room. He didn't need to pee, just to put his foot up and rest it. He entered one of the stalls, closed the door, smacked the stool top down, sat down, then stretched his foot up until it reached the stall door. The right ankle was blue-white and boggy, its flesh seeming to flow out and over his shoe. He thought the syrupy flesh would drip off his ankle if he kept it up any longer.

But he sat. Leaving it up and the keeping his weight off it for five blessed minutes,

He sighed, then walked out without washing his hands. He saw where Cassie was and limped over to her. She was putting him on about what she didn't know, he thought. But why?

"What about the shareholders?" Cassie asked when he came out.

"The dirty not-so-secret," he announced as he plopped down in one of the seats near the jet way, "is that as long as the shareholders receive their dividend checks, they ignore how the company conducts its day-to-day business. That's how the companies survive these drug failures. The sensational testimony at trial, the screaming FDA investigations of the company, the lurid headlines by the insipid press—none of that matters at long as the company cranks those div checks out to their shareholders."

"It's not that easy," Cassie said. He watched her shift her carryon from her left hand to the right. Smooth as silk, he thought. "For example, the Hewlett-Packard CEO had to resign along with some of her board members."

"Not a drug company, but that's exactly my point, Rhodes," Giles said roughly, shaking his head. "So what? Sure there was some musical chairs played in the boardroom for a week. In the end, the company survived, because the dividends weren't affected. The shareholders didn't care who bugged who as long as they got their money."

"And as long as the company kept the shareholders happy," Cassie said, nodding, "the comp—"

"Keep the stockholders fat and full, and they'll stay deaf, dumb, and blind when it comes to the day-to-day dealings," Jasper finished.

"Some get upset."

"Sure," Giles said, slowing his voice down. "There's always a nut or two who squawks at a meeting, but do you know what the rest are doing? I'll tell you. They listen distractedly, totally absorbed by their dividend statement and checks. That dough says it all. The bucks beat back honesty, morality, all of it. Those checks are like blessings from the pope—they cover a multitude of sins."

"But, Jasper, on the other hand—"

"Should the stockholders lose confidence in the company," Giles cut in, "then they cash their shares in, the company loses its money, as well as its ability to raise more. At that point, it's 'hit the bricks, pal.' Game over."

"So we're going to BWI to keep the shareholders happy?"

"No."

"Then why did you drag me here today?"

He looked at her, grinning. "To see the Sister."

# OFFER SOMETHING UP

Cassie, stunned by Jasper's last statement before boarding the BWI flight, strapped herself in tight as the jet's two engines started their whining.

Why would the CEO need to see them?

She set her plan aside to worry through the new factoid Jasper had thrown out there just before they boarded. As the plane pulled onto the active taxiway, its engines now throttled higher, and she assiduously reviewed their conversation in detail for the eighth time, it fell on her that Jasper didn't seem worried. That was good, and her head cleared.

Besides, something else was bothering her.

What exactly did Jasper know about CiliCold? SSS could either support the tiny company or squash it, yet . . .

Wasn't there another option?

She couldn't see it.

Yet.

One thing she did know, though.

She didn't want Giles in any of it. This was going to be her idea, her ticket out of the grind of litigation and away from Jasper forever.

"You all set?" she asked when he finally waddled down the jet way after landing. *I need to know*, she thought, wondering how aggressive to be.

"Yeah. Damn foot," he said.

Cassie watched him make one final adjustment of the right shoe a minute after they deplaned. Standing above him, her arms tight across her chest, she watched the living mud-river of people stream by, going who knows where for who knows what.

Need to be careful, she thought. Too little conversation about CiliCold, and I will have learned nothing. Too much, and he will get curious. He needs to be relaxed enough, distracted enough to have his guard down and give me honest answers.

Blow this, she reminded herself, and I'm litigating the rest of my c—

"Damn it," he said, adjusting his shoe. "There."

He rose to his full height. "Let's get going," he called out, starting to limp down the wide concourse.

In two steps, she caught up, and they walked together through the Baltimore Washington International Airport domestic terminal. Cassie easily kept up with the broken gait of the lumbering giant. She noticed that he wasn't grimacing with each step.

Now, she thought.

"Did you read what I sent you about CiliCold?" she asked.

She saw that he kept looking straight ahead. "Yeah. It's where the deponent worked. You were at the depo, right? They make vaccines or something."

Not enough. She needed more. Time to offer something up. Cassie swallowed.

"They do more than that, Jasper."

He stopped and turned to her, shifting his center of gravity away from his right leg.

"What do you mean?"

His look betrayed nothing.

"Well, they're not hitting up donors up and down Indiana just to make vaccines."

He looked puzzled. Cassie didn't see that look often. Like he swallowed something before figuring out what it was.

This info was new to him.

"How do you know that?"

She stepped closer, ignoring the people jostling by them. "Donors to our firm have contacts, who themselves have contacts. They all belong to me."

He squinted, licking his lips.

She held her breath. Did he have his own plans for absorbing CiliCold?

"Does it affect our case involving their cripped-up accountant?"

"No."

Cassie held her breath as she watched him. She could almost feel him calculating, the silence passing like the long wait to board a plane.

"Well, what are you bugging me about this for, Rhodes?" He stared for a moment, then, of all things, smiled before he limp-marched on.

Damn it, she thought. He knows something. Time to change the subject.

"What does the Sister want to meet about?" she asked. "The Tanner demolition is well planned. Reductions in staff are as we've done in the past. I'll work up the specific targets later."

"Tanner was suicide by stupidity," he said, looking straight ahead, continuing to walk. "All we did was preside over the pronouncement."

"And pick the very best meat from the corporate bones."

"No shit," he said. "Can we sit for minute?"

"It's lunchtime. Let's get something to eat." The notion of absorbing a company like CiliCold wasn't new, she thought. Big companies swallow little ones all the time. But if her preliminary conclusions held up, it would be transformative. Like moving from renting cars to building them.

Or like moving from Maryville, Washington, to Chic—

She killed the thought before it finished. "There," she pointed.

They cut left across the foot traffic to the Green Turtle at the beginning of the wide concourse with its short ceiling.

*Did Jasper just head fake you?*

She blinked twice at the thought. But like a hooked fish, she couldn't shake it.

I bet he does know. His rule was "always know more than the other jerk." *Maybe I'm the other jerk*, she wondered. *I should have pushed him harder.*

Jasper began to walk to the closest table.

"Let's not sit here," she said, turning from the table. "It's too close to all the foot traffic." She twisted, then pointed to a small empty table nearer the bar. "How about there?"

If I bring it up again, she thought, he'll get suspicious. He may be suspicious already.

"Kinda far, but whatever." He shrugged.

Once they got to their new seats, she sat down and released one shoe from her heel, letting it dangle back and forth from the foot of her crossed leg.

*Stop beating around the bush, Cassie. Just fuck him for the information.*

An internal explosion went off in Cassie.

*OK,* her thought stream continued, *I get that that was your first reaction. But seriously, he probably has a lot more of the information that you need about CiliCold. You know you won't outsmart him.*

Cassie shuddered as she looked for a waitress.

*And he's always wanted to fuck you. God knows he tried God knows how many times. Look, you're out of options. Embrace the horror for just a night to finally change your career—*

"Tanner shareholders staying in line?" Jasper asked, jarring her out of that terrible thought-train. She saw something like blessed relief cross his face when he deposited his great mass on the thin wooden stool.

"There, uh, there was, uh, some noise at the meeting," she said, leaning across the table, "but—"

She fell silent as he waved a hand at her. She watched him bring his massive head closer and closer to the menu, like he was going to eat it.

"Hey, sweetheart," he said, grabbing the wrist of the hostess who was just to his left. "How about a double burger with everything on it, and a beer?" He shot a glance at Cassie.

*If I do this, his hands will always be all over me, wanting more,* she thought.

*Maybe you haven't noticed, Cassie, but he's been leering at you and touching you for years. Besides, afterward, maybe he'll stop. You never know.*

"I think, uh, I think Cobb salad is fine with me," she said, shrugging.

"Thank you, sir," the hostess, wearing a white blouse and short black skirt, said, pulling her wrist free. "I'll tell your waitress."

"Doesn't matter to me who you tell," he said, shoving the menus into her hands. "Just get us our food. Unlike you, we don't have all day to hang out at this shithole."

Cassie watched him turn away from the hostess, who walked off, directing his gaze to her.

No way I'm doing it.

*Then it's my sad duty to inform you that you are stuck. The CiliCold opportunity will fly by, and you'll stay in litigation until they put you out to pasture. And while you're drooling on your SpaghettiOs in the nursing home, you'll remember with your last brain cells that you had a chance to finally do what you wanted to but gave up. You're the worst type of quitter—a coward.*

"It's not about the individual shareholders much anymore. Besides," he said pushing back from the small table as the waitress arrived with their meal, "we don't need them."

"Of course we need them," Cassie said, turning her face from him. "You just said so this morning. We operate on the money they provide."

*Besides, look at him. Can barely walk. The geezer will probably be happy with just a blow job.*

"Used to be that way, sure, but not anymore. Time was when the long-term shareholders were the basis of our operation. But two new things are now in the picture. First, the banks."

"You're making no sense, Jasper." He leaned over to the left, and for a moment, she thought he was going to grope another hostess who walked by.

He will want much more than to be blown, her mind asserted.

*Then give it to him. What are you? A virgin?*

"We both know we borrow from banks. Always have?"

Probably wants anal.

*And maybe you'll like it.*

"Listen to me, Cassie." As he bit down, she saw a piece of hamburger coated with yellow mustard dart out from between the buns onto his tie. Goodness, he was already half done with the mess on his plate that three minutes ago was a burger. "They're now part of us."

*No way I'll do this*, she thought. It'd be like eating a live rat. As bad as the first bite would be, you know it will just get worse.

*Then don't marry him. Screw him, learn what you need to learn, then leave. Won't kill you. Plus, you still have your merthiolate, right?*

Cassie didn't touch the salad that sat in its clear bowl in front of her. She always carried a bottle of merthiolate in her purse. The mercury-containing compound would make her ill at once. It was an ICE that she never wanted to use again.

"Of course banks loan to us. Commercial paper plus long term," she said.

And maybe he'll give me no new information, she thought.

*You're the one who said you need more info, not me. I'm just saying that this is how you get it.*

"Forget loans. Cassie. Banks now invest in us. J. P. Morgan, Morgan Stanley, Bear Stearns before they got gobbled up. BOA."

*And by the way, Cassie girl, it's got to be tonight, right?*

What?

*Do the math. You're both in the same town, and no late meetings. Plus, you need the CiliCold info pronto, right?*

She felt all twenty-two feet of her bowels squeeze.

"You with me?" she heard him ask.

"I know you're not saying that individual investors don't matter much anymore," she said.

He rose up, and she swore he was farting. She closed her eyes.

*I just can't see it*, she thought.

*I'm not saying that a picture of you two fucking should be hung in the Louvre. Just do it, learn what you need, and get out.*

"They matter more than ever," he said, gulping down his beer. "But not the way you think." He shot his chair back on the tile floor, almost hitting a black woman and her toddler. "I'm ready to go. Are you?"

She took a sip of water and stood as well.

"You got this?" Jasper asked, glancing at the bill, then looking at Cassie.

"Sure, why not?" She shrugged.

*Should have made him pay, considering you're giving it up to him tonight.*

"Let's catch a ride out of security today," he said, flagging down an electric vehicle. "It'd be good if I got off my feet."

Not tonight, not ever, she thought.

*Fine. Don't. Don't learn what you need to about CiliCold. Miscalculate and lose the opportunity of your career.*

He climbed up and onto the cart, his weight swinging him first backward, then left. Cassie walked around to the other side of the cart and got in, next to the carry-on luggage that he placed between them.

*You have never shrunk from doing what you needed to do. Never. And you have survived and succeeded. And here, at the endgame, when you are so close to becoming a corporate player in your own right, you quit? One damn night is all. Fuck him hard. Give up tail, rather than tuck it and run back to litigation.*

She coughed to hide the heaves rolling through her.

"Cassie, maybe you've been spending too much time in the acq side of events," he said, wiping his face with his hand, "but things have radically changed. This is 2016, not 1996 . . ."

*You pride yourself on being practical, right? Then be practical, Cassie.*

There's practical and then there's stupid, her mind reacted.

*And stupid is not getting what you need.*

"Now, we don't even need much in the way of shareholder money at all to operate. We can run all our deals on what we retain from our profits and the investment bank money. Shareholders still provide us dough, but it's the short-term investors that get us the maneuvering money we need."

*All you have to do is say yes. He will make all the arrangements. You know that. Go along for the ride. For a night, to save the rest of your life.*

"You mean the folks who sit around in their underwear and bathrobes all day, trading in and out of stocks? You can't be serious." More rope-a-dope, she knew, but he was buying it.

"The very ones," he said. He burped, and it was all Cassie could do to keep a straight face through the beer and hamburger odor that enveloped her.

*Cassie, the calculation works. Why are you resisting?*

"Way back when you were in school out west," he continued, "shareholders held on to their stock for six years or so. Now, they hold it for six weeks. Or six hours. For us, that means people are always buying in, and that's what keeps us liquid."

*Let your future open. Just like before.*

Yeah, to this despicable place, she thought.

They arrived at the end of the secure area.

"Another nice thing about these 'churn and burn' folks is that they don't want to give us advice on how to do things," he said, disgorging himself from the thin seat.

"Good thing, because their advice is atrocious."

She'd go to hell before she did this.

*You've got a ticket already.*

He nodded. "These short-timers invest to make money, not to demonstrate how inept they are in understanding our business. It's one thing for someone to buy twenty K worth of stock. But to think that the same clown who sits for ninety minutes a day on the Triborough Bridge on the way to his Kew Gardens dump of a walk-up can tell us how to spend those funds is a joke. We don't need their advice. We just need their money."

*Look at how sick you are of what you do. Break out. Forever.*

"And they make it back when someone else buys their shares."

"Yep. They're in it for the quick buck. As for everybody else, dividend checks are fat. And when there're fat, nobody asks questions. All they want is the dollars—nothing but the dollars. That's what Tanner didn't get," he said. "Oh. Hold on a sec."

She watched him gingerly step down from the cart, with all of the grace of a walrus trying to play the piano.

*The answer is no,* she thought.

*I know differently.*

*And so do you.*

"Those stupid presentations that Tanner used to give at shareholder meetings," Giles said, turning to walk out of the secure area. "What an ass. The shareholders want money—not clinical trials, not cheaper drugs, not more effective drugs, not safer drugs. If they get those too, then great. But if they get their money, then who cares? Here we are."

He pointed to his limo outside. "Cassie," he said, "You do good work. I will have the best bottle of Scotch waiting for you and me tonight. All you need to do is say yes."

*Cassie, if you are to learn what you need to learn to go where you want to go in life, the time is now.*

"You know, Jasper, I—"

"What? Damn."

Cassie looked down, ignoring all the admiring eyes studying her as Jasper took his call. A movement caught her eye. She turned to the left in time to see a tiny mouse scurrying into a small hole in the wall between two stores.

"Shitfire," he said, jamming the iPhone into his pocket. He missed, and it clattered onto the tile floor, shattering the screen. He kicked it against the wall not ten feet away, watching it splinter.

"I have to go to Miami when we're done here."

She watched her right hand move, taking his. Heard her whisper into his ear, almost sneezing at the rank combination of cologne and body odor.

"I'll cancel one of the limos," he said.

# THE GRAND TOUR

Cassie stood for a moment outside Jasper's apartment, her breath coming in irregular, ragged gulps. After one big gasp, she shuffled to the right, down the hall with its golden lights, lit like a heavenly corridor, then turned to the right.

Where the tall elevators stood.

The ones she had ridden up here five hours ago.

Leaning against the light green wall, she pressed the large silver button with her remaining strength.

Nothing. No light. No *ding.* Dead.

We go down the hard way, she thought.

Cassie took a step, then fell back against the wall, sliding down to the floor, her newly yellow skin and fetid breath shouting death was close.

Have to stand, she thought after lying on the cold floor for twenty. She couldn't do it, and the tears spilled out of perfect black eyes, followed by a rough sleep.

She jerked.

Jasper.

Coming out of his apartment, limping down the long hallway to the elevators.

To find her.

To finish.

Forcing herself to stand, Cassie stumbled to the floor 12 steps, beginning the long descent to the lobby.

*Clat-clat, clat-clat-clat, clat-clat* went the stilettoes, echoing off the gray walls lit with bright fluorescents, leaving no place to hide.

On floor 7, she vomited in the corner of the stairwell, the Merthiolate's mercury doing its job.

Have to hurry now, she thought. Cassie regained her bearings, walked down two more flights of steps, holding the grey painted iron bannister with both hands. When she was sure he wasn't following her, she stopped to call Uber. Reaching in her bag, she felt around her bunched-up, wet underwear for her cell phone and stared at it.

No service.

*Of course not. I'm in a stairwell—2:00 a.m.*

She leaned against the wall, her coat collar up high, hiding her hair.

As she dropped the phone back into her purse, she saw the blood dripping onto the stairs from between her legs. She whirled away from it, vomiting again, then wiped her mouth.

So simple, she thought.

It was supposed to be so simple.

Sex for a little surreptitious intelligence.

Fluid exchange for information exchange.

She inhaled. No simple blow job tonight. *He wanted (and I gave up) everything.*

The grand tour.

She gasped at the vision.

*Tried not to fake it. Saying what he wanted me to say. Lying still when he wanted. Standing when he wanted. Sucking when he wanted. Squatting when he wanted.*

*I really put my back into it.*

*He inspected, licked, bit, and inserted in every hole of mine except my ears.*

*What he demanded, I gave up. And when I complained, what did he say?*

"Shut up. That don't hurt, bitch."

*It was good that I swallowed the merthiolate, then. Bet he thought it was a stash of alcohol in my purse. Made me feel sick and, more importantly, looked worse.*

*That he couldn't handle.*

*That's when he decided he was done with me. Guess he doesn't go in for callow women.*

*I was wrong about eating the rat, though.*

*This was much, much worse.*

*And what did I learn—*

Finally, floor 1.

She put all her weight against the heavy door; it groaned open into the lobby.

He didn't care about CiliCold.

And given the smack across her face when he finished with her, he didn't care about her.

Calling for Uber, she searched her mind for the smooth voice that had egged her on—nothing to be found.

Cassie put the phone away and, pressing her head against the thick glass that separated her from the freezing Baltimore rain, suffered through her defeat alone.

# DA DOO RON RON

"Yes? Who is it?" Jon said into his S4.

He pulled himself up in his bed, taking the phone from his ear for a quick look at the time—5:30 a.m.

"It's Rayiko."

"What's up?" His head pounded whenever he moved, but he knew that was just the dehydration talking. Some water and juice would fix that. Plus, it felt so good to be in his own bed, and warm.

"Snowing hard, probably for the rest of the day."

Jon closed his eyes, exhaling all the way. "If we don't get in soon—"

"That's right," she finished. "We won't keep the schedule. I can stay until midnight tonight, but we won't finish up—"

"Unless we come in now. Can Robbie pick us up?"

"She already has Breanna, Dale, and Luiz. Wild Bill is already here."

"Outstanding. When can she get here?"

"In ten."

Jon smiled. "Thanks for the extra sack time." Then he remembered their conversation the night before. "Sorry about last night. It was the best I knew how to do."

Quiet.

"There's hope for you."

"Tell Robbie I'll be outside."

Jon jumped into the car as soon as the red Excursion crunched to a halt, noticing that the new snow had already covered the grey mounds of what had fallen before.

"Snowing hard," he said, piling into one of the back rows.

"What did you expect?" Dale said. "Tulips?"

"Somebody pee in your Wheaties this morning, Dale?" Luiz said, winking at Robbie.

"No smokes at home," Dale replied, rolling down the window to spit.

"Well," Jon said, plopping down next to Breanna, "at least he rolled the window down first, then spit."

He turned to her. "Welcome to virology. How are you feeling?"

"Not the best, but I'm game."

Jon saw that she didn't bother with false bravado or beauty-queen perkiness, just grit. She was committed to this—just like him.

"One more long day and night," he said.

"Well, that's all I can take," Luiz added, turning around to face the two of them. "I'm not sure we'll have enough tissue culture media to last anyway." To Jon, he almost sounded relieved.

Dale, turning around from the second row, snapped his cellphone closed. "Well, we do now. That was Rayiko—she said we just received a fresh delivery."

Luiz pulled back, wrinkling his nose. "Who ord—"

"She did. Yesterday, when we started this express-train-to-hell-frozen-over." Dale shook his head. "That lady's on top of it."

"Wild Bill's already there," Jon said, trying to picture who was on tonight's team.

"Must have had one of his lady friends drop him off," Dale said. "Other guys have a girlfriend, maybe two. Wild Bill's got a whole damn support group."

"Yeah," Luiz said. "And that's just in this state."

Nobody slept because it was just too cold. The basement stayed warmer, helped by all the bodies moving around. Robbie kept the hot tea and coffee coming from the upstairs kitchen. For a few minutes, every now and again, it seemed to Jon that everyone was enjoying themselves—still feeling the cold, just not letting it get in the way of each other.

That lasted until about 8:00 p.m., when the real fatigue burned through.

Rayiko was standing at the entryway to the incubator room, looking at the ceiling as she rubbed her neck. Breanna was just coming down the steps with two cups of tea, thick steam rolling over the tops of the cups in the cold air.

Jon had just returned from carting several inoculated tissue cultures to the incubator and was standing at the hood next to Wild Bill, trying to ignore the hundredth argument that Luiz and Dale were now engaged in for the day.

His head was splitting. He couldn't remember the last time he ate that day. He only knew that that if he couldn't feel his fingers, he couldn't work at the hood.

He picked his head up, not sure what he was hearing. He cocked, straining to hear . . .

Humming.

He looked over to Wild Bill just three feet away, who, head down, in the midst of inoculating yet one more of hundreds of tissue cultures, said clearly, "Da doo ron ron."

Jon, his energy needle on "E," wondering every few seconds why he just didn't sit down somewhere and sleep, thought it sounded familiar.

Listened. Listened.

Then, he got it.

Jon said clearly, "Da doo ron ron ron."

Wild Bill looked at him. Jon laughed and nodded, Wild Bill smiled, and they both sang in rising voice.

I met him on a Monday and my heart stood still
Da doo ron ron ron, da doo ron ron

Luiz, Dale, Rayiko, and Breanna looked over at the two. Even Robbie came down from upstairs to see what was going on.

Jon, now fully awake, raised an arm of invitation to Wild Bill, who continued.

Somebody told me that his name was Bill.
Da doo ron ron ron, da doo ron ron.

Dead still.

Then to Jon, it seemed like the entire room filled with the noise air makes when it is sucked down a huge vortex, followed by the explosive chorus.

*Yeah,* my heart stood still
*Yes,* his name was Bill

Aaaaaand when he walked me home
Da doo ron ron ron, da doo ron ron!

They all laughed, and Wild Bill, the only one of them who knew the words to the song, led them in another chorus. Then again and again, each a touch more ragged than the last, until their voices were raw, midnight had come, they'd finished their work, and it was time, finally, to go home.

Jon arrived at work at seven thirty that next morning. The white truck was already waiting. The driver, wearing thick coveralls from neck to foot leaned against one of the cab's huge black tires, smoking a cigarette. Jon saw him peer into the Cherokee, then wave as the Jeep crunched to a halt beside him.

Jon opened the door and got out, grimacing as smoke from the man's cigarette whipped into his face.

"Hi, Jeff."

"Hiya, Doc. You got a fresh batch for us?"

"C'mon. I'll show you where they are."

Jon walked through the four inches of new snow to the front door of CiliCold, Jeff trudging behind him. He held the door open for Jeff to walk through, closing it quickly after the two had entered the dark living room.

"This way," Jon said, leading him down to the cellar.

"Man, it's freezing in here," Jon heard him say behind him.

"I hope you're going to remedy that," Jon said. They arrived downstairs, and Jon led him over to the incubator room. Jeff opened the door and stuck his head in.

"You have a lot of product. How long did it take to make all this?"

"Two days and a night."

Jeff whistled, a low, warbly sound. "Got your temp logs?"

"Right here." Jon handed over a flash drive. Jeff pulled out a piece of equipment, circular blue-and-white plastic thing with a belt clip and a small screen. Ramming the flash drive in, he squinted, staring at the tiny display, twisting around to let the light of the small incandescent bulb shine from behind.

"OK." He nodded his head. "Some temperature variance but nothing to write home about." He pulled a cell phone out of his pocket and snapped it open.

"Yep, the consignment looks to be in decent shape. Let's get those transporters down here." He closed the phone. "Here you go, Doc." With his free hand, Jeff pulled a folded envelope out of his pocket and handed it to Jon. "Hope this gets you warm," he said as two other men with the same coveralls came down. "You doing OK?"

"Why?"

"A little thin in the face is all."

"I'm good, and about to get better."

Jon took the check, then while the cultures were carried up the basement steps, stood in the living room and called the HVAC office.

While he was on hold, he watched the workmen move each culture set, wrapped and heated, though the living room. He noticed that each man wore the same gloves, fingers cut off at the bases, keeping the hand and wrist warm but exposing the fingers.

What happened to the fingers part of those gloves, he wondered. Did they throw them out? Were they of no val—

*Hey,* he thought, *get it together and get the check to the damn bank.*

Driving through the snow, Jon realized there was no point in having people come in today. After two days of deep cold, it would take all day and half the night to get the office warm and workable again. He reached inside his jacket for his phone, and hit the letter "R," speed dialing Rayiko.

No answer.

Odd, but it was still early.

After pulling into the CiliCold parking lot, he stayed in his car, scripting a broadcast email to the team. When he was done, Jon saw it was snowing again. He closed his eyes.

Ringing.

He sat up straight, digging the S4 out of his pocket.

HVAC guys.

There they were by the door, encased in their trademark red-and-gray thick overalls, waiting with their new equipment to get inside.

Jon took a breath, bracing for the cold, then stepped out of the Jeep to let them in. He stretched his neck, face in the grey sky. Then he exhaled, suddenly disoriented.

Cutoff gloves.

He'd been in the car, asleep, dreaming of the workman's cutoff gloves.

# PROMISSORY NOTES

"Thanks for—"

"Oh," Breanna said.

Rayiko, seeing the accountant jump, put a hand out to steady her.

"I frightened you," Rayiko said, at Breanna's desk, keeping her hand on the accountant's arm. "And the baby, I'm afraid. How are you both doing?"

"Taking it day by day," Breanna said.

"Nice that it's warm inside again."

The project admin noticed that Breanna was quiet for a moment, then she said, "This is quite a group, Rayiko. It always has a struggle on its hands."

"I always like this office," Rayiko said, walking around the front of Breanna's desk. "It's so bright." She knew that Breanna had bad news for her that would lead to hard choices. Rayiko's stomach churned, and she made a face. There was no way out of the interminable money issues.

"Pull up a chair, Rayiko." Breanna scooted over, making space for her. "You're going to need a ringside seat to understand this spreadsheet."

"You mean this financial wreck we gave you?" Rayiko said, sitting to Breanna's right as they both focused on the screen.

"So you know?"

Rayiko, continuing to look at the display, said, "Sometimes you don't need a weathervane to know which way the wind is blowing. How bad?"

Breanna swiveled her chair to look at her. "Gale force now, F5 in about two months. If we're just going to make flu vaccine, we're good for six months. It's—"

"That's all we've ever been good for."

"The extracurricular work that really costs us."

"Where are your projections?"

"Look at cell AA77." Breanna pointed to the Excel table. "Here . . . then here."

"Here?"

"No. That's without animal costs. Look here."

Bad. Rayiko sighed, then pushed her chair back on its wheels to the wall two feet behind her.

"Breanna, it's never been this grisly." She scooted forward. "Is that with committing all our funds?"

Breanna turned the monitor to the side. "I even assumed Jon would continue to bring in $10,000 a month." Breanna turned to look at her. "Listen, it's for me to run the numbers," she said, putting her hands up, palms up. "Not to pry."

"Today," Rayiko said, leaning forward, "you can pry."

"Jon's out on cold calls in Indy today. At least I think that I heard that."

Rayiko nodded.

"Has he ever raised this much in two months?"

The program administrator just looked at her.

"I understand," Breanna said. "It's a big ask, even from multiple donors."

"I'll talk it through with Jon today."

"Maybe he'll tell you he raised the 195 K, and our problems are over."

Rayiko smiled.

"Thanks, Breanna." Rayiko sat still, working to move air into lungs that seemed like plastic. For a moment, she was a teenager again, at the neighborhood pool, coaxed for the first time to climb the ladder to the small board, way up to the top. Once there, she peered down at the distant water like it was death. Suddenly, strange hands on her shoulders pushed her out from the board, out over the water.

Flailing at the air. Screaming all the oxygen out of her—

Rayiko closed her eyes, then, opening them, said, "We're all glad that you are working here with us. Jon said it was one of the best decisions he has made in a long time."

Rayiko watched Breanna study her face. She knew what that look meant, had seen it many times before. Her own mild lip droop always became more pronounced as the day wore on. And on stress-choked days, it was unmistakable. Still, only someone that watched carefully would notice.

And Breanna, she knew, was a careful watcher.

Rayiko nodded.

"It was a pool accident. Bled into my brain as a kid. Not too much, just enough to affect some of my facial muscles. This is the result."

Breanna leaned forward. "Rayiko, it's not that. I was wondering why you work here? Luiz said you trained in virology. At Stanford, right?"

"Yeah." Rayiko exhaled slowly, working to hide her surprise at the question.

"A master's degree?"

Rayiko nodded. She knew where this was coming from and where it would end. "Family's here."

"OK. But so is Lilly. And Purdue, and IU at Bloomington. "So why knock yourself out here?"

"Money doesn't drive me. It's not that I don't like it," the program administrator said, shrugging. "I just don't have the drive and the ambition to do things with it." She put her hands deep into her lab coat's pockets. "I am thirty-five years old. I have had times in my life when I had no money at all: school, the first days of our marriage. Could pay no bills until my next check. Couldn't drive because there was no gas in the car. Nothing."

She pulled her hands out of the lab coat. "There were also times when I had more money than I knew what to do with."

"What did that feel like?"

"Different money questions. But money questions nevertheless. I've been in both places. And both times, money was just a pain in the ass to deal with. My husband likes it. Maybe one ambitious family member is enough."

"So you're here because you don't need a lot of money, and they"—she waved her hand toward the hallway just outside the door—"need you."

Rayiko knew Breanna had reversed it. But that was OK. Rayiko knew why she was there. That was what was important.

"Uh-huh." She got up, "Thanks, Breanna. And I promise you, I'll get this worked out with Jon today."

Rayiko walked out into the dark hall. She thought about going downstairs to her office, but it was tough to have a discussion with Dale and Luiz arguing.

And they argued more now.

She turned left and walked into Jon's office, closing the door behind her. She dialed.

"Rayiko?"

"Jon, how are you doing?'

"Some promissory notes. No certain donors." She could see him shrug in her mind's eye as he said it.

"Where are you, Jon?"

"Indy."

She was quiet.

"I know what you're thinking, Rayiko. No. I am not seeing Alora. Actually, after I get turned down by a few more donors, I'm going to have dinner with her brothers." He laughed.

"Can you make some time for me?"

"You're here in Indy as well?"

"No, but I can be there by about three."

The line went quiet.

"Care to tell me what this is about?"

She wouldn't. He would spend the next ninety minutes struggling to think his way out of a financial box that he could not escape. She needed him open.

Raw.

"No, Jon. How about the Cold Spring Road VA?"

More silence. "I was thinking the same thing. It's where we—"

"See you there."

# MESSAGE IN THE WATER

Cassie stepped into the car silently, dropping the umbrella on the street for one of the attendants to pick up. She noticed nothing, eyes turned inward, running the forensics on the just-ended CEO meeting.

In fact, she thought, it had been two meetings.

Three days after The Horror. The night of—

Cassie shut that thought off and, leaning back into the town car's plush seatback, ran her mind over the day she just finished. Left hand in motion, thumb running through her fingers. January 25. Over and over. Not closing her eyes for fear of where her mind would take her, she forced them to focus on the wet, grimy streets of south Baltimore.

The first meeting with her, Doucette, and Jasper went well.

Cassie had not met the CEO before, and struggled for the right sense of this woman. Her reputation as an enigma was on full display today.

Don't project onto her, she chastised herself. Just describe her.

Straightforward.

Straight-talking.

Soft?

No. Just not abrasive.

Cassie stopped.

This wasn't hitting the mark either.

She turned her focus outside as the limo slipped in and out of traffic around Cherry Hill, coming up to the 695 exchange.

Wouldn't be long to the airport now.

She started again.

Doucette spent the first fifteen minutes of the meeting asking them both about the Tanner merger. At first, both Cassie and Jasper talked, she thought, tag teaming as they had a hundred times before. But then Jasper fell quiet. Maybe his leg, maybe—well, who knows?

Anyway, more and more of the questions came to Cassie. What were her thoughts on absorbing Tanner, Doucette wanted to know. What did she think of Tanner's product line? Could she give her any ideas about the integration timeline?

"How do you see your role in all this?"

She actually asked that.

Not of Jasper. Her.

Cassie, ready for everything and anything, played it cool. Questions were easily answered. Hitting all the right spots, yet she felt no confidence or assuredness. Instead she felt uncomfortable.

Yes.

Uncomfortable and unsteady because she didn't know if her ideas were impressing. Doucette didn't smile, didn't repeat back what she heard, ask any questions, or talk over her. Didn't even nod her head. Yet Doucette was attentive.

Yes, and disarming.

But not communicative.

Like she knew the answers Cassie was going to offer.

The CEO took everything she said and left Cassie with . . .

Acceptance? Acquiescence?

She shook her head. It was like Doucette left a message for Cassie written in water. She couldn't see it.

Well, her eyes were a little blurry anyway. But at least there was no vomiting today. It was starting to really hurt, three days after—

Then Jasper found his voice.

That was the end of that.

He wasn't a sycophant. He was worse. He raised his voice as he told Doucette how lucky she was to have him and Cassie. Then he told the CEO her job, ranted about the new world order of the corporation. How he had evolved (yeah, he used that word) to be the protector of SSS. Wanted a larger role.

The thing of it was, the CEO spoke to him.

Doucette asked him questions, nodded her head at the right times, treated him politely.

And the more polite she became, the angrier he got. The louder he got.

Finally, she got up, thanked them both for their time, and asked them to leave.

So strange.

Then the second meeting, just her and him.

After they arrived at his office, Jasper tore into Cassie—demanded to know why she didn't support him in the meeting, really got in her face.

But this was the meeting for which Cassie was ready. Always ready. Right back in his face. The hell with the Horrible Night. That was her fault, but it wouldn't be the lever used to pry her open. He was insipid, she had said. Couldn't read a room. Didn't learn anything new about people. Should remove his crown and listen. People owed him nothing. In the end, they were screaming in each other's faces.

That should have felt good.

But not today.

No idea why.

"Here we are, ma'am."

Cassie got out, taking the umbrella left on the seat for her, and walked across the wet street, through the tangled mass of human confusion, into the terminal.

# RUNWAY

An hour later, Cassie boarded her American flight to O'Hare and, ignoring the greetings of the flight attendants, walked to 3A, where she pushed the black-and-gray carry into the storage space above. She inserted her ear buds, turning to face the window.

The crew all knew the First Class drill; all would read and respect the "Do Not Disturb" body language that she learned to speak so well.

And while she turned her face to the outside world, she shut out the detritus; humans moving in lines, workers tossing luggage, flight crew deadpanning memorized speeches, while she digested Tanner Pharmaceuticals.

Tanner failed, she thought, not because it stayed devoted to its principles, but because it had the wrong ones. Dr. Tanner thought its principles were its mission statement—what was it? "Integrity, Strength, Honor and Service for Better Products."

He wasn't stupid, just misguided and behind the time. Profits and dividends used to be the result of good products. Now they themselves were the product, the only product that counted.

Missing this simple point cost him his company. This was the first time she'd seen it.

All the other acquisitions were simply generated by fiscal incompetence. Janus lost their company because the shareholders learned the books were cooked. Nysus lost their heads to them because their leadership team warred against each other. When was that? Five years ago—wonder when they get released from jail? The others, TTR, Cronos, Figold—they all threw money down the R and D pipeline and never saw it again.

*Well, the Tanner reason's different, but another one bites the dust.* She reached forward to pull a legal pad out from her overnight.

"Care for a beverage before we depart?"

"No, and don't disturb me again."

The attendant moved on as Cassie leaned over her legal pad, slowly drew out her platinum-line Mont Blanc, and began drafting the memos for the continued absorption of Tanner by SSS.

She worked through each of the major departments: Accounting, Advertising, Human Resources, IT, Legal, Research and Development, Regulatory, and Safety. She used to pride herself on memorizing the major people in each of these areas. But she stopped years ago. Just got in the way. Easier to target someone for termination if you have no clue who they were.

Anonymous assassination.

She started with legal, wrote "100 → 0."

SSS could manage what was left of Tanner with in house legal, so Tanner legal could be exterminated. She twisted in her seat and began to look over her notes for the other departments.

Two hours later, she was done.

Accounting 100 → 0
Advertising 100 → 130
HR 100 → 80
IT 100 → 50
Legal 100 → 0
Safety 100 → 20
Regulatory 100 → 100
R&D 100 → 50

She closed her eyes. Substantial saving would accrue to Triple S if they followed these recommendations, she thought. The increase in advertising that SSS lived on would be more than made up for by reductions in accounting and IT. No imagination there. That was the way to make money—the Triple S way, the Jasper Giles way.

Her stomach rolled over. She wasn't sure where Giles ended and Triple S began.

Anyway, safety cuts go right to the bottom line. These cuts were golden.

But nobody touches regulatory. Once the FDA says no to a product, the reg dweebs come back and say it was because we cut their people. Everybody's afraid of the FDA, even though we pay them tons in user fees. The reg folks parlay fear of the FDA into fear of themselves.

Well, she thought to herself, smiling. Their day would come, just not today.

She lifted her eyes from reg to the next line—R&D.

She wanted to cut more than 50 percent. It was so wasteful and messy. Chemistry studies begat animal studies, which begat human volunteer studies, which begat phase II clinical trials, that begat phase III clinical trials, which occasionally begat FDA approval.

Most times it never got that far. Chemistry looked good, but the compound fried the mouse brain, or the rat brain. What the hell ever. There was a ton of money the company sank into research and development and damn little return on investment.

There wouldn't be much pushback on the fifty percent cut—that was just Triple S's way, its introductory offer. Smiling at herself, she let her eyes roll left and right to the clean yellow margins of the legal pad, as if she could see a solution to what she thought as the R&D hole that money never filled. Research and Development meant you were paying for fail—

She jerked, eyes flying open as the plane smacked something hard.

The runway—

Chicago.

Had it.

Right there.

Saw the idea clear as a bell. It was like the physical shock of the landing jarred some mental obstruction loose, and the idea like clear mountain water poured out and over her.

Then the Jasper text.

# "MY DEAL"

"You and I need to put our heads together."

It was two days later, and Cassie was never more grateful for video call technology. The thought of that man in her immaculate office, or worse, being in his office, with his stink everywhere, was revolting.

He'd asked for this meeting by text, she thought, staring at a blank display. She almost got down on her knees to pray that he'd be professional to—

Suddenly, Giles' face filled the screen.

That was all there was. Her mind's eye showed her a small lizard with a giant human head, and she fought against the urge to back away.

"It was a debacle," Giles said.

"A money leak?"

"Meeting yesterday was total chaos. It took us half the day to figure out which numbers to believe. Profit estimates will undergo a 'correction,'" he said, waving quotation marks in the air.

"It's already January 27. What's next?" Cassie said. Her heart was pounding.

"After the usual threats, 'heads will have to roll,' 'careers prematurely terminated' ad nauseam, leadership has turned to us for solutions."

She turned away, trying and failing not to bite her lip.

"Hey, what are you looking at?"

She coughed. Out of the corner of her eye, she saw the giant head twist left, then right, its huge eyes darting desperately around to see what was going on in her office.

She hated this man more than she hated all men.

"Nothing." She'd been waiting for this moment. The idea she had on the Chicago plane had taken only two days to go from a seed to a tree, plunging its new roots deep into her. She'd done her homework. No pharmaceutical company had ever made it work.

"Well, Jasper," she said, facing him again, her voice resuming its low, neutral tone, "the bleeder is Research and Development, right?"

"Yep, and we're not the only ones with the problem. All the majors are having the same issue: weak internal pipelines, plus downward pressure on drug prices from the generics." He wiped his big hand over his head wet with sweat, then shook it. She fought the reflex of covering her head to protect it from the flying-sweat image.

"Litigation side of things?" he asked, sitting back.

*Thank heavens we're hundreds of miles apart.* "Don't remind me. Plaintiff's bar is getting hot and bothered on Banyial, but I'll manage that."

"How will you do that? The concerns about its relationship to GI bleeds have strong literature support."

"Didn't know you were keeping up with the ongoing work." *What else was he up on*, she wondered. Her stomach turned as his face moved closer to his monitor, squeezing out all but his eyes and nose.

Suddenly, she remembered sharks.

She punched.

"Not your concern," she said, "It's covered. My deal. We straight?"

She saw his eyes narrow, sparking a vestige of combat in her. She stared back.

"Straight," he said.

"OK, then." Get him back on track. "So how do we solve the bigger problem?"

"That's why I'm here," he said, exhaling. The display clouded up with each of his expirations.

"So we purchase these companies, between one and two a year—"

"For millions."

"And we get them lock, stock, and barrel."

"We trim them down and then let what's left service us."

Cassie wanted to throw the paperweight award on her desk at him. "But we buy everything," she said. "The up-and-coming drugs, including the stinkers that they can't move. We buy it all and sort it out."

"Of course."

Now, she thought. The pump is primed. "Then let's buy something else?"

She explained her plan.

He shook his head. "Pretty crazy for a drug company."

"It's a crazy world."

"Well," he said, then burped, "sounds like you've done your homework."

He almost sounded like a colleague, she thought. "So what do you think?"

He was quiet for a moment. Cassie was pleased that for once, he couldn't find the words. Then he answered, "Let's take it to the Sister."

This was what she had in mind. She counted to five, giving her the opportunity to seize control of her pulse rate again.

"Want me to arrange it?" Giles asked,

"No. I'll do it. This is my deal."

# THE SHADOWS

One hour and fifteen minutes later, Rayiko was walking to the white-and-brown house at the Cold Spring Road VA when she saw movement beyond it, coming over the hill with its patches of dirty snow and hard brown dirt.

Jon.

She gestured for him to follow her, then checked her watch.

Thirty-eight degrees.

And this was the high-temp time of the day. She looked up.

Clouds coming in from the north.

An early nightfall.

She sat on the bench. The wood had actually had time to dry off. That was a blessing. Wet, cold wood and wool were a bad mi—

"Rayiko, that was a long way to drive. Tell me."

She turned to see him focused on her. His face was set, mouth straight. No smile. She realized that he didn't know what he was getting into. Good.

"You know we are within a month of CiliCold tanking, don't you, Jon?"

"Yes, I know." She could sense a dead sadness behind his eyes. "You're informed?"

"I spent the morning with Breanna."

He blinked twice. "OK. Good. I'm glad that you know."

She sat up straight. "It's a big hole, and I'm guessing that you won't tell me that your money raising today will fill it."

Jon looked down. With a strong voice that she heard less and less, he said, "I got five K. It won't even cover the bottom. But"—and he looked at her again, leaning closer to her—"the CTSA here at the IUPUI may do something for us."

She shook her head. "Sure, but those translational science people like solid pedigrees plus data, not eccentric scientists and theories."

She saw him look away.

"Jon, let's get real here. Your major affiliation is in West Lafayette, not here with faculty in Indianapolis. And you know they don't have the money they used to have to spread around."

She watched him as he turned, slumping forward on the bench, looking straight ahead. "Rayiko, I can't blame them. I just have a bag full of ideas that I'm shopping around, to produce a result that the field has given up trying to find."

He rubbed his left hand with the right, back and forth. She blinked a tear away. "Jon, that's not it. Nobody believes your ideas. They—"

She sat up straight—as straight as possible, trying to become part of the wood.

The speeding frozen mush ball flew by, catching Jon in the throat and chest.

She looked to the left.

A young girl, with a guy whom Rayiko guessed was the girl's brother, stood frozen. Both looked like they were eight. All four eyes were wide open in horror.

Jon jumped up. "Do you know what you just did?" He pointed to the kids. "To me, a virologist, an epidemiologist, a *freaking* PhD." He bent down and made a small and badly formed mush-dirt snowball, bellowing, "Revenge is coming. Get ready for war." He took a step, with a grotesque look on his face.

The kids, bursting out in laughter, took off running up and over the hill.

He looked down at Rayiko, frozen mud and dirt on his black jacket. "Well, you know, I always thought I should have been a Viking."

She laughed. "More like a snowman. Sit."

He sat to her right, turning to face her. She saw that his face caught the last rays of a sun being inexorably rubbed out by dark and lifeless clouds.

"It's both better and worse than you think," Rayiko continued. She struggled to keep her voice even. "They don't believe your ideas, Jon. Nobody does. They believe you. They know you don't have the idea that you need—that we need—but if anybody gets it, it will be you. They don't trust much, but they do . . . trust . . . that."

"Do you, Rayiko?'

"I've always known it."

At the touch of his arm on her coat, the project administrator's pulse raced.

"But, Jon, that conviction is hurting them now," she said, leaving his arm on hers. "They can do the math, not to Breanna's precision, but—"

"They know time's running out."

"And you have to decide. Give up the quest and just make flu vaccine, or go for broke and risk it all, putting everybody out on the street if you fail. That is your decision. Don't put it on them. You will need to go a—"

"You folks work here? Visiting somebody?"

Jon stood up. "No, sir. We were just leaving."

The security officer smiled. "Don't blame you much. Getting cold again." The guard waved, then turned and walked down the hill in the snow.

She got up to leave.

"Rayiko."

She turned, looking up at him. The sun had fled, banishing them both to the long shadows.

"I understand you," Jon said, "And I will carefully consider what you've said. But know this. We both give our best to CiliCold. For you, that means committing your organizational skills and your diplomacy. For me, it's my heart and my hunches. I don't understand either but . . ." He put a hand on each of her shoulders. "Rayiko, that's all that I have ever had that I can trust. I am nothing without them, and I commit those to our efforts."

"Jon." She looked up at him, this man of contradictions, childlike weaknesses, staggering intellect, crippling vulnerabilities. He was held together by his connections not to himself but to others, including her.

She had tried and failed to love him. There was only her family for her now. But she was in awe of this thing with Jon, this emotional web, through which poured his pain for her to see, and from which he received her quenching relief, balm for the anguishing fire always threatening to consume him.

She loved her husband, but she marveled at Jon.

She stepped back. "See you tomorrow, Professor. Don't have too much fun tonight."

"Bright and early."

They walked their separate ways in the dark.

"Just couldn't keep her happy, Will," Jon said three hours later, walking outside Appleby's, just behind the two men wrapped tight in thick jackets.

"Yep," the taller one said, blowing air through his frigid fingers. "Alora's always stepped on her men during her life-climb. I'm really sorry you're the latest casualty."

"Whatever," Jon said, clapping Will on the back. "The fact that we're divorced doesn't mean that I can't hang out with my ex-brothers-in-law."

"I love it," Tom, the younger of Alora's two brothers, said. "But I have to say, Jon, you are looking a little on the ragged side."

"Sure enough," Will added.

"Divorce will do that," Jon replied.

"Yeah, but that was six months ago, man."

The three men faced each other just outside the building lit by the overhead bright incandescence.

"Glad you brought that up, Tom. I am reopening the divorce negotiations."

"What?" Alora's two brothers stared at each other.

"Yep. I'm just letting you know that I am getting the best divorce attorney around, because this time, I want custody of you guys."

They all whooped and high-fived. Jon wanted to talk some more, but he had seventy miles to drive. They broke up and headed to their own cars and into an unforgiving evening.

He cranked the Cherokee's engine, which started strong on this cold night. Ten minutes later, he was passing Fifty-sixth Street on I-65. New snow was coming this night, probably six to eight more inches by the time the small yellow orb rose the next morning. He would be home—

Alone, he thought.

By 8:00 p.m.—

Alone.

And get some work done.

Alone.

"No," he said aloud to no one.

With all the waning self-discipline that he could muster, he kept from walking through the huge Divorce door in his mind, now yawning open, beckoning him like a friend in pain, forcing his mind down the other remaining narrow hall.

At the end of it was a phone.

Of course.

He snapped out the S4 and made the call.

"Thanks for coming down to me today," he said. "You were saying that I should be true to the dollars or true to the team's beliefs in me?"

"Can't talk now."

"I just wan—"

"Tomorrow."

The line was dead.

He exhaled then let his drifting mind pull him north through freezing Indiana farmland to dark West Lafayette.

# MOLECULE MANAGEMENT

"I don't know why you're so upset," Jasper said, as they caught the elevator to CL-4.

"I'm simply saying that I expected this meeting with Doucette to be just the three of us." Cassie replied, not looking at him, too stunned to learn that her acquisition idea was the topic of a wider discussion. "It's just a trial balloon. Not a presentation before corporate leadership. Goodness, Jasper."

Things are getting worse all the time, she thought, swallowing what tasted like blood.

"The Sister has strange ways," Jasper said, shrugging. They stepped off the tiny elevator out into a small foyer then took a right. Ten steps later, they were at Doucette's outer office door.

"I love these corporate floors," he continued. "No minions scurrying around."

"Good for you," Cassie said, unable to shake the impression that Jasper was sneering.

It didn't matter. At least she had some warning up front. Cassie's excitement about the idea surprised her. She didn't think she'd get excited about anything after last week.

But she could handle that, she thought. Old lessons don't die. They're harder to find when you need them, but they're still down there.

It was February 1, and she'd spent the last three days reviewing her material again and again, studied it so much until she hated it. Then she memorized it. By the time she had every factoid investigated and scrutinized, every nuance of the presentation absorbed, she didn't care if it was accepted or not.

Cassie watched the CEO's exec sec stand as the pair entered the conference room. Around the maple wood table were six matching chairs. Cassie inhaled the leather smell of the room.

Jasper sneezed. At least he covered his nose, Cassie thought. She saw that only a little leaked from his fingers to the palm of his hand.

"Hello, Zita? I hope you're well," Cassie said. It was good to focus on someone, to say something, anything, to get this meeting moving.

"Good as can be, Cassie. They're ready for you in her conference room." Cassie saw Zita look at the back of Jasper's head as he, not waiting for an invitation, limped directly ahead to the smaller area. Shrugging, she beckoned Cassie to follow him.

Cassie entered the inner sanctum.

The room was a simple rectangle and utterly without any affectations. Harsh fluorescent light shone off white walls, with the three white tables configured into a "T." Ms. Doucette stood at the center of the T's crossbar. "Hello, Cassie. Nice to see you again."

Cassie reached her hand out, giving a perfunctory shake. "Thank you for seeing us, Ms. Doucette."

"After the financial news that I just received from Nina," the CEO said, turning to acknowledge the chief financial officer, who was just entering, "I am looking forward to some better news from you."

Cassie turned and smiled. "Nina, very nice to see you again."

Nina smiled and shook hands. Cassie noticed that her niqab was the purest blue that she had ever seen, perfectly accenting her white blouse.

"Let's all be seated," Ms. Doucette said. "I've allotted an hour for this conversation and, given its sensitive nature, did not ask the heads of the other divisions to attend."

"Especially R&D," Giles said, moving his head left and right, all the while twisting his right wrist like it was screwing a bolt into the wall.

Cassie, pleased that everyone ignored him, was surprised at the hammering of her own heart. Damn these feelings. She turned her mind back to the past, to Washington State. She thought the Unthinkable Things from long ago. It took just a moment to readjust.

Her pulse was now low again, pushing blood through cold skin. Those thoughts always worked.

"Should Nina and I conclude that this idea of Cassie's has *prima facie* merit," Ms. Doucette said, removing a pen from inside her black jacket, "we'll involve the others as needed."

"Don't forget the board of directors and perhaps the shareholders," Giles added.

Jasper.

Cassie saw that the CEO, ignoring him, turned to Nina, beckoning her CFO to start.

Cassie heard Jasper grunt.

"So far, I have heard nothing about this," Nina said. She was living up to her reputation as head of Quantitative Assessment and Planning-Financials. All business.

"Well," the CEO said, "let's change that. Cassie?"

She had thought that she might start with some of the background, but read the room as too grim for the review. Just say it.

"I think Triple S should get out of funding R&D."

The only sound was the hiss-hum of the florescent lighting.

"Cassie," Nina said quietly, "that idea is quite, uh, unusual, but not very practical." She raised her hands. "After all, what we at SSS do is R&D. Are you saying that the solution to our fourth quarter declining profits is for our drug company to leave drugs behind?"

Cassie, hearing Jasper snort, leaned over the table toward the CFO.

"We've already started the move, Nina. Fifty years ago, drug companies developed everything in-house. Early drug development testing, CMC, pharmacology, metabolism studies, PK—"

"And toxicology," the CEO added.

"Yes," Cassie replied, nodding to Meredith. "We did all that in-house. We've come to call that preclinical. In addition, we also managed the required human studies."

"The clinical side of the floor. We know that," Nina said, looking to Doucette like she was bored.

"And we paid for all of it," Cassie continued. "But the industry moved away from that model. We now turn over the human investigations component to outside groups that do the clinical research. We give them direction in protocol development, sure, but it's their responsibility to write it, get it approved by the FDA, and find clinical sites, which themselves find the subjects who will take part in clinical trials. Nowadays they even do all the statistical analysis for us."

"And we pay them a handsome sum too," Nina said, flipping through pages of printed spreadsheets.

"Not if they're academic we don't, Nina," Cassie said, now opening a manila folder that she brought. "We pay a fraction of what a for-profit solution would cost."

"Even if you add the indirect costs?" the CEO asked.

"With those funds that we pay the university factored in, we still pay hundreds of dollars less per patient than if we went with a private-sector clinical research organization," Cassie said.

"We pay academics less and let them write a few papers. That keeps them happy," Jasper said, shrugging.

"And," Cassie said, turning back to Ms. Doucette, "we keep the cost down by sponsoring a competition for the group that organizes all this clinical research flotsam. These academic centers fight over the chance for us to pay them peanuts."

"Yes, yes, yes," Nina said, letting her hands fall to the table. "You just defended the rationale for our modus operandi. Now, just how does this get us to pulling out of R&D?"

Cassie saw that Nina was focused again. So much the better. "What we do is only a halfway measure, Nina. It deals only with the clinical. But the other money loser is preclinical. We are still vulnerable there."

The room was quiet.

"You mean treat preclinical like we do clinical?" the CEO asked, elbows on the table, chin resting in her palms.

"Why not?"

"I'm not sure I'm following," Nina said, shaking her head. "How would the preclinical side of things work?"

"Well, there we have the molecule identification and development," Cassie, said keeping her eyes on Nina. Turn Nina and you turn the room, she thought.

"We work both ends at once," she continued. "First, make different groups compete for the right for us to buy their molecule from them." She paused for a second, making sure that she had everyone's attention. "Then, we find external working groups willing to compete for the right to study it."

"You mean these working groups do all the preclinical?" Nina asked, looking around the room. "Who are these people?

"Academics."

"Sure, for now," Jasper said, "but once the word is out, private labs will jam their snouts into our trough,"

Meredith let her mind shift to auto, listening to Cassie and Nina discuss the various roles research groups might play in the new project Cassie described.

Jasper, as usual, contributed nothing of importance.

He was an obstacle. In the past, she'd have tuned out his middle-school sarcasm, given him an important role in the project, and thanked him for being a Triple S player.

Now, he grated on her. With every passing month, he was more insolent, less respectful, singing a self-serving song about the benefits of corporations that was strident and out of tune with her. Now, he was under her skin, an abscess that had been slowly swelling, but suddenly on the edge of explosion.

The abscess needed excision.

But just like abscesses, Jasper would leave a smelly, disgusting mess behind.

But . . .

It would be delicate, she knew. His question about the board was a gambit. There were some on the board of directors who loved his arguments, loved him. And of course, shareholders were focused only on profit. No moral compass there.

Meredith shifted restlessly in her chair. Any move against him would make him her enemy, a powerful enemy with powerful allies.

No, he was already an enemy, she thought.

Maybe the Virgin Mary was listening, maybe not. But of one thing she was sure.

Whatever happened would be up to the CEO, who alone would face the consequences.

"We would probably need to stay away from private labs," Cassie continued, bringing her new knowledge to bear. "They game the system and will cost us too many dollars for just par work. Academics value their reputations more."

"And people will sell us their precious molecules because . . ." Nina asked

"Because they're broke and they can't afford to continue to study all the necessary properties of their own molecule to get it to market," the CEO responded.

"And how much will these molecules cost?" Nina asked, head down, taking notes.

"A lot less than identifying and working up the molecules ourselves," Cassie said, leaning forward. "Plus there's no internal bias. We would have a purer selection process."

The CEO leaned forward. "What do you mean?

"When we develop molecules in-house," Cassie said, turning to Doucette, "we invest in them. It is sometimes hard for us to walk away from that investment."

"Not following, Rhodes," Jasper said, thumbing his iPhone.

"We spend so much time on its development, or an influential internal team believes in it too much," she said, putting air quotes around *believes*. "We stay committed to these loser compounds longer than we should."

Cassie looked around the room. "We are not as discriminating and objective about their chances for success as we should be, driving up the costs."

"How so?" the CEO asked.

"By continuing to pour money into the development of molecules that others would rightly have rejected much earlier?" Nina asked.

Cassie nodded. "On the other hand, if you buy the molecules from the outside—"

"We are more objective for the chance of failure—"

"Because we have no vested interest in the molecule's prior development."

Cassie nodded back at Nina, who was clearly getting it.

"Cassie," the CEO said, looking straight at her. "I do know our competitors buy molecules, but only to augment their own discovery process, not to supplant it. I know of no company that has abandoned its own preclinical program." She pursed her lips.

Cassie turned to Ms. Doucette. "How many molecules are we working up in preclinical now?"

"I can't tell you exactly, but—"

"Nine."

Nina is sharp, Cassie thought.

"And of those nine, how many will blow up before they make it to the clinical side, Nina? You know, fail metabolism studies or the toxicology studies. Or kill the animals."

"Six or seven."

"Say six," Cassie said, looking at the CEO. "Then those six are money losers for the company. Each costs us $9 million to work up in-house. So the company loses $54 million dollars. And we are always trying to fill the pipeline, right?"

"Yeah, following losers with more losers."

Jasper, of course, Cassie thought. Always Jasper.

"Now suppose," she continued, "we have people compete to sell us the right to study their molecule. We pay $5 million each for four of them, $500 K for the molecule, then $2.5 million for toxicology and animal studies that we turn over to outside groups to perform. Do the math."

"Saves thirty-four mil," said Nina, scribbling some numbers down.

"But Cassie, are there enough molecules out there?" the CEO asked. "Who has them?"

Cassie turned to face her. "Who doesn't? Academic labs, small biomed companies. The country is teeming with them. And they are all the same—dedicated researchers devoted to their molecules but always strapped for cash because they have neither the resources nor the know-how to generate capital."

"So we buy them?"

"Only the ones with solid biochemical profiles that win our competition. And they come to us in a package, which we then turn over to outside groups to carry out the preclinical investigations. In doing so, we will be moving from the molecule development business—"

"To the molecule management business," the CEO finished.

"Yes, Ms. Doucette. One other thing," Cassie said. "If we decrease drug development costs, then that's more dividends for shareholders."

The magic word, Cassie thought, noting that all were silent. Then Nina asked, pen hovering over the page, looking at Cassie, "Where do you suggest we get the money to pay for these molecules?"

There it was.

Cassie inhaled slowly, savoring the moment. "What's our R&D budget?"

Silence again. Then they all began talking at once. Ms. Doucette cancelled the next appointment, then the next. Ninety minutes later, they broke up. Then, as they were leaving, Meredith asked, "Jasper, can you stay behind, please? I have some questions for you."

# "SHE JUST DID"

She watched Jasper as he let go of the door handle. When everyone else was gone, he asked, "What can I do you for?"

"Are you feeling all right?"

She saw his mien drop into expressionlessness, his famous "flat face."

Finally, he deadpanned, "I have my problems."

"Stop being one of mine."

He stood up straighter, she noticed. "Did you think that I wouldn't hear about that Sherman deposition? It was shameful."

"Sorry, I didn't know you were a lawyer who actually took depos."

She let it pass. "I don't have to be to recognize despicable conduct."

"It was necessary, in my view." He leaned forward, stretching his pudgy arms on the table, putting his weight on his hands. In a guttural voice, he said, "Stay in your lane, Meredith."

"I am, and you know what? You're in my headlights."

She sat down, looking straight on into Jasper's glowering face.

"The interviews that you give are your business, Jasper. Management of this company's affairs are mine. Your job is to make my job easier. Not harder. And certainly not embarrassing."

He dead-faced her.

"Are we going to have a problem, Jasper?"

"No."

"Because if this happens again, I—"

"Because we already have a problem, Doucette."

"OK," she said, leaning forward slowly, voice low and even. "Do tell me what you think our problem is."

"You don't have the balls for this job."

She looked at him for a second. Then she nodded. "Which means I don't think with them."

He took a step toward her. "I can have you hung out to dry, you know."

She smiled. "I know that you have friends on the board of directors. Rumor has it that you are angling for a CEO job somewhere, maybe even here. And heaven knows you have the knowledge, Jasper. But"—she leaned forward over the table—"you are clearly missing most all of the humane components of leadership. Corporations aren't chess pieces on a brick-and-mortar board, Jasper. They are human endeavors operating by and for people."

Giles flat-faced. Meredith watched him fish out a coin—looked like a quarter—from his pocket and place it on her desk.

"For your collection plate, Sister." He stood up straight, then collapsed his weight on his left leg. "Don't worry. You get to keep me. Cassie can't take my place."

Meredith cocked her head. "She just did."

Giles glared, then banged the table and took a crooked, malignant step toward her, the hot, contorted look from his twisted face chilling her blood.

"Oh sure, Jasper," she said, standing up, then rounding the table so there was no furniture between them. "Please give me a reason to call security. Your friends on the board won't ride to your rescue if you assault me."

He leaned down, snatched his satchel, then turned and walked out of the office, raising his middle finger backward over his head as he walked out.

Meredith walked to the wall to turn off the lights. Then falling back into her chair, covered in the soft light of the orange sun, she sighed. After her pulse rate dropped, she called Cassie, her new VP-Legal, to explain the new change in reporting responsibilities.

# N OF 1

Ugh, Cassie thought as the United 757 bounced twice, then settled on the runway after its landing at Atlanta Hartsfield.

She opened the tiny window shade to see the leaden sky throw sleet at the airport. At 3:35 p.m., it looked that what natural light was left was willing to call it a day, giving itself over to another cold and sullen February night.

She gave in to the temptation to scratch her head, really looking forward to sleeping during the hour limo drive to her home in Clayton. When the flight attendant announced they could deplane, she waited in her seat as she always did for the rest of the first-class passengers to struggle off the plane with their stiff necks and swollen ankles. Then she stood and walked down the jet way alone, ahead of the economy dweebs flying in steerage.

Walking quickly past the crowded baggage claim area toward the driver she recognized, she felt her cell vibrate. Pulling it out of her long, black, winter coat, she was surprised to see who the caller was, and put the phone to her ear, slowing down.

"Cassie? This is Nina. Are you back in Atlanta?"

"Yes."

"I was wondering if you could head back to BWI."

"Just left there."

Silence.

Cassie closed her eyes. "Of course. I'll check the flight infor—"

"The same plane you were on turns back around in an hour fifteen."

"I need to physically be there?" She couldn't help herself. A killer week shouldn't end like this.

*Tell it to the universe.*

"Cassie, Ms. Doucette gave your and Mr. Giles' plan quite a bit of consideration after you left."

Mr. Giles' plan? Cassie's stomach turned brick-hard. She counted to seven, her eyes focused on the baggage cart revolving again and again, her lips still. Finally, when she could trust her voice, she said, "Yes, of course."

"We are calling it the molecule management system. The idea is quite an attractive one," Nina said. "However, it's not something we could switch to right away."

Cassie walked over to the concourse wall, letting the human river flow by her. "I imagine. It's a lot for the company to absorb."

"Mr. Giles suggested that we might start with a test case first. 'An *n* of one,' as the research guys say."

You mean as they used to say, Cassie thought. Their jobs were already terminated. They just didn't know it.

"I think that I know just such a group. They work out of northern Indiana. They are making some incredible claims, but apparently believe that they have all of the early lab work to back them up."

"What else can you tell me? No competition for them? Are they ready to sell so easily?"

Cassie thought for a moment. "Let me do some more homework and get back to you."

Cassie was back in a BWI hotel by midnight. Rain and meetings all day Saturday. And Sunday.

A week later, she was presenting the idea to senior management.

It was coming together. But she knew that she required information about the target. A hook.

# DARK ROPE

"Yeah. We saw that. There's blood in the water, that's for sure." Then, after a moment, "Boss."

"I know that," Beom screamed, his bulging neck muscle stretching his white shirt to the breaking point. He saw the fear in his traders' eyes, those unlucky enough to sit in the front row, their thigh muscles pushing the cheap chairs back and away from him despite themselves.

*Byeong-shin*, he thought in his native Korean. Such imbeciles.

Cell phone vibrated in his pocket—two long vibes, a short, and then a long one.

No. Couldn't be.

He ignored it.

"What I don't know is why you aren't killing these sonsabitches." The chief broker/dealer glared at them. "You each picked the way wrong week to be lazy. The thirty-fifth floor just increased your buy quotas."

Hearing the groans from the room, he stomped over to the trader sitting in the first row, kicking the chair out from under the young scruffy man. The bearded thirty-year-old fell over and clumsily sprawled all over the floor.

"Nobody gives a fuck what you think," Beom screamed into the face of the young trader who was now trembling, eyes closed. Beom looked up. "You all remember that. Your asses aren't glued to these seats."

He leaned down into the face of the trader who was struggling to right himself. Puffing his face up to fill the field of vision of the insipid *chon-nom* on the floor, Beom said, "If you don't like this place, boy scout, leave."

Beom stood up straight. "There are always new butts out there waiting to take your chairs. Any takers? Raise your hands."

Cell phone vibrated.

*Jen-jang*. It could wait.

Beom walked back behind the wood table and the white Target plastic bag on the floor under it. Ignoring the bag, he turned to face the paralyzed traders. "Sweet knees, kindly explain to this group what higher quotas mean."

He pointed to the woman at the end of the first row, the only one of the three female traders who ever wore skirts.

"If I leave my knife at home, I don't get no bonus," she said. She almost spat it out, eyes on fire.

He liked that. This was a tigress. He could smell it. She'd eat a seller's newborn, lapping up every last drop of fresh blood.

"Right," Beom shouted. He leaned down and picked up the white plastic bag, placing it on the table, "and 'no bonus' is one big step down the gangplank to getting canned. You hearing me?"

He noticed that some said yes but all had their eyes on the bag.

"If too many of you get canned, then I get fired. And I am telling each and every one of you, that—"

He opened the bag, pulling out what looked like a dark rope with a handle and thinner strands at the other end.

"I will personally horsewhip each of you within an inch of your damn lives before that happens." He cracked the lash. Everyone jumped to their feet.

"I will go to fucking jail for whipping you before I get fired for missing these quotas."

He cracked the whip again against the wall.

"And I will horsewhip the cops trying to take me down. You hear me?"

Silence.

"You fucking hear me?" he bellowed, arms raised high, face flushed, eyes bulging.

"*We hear you, Beom.*"

"Then go rip the faces off these sellers." He hurled the whip to the ground, whose every bounce protested that it was not flaying open a vulnerable back.

His cell phone rang again.

"Get out of here, all of you!" he yelled.

Even his oldest traders stood frozen in place, mouths open. Beom slammed his giant fist into the table, which cracked with a hiss on impact. "Move your asses."

When the room cleared, he hit Talk on the iPhone, taking a deep breath. "That better be you, Hugo, with those July 50s."

"No, it's Rayiko."

He pulled the phone from his ear, gaping at it like it was an alien device. After a moment, he sat down in one of the traders' empty seats, speechless. Then, he said, "Not here. Not now. Tonight."

She hung up.

*Jen-jang.*

The rest of the day would be ruined. That always happened when he became almost human.

Ordinarily, Beom was home at 8:30 p.m., ready for a meal and one of his favorite *maechunbu*. Not tonight. Instead, after removing his jacket, tie, and white shirt, he kicked off his pinstriped slacks and sat on the bed. Body breaking through his T-shirt, sock garters still on.

The phone rang.

Same number.

Beom watched it ring, the screen pulsing with light, with new energy. It rang on and on.

Just do it.

He picked it up.

Nothing.

Just as well. He didn't want to speak anyway, he lied.

Still . . .

"Hello?" he said.

No answer.

"Rayiko?"

"Yes. It is me. I had a tough time finding you. When did you move to New York?"

Don't let her question you, he said to himself. "I thought it was your mother's attorney on the phone."

"Since when does he call you about futures prices?"

"Yeah, yeah. What can I do for you, *ttal*?" She was always smarter than him, he thought.

She explained.

He shook his head as though she could see it. "No. These people don't make a lot of money here, regardless of what you may have heard in Illinois."

"Indiana."

She thought to call me, and I couldn't remember where she lives. "They are only traders, and not good ones. Most of them will lose money by the end of the week."

"Not talking about the traders, Dad. The firms for whom they work."

He thought for a second. He always misjudged Rayiko.

Like he misjudged her mom.

"And what do I tell these institutional peop—"

"Rich institutional folks," she interjected.

"When they ask why they should pitch in?"

"Tell them your daughter is good for the first thirty large."

"How is that possible?"

"I plan and I count, just like you taught me, *abeoji*."

Beom smiled, unwilling to strangle the warm feeling that threatened to overcome him. If only he could hold it—*yeong-wonhi*. "Anything else, or can I hang up and just carry out your orders?"

"The commitments have to be made by EOB tomorrow."

"That's impo—"

"You always do the impossible. Now do it for something more worthwhile than a second high-rise Manhattan apartment. Call me tomorrow, *abeoji*." A moment later, she added, "Please don't fail me."

They hung up.

Beom shook his head. How could he hate family, but love his daughter?

But he did.

No matter.

There was new work to do.

◆

By eleven the next morning, Beom had a $90,000 commitment from three execs.

By 1:30 p.m., another $45,000.

By 3:00 p.m., a new $20,000 was in.

One more check to get.

By 4:00 p.m., done.

Hyperspeed Courier had the checks delivered to his office by 4:30 p.m.

"Rayiko, it's all there,' he said when he called a few minutes before five. Plus, I'm kicking in the thirty K, so you can keep your buy-in."

"Thanks, Dad."

He couldn't help it. "You owe me now, *ttal*."

"I always owe you, Dad. And we all have debts we can't repay."

His heart swelled. He only said, "Yeah, yeah, yeah. Talk to you soon."

"Call Mom."

Rayiko put the phone down. She would have the money by that evening. That was how he did things. She didn't expect that he would replace her buy-in with his, though. That really simplified things at home. And home was going so smoo—

Phone.

Jon.

"Rayiko. How are you? Is this a good moment?" She heard him cough.

"I'm fine, Jon. How are you?"

"Great, and back in the office." He paused; she could feel him gathering his thoughts.

"I considered what you told me. You were right. I have two and only two choices."

She was quiet.

"I can't let them suffer for me."

Motionless, phone tight to her ear.

"I will cure this son of a bitch. And we will move rapidly because we have to."

"You just come up with the right idea that we need, Jon. We will work on the money side of things."

"Well, we are way short."

"You're not the only one who can make an ask. We know that you are a genius. So go be one. See you soon."

She hung up. Beom and Jon were so different, yet she was connected to them both. Each could move mountains if they wanted. It just took her to make them want it.

# C

"Did I tell you that you could work late?"

Breanna watched Ethan's eyes narrow. Her own throat tightened. It was so hard for her to breathe, to think.

"Everybody had to work late. I texted you about this yesterday afternoon."

"Breanna, we have a kid here. What am I supposed to do when you're gone?"

She was tired. And at once, she was sick of being bullied. She worked hard, and now, Ethan was pulling this shit. This clod, this ignorant man wanted more. She lifted her left foot off its heel to step closer, get in his face.

Instantly, nausea hit her like a wall. She clutched her stomach, bending over, trying to stop the words that flew out anyway.

"Well, how about lifting a finger to take care of her, Ethan? Did you feed her last night?" she asked, trying and failing to stand up straight, barely getting the words out.

"Well, some." He took a step back. If the nausea had ended, she would pin his arms. Get up into him. Penetrate beyond that stupid, sleepy smirk that he smeared all over his face.

Instead, she remained bent, arm and fingers pointed in his direction.

"Ethan, you expect me to work all day, when you do no work. Then, I make dinner. Then take care of Jackie while you are sleeping in front of the TV."

"Look, Breanna, you know my situation," he said, raising both his arms.

To her, Ethan, unkempt, short hair growing on his scalp in patches like weeds, looked like a six-foot scarecrow, arms flapping, thin wood jaw rising and falling.

"I know your situation means that you have nothing to do all day. If you're looking for work, then fine. Another faculty position, fine. But as long as you are doing it at home, you should take care of dinner and help out with Jackie. Don't put it all on me."

She didn't remember feeling the punch but cried out when her head bounced off the floor. Heard it "gunge." She lay there, flat on her back.

"You deserved that, Breanna," he said, leaning over her. "Don't pretend you didn't. You had an ass-kicking coming."

She pushed herself up, then rolled to get on her knees, her eyes always fixed on him. "I'm leaving."

She threw up, the thick yellow-green expellant splashing off the wooden floor. Wiping her mouth, she said, "And I'm taking the baby."

She stood, one loafer in the vomitus, the other a step closer. Clenching her right fist, she fully expected him to come at her. She didn't care. Let him. Let him kill her. She was fighting back. *As God is my witness, I'll kill the pig before he hurts me or my baby.*

"Get the hell out of my house, and take that damn kid with you."

Breanna stepped backward, eyes on him, reaching with her right arm for the couch where her heavy brown coat was. She then turned and rushed around the corner to where Jackie was, lying in the portable crib by the breakfast table.

She grabbed the two-year-old, astonished the baby had slept through the fight. Usually she cried at the drop of a hat—any hat.

Now, fast asleep.

Breanna ran by Ethan and out the front door to her car. Turning the engine over, she headed out of the apartment complex, the bright sun lighting her way.

But where should she go?

She turned right on Elmwood Street, then took 52 south. She belched, the hideous smell igniting another nausea attack. She stayed on 52 until she got to the old deserted mall, and parked in the empty lot. One car in a parking lot field full up with dirty snow.

Breanna dialed her sister, explained.

"Breanna. He's no-account. Always been, always will be. Staying with him trashes your life and trashes Jackie's. Lose him. Pure and simple."

"I know what he did, Rita, and I know why I left. But I can't have Jackie without a father."

"Really? She hasn't had a father who cared for her one day in her precious life. Is he using?"

"How could you even suggest that?"

"Why wouldn't I? He's out of work, irresponsible. Time on his hands, no coins to rub together. I bet he is."

The worst of all possible worlds, Breanna thought, dropping her head into her hands. "Maybe he—"

"Has he given anything to Jackie?"

"I-I don't kn—"

"Has . . . he . . . given . . . drugs . . . to . . . Jackie?"

"What? No. Of course not." Then she thought. Jackie was quiet during the entire fight. In fact, she was quiet last night. In fact, she was still—

"Jackie!" she cried, looking over at the child, whose arms and legs twitched and jerked. It was as though her baby was on a scalding oven, trying desperately to get off and not knowing how. But Jackie endured the muscular agony without a sound, totally out of it.

"Breanna, take her to the ED at once."

Breanna fired the car up, reversed out of the parking lot, and headed onto McCarthy Lane.

Jackie was admitted to Indiana University's Arnett Hospital at 9:07 a.m.

Nine hours later, Breanna took her precious one from the nurse back into her arms for the drive.

Anywhere but home.

◆

Next morning in a newly rented apartment, Breanna called Rita. As she started to talk into the cell, she looked over at Jackie, who was crying while trying to crawl-roll over to her. The mother walked over, scooping her up, and with her free hand, reached down for the phone to hear her sister talking.

"Don't know where—"

"Hey, Rita, I just got home. We are in an apartment."

"Not the same one?"

"Good Lord, no. A different one, far from Ethan. Not like he cares where we are."

"Jackie was OK last night?"

"Yeah. I know that I just gave you the text highlights. But she's OK."

"What did they find?"

"Cocaine."

"In her urine?"

"Yeah."

"How much?"

"Goodness, Rita. How do I know, and what do I care? It—"

"Sorry, I just meant—"

"Doesn't matter how much. What matters is that Ethan gave our baby coke to shut her up. His daughter," Breanna finished, sitting down to stave off more nausea and to rock Jackie, who was really crying now.

"I'll send you some money."

"I don't need the world. Like I say, I have some, but I've got to figure this out."

Silence.

"Breanna, what are you really going to do?"

"One thing I'm sure of is that I'm keeping my babies safe. I have spent my last night with that animal."

"Don't you have to go back to get some clothes and things?"

"I'll buy what we need."

"I hope that's right. It can be complicated. Remember, that's his kid your pregnant with."

"It's my baby, and I will take care of it," she said. She would do everything for her children. The thought anchored her, as though her feet had finally landed on the solid ground she'd been struggling to feel. "I'll call you soon to update." She hung up to play-tickle Jackie to sleep.

Next morning, Breanna called in sick, then got Jackie up.

It felt like the first normal day in months. The nausea had vanished, and with Jackie on her knee, she started a list of all the things that needed doing.

Sixty-two items later, the list was done.

Furniture, kitchenware, food, medicine, follow-up appointment for Jackie. Hospital bill. Prenatal for the new baby. Underwear. Bras. Shoes. Slacks. Jeans. Blouses. Car maintenance. Wi-Fi. Vacuum cleaner. Internet. Plates, silverware. Lawyer. A new laptop. Small TV. On and on.

She had no idea how she was going to get this all done, then remembered how a minnow eats a whale.

"One bite at a time," she said nuzzling her nose against that of Jackie, who clapped her hands and kicked her feet with delight.

Six hours later, Breanna stopped her car brimming with mops, towels, soap, dishware, toilet paper, and toys for Jackie, to check her mail. She just wanted to see if the box key worked.

No mail.

When she got to the door of her apartment, she saw a thick envelope on the ground. She walked over, picked it up.

Her name on it.

Bet it's Ethan.

Damn it.

Breanna opened it.

She bobbled the cell phone that came sliding out of the envelope but trapped it between her index and middle finger. Placing it under her chin, with Jackie in her left arm, she held the remaining folded piece of paper to the light with her right.

> I know your pain. Will call you tonight. Let's make this right. C.

# RAGGEDY

That message.

Breanna just couldn't figure it.

She knew not to count on what she couldn't see. Still, it just might b—

Suddenly, she heard the wood floor creak and groan and felt a hard cold breeze on her neck.

She spun around. "Who's in my office?"

"Hello stranger," Rayiko said. "Hadn't seen you for a couple of days."

Breanna sighed, shaking her head. "Well, it's been raggedy."

"I just got here myself. Here." She saw a check in Rayiko's hand.

"What is this? I—" Breanna studied the check: $190,000.

She bit her lip, mind overflowing with a thousand questions.

But this was Rayiko.

Rayiko would tell her what she needed to know.

"Well, I think that I know what to do with this," Breanna said.

"We'll have to pay tax on it."

The accountant laughed. "Listen. With the bills we have, a large taxable income is not anything that we have to worry about." Breanna looked long at the check and looked at Rayiko.

"You look tired, Rayiko."

"I'm much better now."

"I'll let you tell Jon what he needs to know."

"Done," Rayiko said, having turned away, already headed out of Breanna's office.

# PING, PING, PING

"Come on. You kick your feet for me, J baby."

Breanna knew, she just knew, that her Jackie understood her. Just one more—

"C'mon. Yes! There you go."

Jackie kicked her right foot, squealed her delight, and kicked both feet twice, abandoning herself and her wet bottom to a joy moment that cold evening.

Mom wasn't far behind. Breanna loved this. She was one with her Jackie and one with her unborn.

Ethan.

And his notification letter that was in the mail, waiting for her today.

Ugh.

She knew there would be no reconciliation. Forget that. But now she had to find time to get in a court fight over custody. And didn't she have to tell him about her pregnancy? Don't know. Just don't know. Would he use her silence against her?

Too much. She put Jackie down so her sweet one wouldn't sense how upset she was becoming. Just didn't know—

*Ping ping ping.*

Her head jerked up. What was that? Her phone was right next to her and silent.

The doorbell ring was nicer, the fire alarm much worse. Refrigerator door open? What—

*Ping ping—*

The other cell phone.

The phone with the note.

Breanna ran to the closet, where her coat was.

Where the phone was.

*Ping . . . ping . . . ping.*

There, in the pocket. She reached down deep for it, but its slippery plastic slipped between the lining and the wool, down to the bottom of the seam of the coat.

Damn.

*Ping ping—*

Almost . . .

*Ping ping—*

Got it.

*Ping . . . ping . . . ping.*

Breanna held the phone, an old iPhone whatever, just watching it.

What was going on here, the accountant wondered.

Nobody she knew would ever be this mysterious. How about someone from work?

No.

Why would they need to disguise th—

Jon?

Her heart jumped. Maybe he wanted to talk unofficially. Why? He had lots of personal discussions at work. Everybody knew that. In fact they loved it, counted on it. Why would he need to hide—

Maybe . . .

A little more personal?

Maybe to pursue her?

To one day, hold her?

And he couldn't do that with an office-to-office cell phone call, could he?

Hence the burner.

A little diabolical, but hey, he was under real stress and it was a cray-cray world.

*Ping . . . ping . . . ping*

"C"? Why sign "C"? Did he have a middle name? Nickname she would learn?

*Who knows?*

*Answer the damn phone.*

*Ping . . . ping—*

"Hello?" she said.

"Breanna?"

Not Jon.

A woman.

Don't recognize the v—

"I will tell you who I am in a moment, Breanna, but I first want you to know that I have been where you are. It almost broke— No, it—"

Who was this, Breanna wondered, holding the phone tighter, relaxing some.

What did this mean?

Friend of Rita's? Rayiko's?

She didn't know.

"Did break me, Breanna. I have been better since then. Not normal. Just OK, and never the same as before. I will help you through this if you let me."

"Who is—thank you—who is this?"

"My name is Cassandra, Breanna."

# SCRATCHING

Breanna leaned forward, hair hanging down over her face as she strained to hear every syllable the strange voice uttered.

"If you like, you can call me Cassie. Whatever name you want to use is fine. Do you have time to talk with me, Breanna?"

Cassie? She didn't know any Cassie. "Maybe five or ten minutes," she said. "I'm putting my—" She paused. No point in revealing more than she needed to. "Some things away."

"Breanna, how are you doing? More importantly, how are you feeling?"

*Who is this?* she wondered, eyes closed, with a tight grip on the phone. "How do you know me?"

"I know that you are a fine accountant and that you have a husband who can't shove enough coke up his nose. I know that you have a baby girl named Jackie, and one on the way. And, Breanna, I know that you are all in danger.

"You are doing all that you can," the voice continued, "but you will lose. I think you know that too."

*She's right,* Breanna thought, eyes suddenly wet with tears. *And I'm sick over it.*

"How are you sleeping now that you left him?"

"First night or two after I left, I slept well. Now, I'm struggling some." Breanna felt better just letting that come out.

"Most days I can forget," Cassie said. "But it always comes back in the evening. The night owns me, Breanna. We can't let that happen to you."

To the accountant, Cassie's voice was calm, nasal, and melodic, like it knew its fate.

She settled down some as she realized that this was an older woman, one who'd been to school.

She needed to know more. After a long inhale, she asked, "Cassie, what happened to you?"

"I wanted to hear about you, but if you're OK with it, we can begin with me."

She paused.

"I am not from here, Breanna. Washington State was home for me. Logging country. I remember cold rains on short winter days, and of course, the rest."

The breathing on the phone was rough now. Not threatening. But labored, difficult.

"Was it your husband too, Cassie?"

"Much closer."

"You sound like you're still in pain. Have you seen somebody for help?"

"You mean a counselor?"

"Yes. Therapy."

"Yes," Cassie replied. There, and in Illinois. If you decide to see someone, I hope you have a better experience."

Breanna was quiet. *Doesn't feel like I'm hearing lies here*, she thought.

"Was it your boyfriend? Uncle?"

"My therapist? No."

They both laughed.

Then after a moment, Cassie said, "Dad. It was my dad."

Breanna ran her teeth back and forth across her lower lip. This was somebody who knew pain. The education couldn't hide the change in Cassie's voice. Whatever this woman did during the day, the anguish was waiting for her after dark.

Breanna walked back over to pick up Jackie, who was whimpering now, then came back to the phone.

"How old were you, Cassie?"

"Sixteen."

"Do you hate him?" *I hate Ethan*, she thought. Usually her head hurt at the thought, but not tonight.

"Not at first," Cassie said. "I hated me." The voice changed, the melody gone. "So . . . disgusting. Dismembering."

"Cassie, why did you write me?"

"Because I did not want to see you irretrievably damaged as I have been."

Jackie started crying.

"I have to go, Cassie. But let's talk again."

"I'd like that, Breanna. When can I call?"

"Tomorrow night. A little earlier maybe?"

"You must be busy, and dead tired."

"Yeah. Right on both counts. And I need to go in to work tomorrow."

Silence, then Cassie said, "Work. Yes." The melody was back.

"Good night, Cassie."

"Good night."

Breanna ended the call, trying and failing to focus on getting Jackie ready for bed. She was captivated by the turn of things.

Twenty minutes later, Breanna turned out her light and lay on her side, facing Jackie's crib. How was Cassie going to help?

She was asleep before she could count the ways.

The next night and the next and the next after that, Breanna found herself a captive, listening to Cassie's background.

Cassie was from Marysville, Washington, a town, in Cassie's words, that had fought and lost the logging wars as the tree huggers ripped the hearts out of the cutters.

"My father," Cassie said, "Carl—"

She even gave his name, Breanna thought. I'd never do that.

"Was as rough as the wood that he cut. He stood for nothing but hard drinking and was tough on my mother.

No, Breanna. He beat her unmercifully."

No voice-melody now.

"'Ain't no good work no more. We need to get out uh t' county,'" Cassie would say, imitating her deep-throated dad who gave these pronouncements between belches at the cheap dinner table.

Breanna trembled just a little—she feared what was coming. Cassie had a voice that could scare.

But this voice also grew on her. Each anguishing sentence brought Breanna closer to her own pain, her own weakness, her own frustrations at what the universe had dropped on them both. When Cassie described how her family watched their world turned upside down, how the milling business death turned proud people into beggars, Breanna felt like she was there.

"I despised being poor, watching my mother break her back to make ends meet. I had to get out of Marysville, to"—and her voice would drop—"'get out uh t' county.' I just wanted to close my eyes and fly, Breanna, into the sky, the light."

Breanna felt like she and Cassie were together, both teenagers peering from a dark, damp corner of the small, cold living room as Cassie's mother anguished over which bill she would pay next.

When Cassie, her parents' trajectory already set for destruction, described a sixteen-year-old's plans for escape, Breanna remembered her many dream escape plans from Ethan. Sobbing into her pillow, she listened to Cassie.

"And a dad who'd always been pulling me, touching me, feeling on me," Cassie said. "I was fifteen when they told my parents they were losing their house, Breanna." The soft cadence was frightening and exciting. "I thought I was smart then, but the world outsmarted me, like it's getting ready to do to you.

"Fall afternoon, I remember my mom caught a ride with a neighbor to a grocery store way across the county. Her goal was to try to convert a twenty, a ten, and three ones into a week's work of groceries. It wasn't to desert me. She didn't know, like I didn't know . . .

"Anyway, I came home from school, hoping to go with her, but she was already gone. I remember the hairs on my neck standing on end, so strange . . . I must have known what I didn't want to know.

"He came out of the bathroom. No pants. Leering at me like I was some animal that he wanted to rut.

"'I . . . I need to go out again,' I told him. My voice was shaking. I turned to leave, but he was across the kitchen at once—so fast. He kicked me in the back, hurling me into the wall next to our dirty refrigerator.

"The blood didn't just flow, Breanna—it jetted from my forehead. I remember some of it landing in the pot of cold stew left on the kitchen counter. Made a heavy sound.

"He grabbed me by my hair, pulled me down backward. Ripped my skirt—it had been so clean. Yanked my panties aside and rolled over onto me.

"I pushed against his chest with one hand and pounded his face with the other.

"Suddenly, his movements in my groin stopped, and I thought I was saved.

"Then he punched me. With his left hand. Twice. I still feel it, Breanna. Can you believe it? I still feel it. Once on my jaw, the next on my eye. When I came to, he had his finger up in me, then his penis.

Breanna closed her eyes tight, twisting in the seat, her knees together. "Cassie, this is—"

"When he tried to kiss me, his mouth open, his snake tongue coming at me, I caught his lower lip between my teeth and bit hard into it. It was the only weapon I had, Breanna, and I used it.

"He tried to pull away. I held on. He tried to rear back and headbutt me, but I just clamped down and down and down on that loose skin.

"Finally, he pulled away, and the disgusting animal meat partly ripped off in my mouth.

"He howled so loud, Breanna. It was savage. Like a beast. I jumped up. I . . . I swallowed it. But I was free. I crawled away from his grasping, flailing hands and heard the outside door opening. I cried out, 'Mama,' and the door flung open.

"It was Luther Hookson, Breanna, my dad's friend. Dirty overalls over a dark shirt. Big man. Stupid man. But the same look in his eye."

"He said, 'What have we here?' I cried out, 'Mr. Hookson, help me leave, please.'

"He picked me up like I was a rag doll and took . . . took—" She stopped.

"Cassie," Breanna said, exhaling. She'd been holding her breath, she realized. "Listen, why don't—"

"He took me back inside, slobbering on my neck. Between him and my dad, they both raped me. Again. Again. Again. I remember Luther's breath, thick with alcohol and cigarette smoke. Somewhere in there, I lost consciousness.

"After that, I, uh . . ." She stopped again.

Breanna didn't want to talk to her anymore. She wanted to hold her, to protect her.

"Uh, I gathered some clothes and ran to a friend's house. Nobody was there, and it was getting dark. I walked around the house's corner, you know, out of the way? Sat on the ground. It was cold, so hard. Unforgiving. Dark came and, with it, rain. I thought the rain would clean me, but it couldn't clean the insides.

"I remember thinking about the night before, when everything was normal, the rain outside, us inside, my mom there cooking, and Dad passed out, and I was doing some homework. I remember thinking, 'I felt human last night.' And then I thought I'd never feel human again.

"I was right, Breanna. I never have."

Cassie exhaled, then said, "I hitchhiked my way to Spokane. Never been back."

Breanna said nothing, her brain spent, her mind's eye exhausted. This woman—

"I brought the worst of it with me, Breanna. And it comes to visit, every night. Has it gotten this bad for you yet?"

"No, Cassie." Dear God, she thought, her forehead leaning into her other hand.

"From what I hear, you left your husband and took your babies."

"Yes."

"Then I will keep— Oh." She paused. "I've been talking too long."

Breanna, heart thumping, could not let this new, young relationship die. "Maybe we could meet? Would that be possible?"

"I'd like that, Breanna. Call me on the cell I left with you. One final thing?"

"Yes, Cassie?"

"What I have said these past minutes I have told no one. Not counselors, not friends, not family. Nobody. I want you to know the worst about me."

"I . . . I know."

"I am naked to you now, Breanna, defenseless, but know this: whatever small honor I have left, I use it to fight for you and your babies. Whatever the future holds, I stand with you, unworthy as I am, if you will have me. We must not let this happen to you."

Breanna, scared and strong for Cassie, clenched her fist. "Good night, Cassie. See you tomorrow."

"I will be where you tell me to be."

# DESTROYER OF MEN

The next night, Breanna pulled into a Perkins on Route 26 near Veterans Memorial Parkway, the leaden sky beating the small red sun into its western retreat.

She asked for a booth in the back corner and, after ordering some water, reflected back on today's conversation with her landlady about babysitters. The landlady not only knew about them but enjoyed being one, agreeing to look after Jackie for the evening. Enjoying the moment, Breanna leaned back in the booth.

This shouldn't take too long, Breanna thought, maybe about an hour.

The conversations this week with Cassie had been both draining and transforming. This woman had endured hardship, yet she had built a life, had made something of herself.

Still, such pain, the accountant thought, shuddering.

Breanna forced herself to look around, noticing that the restaurant was emptying, many patrons having finished an early dinner and now heading home after the rush. She turned to look for the restroom. Even sipping this water was—

"Breanna?"

Breanna turned back to look up into the eyes of a svelte olive-skinned woman with long dark-brown hair that swept into and around Cassie's face, almost hiding it, looking down on her. Breanna thought she was looking up into a sweet-smelling cave.

"Cassie? Please sit down."

Cassie walked to the other side of the table. "You look good pregnant, Breanna."

The mother jumped. "Yes. How did you know?"

"I'd seen some photographs of you," Cassie said, resting back against the booth. "You were so attractive, eyes bursting with the light of the intelligent. But not as beautiful as you look now. Nature imbues pregnant women with a special beauty that the world tries and fails to steal."

Breanna sucked her lip. "Did somebody write that?"

Cassie closed her eyes. "I did. Twenty years ago. An eternity."

Cassie looked like a woman who'd borne crushing pain and emerged with terrible wisdom, Breanna thought. To her, it appeared that Cassie had to make a conscious effort to lift her own head or to even reopen her eyes after blinking. Breanna exhaled, having no problem connecting the terrible history she heard over the phone the last few days to this mysterious, somber woman.

"Sorry, I am three minutes late," Cassie said. "I'm no good at directions, and my eyes are getting worse. GPS makes it better, though."

"I was really moved by our talk this week." Breanna exhaled. "I think I get you." After a moment, she added, "And you get me."

Cassie looked up at her. "Before I called you, I debated with myself about whether I should say anything at all about my—"

"What would you like?"

Out of nowhere, the waitress appeared, overweight, greying but wearing a warm smile.

Cassie looked up. "Just some hot tea for now, please. Thank you. Breanna?"

The mother just shook her head, glancing at her own water.

After the waitress disappeared, Breanna leaned over the table. "But you did tell me so much." After a moment, she asked. "Why? You didn't know me."

"Because I wanted you to know that I was genuine. But," Cassie said, leaning forward across the short table to Breanna, "it was time. Time to empty myself, pour this poison out of me. I'm sorry if I overwhelmed you, but it rushed out like dirty filth." Closing her eyes, Cassie sighed.

"How do you feel now?" Breanna asked, reaching across the table.

A pause, then Cassie replied, "Different." Cassie opened her eyes now. "If it's OK," she said, reaching into the pocket of her jacket, "I wanted to take some time tonight to tell you what I could do for you. But first . . ." She handed a card over the table.

Breanna studied it.

Cassie Rhodes
Attorney at Law

Breanna shook her head, then looked up at her "You're an attorney?" After the mess of her early life, she thought, Cassie had become an attorney?

"Yes, I am. And you will need one." Cassie shrugged her leather coat off her shoulders. "Your husband is starting to come after you. He has an attorney—aggressive, but weak-kneed."

Breanna put both hands down hard in her own lap. "What's he going to say about me?"

"Thank you for the tea."

The waitress left as suddenly as she appeared, and Cassie turned to Breanna. "He says you are not a proper mother." After a moment, she said, "Plus abandonment."

"What?" Breanna said, raising her right hand out of her lap and above the table. "I took Jackie with me. How can—"

"I know," Cassie said, leaning over the table. "But he will say it anyway. He wants to make things as difficult for you as possible. Plus, he wants your daughter back."

"Why?" Breanna said, right hand now clutching her chest. "He can't raise her. He did next to nothing for her."

Breanna watched Cassie wait until a customer passed their table, then whispered, "He thinks that he and his girlfriend can."

Breanna though somebody had grabbed her hair and yanked her backward, away from Cassie, away the table, away from the restaurant. Her breath came in ragged gasps. She covered her stomach with her left hand.

"This is new to you. Breanna, I am so sorry, but I wanted to be the one to tell you." She reached out and covered Breanna's right hand with her left. "This is the kind of thing that these animals do."

Breanna pushed back from the table. "I need a moment."

"Of course."

She was going to ask Cassie for a cigarette but thought of the baby. Instead, she got up and walked to the restroom.

Her head was pounding like someone was in it, slamming a hammer to get out. In the restroom, two waitresses were talking at the sink. Breanna rushed to the nearest stall, then sat for a couple of minutes.

Waiting for the waitresses to leave, which they did.

Waiting for the tears to come, which they did not.

What did come was anger.

She trusted him.

And he had a girlfriend on the side.

For how long?

Did she hook him on coke?

Probably both of them were using.

And all the time, I was taking care of him in that apartment, looking out for him, bringing money home for him.

How he must have laughed at me while he was fucking her, telling his bimbo about me and his plan to go to my parents to get money.

Both of them laughing.

Her pulse raced, and her breath came in torn gulps of air as she pounded the stall's thin wall three times, then turned and threw up on the floor, not able to stand up and turn around to use the bowl.

Fuck Ethan.

Why did God make such vile creatures?

To destroy them.

Fuck them all.

When she came out, she saw that Cassie was watching the restroom from where she sat. *She's concerned for me,* Breanna thought, *a hell of a lot more than anybody else.*

Breanna, sitting down, closed her eyes, saying, "I'm glad you told me."

Cassie reached her hand over, and Breanna grasped it, holding on for a few seconds.

Breanna removed her hand and sat up straight. "I'm going to need help, Cassie."

"Tell me what you want me to do."

Breanna answered at once. "To help me raise my children on my own."

Cassie moved her left hand to her chin. "Then I will help you. What about Ethan?"

"The hell with him. I'm divorcing the bastard." She held Cassie's gaze. "But, Cassie," she said, hands out to the attorney, "I have no money for—"

"Breanna, you don't need it. I am here for you now. I work with the best, most expensive divorce attorneys, plus super-sleuth private eyes, expert forensic accountants. Plus, we know the judges."

Breanna watched as Cassie leaned over toward her, pointing an exquisite, long index finger her way. "When we're done, Breanna, Ethan will be a ghost. And," she said, letting that index finger touch the back of

Breanna's left hand, "you will finally have the life that you want. Plus, no cost to you."

"What?" Breanna leaned back.

Breanna watched her Cassie's shoulders tighten as the attorney stirred her tea silently, slowly. Then she said, "Men are God's punishment upon the earth, Breanna. They are driven by primitive hormones and a sense of superiority. They torment animals, us, each other, and finally the planet. It's a pleasure to destroy them, if only one at a time."

Breanna stared at her as Cassie put the spoon down. "There is more. We will pay your day-care bills, putting Jackie and . . . what's the name of your unborn child?"

"Karen."

"And Karen in the best day care in Lafayette when they are ready. They will be dropped off and picked up each day. Any questions at all, you call me. My card, please?"

When Breanna handed it over, she watched Cassie flip it, draw a Mont Blanc from her coat, write, then hand the card back. "That's my cell."

This is a dream, the mother thought, turning the card over.

"Can I take your orders?" the waitress asked, smiling at them both.

Breanna saw Cassie study the waitress carefully as if she knew her, then say, "Breanna? You first."

"Vegetable plate for me, please."

"I'll have the same, plus another cup of tea, please."

Breanna, head no longer hurting but heart bursting, sighed.

"Do you like where you are staying, Breanna?"

"Yes, we love it," she said, cocking her head. "Why do you ask?"

"I will make a phone call, and your rent will be paid six months in advance. Plus, utility bills come to my office direct."

The accountant looked down, shaking her head.

"Breanna, I am serious. Look at me."

Breanna looked into round, soft, unblinking eyes.

"I want you to be a success without taking another fifteen years to get there like I had to. To that end, I want the company."

Breanna tilted her head. "CiliCold? Why?"

"I can develop it, Breanna. We know that it's struggling now. But CiliCold has great ideas. I want to save it. And you will play a role in that. With our help, in a few years, you will be independently wealthy."

"As an accountant, Cassie?" She smirked.

Cassie nodded, not breaking eye contact.

"Yes, secretaries made $80,000 a year at Microsoft, and that was twenty years ago. When we are done, Breanna, your secretary will make more than that."

"And the people I work with?"

"Excuse me. Here are your meals."

Cassie sat back, letting the waitress place the steamy platter with carrots, broccoli, squash, and bread.

"They become rich." She leaned closer over the hot plate. It looked to Breanna that she was emerging from a fog. "Including Jon. Perhaps Jon most of all."

The mother watched Cassie lean back, continuing, "He's interesting, isn't he?"

"Cassie," Breanna said, shaking her head, "he's a counter example to your view of mankind."

The lawyer closed her eyes. "No. He's just not there yet. You watch. The more rested and confident he becomes, the more of his disgusting nature will be revealed."

She stopped, then said, "Don't be fooled, Breanna. It's his destiny. But," Cassie said, sighing, "don't worry. He will do well financially also."

Breanna sat quietly for a second, then asked, "What happened to you after you left?"

Cassie's fork stopped in midair. "Left where?"

"Maryville."

"I will tell you—right here—if you really want to know."

"Yes, Cassie," Breanna said, reaching her hand out. "I would."

She saw that Cassie returned her gaze. Then, putting the fork down, Cassie rose, came over, and sat next to her. At the touch of Cassie's thigh against her own, Breanna's breath caught, and her heart started racing.

Cassie in a low voice, said, "Spokane wasn't working for a sixteen-year-old unskilled girl like me, so I hitched myself to Skagit, just south of the Canadian border. Thank God I wasn't pregnant. I worked for a cleaning service for hotels and scratched out a living for a while, if you can call it that. Focused on getting my GED."

Breanna felt Cassie's hand on her left arm and inhaled.

The attorney stopped talking, staring straight ahead, then said, "There was a new smell that followed me now."

"Smell? What was it?"

"Defeat. What I then called death."

Cassie stared across the table and down the long restaurant aisle for a moment then sighed and continued.

"I received my GED in 2000 and enrolled in Skagit Valley College. I wasn't 'out uh t' county' yet—" Cassie's voice affected that same tone as it had on the phone when she uttered that phrase.

Her father is with her, even here, Breanna thought, relaxing her arm under Cassie's touch.

"But closing in fast on an escape route," Cassie continued.

Breanna looked over and saw Cassie watching her. The mother realized that she enjoyed looking at this aging face, full of wisdom and wonder.

And she hoped Cassie's hand would stay on her arm.

"Money was never easy, Breanna, and I took terrible jobs to make the hard ends meet—washing dishes in lukewarm dirty water, serving as secretary for lecherous bosses whose salacious glances transmitted the incessant message that only my body counted."

Breanna noted that Cassie started drumming the fingers of her left hand on the table. Suddenly, she removed her arm and turned to Breanna.

"I decided to spoil my looks. I became an expert at ruining my hair with harsh, abrasive, and terrible hair color, a master at mangling my makeup, a pro at putting grotesque rings through my lips, nose, and finally, both eyelids." She inhaled deeply.

Breanna only nodded.

"The combination of distorted appearance and my frozen dumber-than-dumb stares finally beat the vermin back. But, Breanna, I paid a price. I lost myself in all that. I didn't know who I was."

Breanna wondered if Cassie knew even now, then wondered if she could help her.

"Anyway, after two years, the University of Washington accepted me as a junior. That was— Oh. What time do you have to leave?"

Breanna checked her phone. "Right now." What this woman had been through, Breanna thought. And what she's made of herself. She put the card in her purse.

Cassie touched her hand. "Think about all that I offer you, Breanna, and why I do it. You will have lots of questions. I want to answer all of them."

Breanna stood, but noted that Cassie stayed seated. "Aren't you coming too?"

Cassie looked up, and to Breanna, she seemed to blink in slow motion, with lids that must have felt so heavy. "You go, Breanna. I've got no adorable waiting for me at home like you do. I will take care of the bill and follow in a few minutes."

"Will you call tomorrow?"

"Yes," Cassie said, touching Breanna's hand. "Let's talk some more."

# NOTHING PERSONAL

With the first swallow this Tuesday morning, Jon just knew there was trouble.

Sleep had been good though. He'd been dreaming.

A deep one and a strange one.

Gloves with no fingers, floating around, detached from the empty finger pieces that were themselves adrift.

Head buried under the comforter, deep in the warm bed with the wooden frame that Alora had loved so much, he closed his eyes and swallowed again. The raw hollow pain started just below his jawline and followed the saliva all the way down his throat.

He'd felt fine the night before, although another long night of work kept him up late. He swallowed again, having to bear down to get the saliva down his raw throat.

No such luck.

Common cold had come a-callin'.

Although he wasn't a physician, he had learned all that he could find about these viral infections: what caused them, how long they lasted, how many people were affected, how much work time was lost in the wake of its suffering, the fortunes the country expended in vain to reduce its effects.

Yet he took particular offense when his turn had come round at last, as though knowledge of the virus's wiles and ways conferred a special personal protection, an intellectual immunity.

But the virus didn't care about what he knew.

Nothing personal.

Hopefully, it wouldn't take too long for his antibodies to kick in.

Once the Ts and Bs knew they had the right formula, they poured it on.

First the viruses were everywhere. But soon, the antibodies were, and ignoring Jon's ailing tissues, they converged on the viruses, like chemical iron bars drawn to a chemical magnet.

There was no escape for the viruses at this point. They were sensed, trapped, and targeted for termination.

Nothing personal.

The antibodies were like anti-species missiles that once released, locked on, bore down, and tore through the viral coats. Sometimes the antibodies lurked outside an infected cell, waiting to pounce on the newly born viral particles as they were emerging, tearing them to pieces, spilling the useless and deformed viral contents on top of the dying epithelial cells.

Then his immune system really got nasty.

It released substances that allowed the immune cells to communicate with each other, a chemical web link that the virus could not hack. The attack became more coordinated. Cytokines and interleukins facilitated communication between the different immune cells, helping them to work together—a cellular correlation of forces.

Leukotrienes amplified the antibodies' homing ability. A variety of interferons were generated, throwing the viruses off their usually reliable chemical scent for uninfected cells. These disoriented viral particles waited around, oscillating in confusion until specially made compounds called complement, like molecular wrecking balls, slammed into them, collapsing the virus particle in on itself.

What started as a serious infection threat ended as a microscopic turkey shoot.

But hey, nothing personal.

Any army battered such as this would have surrendered. Of course, the virus particles had no such understanding, but Jon knew it didn't matter.

The immune system would take no quarter.

It wouldn't stop until the last viral particle was liquidated, the antibodies circulating for days, even weeks, to make sure not a single particle lingered. It was brutal, efficient, and complete.

It just wasn't per—

He sneezed three times—harsh, nasty ones.

S4.

Getting up, he walked to the dresser and connected the call.

"Yes?"

"Hi, it's Robbie."

He pulled away from the phone for a rat-a-tat-tat cough into the crook of his arm, then cleared his throat. "Hi, Robbie. How are you?"

"Toasty here in my office, thanks to you."

"Thanks to us all, including you." He rubbed his eyes.

"You sound like you have a cold."

He'd just cleared his throat. How could she know? What did he have, a camera in his bedroom, for heaven's sake? "A little one. What's up?"

"Just wondering where the agenda was."

"Oh."

Tuesday.

Staff meeting.

In a flash, he didn't feel his symptoms.

"I'll have it emailed to you in five minutes. I should be there in an hour."

"Great. See you then."

His body would have to do with gargle, fluids, and some Tylenol. The idea of rest, so tempting a moment before, was banished to the back burner. He turned to head to the shower, scratching his head.

At the shower, he leaned over to turn the water on, letting it run to get hot. After thirty seconds of its thick white steam, he turned to step in, adjusting the temperature down a tad.

Nothing better than a hot shower during a col—

He stopped, one foot in the shower, the other on the outside, waiting to join it. He didn't move a muscle, and for a moment the cold was gone, all symptoms overrun by a new powerful, almost violent surge of emotion.

He knew what the dream meant.

How about that, he thought.

It was personal, after all.

# FULL BITCH MODE

"Rita, I was just heading to the car," Breanna said, walking to the Toyota after kissing Jackie goodbye at the babysitter's.

"No worries. Call me when you're in the car. How're things?"

"Diarrhea."

"Who?"

"Your favorite niece. And your favorite sister. But better now."

Rita's snarky laugh filled her ear. "Call me."

A few moments later, Breanna got into the car and cranked the engine. It roared to life. She backed out of her spot through the slush that was starting to freeze again and started out to Route 25 and CiliCold.

The car ground to a halt at a traffic light, and Breanna waited, tapping her thumbs on the steering wheel. She'd looked Cassie up. Impressive CV at a distinguished law group. Lots of work in pharmaceu—

Phone.

She picked it up.

"Hey."

"Hey back. What did you learn, Rita?"

"You latched on to a quite an attorney. Or should I say she latched on to you."

"I was also impressed with her CV. Plus, she had quite a reach with other specialists." Breanna paused, then added, "I'm inclined to believe her."

"So, Breanna, what's the story here? Manna doesn't fall from heaven anymore. What does she want from you?"

"To buy my company. I mean the company where I work."

"And she really needs your help for that?"

"She said that she needs information."

"Accounting information? I guess that makes some sense."

"No, information on how the work is going."

"Technical things? Like science?"

"Yep."

Rita was quiet. Then "So this means clandestine drops, and secret meetings with the attorney? Deep Throat stuff?"

"No, actually. We do it by e— One second. It's starting to sleet." The mother inched the car across two lines of traffic, then pulled into a gas station. The sleet slammed into the car like needles, trying to get at her.

"We'll do this by email."

"Email? C'mon, Breanna. Even Mom knows not to trust it. Talk about hackable."

Breanna sighed. Rita could be so frickin' patronizing. But the accountant knew that she was just trying to look after her little sis. Breanna pushed away her irritation. "Not the way you think. She and I will both have the same email account. Same username and password."

"Uh, OK."

"I compose a note to her but don't send it."

"Then—"

"I save it instead to the drafts folder. Then when she logs on, she goes not to the inbox but to drafts. Since we are sharing the account, my draft is in her draft folder. Same thing when she sends me a message. We communicate but no emails are sent."

"Hmmm. I tried something like that. Write a draft from my home notebook, then try to find it on my phone. Could never make it work."

"You have to go into the settings to share the draft folder." Breanna raised her voice against the sleet now coming down hard on the car.

"Well, OK. So assuming that you can get this—what? Data? You know my three questions. First, is it legal for you to do this?"

"It's not data, just the ideas that are being discussed, and people there talk freely. Anyway, I spoke to Cassie about the legality of this. If CiliCold were a public company, then absolutely not. It's illegal. But it's privately owned, so no legal problems."

"OK. Question 2, is it ethical?"

Breanna sighed. Rita could be oppressive with these interrogations.

"Yes. Private companies try to learn what another is doing all the time. Sometimes it comes out in conferences and papers, sometimes in site visits. If our company is going nowhere, Cassie's team won't buy, and no real harm done. If the scientists are on to something, then all CiliCold employees stand to become rich. Nobody at the company will sue over that."

"And number 3, morals?"

"Yeah, sis. My personal morality. I think I'm OK with this."

Silence, then Rita said, "If someone had asked you three months ago about doing this, what would you have said?"

Irritation surged through Breanna. "What does that matter, Rita? Three months ago, I wasn't pregnant and didn't know that my husband was banging some stripper named Holly Hooters."

Breanna took a breath. "Listen, I'm in a tough fix. I can't afford a good attorney. Without Cassie's help, I'll have worked myself to the bone, with all my money going to Jackie, Karen, bills, and legal fees. I may survive, but I'm guessing two years down the road, I'd be a wreck."

Silence on the other end.

"Rita, how many times have you told me that one of my weaknesses is failing to be a bitch when I need to be? Well, you know what? I'm in full bitch mode now."

"OK, OK. I give. Bottom line, then, Breanna. You going to do this?"

"Bottom line, do you think that I should?"

"I think you have to look out for yourself. God knows nobody else will."

"You sound like Cassie. I'm all in with this. Gotta go, Rita."

Breanna hung up, and as the sleet turned to rain, she let the car run, but stayed at the gas station. She decided that she could be late this morning.

# SOMETIMES A GOOD LAUGH IS WORTH THE TROUBLE

"Milk."

Rayiko watched her husband, Richard, peer from around his newspaper, wearing his pretend scowl toward his son.

"What's the magic word?" Richard said, staring across the breakfast table of Cheerios, orange juice, forks and spoons. "When you ask for something, you need to say the magic word, Gary. Now, after me, OK? Can I have the milk . . ."

"Now," Gary shouted, banging the table and laughing.

"That's my boy," Richard said, laughing and slapping the table in unison. She watched the smile vanish from his face when he saw that she had entered the room.

"We're just foolin's all," he said.

"Long as you know when to stop." She tried not to smile but couldn't hide it. At four years old, Gary adored his dad, and it was good to see Richard embrace his role. Didn't always do things by the rule book, but the two of them were tight, and she was just fine with that.

"Is there room at this messy table for me?"

Rayiko stared at Richard and Gary as they looked at each other. Then, both laughing, they shoved the cereal boxes, dirty spoons, used napkins, paper cups, one with chocolate milk, another with orange juice, to the floor.

"Lots of room now, Mom," Gary said, smiling behind an arm that failed to cover his face.

Father and son broke up in heaves of laughter as Rayiko stared open-mouthed at the mess.

"Both of you are going to be late cleaning up that mess this morning." Her Android buzzed and she glanced at it.

"Yeah, you're right, hon, but sometimes a good laugh is worth the trouble," Richard said.

"I'll be laughing as you clean up your mess. Think I'll skip breakfast this morn—" She scanned her email. She read mouth open, then sat down at the breakfast table crushing a box of Cheerios that was lying on the seat, and read some more.

Richard and Gary looked at her then at each other. Richard then stood up, walked around Rayiko to read over her shoulder. After a few seconds, her husband walked to the sink to gather some cleanup cloths. His son followed, not making a sound.

"Rayiko," Jon said, selecting the incoming phone call in the Jeep. "I'm heading for work. Listen. I was thinking last night and this morning. I know how–"

"I know that you were, Jon."

He pulled over to listen to her, letting her voice enter him. Comforting. Stabilizing.

"But I am afraid that I'm going to miss your thoughts. I have a family emergency I need to deal with."

"Oh no. Richard? Gary? What can I do?"

"Nothing for you to do. I have to manage it, but it's not them. It's my brother. I'm packing now."

Yes, he remembered. Her brother, the smartest one in the room—with a coke habit.

He listened. She sounded stressed and alone. She was pressed, pushed, and pulled by events that were out of her control. He tried to figure out how to be there, to race there.

"When will you be back? Our experiments will really ramp up—"

"A month."

Jon froze, thought-shocked into a new oblivion. He mouthed the word—a month, a month, a month. Instantly, his left ring and little finger went numb. New thoughts wandered in, wondered and then demanded to know why she had to be gone so long. Deaths didn't take that long to arrange. What could—

"Stop," he said to no one.

This was Rayiko. She wouldn't have called if she hadn't thought it through. She kept control. But he knew that keeping control meant living on the edge, always being just a thought away from being pushed over the brink, into the darkness.

But this was who she was.

He took a breath, then spoke.

"I understand, Rayiko. Not everything, but enough. Take the time you need. We'll work out any leave of absence issues. Are you coming by this morning?"

"Richard is taking me to the airport now."

"All right, then. Take care. Don't think about this place. We'll be fine."

He knew what he had said was a lie. But he knew she knew it was.

# THE STEM OF THE Y

"I drive myself and drive you to the brink," Jon began, at the staff meeting later that morning.

Breanna saw him lean forward, nose running, stiff index finger jammed hard into the tabletop. She knew that he had to be bone tired after the last few days. Plus, there was now redness around his eyes, and he had this new cough.

Sitting away from everyone, down at the end of the table by himself, he spoke in low hoarse tones, but emphatically, earnestly. His energy flowed from him in waves like heat from a hot radiator She noticed everyone leaning forward to hear a voice barely audible.

"I used to believe, in fact was raised to believe, that I could do anything," he was saying as Breanna saw him look at each of them. "I know better now," he continued. "Many jobs I can't do. That's why I'm so pleased that I have each of you as my colleagues, my companions, and my friends."

Breanna saw both Luiz and Dale smile.

"Thanks for that, Jon," Wild Bill said in a quiet voice.

"Where's Rayiko?" Dale asked.

"She's out," Jon replied, then coughed.

"Everything OK with her? And with you?" Luiz asked.

"I just have a cold. That's why I'm sitting down here away from you guys."

"We thought it was us," Bill said, smiling.

"Well, my cold, and Dale's aftershave."

Everybody laughed.

"Rayiko has to deal with a family issue," Jon said. To Breanna, his voice had changed. Flat now. No anger. No anxiety. No humor. Nothing to give away the feelings she knew that he must be having about Rayiko's absence.

"Her son?" Dale asked. Breanna couldn't remember Dale ever speaking in such a soft voice.

"I assured her that we would all be fine without her, but," he said with a smile, "she knew better than to believe that. She will be gone for a while though. A month. Back in early March."

Everyone was quiet. Then, from Luiz, "She's important around there. We're going to miss her."

"And," Jon continued, moving his hands from the tabletop to his lap, "you all have been patient with me as I let my demons push me, and through me, push you and this company. I want the cure."

"So do we," Dale said.

Breanna was pleased. She didn't even think Dale had an "inside" voice. But he did, and the accountant felt this group of outspoken people come together now, letting themselves be bound by Jon's strong emotional ribbon.

"You're right," Jon said, smiling across the table at Dale. "Both you and Luiz have been working with me on this idea of mine. Meanwhile, Wild Bill has been covering our regulatory backsides."

"Oh," Wild Bill said, rocking backward in his backwards chair while pushing his glasses up onto his nose. "Don't worry about those folks. They don't believe you can do what you're working on, either."

Everybody laughed. Breanna felt the tension break.

"Yeah," Jon said, "I guess we haven't given them reason to worry about us. While we have sacrificed the occasional rodent, we've been careful with our monkeys."

"Hope we keep it that way," Luiz said.

"The only thing that I'm going to kill is my own soggy ideas," Jon added. Breanna watched him draw a deep breath. "I thought the way to beat the virus—"

"Viruses," Dale interrupted. "There are over a hundred different virus types that cause the common cold, and they are changing all the time."

"That's why you can't beat them," Wild Bill added. Breanna watched him move his index finger back and forth across the tabletop slowly like he was rubbing a stain out of it. "They change so fast the immune system can't keep up."

"Yep," Jon said. "And I tried to help expand the memory of the immune system's memory cells." He paused. "And failed. A memory cell, Breanna," he said to her, his soft voice raising the fine hair on her neck, "retains a memory of the virus against which it has made antibodies.

What I tried to do, and failed, was to get them to create antibodies for viruses they had not been exposed to."

She cocked her head. "From what we discussed, I'm not sure how you even do that."

"Actually," Dale said, "neither are we."

"We tried a few things. Injecting them with viral fragments. It's a nice bit of intracellular manipulation, but the B cells didn't do anything." He paused for a minute. "Except die."

"But even if that had worked," Dale added. "I mean, how useful is that? Every few weeks, you'd have to inject pieces of the virus of the month into the B cells. Doing that with people on a population-wide basis is a nonstarter. Probably, folks would rather go ahead and have the damn cold than go through that. Oh, sorry."

"You're such a potty mouth," Robbie said, wagging her finger at Dale. Breanna joined in the laughter.

"I also asked Dale and Luiz to try DNA manipulation. If we could change the instructions that the B cells follow to guide their antibody production, we could get them to produce any antibody we wanted."

"And we were able to do that to some degree," Luiz said.

Wild Bill's chair rocked forward, all four feet hitting the floor. "We tried that?"

"Yep. But only in rodents. Things started off ugly. Know what amyloid is?"

No one answered.

"It's when these B cells stop making helpful proteins and start producing trash protein," Jon said. "No one knows why. But they laid the stuff down everywhere: lungs, heart, stomach, and esophagus. It gets in the way of your organs doing their job." He paused for a second. "Gets in the way of life, I guess. My dad died of it."

Everyone was quiet for a moment. "We moved past that phase pretty quickly," Jon continued. "Soon, we got the B cells to produce new antibodies. But we didn't know how to configure them."

"I don't know what you mean," Breanna said. She felt a little unanchored. These attempts by sincere scientists all seemed so, so desperate.

The phone rang, and Robbie got up to answer it.

"I didn't know we had phones here," Wild Bill said. "Haven't we given up on land lines?"

Robbie walked back in and took her seat. "I took a message." She smiled at Bill. "Cell service is still pretty twitchy around here on some days. Need a land line for backup."

"You would use semaphore flags if you could get away with it."

"Maybe you'll buy me some, Dale," Robbie said, aiming her sweetest smile at him.

Breanna saw Dale blush and hid her enjoyment of the moment.

"Well," Jon continued, looking straight down the table, "we could get the B cells to construct these antibodies, but we didn't know what these particular antibodies would be good for."

"To be useful, they'd need to respond to something—like a virus," Dale said.

"Yes," Jon said. "But we didn't have a virus in mind. It was like writing out map directions without having a destination."

"We were pretty lucky," Wild Bill said, licking his lip. "It could have been an antibody against the rodent itself. A whole new autoimmune disease—that would have been real trouble."

Jon nodded. "A few weeks ago, I thought we had it. And we moved to monkeys. After the treatment, the monkeys' immune systems were fired up, churning out antibodies, which was good."

"Only problem was that the antibodies never destroyed any viruses. We were making antibodies to nothing," Dale added.

"And that, ladies and gentlemen is the nickel tour of CiliCold," Luiz said. He scratched behind his right ear.

"Till now. I see where we've gone wrong."

Breanna saw Dale roll his eyes. Anger flashing, she pursed her lips. This super-cynic enjoyed trashing everyone's ideas. She looked at Jon, who was running his left hand through his hair, deep in thought. If he saw Dale's reaction, he was doing a great job of ignoring it.

"What we're missing," Jon said, "is that the B cell can't do it all. It is a two-phase pro— No." He corrected himself. "It's a relay race. The B cell starts, but it's got to hand off the baton."

"What?" Breanna said.

Luiz jumped, hitting his coffee cup. A lump of brown liquid leaped into the air and splatted on the worn table. "Jon, I don't—"

"Just a sec, Luiz," Jon said, holding his hand up. "Let me lay my idea out totally." He turned his attention to the group. "The B cell can't make what it hasn't been exposed to, and we can't get it to make anything worth making, because while we can get it to make an antibody, the antibody isn't directed at anything worth killing."

"Yep," Dale said.

"But isn't what we're saying that nobody, not us, not the B cell, not the immune system, can make antibodies until they know what they are making them for?"

"They can't make a killer unless they know what it's going to kill," Wild Bill said, chewing his gum.

"Second amendment folks will add you to their list of targets if you keep that kind of talk up, Bill," Dale intoned.

"Well," Jon said, "maybe we should let the B cell start—but only start—the process."

"What?"

"If the B cell starts it, then, I mean, what's going to finish?" Luiz asked, mopping the coffee up with a handkerchief.

"The ECF."

Breanna couldn't keep up, and the frustration was gnawing at her. "What's the E—"

"How is the extracellular fluid going to get this to work?" WB asked. Breanna saw that the regulator was watching Jon carefully.

"OK, OK," Jon said, standing up. He sneezed again. "We'll have to work out the details, but here's the general idea." He walked over to the old blackboard, full of math and chemistry scribbles.

"Hey, don't erase that," Luiz said. "I was looking for it."

Jon looked confused for a second.

"Hold on," Breanna said, taking two pictures with her phone.

"Got it," she said. "Can he erase now?"

"You bet," Luiz said. "Let me get those later."

"No prob. I'll have them in the cloud before we're done here."

Breanna saw all eyes were on Jon, who had just finished erasing the board. Then across the top, he wrote "Antibody Structure." Below it, he drew a huge "Y." Then he doubled the stem of the Y and both of the two top lines so that each of the three original segments of the Y had a line parallel to it.

"This is what I have in mind."

He drew a straight horizontal line through the "Y" where the three original lines joined. Below the line, he wrote "B cell." Above the line, he wrote "ECF."

"What the—"

"Partial antibody construction?" Luiz said.

"Right, and the top part is made—"

"By the ECF."

"After the B cell makes the bottom," Luiz said.

"Hot damn."

"Meeting adjourned," Dale said, getting up so fast he knocked his chair over. "We got us some work to do."

"Ahead of you," Luiz responded.

"What are you sitting there for, Robbie?" Dale said, pointing at the exec sec. "We got some supplies to order."

"Right behind you."

"Wait, wait," Breanna said. She looked over to Robbie, who shrugged and said, "I just work here," as she followed WB out the door.

The stampede ended, and Breanna saw that only she and Jon were left in the room.

# FINGERLESS GLOVES

Breanna lifted her arms, then shaking her head, dropped them to her side. "What just happened here?"

"Maybe nothing, I don't know," Jon said, leaning against the table, which scooted back an inch. He rubbed his eyes. "Anyway, can you stand another five-minute immunology session?"

She knew how busy he must be, but really wanted to know. "Whatever it takes to understand what occurred here."

He erased the board and redrew the "Y."

"This is what the antibody looks like when it's fully constructed by the B cell. Now of course, this is only a two-dimensional representation, but the idea is that once released, this Y structure gets pulled in the exact shape it needs to latch onto a virus. Several hundred of these Ys latch on, and the virus is toast." He looked at her. "You with me?"

"With you," she said, drawing a step closer.

"So the three-dimensional shape is everything. It must be a perfect match. That's why the B cell can't make an antibody until it's exposed to the virus. It has to know what shape it needs."

"It has to see the lock before it can make the key," she said.

Their eyes met. "Yes, yes, that's a great metaphor."

"Well, if that's the case, why did Luiz and Dale just tear out of here?"

"Because they saw what I saw."

She shook her head. "Which was?"

"What if we rely on the B cell for only half of the key?" He sat down, and to Breanna, although she knew he was tired, he looked younger. "Many of the cold-causing viruses are related—very similar structures. That means the antibodies that react to them are similar. Now, what if we get the B cell to make just part of the antibody, say the stem of the Y. This partial antibody gets released.

"Once released," he continued, "means it gets into the extracellular fluid among other cells, proteins, hormones, transport proteins, amino acids. The building blocks for larger molecules. Then when the partial antibody comes close to the virus, the antibody construction is completed. The missing amino acids are added on, completing the Y, and the resulting antibody is tailor made to the virus that it's in proximity to."

She rubbed her forehead. "So the B cell doesn't have to make the entire antibody? Not sure I get that."

Jon held his right hand up, then covered the fingers of his right hand with his left one. "The part of the antibody that's constructed within the B cell is like a glove with no fingers." He removed his left hand. "The fingers get stitched on later, when the right size for them is known."

"How does that happen?"

"Well," he said, standing again, staring at the board. "Antibodies are proteins. That means they are sequences of small organic acids called amino acids. Now, we used to think that these proteins were constructed from the amino acid building blocks inside the cell. But we now know that some of that construction takes place in the ECF as well. That's what this idea relies on."

"Pretty clever."

"Maybe it's just fanciful," Jon said, blowing his nose. "Sorry. It's asking a lot of the extracellular fluid environment. The ECF construction must match the pattern of the virus. That means it can't add just any old amino acids; it must have the right ones and add them in the correct sequence—directed synthesis.

"But"—he scratched his head, and their eyes met again—"it should work. I mean, it's all chemistry. Things like London forces, van der Waals forces work for us to essentially train the ECF ribosome for what amino acid sequence is needed for the 'Fab' segment." He shook his head. "I mean the other missing ingredient of the Y."

"Well," she said, walking to the board, "why won't they make antibodies to match say, another white cell or a muscle cell if that happens to be close as well?"

"Because the base of the antibody, the part made inside the B cell is primarily antiviral. That's what I'm counting on anyway. Otherwise, I just don't know." He sat down and closed his eyes. "I'm sorry. I'm really beat."

She stood over him for a second, resisting with all her might the need to hold his head in her arms close to him, to help him finally to rest.

"Plus," he said, looking up at her. "It's my last idea."

Date: February 8, 2016
Subject:

Cassie,

This is my first note to you, Cassie. I hope that it helps.

Lots of excitement today. We learned that we lost our project administrator for a month because of personal circumstances. We will all miss her. Plus, Jon came up with a new idea. I don't understand it all, but it involves allowing something called the extracellular fluid to finish the antibody construction the B cell starts. I will take good notes as we work through idea. In the meantime, my notes on what Luiz does follow below.

Will keep you posted. I hope that we can talk soon. Gotta go. Thanks for help. Breanna

# YELPING

The wind sharpened its teeth on the dry air, biting into his exposed face.

It was two weeks later, and Jon knocked for a second time on the old wooden door of the small house just south of Lafayette, west of state road 52.

The scientist put his thick brown glove back on, then stepped away from the door and moved to the right on top of the old brick landing and looked around the side of the house down the wet driveway.

There it was, the Camaro with the distinctive white lightning bolt on the red side panels and even more distinctive wide white walls on the front, blacks in the back. Jon laughed while he walked to the car, careful to avoid the muddy puddles that reflected little of the thin late afternoon February light. Crunching over the gravel, he pulled his right glove off and felt the hood.

Warm.

Still, somebody could have taken his car and—

"Hey, man."

Jon spun around to see Wild Bill's head hanging out of a second-story open window, his image appearing to ripple as the inside heat passed in waves over him as it moved from the warm room into the cold air.

"What're you doing down there, Jon? Taking my car's pulse?"

"Don't have to," Jon said. "This thing is dead."

"Be thankful I'm not my daddy, or you're the one who'd be dead."

"I know," Jon said, shivering at the wind's new bite. "The last two things you want to mess with on a South Carolina man are his car and his woman."

"Dog. A car and his dog. You'd have never been a good Confederate."

"Up for a ride around the 'plantation'?" Jon asked, whirling his right hand in the air, signifying the 465 loop.

"You said it. I need a minute. May have to make a stop. And," he said, pointing a finger, "just because you insulted my South Carolina honor, we're taking your car."

"Bet. Just get your narrow regulatory ass down here."

Jon walked around to the front of the house. Although two stories, it was on the small side. Only thing big was the yard, with a windbreak of trees to the north and west—textbook Indiana.

The drizzle stopped, but the wind continued its mournful howl out of the west. Jon turned his back to the front door to look at the brown front yard across the street, junked up with old car parts.

The front door snapped. He turned. "Ready, B—"

A woman.

Jeans, short boots, and a fur-lined leather jacket half way zipped up.

"Oh. Hi," Jon said. He swallowed.

"Hi, back." Her lips were straight, but eyes alive with a smile. Jon guessed that she was 225 pounds, and all of 5′6″.

"What're you and Bill doing tonight?" she asked, keeping eye contact.

Jon felt like he was staring. "Uh, not much really. Just ride the loop. Talk some things out, I guess. Listen, Bill didn't say that he was entertain— I mean, that he had company. I hope I'm not interrupting anything." He smiled at her and sighed. "You know, I am really messing this up."

A smile appeared below cheeks stung with pink from the wind. "You're sweet. He said that you'd drop me off."

"Of course. Be my pleasure. By—"

"And that's because my friend is a true gentleman," Wild Bill said, appearing behind the woman. Jon watched Bill put a hand gently on both her shoulders, then nuzzle her ear. A new deep smile spread over her face.

"Are you really going to leave me tonight, Em?" Wild Bill said.

"Bill," she said, her face bright with new fire, "you know that I have to be in Evanston tomorrow."

"How about if we go to Louisville next weekend?"

She turned to look at Bill with a face that told Jon she would go to Louisville, hell, or anyplace else with the rangy South Carolinian.

"Let me call you," Wild Bill said.

"Tomorrow?

"Count on it." He slipped an arm around her.

"Not in front of your friend," she said. Jon felt her gaze, receiving her signal that it was fine with her if Jon took a walk for an hour or two.

"OK," Wild Bill said. "Let's go." He gave her a gentle push toward the steps.

Jon hustled down then around to the Cherokee's driver's side, flipped the locks for everyone, and all clambered in, the wind howling hard at their back. Jon saw that Wild Bill let Emma sit in the front.

The wind died down enough for Jon to hear the tiniest of groans from Wild Bill as he scooted over behind the driver's seat. Had to be his leg. Winters usually bothered it, and this winter . . . goodness.

"The weather's never like this in Monetta," Bill said.

"Your hometown is a long way from here, partner. And where are you from?" Jon asked, turning to Emma as he fired up the engine of his Cherokee.

"From around here," she said. Her smile had vanished, replaced with a hard winter face.

"Around here's not so bad, Emma, 'specially in the spring and summer," Wild Bill said. Jon noticed that he had leaned forward between him and Emma.

The smile was making a comeback.

"I'm glad I'm here, Em," the regulator continued.

Jon saw that the smile was all the way back now.

Jon nudged the car back through the wet driveway and onto the street, as Em talked of how anxious she was to be on the other side of frozen February. Ten minutes later, they pulled into an apartment complex just off SR-52 in Lafayette.

"Nice to meet you, Jon."

"You too."

"I'm calling tomorrow," Bill said, kissing her neck.

"Talk to you then." She got out, turned, blowing him a kiss. She ran inside as the cold rain began to come down again.

Bill fell back into the seat. "South, boss."

"I know the way."

They headed out SR-26 east to I-65. The rain was now pounding on the roof, but the February light was holding.

"So how's Alora doing these days?"

"Well," Jon said, shrugging, "we'll be passing her soon." He leaned forward to adjust the heat.

"What are you talking about?"

"She's with her family in Zionsville."

Bill was quiet for a moment, then he said, "You going to give up the house?"

"Yeah. No point in my keeping it. I have a nice place I'm in now anyway."

"When's the shared house going on the market?"

"I don't kn— whoa." The car in front to the left suddenly veered right, into their lane. Jon hit the pedal, and the brakes squealed as he pointed the Cherokee to where the swerving car had been a moment before. The grey BMW kept sliding to the right, straightened for a second, then suddenly turned hard right, into the service lane, and from there, plowed through the thin, soaked winter brush.

Jon pulled into the service lane, turned his engine off, then clicked on the emergency flashers. He and Bill got out at once and headed the few feet back to the BMW sitting askew in the brush.

"Hey, buddy," Wild Bill said, tapping on the thick glass of the driver's window. "You all right in there?"

The door opened, and the reek of alcohol and vomit hit them. Jon took a step back, but Wild Bill stayed where he was. He saw the regulator turn away, then taking a deep breath, turned back and said, "Like to try to help you if we can."

Jon watched over Wild Bill's shoulder as the driver lunged at Bill. Suddenly, Wild Bill fell back into Jon, and Jon found himself holding his friend, who had almost bowled him over.

Wild Bill struggled up in Jon's arms then stood up straight, spat, and stepped forward.

"Drunk son of a bitch."

Jon saw Wild Bill's fists come up. With two steps, he was in front of Wild Bill. Turning his head to face the driver, who was now giving them both the finger, Jon said, "We're out of here, friend."

Then he placed a hand on Wild Bill's chest. "We don't want any of this, Bill. The rain's letting up some, and the rest of our drive will be good. A slugfest with a drunk will ruin it. You with me?"

Wild Bill looked away.

"You with me?" Jon's face was now in Wild Bill's space.

"I should ruin this guy for what he did to me." Bill shoved Jon aside. He twisted to the left to reach inside his coat and came back around, holding a knife.

Jon gasped, then lunged toward his friend. He grabbed Bill's knife-holding right hand by the forearm with his right one, planting both feet in front of him.

"Bill," he shouted. "Listen to yourself. You want to ruin him? For what? Because he shoved you? He's drunk, for heaven's sake."

"He won't do that to me again."

"Right. Because he won't see you again."

They stood that way for what, to Jon, seemed like forever. The two of them in the rain, hands on each other. The drunk driver, sitting in his car, door open, his legs out, his left shoulder and neck resting on the upright seat.

"You can let go now," Wild Bill said.

Seeing his friend's eyes clear, Jon stepped back, taking deep breaths.

"Spending the rest of the evening dealing with the Lafayette police wasn't what I had in mind anyway," Wild Bill said, putting the blade away, then adjusting his dark-gray leather jacket.

The two walked back to the Cherokee. In thirty seconds, they were strapped in and back on the road, driving in silence.

"Shit happens," Bill said.

"Well, shit almost happened," Jon said, adjusting the thermostat up a notch. "It doesn't take long for a car to get cold."

Turning to his friend, Jon said, "You stopped in time."

"Like hell I did. I was going to feed him the whole can of whoop-ass. You stopped me."

Jon turned and saw Wild Bill with his glasses off, scratching his forehead. He had come to know that when the glasses were off, something was up.

"If that would've made a difference, I'd have fed him my can too. Here we go," Jon said, turning right then slipping into the left entrance lane onto 65 South.

"Yeah. Well," Bill said, sitting up in the seat some.

"I was telling you about Alora." Jon wanted to change the subject. "She thinks I'm porkin' Robbie."

"What?" Bill sat up in his seat. "Robbie? Are you? Damn. Well, she is avail—"

"'Course not," Jon said, shooting an angry look to his right. "C'mon, Bill."

"Well, that's a relief. I don't see how you'd have the energy for that extracurricular anyway. But I had to ask." Bill shrugged. "People fool you."

"Well, I'm not." He was going to say the worst thing in the world was to have affair with someone at work, but he choked it back, not really sure why.

"Anybody else?"

Jon looked over again. "Damn it, Bill. No."

"You brought it up."

"No. Alora brought it up. She's wrong too."

"Well, why'd she think it?" Out of the corner of his eye, Jon saw Bill looking at him. "Women can smell that stuff a mile away."

"Hey, look, I told you—"

"OK, OK. I get it," Wild Bill said, holding his hands up. "Long as you're not dipping your pen in the company ink, I'm fine."

Jon laughed. "Hadn't heard that one." He was going to ask Bill why he didn't go after Robbie, but instead asked. "So you and Emma tight?"

"I really like her."

"Well, it's clear she likes you. She'd have been perfectly happy if I disappeared as fast as I appeared back at your house. How long you and Emma been an item?"

"Three months. It will last a little while longer, then I'll move on."

Jon looked over. "She's not the one?"

He saw Bill flick his right wrist. "It's not that. But she'll get used to the attention. Then she'll get tired of it."

Jon tapped his hand on the steering wheel and frowned. "Relationships change. They can't be frozen, WB, always playing out the first day's pleasure over and over." Jon shrugged. "Give the next phase a chance. You say, 'people surprise you,' right? Well, life surprises you, Bill, if you give it a chance."

"You really giving me advice on relationships?" Bill said, rolling his eyes, shaking his head. "I'm really in the shit now."

They both laughed. "But," the regulator said, "the next stage isn't so hot. Things will lose their freshness, and it'll be time to move on."

"So it sounds like you're OK with this . . . this imminent breakup."

"Always disappointed when the day comes. But expecting it makes it easier."

Jon caught Bill wiping his eyes. Then the glasses were back on.

They were quiet for a while, the only sound being the Cherokee's tires slashing through the rain on their way south to Indianapolis.

A few minutes later, Jon asked, "Usual stop?"

"Hungry already?"

Jon nodded. "Thirty-eighth Street exit up ahead. Let's do it."

They pulled into the near-empty Wendy's parking lot, ran inside, and ordered.

"That all you getting?" Wild Bill said, pointing to Jon's Frosty.

"Not too hungry these days."

Wild Bill shrugged and led the way to a couple of seats. "So was Alora always the way she's been recently?"

Jon finished a gulp. "So good. Why do you ask?"

"Just can't imagine you marrying someone so self-absorbed, s'all."

"She changed after the university thing."

"But you were exonerated, right?" Bill said, pulling a WB with his chair. It was your colleague who copped the data, not you."

"Yeah, that's all true enough. But it was big, public, and embarrassing. I chose to leave the U, then she chose to leave me. Really didn't fit with her career trajectory."

"Pardon my French," Wild Bill said, lacing a French fry back and forth through the ketchup until it was a dripping red blob.

"Man, that's disgusting. Should be a second-degree food crime."

"What would be a first-degree crime?"

"Whatever the hell you're going to do next."

"Well," Wild Bill said, popping the red French fry into his mouth, "you and Alora didn't seem to fit. I mean, I see some couples that are just natural, the whole 'two becoming one' thing. My brother and his wife back home are like that. After a few years, hard to see where one ends and the other begins. You and Alora . . ." WB paused.

"More pulling apart than coming together?" Jon asked.

Wild Bill shook his head. "I think of it more like a case of different dreams. Alora's a climber. She wanted to walk a well-trodden path headed to the comfort zone. Nothing wrong with that, either."

Jon looked outside, just chewing.

"And in case you're interested, my tight friend, you are a struggler. You have to make your own path. Because— Hey."

They both scooted their chairs back from the three-year-old at the next table who knocked over a cup of Mountain Dew.

"Well," Jon, taking a napkin to dry his jacket, "when you're done painting that last French fry, you think you'll be ready to go?"

Wild Bill held the fry up, smeared in ketchup and covered with Mountain Dew foam. "I should take a picture of this thing."

They headed back to the Cherokee, and after Jon fired it up, they pulled back onto 465, now heading south before east.

"Well," Jon said, checking the heat, "I saw your last email. All quiet on the FDA front."

"We're shooting blanks, so they're not worried."

Jon's grip tightened on the wheel.

"I don't mean harm by that, Jon," WB said, turning to face him. "But what we're doing is standard. We manufacture vaccine. We're within standard operating limits, normal parameters. Bladdy, bladdy, bladdy. You know. That's where you want to be with the feds."

After a few moments, when they were swinging by the new airport, Wild Bill said "I like your idea. That 'stem of the Y' routine. Still a long shot though."

Jon licked his lips. "I think the partial antibody approach will be OK for us, seriously. After all, it's about the chemistry. Once the partial antibodies get out in the milieu, they can produce the exact protein structure they need. London and Van der Waal's forces are pretty powerful at the atomic and molecular level. Actually—"

Wild Bill snorted, slapped his hand on his thigh. "I heard you telling Breanna that. Man, you're shit-rippin'."

"What?"

"Pulling it out of your ass."

They both cracked up, Jon laughing so hard he had to bring the car across the road into the service lane.

"You know, the idea is very good, and heaven knows you invented sincerity," Bill said, playing with the window control. "But I also have to say that you don't know what you're talking about. Fact is, you've got no clue how any of this is going to work." He shook his head. "Van der Waals forces." He yelp-laughed again.

"Yeah," Jon said, staring into the dark. "I really don't know."

"Yep." They both stared at the Tenth Street lights off to the left for a few moments.

"So let's you and I play this out, Jon."

Jon's vision blurred, and the new beast in his stomach stretched, now wide awake. "I don't want to do this, Bill."

"What happens if it doesn't work?"

Jon looked out the front window then turned his gaze to outside his own. All was blackness. "Well, we continue to make vaccine, for a little while longer."

"Probably only for a couple of months, right? I mean, the flu scare is over, so the companies won't need our help with production until late summer when the new season's viral template is set."

"Uh-huh."

"Plus, we don't have the pedigree for a Purdue grant, much less a national grant. The application process alone requires a ton of work, plus, it can take nine months from submission to getting the federal wampum." Bill adjusted himself in the seat.

"It's not just that," Jon added, turning to look at Bill. "Only seven out of a hundred are funded." He started the car up. "Forget that."

"Well," Bill said, "they've already forgotten you. Turnabout's fair play."

They drove a few more miles.

"Then that's it," Wild Bill said, looking out of this window. "We going east now?"

"Yeah to both."

"Thing is, Jon, you're going to have to be straight with us. We depend on you, maybe a little too much. But you deliver. You'll ruin it all if you lie to th—"

Jon snapped his head around. "What do you mean by that? I'm not going to lie."

"If you don't tell them the truth, then you're lying to them about the company. They deserve better than that, right?"

Jon saw Rayiko's face for a moment. The two of them would work up something. They always had. But tonight, he put that hope aside. He sighed, and felt a new sting in his right eye.

"Jon," Wild Bill said in a low voice, "something to think about is giving up the company. I mean selling it to another group."

Jon licked his lips. What was Bill talking about?

"Listen, you and our virology boys have come a long way," WB said, looking out of the window. "You've made incredible progress on memory cell manipulations. Shoot, I think you can get those B cells to pick cotton for you. That's great technology, and I'm here to tell you that big pharma is desperate for that."

"Just sell out?" The car had gotten very warm for Jon, and he cracked a window.

"Why is that selling out?" Bill asked, turning around to look in the back seat for a minute. "Yeah. There they are." He reached back then turned around, gloves in hand.

"You and I just agreed that the company doesn't have the money to tide it over until next season," Bill continued. "And you've raised a ton on your own, but you can't keep doing that. Eventually, people will want a return on their investment. You hearing me?"

"I have one more card to play," Jon said, swallowing. "And I think it's a good one."

"And I'm there with you. But the best card players know when to fold. Just sayin'."

Jon said nothing. Wild Bill's logic was dead on, and he knew it. He'd been avoiding it for weeks, ever since the last series of experiments failed. And he had to deal with Alora's "I told you so" taunts, the disappointments of his people. Damn, those experiments should have worked. But—he sighed—science, hard, cold, and ruthless, didn't give a damn.

Nothing personal.

And fact was, the company couldn't survive another failure. He turned to Bill.

"Can you help with the sale of the company?"

"Maybe." Wild Bill shook his head. "I don't know. I mean, I can get the word out, invite some folks down to see us in action, but that's as much as I know to do."

"OK," Jon said, holding his open right hand out to Wild Bill. "Let's say nothing else about this until after the partial antibody idea is tested. If it comes up dry, then I'll . . . I'll throw in the towel. I mean, really. What choice do I have?"

Bill's right grasped it.

"Thick and thin, man," they both said.

"This Castleton?"

"Yes, sir."

"I got a stop to make," Bill said. "You don't mind finishing this ride without me, do you?"

Jon threw both hands in the air, letting them plop into his lap. "You're going to stay here? What is it? A girl?"

Bill buttoned his coat. "Well, they're all single. I'm single. What are we supposed to do? Virology?" He yelp-laughed. "Plus, I really like her."

Two rights and a left, and they pulled up to a small house.

"Let me guess."

"You don't have to."

"Just don't be late tomorrow, WB."

"I'll be there before you."

Wild Bill closed the door as the porch light came on in the small house. Not looking back at his friend, Jon turned around in the light projected from the high-amp parking lamps of Castleton Mall, heading back to the highway.

By the time he reached the 465-65 split, the Cherokee pointed north to Lafayette, and the scientist lost himself in thought, bending the antibodies to his will.

# NOT CLOSE ENOUGH

The headache of her life awoke her.

Cassie groaned, choking back a sob as she tossed on the oak bed. Then, VP-Legal, drenched in sweat, leaned over to pick her gold phone up from the cherrywood end table.

2:17 a.m.

Her new routine had roused her.

Nightmares. Sweats. Middle-of-the-night heaves.

Two nights ago, she wet the bed.

All thanks to the Jasper Night.

But the headache, now that was new. Able to find only one slipper, she stumbled to the bathroom, the one expensive Sophia slapping on the tile.

When she finished heaving, washing, then heaving again, she walked to the kitchenette to make some tea, then on to the living room. Sinking into one of its three soft leather chairs, she pulled the phone out of her robe pocket and started a Breanna draft.

These had been good notes, she thought. The plan was working. Cassie and SSS were absorbing all they needed to know about CiliCold.

Yet there was something el—

She pushed the thought aside, and began to write

> Date: February 8, 2016
> Subject:
>
> Breanna
>
> Thank you for your messages this week concerning CiliCold. We now think that we have a good sense about the direction of the company. As you know, we

> have not been so interested in the flu vaccine production component of the company's work.

Cassie paused. Her headache was shrinking. She'd have to remember this brand of tea.

She looked down at her waiting iPhone. Something was missing from the email.

It was confidential, she thought, so why not take Breanna further into her confidence?

> You should know that we are moving ahead with plans for the acquisition of CiliCold. The notion of programming immune cells to react to certain viruses, to make a super-vaccine, would be a practical application of Dr. DeLeon's work. We would of course need the worker materials of Luiz and, to some extent, Dale, although his contribution to this aspect of the project is unclear.

Breanna would like that last part, she thought. She doesn't think much of Dale.

But if this email was going to build Breanna up, then Breanna would need to hear more. And Cassie knew that she needed to say more.

> You have been through so much these past months. Since our first meeting last week, I have reflected on whether there is anything else SSS can do for you. Despite my best efforts, I am falling short of providing all that you need.

Not good enough. Cassie licked her lips. Breanna was going through hell at work: the infighting, DeLeon's distractions, Rayiko's absence. Breanna needed support. Not like a sister far away, but a friend.

Closer.

> You should know that I think of you and Jackie often. You are so helpful to me. I am here for you. You have my number if you would like to call me.

Say what you're thinking, Cassie, the urgent voice whispered. Write, write, write.

> I want nothing more than to have you with me, holding you. Sweet mouth on mouth. Running my tongue along your long neck and then your delicious breasts as you stretch out next to me. Our naked bodies as one. Wetting my fingers. Putting them on you, in you. Be my love and come to me soon.

Headache gone, Cassie studied the message for a minute. Then she deleted all but the first paragraph, saved that part in the drafts folder for Breanna, and headed back to bed.

# IN THIRTY

Jon opened the Cherokee door in the CiliCold parking lot, leaning into the warmest air that he'd felt in weeks, He stepped out into—

Mud.

Tuesday, February 9th, wet-cement-like Indiana mud.

Couldn't break the shoe loose, so he hopped to the front door, then balancing, hopped through it.

Into Robbie.

"Thought you'd never make it, Dr. DeLeon," Robbie said, breathless as always when he entered. "Purdue called. They need to see you about your adjunct professorship. Hey, what happened to your foot?"

*What adjunct professorship?* he thought. He'd forgotten all about it. "Don't ask, don't tell. I'll give them a call."

"Sounds like they want to see you," she replied. "City inspectors were here this morning as well. They said they were concerned about the water consumption."

"Water?" He shook his head. "We use a lot of water, but we pay for it."

"Think they want you to pay more. A higher rate for higher usage. Also—" She thrust a letter at him. "*Annals of Virology* rejected your manuscript."

He almost smacked his hand against his leg in disgust. That was the fifth rejection so far. There were still other journals to go to, but the submitted paper would have to be reformatted, maybe even shortened, and the references reorganized. All of that would take time, about a week.

Less if Rayiko was here.

Suddenly, the urge to call her filled him.

No, he thought. She had her own troubles. She would call when she was ready.

"And Luis and Dale have been yelling for you. Something about getting the B cells to release the FC incomplete somethings. Hey, Dr. DeLeon," she said, drawing closer to him, "will we get paid this week?"

Jon drew back, surprised. "Sure you will." He hopped closer. "Remember our deal? Why would you ask?"

"Well," Robbie whispered, "Breanna wasn't in yesterday. We're afraid that she found a new job. I think her husband got fired or something. Nobody's heard from her. Dr. DeLeon, I just can't afford to not—"

Jon flinched at the new brisk wind blowing in from the suddenly opened outside door. Turning, Jon saw Breanna. A black coat and scarf, with red cheeks and the thickest hair.

"We were just talking about you," Jon said, now facing her. "How are things?"

Jon noticed that she hesitated for a moment, then said, "I'm doing OK."

"Well, there's a touch of spring in the air," he said with a smile, "usually accompanied by a ton of mud, which is where I left my shoe."

He couldn't call that slightest move of facial muscles on her face a smile. "Well, we're due for your six-week review today," he said.

He saw her eyes focused at once, and for the briefest of moments, Jon thought she frowned.

"I'm not in trouble, am I?" she asked.

He felt like he was striking a match, only then recognizing a kerosene smell in the air. "No. I—"

"You'll want to see the virologists first, Dr. DeLeon," Robbie said, flicking her notepad back and forth with her wrist. "Luiz and Dale are anxious to talk to you."

*Just take yourself home*, he thought.

He shook it off. "Breanna, let's just go ahead and do your review now."

"That'd be fine," she said.

"Up to my office, then, where I have some sneakers." He turned to face Robbie. "I guess Dale and Luiz are impatient?"

He watched her eyebrows go up.

"I'll call them in just a minute and schedule a time for a serious conversation."

Robbie's phone rang.

"No need," she said. "I bet that's them now."

"OK," he said, turning to the steps. "Breanna? After you." Twisting toward Robbie, he said, "Tell them I'll call in a bit."

"I imagine that I'm interrupting your schedule," Jon said as they walked into his office. He held the door, letting her pass under his arm, noticing again how short she was. She wore no perfume, unlike Robbie, whose perfume level was way up. Dale once said he saw a bird fall from the sky when Robbie emerged outside to get some lunch for everyone.

Luiz and Dale.

Damn it. Gotta call them.

Jon, motioning her to sit in the chair next to the beige wall, sat in the chair next to her, on the same side of his desk.

"Just a moment," he said. He dialed Luiz.

"Luiz. Hi. Jon. Robbie told me you wanted to talk with me . . . No, let's just go with the heavy chain-only model . . . Well, Dale thought it was a good idea a few days ago . . . OK . . . how about in about thirty minutes? Bye."

"Before we start, can I ask you a question?" Breanna said. He saw that her eyes were now fixed on his.

"Sure?"

"How do you do this?" she asked.

"Do what? Work?"

"Face cease—"

S4

"Dr. DeLeon, Dr. DeLeon."

"Robbie?" He'd never heard her so out o—

"Dale just quit."

# CRAY-CRAY

Breanna watched as Jon turned, offered her an apology, and rushed out. She took a deep breath, looking out the door through which he had just hurried. She liked Jon. He was kind and devoted. He did his best to answer all her questions. And he was smart.

But this was a madhouse.

Rayiko suddenly disappears. Jon phases in and out of relevance. Dale takes off. Wild Bill waltzes in and out. They were great as individuals, she thought as she rummaged through her Madewell bag, but as a group, they were flying apart.

She preferred to send these messages from home, but Breanna went ahead anyway, navigating to the draft section of her new private email account.

This was going to be a cray-cray day.

If it weren't for Jackie and Cassie, she'd be out of her mind.

> Date: February 9, 2016
> Subject:
> Cassie,
>
> We continue to be in turmoil here. I have just heard that Dale quit. While he can be an irritant, he continues to be a necessary cog in our machine.
>
> I have taken some detailed notes from our discussions here about experimental plans. We are going to begin the

B cell altered production of antibodies soon, although Dale's departure will change that.

It is good to hear from you, Cassie. I rely on your help and friendship. B

# SWISHER SWEETS

"Well," Dale said, walking up the steps, "you go ahead and do your chem run, amigo, because I think I'm quits on CiliCold, man."

Dale saw Luiz reach for the phone, then the bald virologist turned around to climb the basement steps. Once upstairs, he snatched his coat, walking to the building's back door. It was all so useless, he thought, so aggravating. How many weeks had they spent trying to conduct experiments based on incomplete, jacked-up theories of a—

*Of a what?* he thought.

An unstable scientist.

He might as well just run with that, because that was what Jon was—brittle, unpredictable, even emotional.

An anti-scientist.

*Time to shop my resume around*, he thought. *Select zone five and run for my professional life.*

He looked through the door's window, hand on the single brass handle.

The sun didn't spend much time in the alley this time of year, but it was there today.

But so was the wind.

If he was lucky, it would be blowing from the north, and the north-side building would protect him.

If not, well, just a quick smoke.

He poked his head out.

"Praise the gods," he said, walking the short distance to the chain-link fence. Turning his back on the door, he leaned against the fence, took out his matchbook.

A lone match.

"The mark of a professional," he said. Even in the winter, a professional can light a cig with a single match.

OK. He pulled the last match free. For the victory, and the gold, he thought.

One . . . two . . . strike.

The match flared, the door behind him banged closed, and Dale jumped, dropping the lit match to the frozen mud.

He turned. "Hey—"

Jon.

*What the hell does he want?* Dale thought. "You just spoiled my record for lighting a winter cigarette with a single match."

"Well," Jon said, "let me make amends."

Jon took out a thin cigar, lit it with one match, then with it still burning between his hands, said, "Bring it over."

Dale leaned down, cigarette in his mouth, and the cigarette ignited.

Dale inhaled. "I'll consider my streak unbroken."

"Then I want an assist."

They fist-bumped.

They both turned to face the north building wall, backs leaning against the chain-link fence, pulling their smoke in.

"You know, Dale, I always wanted to ask you, but didn't want to give you the satisfaction of my curiosity. Why on earth do you wear clogs?"

He pointed to the light-brown wooden shoes, now mud and ice flecked, on Dale's feet,

"Well, why do you wear sneakers?"

"In the lab, we're on our feet for hours at a time," Jon said, eyes closed while leaning his head against the door. "Sneakers are comfortable, and that comfort comes from their flexibility. That's why everybody wears them," he added, straightening up against the fence. "But those things on your feet are wooden. What's the story?"

Dale looked up at the sky. If Jon wanted the answer, then here it came.

"I wear them because my grandfather wore them."

"What? He was from Holland?"

"No. Jersey."

The virologist watched Jon drop his head. "I'm not reading you, Dale."

"Well, when I was kid, old Gramps told me lots of stories from the '20s." Dale laughed. "You think things are crazy now? We don't have anything on those folks with the beer and the speakeasies and the girls."

Dale turned his head to Jon, watching his boss blow smoke in silence.

"My gramps was trying to generate some serious money both in his tie business and in the market."

"He told you this?"

"Didn't your grandfather ever talk to you?"

"Nope, and thank God."

"Whatever," Dale said, shrugging. "Course, when the market collapsed, he lost his investment, and his tie business dried up. He told me that one week, he was down to his last forty bucks and had to choose between buying shoes and paying his rent. Rent was $21.50."

"And the shoes?"

"Twenty bucks."

Jon nodded. "A big delta back then."

"Damn right. A $1.50 shortfall was a problem. So he paid his rent, and that left him $18.50. His shoes were in really bad shape. He used to tell me the only thing that kept them on his feet was the blood and the dirt." Dale shook his head.

"So then, he—"

"He found someone selling clogs for $18.25. So he bought a pair, and with the remaining quarter, found a cheap diner where he got a cup of some fish soup. Said it was vile."

Dale watched. Jon didn't make fun of him. No glib off-the-cuff answer of his that everyone seemed to like, and that disgusted Dale.

"So you wear them to—"

"To remember how tough life can be."

"No," Jon answered.

Dale turned. What was with this smart-ass? "Now look, Jo—"

"Don't get me wrong, Dale. What you say is true, but isn't that just part of it? Clogs show you are committed. Whatever else the day throws at you, you are in your clogs dealing with it. They are walking evidence of your ability to commit." Jon shrugged then turned back to look across the alley. "Anyway."

Dale was quiet. Jon had said in four sentences what he was groping toward for years. "Maybe."

They smoked in silence for a minute, then Dale saw Jon turn toward him. "One thing though. Aren't they uncomfortable?"

"Sure, for the first 1,000 miles. Then you kind of get used to them."

They both laughed.

Dale looked down. "Nice sneaks you got there. You going to run home today?"

Jon looked back. "I'm not running anywhere. Heard you have some beefs, Dale."

So he wants to go mano a mano with me. 'Bout damn time. "Want them with the bark on or off?" the virologist said, spitting.

"The rough way."

His heart racing, but his voice icy calm, he began. "You're inspirational but not practical. And your inattentiveness is killing this company. Insight is fine, but pragmatism is better."

"OK," Jon said, exhaling.

*You got his attention*, Dale thought. *Let it all out.* "Plus you've got this . . . this thing. You drift. Can't stay focused. Look." He turned to face Jon, "I don't know where your head goes, but it damn sure isn't Virologyland, and that, boss, is where we need you." The virologist took a drag.

"Anything else?"

Dale exhaled, long and hard. "Yeah. You need a new car. Cherokees suck."

"Any other time, I'd say, 'You make us the money, I'll buy the car,' but—"

Suddenly, Dale was angry. He'd had it with facile humor, these smooth, nonresponsive comebacks from this guy. "Hey, Jon, I'm serious here. Don't try the soft-sell 'I'm a smart guy, just a little off' business. That may work with the XXs around here, not us XYs."

"Dale," Jon said, staring at the lengthening ash on his own small cigar, "there is no question about your being smart. But do you know the difference between being smart and being intelligent?"

Dale stared at him. *Now what's he getting at?* he wondered, saying nothing.

"You stay with me," Jon said, "and I'll try to teach you. In the meantime, everything you say is true."

"About the Jeep too?"

"Especially the Jeep."

Victory.

Dale relaxed. "Well then, what are we arguing about?" Dale said. "Straighten the hell up."

"Sure, I can try to be practical," Jon said, stepping on a fallen ash, "but it only works for a day or two. Then I get bumped back into my rut." He shrugged. "My being practical is like you throwing a consistent curve ball."

"How do you know I can't?"

"Because if you could, you wouldn't be here."

They both laughed.

The virologist saw Jon point to the cigarette. "You gonna smoke that thing, Dale, or are you just going let your frostbitten hand hold it a while longer?"

"Fair point." He inhaled, closing his eyes.

"You know, Dale, I never had one idea worth a damn when I was being practical."

Dale couldn't help it. "So they all come when you're spaced."

"Call it what you will, that's where they are."

"Well, how does this work? Do they call to you?"

Jon looked down the alley, past Dale. "They're not really verbal. Visual. Like watching clouds. Or like writing in water."

Dale watched Jon squint, then make a face. "If you don't get it right away," Jon continued, "you never will. Quiet images. Some I can interpret. Others, I never do. He spat. "That last part's tough."

"So your mind churns out movies without soundtracks," the virologist said, turning to Jon, shaking his head. "Man, you need to see somebody."

"True dat. Should've gone to one when I had the chance. Too much to do now."

They were both quiet for a minute, facing the north wall, turning the air to white with their smokes. Then Jon said, "Laying into me's not affecting me, Dale. I am who I am. But talking to other people about it affects them."

Dale turned to him. "They need to see."

"They don't need your thoughts about me to help them see. You don't give them insight; you just frighten them." Jon turned around, facing CiliCold's back wall. "Did you know that not one of them is afraid to talk to me about any of this?"

Dale just looked at him. Jon turned, staring back.

"The one person who is most critical never confronted me eyeball to eyeball about it, until today. I'm wondering why, Dale."

"So am I."

"Well, let me know, and I'll bring another cheap cigar and we can talk some more."

"That Swisher the best you can do for a cigar, Jon?"

"No. I like Ashtons, but they last for ninety minutes. Why bring an Ashton to a Swisher Sweets discussion?"

"Then," Dale said, "let's make the next one longer."

"Bet. Now let's get the hell inside."

"Bet."

# PRIMED

"Ugh," Jon said, five minutes later as he wiped his mouth with his left hand, putting the coffee cup down. "Last time I smelled something like this, I was changing burnt-out transmission fluid in my father's truck."

Dale took a swig from his own cup. Another swig.

"My nasty coffee growing on you, ese?" Luiz asked.

"Actually," Dale said, smacking his lips, "the brain cells that survive get a hankering for it."

"I'm glad you all called me down here," Jon said, leaning across the table under the old fluorescent light, letting his knuckles rap out a near-silent cadence. "We need to work out some of these design issues."

"If we didn't get you down here," Dale said, walking over from the four-by-four support beam he'd been leaning on, "you'd think your job was to raise money."

"Ugh." Jon shrugged. "I'm getting worse at it."

"Just a bad streak," Dale offered, shrugging. "But now we've got real work to do. First we have to get the memory B cells to make their almost antibodies, then we need to monitor their effects."

"B cells are your babies," Jon said to Luiz, turning slightly to his right under the florescent light that swayed with the passing street traffic. "How close are we to getting the B's to put out incomplete antibodies?"

"There." He looked up from the pad he'd been scribbling in.

Dale leaned back to let Jon study it.

"You're not serious," Jon said, looking up at Luiz.

"Square business. Honed into the right segment of the genome. Then"—he shrugged his shoulders—"just hunt and peck for a bit."

"Shitfire."

Jon, chin resting on his hand, looked over at the younger worker. "Incredible. You are the maestro of the memory cells."

"I call him the bastard of the Bs," Dale snorted.

Luiz scratched his chin. "Actually, the leased equipment makes all the difference."

"Still, if I didn't know better, I'd think you'd have these memory cells singing songs."

"All in their DNA, man."

Jon nodded. That a cell less than a thousandth of an inch long could hold coded chemical instructions for all life functions that would fill hundreds of books, each hundreds of pages long could still made his heart skip a beat. But that Luiz could manipulate the small part of it that controlled antibody construction was like practicing jump shots 1,000 miles from the hoop until you got nothing but net.

"How many codons do you need to control?"

"Sixteen, but they're all regulators. Flip the Supremes on, and the B cell will make the entire antibody, soup to nuts. Flip the Marvelettes on, and I can get it to make the light chains—"

"The top of the Y—"

"On. Turn on the Vandellas, and I can make the heavy chain."

"You know," Jon said, trying hard not to smile, "I don't want to ask you—"

"Sure you do–"

"What's up with these Motown singing groups?"

"Just puts some zing in the work. And I like the old hits."

"He likes those old women who made those hits," Dale said, lifting up for a minute. Jon squinted at the new stink in the air.

"Yep." Luiz sneezed, then rubbed his nose. "It's amazing anything can live down here with those regular detonations."

"What kind of tolerance to you need with the transfections?" Jon stood up, wiping his nose, watching Dale smile. "You know, Dale, you should be thrown in jail for tossing those out."

"I was," he said, "but I was released in twenty-four hours. Can't imagine why." Ear-to-ear smile on his face.

All three laughed.

"No room for error at all," Luiz said, cracking his knuckles. "It's a pretty important part of the B cell's DNA. But our vectors are sharp. They only go after the undifferentiated B's."

"How did you get it that specific?"

"Easy. It's all proteomics. Once I know the protein these undifferentiated B cells make, it's easy to home in on them. Then I turned on the 'stem of the Y' sequence."

"No other tissue is affected? No other cellular injury."

"Not a scratch. Leastways not from my transfections."

"You make it sound easy. I know it's not. Good work," Jon said, turning from Luiz to Dale. "Maybe you can control your GI track long enough to tell us how to measure whether Luiz's work is producing the results we need."

"Compared to Luiz's work, mine's a snap. We just measure the viral titers. Thing is, though, I don't know if we can test this in vitro."

"Why not?"

"I can get the virus and the B cells together, but if your idea is going to work, Jon, the key is the extracellular environment, right? That's where the final antibody construction is supposed to take place. I've got to get the mix just right."

"Why not just extract if from one of the monkeys?" Luiz asked, sitting down.

"Well, if I did that, then the fluid would have to be processed. We don't want the ECF to contain antibodies made by the animal's own immune system."

"Yeah," Jon said. He hadn't thought about that. "That would be a problem. We wouldn't know which antibodies were destroying the viruses."

"You could try to remove the antibodies," Luiz said.

"Sure, and by doing that, I alter the fluid in a way that it's unable to finish the construction of the antibodies," Dale added.

"We don't know what property of the ECF actually instigated the antibody construction, and it's easy to destroy what you need but don't know you need."

"HMS *Salisbury* all over again," Luiz said.

"What?" Jon turned to stare at Luiz and saw out of the corner of his eye that Dale was doing the same thing.

"*Salisbury*?" Luiz looked at Jon then Dale, shaking his head. "Lind carried out that famous experiment on the sailors to prove that fresh fruit cures scurvy. Remember? 1747?"

Dale and Jon looked at each other. "Luiz, maybe you can write a book report—"

"Anyway," he continued, waving a hand at Dale. "Problem was the admiralty decided that it was just too cumbersome to start packing fresh oranges and lemons on their ships. So instead, they boiled the fruit down and just put the extract on the ships for the sailors to take. That made the logistics manageable, but scurvy still spread like wildfire. Turns out boiling the fresh fruit denatured the vitamin C."

"Leave it to the British," Dale said. "No wonder we whipped up on 'em twice."

Jon looked at Luiz, nodding. "I think I get it."

"Anyway," Dale said, "anything we do to help ensure the extracellular fluid will do what we hope it does may produce the opposite result."

"So we have to go right to animal testing?" Jon would know whether his idea worked sooner than he realized. His pulse rate jumped.

"I think so. Once the B cells are treated, we infect the animal, then monitor for new antibodies and viral loads."

"Hopefully we'll show increasing antibody titers and no, or at least decreasing, viral titers."

"What about the FDA?" Dale asked, wiping his forehead with what looked like a wash rag.

"Good point. Well," Jon said, taking a few steps back from the table. "Let's just say design issues required us to go to monkeys sooner rather than later."

"It's a good con," Dale said. "Didn't know you had it in you."

Jon turned and looked at him. "It's also the truth."

"Yeah," the bald scientist said. "Another complication is going to be the number of animals we need to test."

"Well, we need to run multiple animals for each version of B cell Luiz makes."

"Of course." Jon remembered his excitement months ago that was dashed to pieces. "Don't want to be fooled by a fluke again."

"Wonder where that term *fluke* comes from."

Jon stared at Luiz, knowing without looking that Dale was doing the same.

"How . . . many . . . animals?" Jon asked pointedly.

"Ten per experiment."

Jon sighed, and sat on one of benches. "That's a ton."

"Better than taking time trying to replicate a false positive," Dale said, coming over to Jon's side of the table.

"Agreed." Jon sat quietly for a moment.

"If your idea is right," Dale said, "these partial antibodies will get released and construction will finish in proximity to the virus. That's likely going to require interaction with many substances in the ECF we may not know about yet," Dale said.

Jon shrugged. "It's not exactly guaranteed to work."

"Well, it's not exactly a shot in the dark either. Pretty clever, actually," Dale said, reaching for the coffee pot.

Both men turned to Dale. "Damn," Jon said. "Dale, that's fulsome praise coming from you."

"He got a few smokes in today," Luiz explained.

"Always makes me garrulous and generous," Dale said. "One thing though, if—"

"What?"

"These antibodies are to finish their construction in proximity to the virus. How do we know that the ECF won't put the wrong finishing touch on them? For example, create an antibody that reacts to endothelial surface, or kidney tissue, or the optic nerve."

"Two things, I think," Jon replied. "First, our maestro Luiz is targeting memory cells that make the heavy chain that go after viruses. So the partial construction within the B cell will be targeted for viruses. I can't believe that the crowning touch is going to make it veer off and head for the first chief cell or neuron it can find."

"OK. And the second?" Dale asked, rubbing his chin.

"Yeah." Jon wondered whether he should finish his answer, not knowing how they'd react. But their careers were on the line too. They deserved to know what was on his mind. "I'd been thinking about this one for a while. The best way I can describe it is something like defense in depth."

"Too much *NFL Today*, man," Dale said, turning away.

"Actually," Jon said. "I don't watch football."

Dale turned back. "You're kidding."

"Haven't seen a game in years."

"That's unhealthy," Luis said.

"Shit. Un-American is what it is."

"Too busy, and not much interest anymore," Jon said. He sat down. "Anyway, the idea is that the body's reaction to the virus is multifactorial. There are responses in many tissues, and these antiviral products are out there in the extracellular fluid. The system is primed to respond to the virus.

"So," Luis said, looking up from the table at Jon, "when the incomplete antibody shows up, it will just know what to do?"

"With some ribosomes and RNA in the vicinity."

"Sounds downright religious," Dale said. "Wonder what the FDA will say about that?"

"The body's power is a force we are trying hard to understand. Not sure that we'll ever get all the way—"

S4.

"Dr. DeLeon?"

"Hi, Robbie."

"Purdue just called. They—"

Cut off.

"When you going to get that thing fixed?" Luiz asked.

"Who knows? Appreciate the talk. When can I see your experimental plan?"

"You'll have them tomorrow. We know you want to see it, and—" Luis paused and looked at Dale.

"We're with you, boss," Dale finished.

Jon fist-bumped them both, then headed up the steps.

# POISONING THE WATER

"You'd better have a look at these, Ms. Doucette."

Cassie handed Meredith a manila envelope across the table in the CEO's office.

"They'd better be good if they are going to help us with our meeting with Jasper in twenty minutes." Meredith smiled. To Cassie, she seemed to be basking in the sunlight streaming through the tall north window of the office.

"No, ma'am," Cassie said, looking across Meredith's maplewood desk. "They are going to hurt you."

Meredith looked up from the envelope, her brown eyes full of curiosity. Then she placed the envelope back on the desktop and pushed it over to Cassie.

"Maybe you'd better tell me what they are."

Cassie took the envelope back. "They are emails between Jasper and the board of directors."

Meredith exhaled. "What do they say?"

"That you are a danger to the company and that you should be removed."

"Well . . ." She shrugged, looking out the window. "That's been coming."

"He wants me out too."

Meredith was quiet for a minute. Then she said, "Of course. You threaten him."

Cassie shifted in her seat. Meredith didn't seem to get what was happening here. "Ms. Doucette, these are not just emails from him. There are one or two responses showing board members are absorbing his message." Cassie thought for a moment, then said, "These emails can make it difficult for you to operate. They poison the waters."

Meredith nodded. "I understand, Cassie, and I am grateful for his heads up. But"—the CEO looked up, stretching her neck for a moment—"I still control a majority of the board, especially after the Tanner purchase. No, Cassie," she said, with a smile, "they don't poison the water, they just ruin the flavor."

"Now," she said standing, "let's not let your subordinate wait any longer."

# A YANKEE'S JOB

"Hey, boss. Storm on the way."

It was three o'clock when Jon arrived back at work. He'd just parked on the side of the house and walked across the ice around to the front sidewalk, newly covered with a rough white coat of salt pellets.

"I heard, Robbie. And it was so warm this morning. What gives?" He looked over at Robbie and pointed his right index finger her way. "Wild Bill, right?"

"How did you know he shoveled?"

"Salt. He always puts down too much salt."

"Yeah," her phone rang and she picked it up, hesitating for a moment before bringing it to her ear. "Don't be so tough on him, boss. What do those folks from South Carolina know about shoveling snow?"

"Zippo. Same thing we know about hurricanes, I guess," he said, unbuttoning his coat. Turning to head upstairs, his pace slowed then stopped. He walked back to her desk and seeing that he had her attention, made a writing motion in the air. She put a pen in his hand, and he wrote out:

> Everybody gets to leave an hour early today because of the weather. Get going at 4. Dr. D.

Robbie read it, gave his a big smile with a thumbs up, then ran to answer her phone.

He walked up the stairs, passing Wild Bill,

"Hey, Bill. Tell the team I said school's out early. Front's coming in."

"You know Luiz and Dale aren't going anywhere. Besides," Wild Bill said, holding out his arms, "that's all you have for me today? Didn't you see that shoveling job I did?"

Jon smiled. "Never send a Rebel to do a Yankee's job."

Bill laughed. "No wonder we seceded. See ya tomorrow. "

Jon watched him inhale, then WB asked, "Any word from Rayiko?"

"No, but hopefully she's back in a few weeks."

"Rayiko and spring. Sounds like a good combination."

"Hope we have some good results for her."

Wild Bill's smile faded. "Well, see you in the a.m."

"Sure thing." Jon turned and headed toward the basement. Looking to the left, he spied Robbie still in her office. She was so dedicated to making this place work. He reversed his steps and walked to her desk.

"Hey, Robbie, how are things going with you?"

Her face lit up like fresh snow at sunrise. "We're doing fine."

"Yeah," he said, leaning back in his chair. "I hear that you need a babysitter some nights now."

"Sure do," she said. She sucked on her lower lip for a moment. "But dating for real is different from your dreams, you know?"

"Well . . ." He thought for a minute. "Life is different from our dreams. You remind me of that when I need to hear it, OK?"

"Let's remind each other," she said, clapping her hands together.

He rested a hand on her arm. "Nobody looks like you when you get that light in your eyes, Robbie. Even spring wants to get here faster just to have a see."

The light got even brighter as she hugged him, then whirled to get back to her office phone.

Jon turned around, then hustled down the steps to the basement. When he got there, he saw Dale with the monkeys and Luiz across the room with his equipment.

Jon leaned back on the chair between them. "You guys tell me something. Why is it that lab seats and bar seats are so similar?"

"'Cause both are filled with the asses of people lost in their dreams."

"Ah," Jon said, slapping Dale on the shoulder. "You nailed it."

"You know, Luiz," Dale said turning to his left, "how are you going to make partial antibodies without killing the B cells that make them?"

"Hey, that's what viruses do, not me," Luiz said, hand up in protest. "Ordinary viruses trick the cell into making something it ordinarily would not make and, in the process, throw off the cell's control mechanism so that the cell dies."

"While you . . ."

"I make the smallest adjustment in the instructions to the cell for antibody construction, not changing anything else that it does."

"So it can live normally, but make these anti-half-bodies," Jon added.

"It's like—" Luiz thought for a second. "Like controlling the song a soprano sings. I don't kill the singer, just adjust the sheet music."

"He means the libretto," Dale chimed in, rolling the sleeves of his lab coat up even higher up his arms. "The soprano reads libretto."

Jon and Luis both stared at Dale.

"I'm a man of acquired tastes," Dale said, bowing to them both.

"My ass," Luiz and Jon said at once, all three laughing.

"So, gentlemen, how we going to measure the success of these experiments?" Jon asked.

"Have to start small," Luiz said. "Let my B cell babies first start producing these partial antibodies and study them. They should all have the common constant sections."

"The stalk of the Y?" Jon asked.

"Yes, yes," Dale said, grimacing at the imprecise term. "'the stem of the Y' for you biochemical aficionados."

Jon ignored Dale. "So you'll do a population study of the shape of these constant regions, these stems?"

"Yeah," Luiz said. "Thing is though, we have a choice. What kind of population of these do you want? Tight or loose?"

Jon had to think. "Hadn't thought of that. You have that much control?"

"What do you think we've been doing in this basement?" Dale said.

"I can make them all the same, or give the Y stems some variability."

Jon thought for a moment, pushing Dale's sarcasm away. "Let's keep them all the same. We can vary them later, depending on our results."

"We can't search forever to get the right answer," Dale said.

"We don't have forever," Jon said, putting his hand on Dale's arm, "just a few weeks, maybe less. Let me know when you have your first aliquots of product."

"Well, I can pretty much guarantee we'll have the product you want," Luiz said, standing to stretch, "but we really should plan to kick it to the next level pretty quickly. The only way we know this will work is if we actually get into the ECF to finish the construction in the wake of viremia."

"Luiz, we should do some toxicity studies first," Dale said, leaning over and in front of Jon to get Luiz's attention.

"Good point. We'll work with non-viremic rodents to check for tissue/organ damage."

"Good idea, Dale," Jon said, getting up to head upstairs. "How long?"

"A full three weeks for the full prep."

"That long?"

"Have to remember that we're also in the vaccine production business," Dale said, taking out a cigarette and turning to walk upstairs.

"Three weeks it is."

Jon headed upstairs after Dale. He took a deep breath. The process was underway. He and, in fact, the world, one way or another, would soon know the value of his idea.

# TEARING THE ARMS OFF THE FRAME

"What's she doing here?" Jasper asked, stopping in mid limp as he saw VP Legal was also in the room with the CEO.

"Jasper," Meredith said. To Cassie, the CEO sounded like she was talking to a seven-year-old truant. "She is your boss. I wanted to meet with her alone, and she recommended that you attend as well." Meredith tilted her head, still looking at Giles, and said, "Was Cassie wrong about that?"

"No, no, of course not."

"Then, Jasper, won't you please be seated?"

"I think that for once . . . there." He fell into the narrow wooden chair. "I will take your advice."

"OK," she said, "We are all busy. How do we proceed with CiliCold?" Cassie watched Meredith lean forward, elbows on the desk, running her hands back and forth over her temples and into her gray hair. "Cassie, can you bring us up to speed?"

"CiliCold is perfect for us. They are small, legally unprotected, and—"

"Unprotected?" Ms. Doucette asked. "No patent?"

"No, ma'am. Because they don't have a scientific process that reliably works, and they don't have a lawyer."

"Cretins."

The CEO ignored Jasper and turned to Cassie. "Just what is their process, so we can all hear it with the same words."

"To cure the common cold by preventing it."

"Bullshit."

"Thank you for not using that language here again," the CEO said, now looking at Jasper. "Cassie, how will it work?"

"By getting cells to, uh, essentially collaborate with the fluid surrounding them to make antibodies to the virus before the virus can attack and kill too many cells."

"But it doesn't work?"

"They will be testing it these next weeks."

"Jasper?"

He shrugged. "Maybe we should wait until we see if it works."

"If we do, then we'll have to wait on line," Cassie said, moving closer to the desk. "They are liquid-low with no collateral and can barely pay their bills for these experiments. They'll accept a fair offer." Cassie hesitated for a moment, looking down. Then she said, "Also, if the process doesn't work, the team there will find the one that does."

"You don't know that," Jasper said, with a loud exhale, shaking his head. "Please."

"Do continue, Cassie."

"The best way I can explain it is that there are moments when it's time for the technology."

"Moments?"

"Yes, at the beginning of the twentieth century, the new concept of the times was heavier-than-air travel. Even though we know that it was the Wright brothers who pulled it off, the fact was that many groups and teams were simultaneously working on it. The materials were finally right, and the ideas were right. It was time for it to work. Nobody knew who it would be, but they all knew, given the expertise and the resources, that someone would succeed and soon.

"In the sixties, it was organ transplantation. Same thing with computers in the 1980s. Apple, Osborne, IBM, Tandy, others were all working to create the first mass-produced PC. Nobody knew who it would be, but they all knew that it was time and that it would be someone. Again, the time was right. Like hot, dry kindling. Somebody would spark it."

"Sorry to rain on your parade, Cassie," Jasper said, both hands on his right thigh, moving it back and forth, "but cold fusion is a huge counterexample."

"Are you feeling all right, Jasper?" Meredith asked.

"Been better, but OK."

"No, it's not," Cassie said after a moment, turning back to Meredith. "That excitement was not driven by undeniable progress, but undeniable fraud."

"Anybody else working on this?" the CEO asked, taking a pen and pad out of her desk. She scribbled for a moment.

"Some European teams are taking a keen interest in the B cell manipulation, but—"

"Can we please get to the fuck—the real point?" Jasper said, dropping his hand on the table.

Cassie jumped, but noticed that Meredith didn't twitch.

Silence for a moment. "Please enlighten us, Jasper."

"Will the board approve this?"

"I disagree, Jasper," Meredith said. "That's not the point at all."

Cassie felt as much as heard the new ice in the CEO's voice.

"The question is whether the board needs *a priori* notification of the purchase," the CEO finished, looking right at Jasper.

"What? A prio—"

"Cassie?" the CEO nodded to her VP Legal.

"We are so used to acquisitions being a money drain," Cassie said. "Buying Tanner cost almost a half a billion dollars. This is going to cost only a half a million, if that." After a moment, she decided to smile. "We've actually never purchased a company so small."

"So you see, Jasper, even though this isn't exactly a petty-cash purchase, it is well below the threshold required for the board's financial approval."

"I think it's wise to let the board know what you're doing anyway," he said, struggling to sit up straight in the small chair. "It's not just about the money."

"You think it's wise, but not required? Am I hearing that right?"

"I didn't say that, Meredith. Don't forget the I clause."

Cassie was suddenly confused. "I don't know what that—"

"You would if you knew your job, 'boss,'" Jasper said, putting air quotes around *boss*.

"The reason you don't know, Cassie, is the reason most people don't know," Meredith said, elbows on her desk, hands rubbing back and forth over each other. "It's never been invoked."

"Not until now, anyway," Giles added.

"And why is that, Jasper?"

"The I clause states that should there be an acquisition that moves the company in a new direction, potentially exposing the company to unforeseen peril and new risk, the board needs to be notified before the purchase."

"No, it does not say that."

"It most certainly does, Meredith."

"Check your language, Jasper," Meredith said, shaking her head. "It says the board should be available for advice in an innovative but perilous venture."

She then turned to Cassie. "The I stands for 'innovation.'"

Cassie watched Jasper leaned back in his chair, attempting but failing to cross his fat legs. "Well, don't you need their—"

"No."

"Wh—"

"The purchase is minuscule, the risk is small, and the reward is great."

Doucette faced Jasper. "The I clause does not apply." Holding Jasper's stare, she said, "Cassie? Move forward with the purchase."

"Right away."

"Questions? Adjourned. Cassie, can you please stay behind."

Cassie watched Jasper's hands as they gripped the chair arms. She thought he was going to tear the wooden arms right off the frame.

# CURE FOR NO DISEASE

"What's your take?"

The CEO saw that Cassie didn't have to think long.

"He will come after you hard, Ms. Doucette."

Meredith was quiet, waiting to hear what else Cassie would say.

The VP-Legal, head up and looking back at her, added, "CiliCold was my idea, but I wonder if it's worth the risk."

Meredith leaned over her hands that were folded on the desk. "Risk? To whom?"

"To you, of course."

Meredith was surprised and pleased, but kept the smile off her face. "It's not your motif to actually care about anyone else, Cassie," she said, rising. "But thank you. I'll be fine."

The CEO walked around the large desk to sit next to her VP-Legal. "Actually, you are the one at stake here, Cassie. Jasper only hates me because I placed you above him. He hates you for what you represent."

"Which is?"

"A threat to the core weakness that drives all that bluster and rage."

Meredith paused. She knew the easy conversation was over. *You've already lost Jasper's support*, she thought. Why run the same risk with Cassie?

Heart thumping, Meredith inhaled. Then she said, "Cassie, I am worried about your load . . ." followed by, in a softer voice, "and you."

She watched Cassie pull herself up straight in the chair. "I can handle it all, Ms. Doucette, as I have so far."

"Yes." Meredith stretched her legs out. "Everybody thinks that they have enough runway, right until the moment that they slam into the mountain. There's not much runway left under you, Cassie, and the mountain is close."

"What are you saying?"

Meredith leaned over to her. "Look at your load. Litigation. How many trials do we have ongoing? Four? Five? Then there's the Tanner breakup and assimilation. And now, this CiliCold matter."

Looking at her silent VP, Meredith had never seen such emotionless eyes. They sent a chill through her, but it was too late to stop now. She swallowed.

"It's not an insult, Cassie." Meredith lowered her voice. "I do not know everything about you, but I know enough to know that you carry hot anger in you. I can understand that in your business, this can be a good thing. But only for a while."

Meredith watched as Cassie refused to look at her, staring at the empty chair behind the desk. "I will not deny what you say to me, Ms. Doucette . . ."

The VP took a deep breath, and Meredith waited through the time in silence. "My pain is my own. It is a force that has served me well so far." And in a voice that was tighter, more forced, Cassie said, "It hurts only me, not Triple S."

Meredith gently pulled her own lower lip for a moment. She had to pursue this. "Cassie? Dr. Franklin may have had another point of view." She reached over to her desk, pulling out a folded sheaf of papers, then handing them to Cassie.

She noticed Cassie's sharp intake of air as the VP-Legal read the top page. "He was our enemy in trial."

"No. He was a plaintiff's expert who disagreed with us. That does not make him an existential threat. He was not there to destroy you, or us. And now he is dead. Suicide."

Cassie sat still.

"Triple S's interests were served by the demolition of only his argument, not him."

Meredith sighed, then continued. "I am no lawyer, but there are many ways you could have taken his points apart. Get the negative reviews of his papers. Collect the testimony of other experts who have criticized him. Find his own comments that undercut his current ones, which is what the attorney representing us tried to do before you summarily dismissed him. That's how you sow doubt in a jury's mind.

"And," Meredith continued, now turning to face Cassie, "you know all this, right? Yet you destroyed him, going way out of your way to do it."

Cassie began to speak, but Meredith held her hand up. Sink or swim, she thought, palms sweating. "I'm showing you a mirror. For your own sake, look into it with me.

"I can't imagine how much energy you and your team put into discovering that jewelry, then tracking down his paramour. You could have driven a stake through the heart of his testimony with only 25 percent of the work. Instead you went out of your way to assassinate his career."

Meredith stood and, turning around, sat on her desk, facing Cassie.

"And what of the collateral damage? His wife? Grandchildren? The attorneys and paralegals who may have disagreed with your approach but felt compelled to follow your directions? That is how monsters start. Insecure people, redirected to a scorched-earth mission from an authority they follow without question."

The VP-Legal stood then turned and walked to the window, the sun's tepid light now failing to illuminate the room. Then turning and pointing to Meredith, she said, "You're trying to destroy me like you are doing to Jasper."

Meredith, heart in her throat, stood and faced her. Now or never, she thought. "No, and you know that. I am trying to keep you from becoming Jasper, and I'm praying that I'm not too late."

"I don't need your help for that," Cassie said, both hands outstretched, balled into fists. "I could never be like that disgusting, hideous creature."

"How do you think Jasper got the way he is?" the CEO asked, gesturing to the seat where he sat earlier. "He wasn't born that way. He had some terrible event happen that led him to think that twisting his emotions and intellect would protect him. I don't know what that was, and it's too late to stop him now. He must face a fate he chose decades ago. But you, Cassie? What about you?"

"I—"

"Don't bother answering me, Cassie. Answer yourself. What disease do you have that your behavior cures?"

"My behavior's a companion that has saved my life."

It was beyond twilight now, but Meredith fought the urge to flip the light switch. "I don't doubt you for a minute," she said, returning to her desk chair. "That was true, at one point. But it's no friend and protector for you anymore.

"Lose what doesn't help anymore, that does nothing but keep you so angry you will explode. Do you know your Melvin?"

She shook her head, saying "No, but I have learned much from life." She licked her lips, then after a moment, said, "Maybe too much."

Meredith stood, heart going out to her injured colleague. She walked up to Cassie, gently holding the VP's upper arms in her hands, saying, "Don't learn so much that there is no difference between you and what you hate."

# ZENITH

What would she wear? Would she show those legs? A hint of cleavage? If so, was it for him?

He had become two Jon DeLeons, one wholly focused on his research, the other focused on getting and holding her attention.

He and Breanna walked to a restaurant on the first real spring day, the first afternoon when the air was alive with rain that turned ice-encrusted mud to warm black dirt, and the occasional buzz of an insect startled.

They talked for two hours that day.

Jon believed that she saw him as a new friend, maybe a kind of a mentor, maybe a fantasy love interest.

He'd known lots of lust days. But that was not how he saw his Breanna.

With Breanna, it would never be about the sex. It would be about the connection.

Yes. Yes. Yes.

That was it. He wanted to connect to her emotionally, to feel an emotional need for her as she would for him.

Of course, if sex came along for the ride, well—

But he knew that sex would ruin it.

Things would never be the same at work.

She would come to hate him, despise him, for what he would represent—his enticement, her weakness. Her failure.

He could not bear the concept, the very idea that she would hate him.

So sex was out.

Yet the absence of sex elevated the relationship, kept it pure. She redeemed him, enlightened him, restored him. That she needed his strength actually made him strong. This was all so transcendental, well above the tawdry and the physical.

And with this nexus established, he connected to himself, and his wholeness poured through on him.

He knew he was tired, but fatigue didn't matter. His weight fell, yet he did not miss food, seeking instead this new emotional sustenance. This tantalizing gift of heaven was his to relish each day that he worked with her. And while he was a little dizzy at times, his work focus was never sharper.

He spent hours with Luiz and Dale, debating the critical experiment's details. Which rhesus should be chosen? Why? Which viral infectant? Why? When should Luiz release the partial antibodies? Why? He was re-devoted to the B cells and the project because he was devoted to Breanna. He could not control her, but maybe, just maybe he could steer CiliCold to a positive course. He would keep her safe by making the company strong.

It would save her and would also save him.

And when she needed him for a work issue, or just to talk things through, he was there.

Wild heart racing, he listened, speaking only in quiet tones, occasionally touching a sleeved arm or tapping her hand in support, providing the answer to her administrative question.

He did not ever pretend to believe that he knew her heart or even what she thought of him. He believed that she knew his, and hoped and prayed that she did not mind the knowledge.

To Jon, this was the emotional golden age. He had never used drugs, but if this was how drug use felt, he got it. With Breanna as the focal point of his life, he was focused, directed, connected to all good in the universe, high on life. The zenith days.

# FULL POWER DESCENT

Wild Bill felt his heart beating faster as he headed down to the basement, the tip-off that anxiety and despair were both moving in at once.

To Bill, that summed up life.

"Welcome back, WB," Bill heard Luiz call out. "What's up in DC?"

"Not us, thank God," Wild Bill said, waving to Dale and Luiz. He pulled a Wild Bill into a seat by the kitchen table. "How's the work going?" He looked at both of them eagerly.

"Slow progress," Dale said, head in a cage. "Toxicity studies showed nothing to worry about. That is, if you're going to treat hamsters."

"Hey now," the regulator said, leaning forward until the back of the chair supported his weight on the table. "That's great. When do we jump to monkeys and really take this idea out for a spin, Luiz?"

"Working on their baby B's right now."

"When the boss gets his head out of his ass."

Wild Bill shifted his weight backward so the chair was resting on all four legs and saw Luiz look up from his notebook and stare at Dale.

Dale pulled his head out of the cage. "Yeah well, I'm just saying that he's acting odd again," the virologist said.

"How so?" Bill asked, voice even. He knew a scientist had to be critical, but Dale could really get under your skin.

"Not concentrating. I go by his office and I catch him dreaming off into space. He doesn't always follow conversations you have with him, and when he does, he fumbles his answer out."

"Always been a bit of a dreamer," Luiz said.

"He sure as shit dreamed this idea up," Wild Bill said, stroking his sideburn.

"You trying to make that ridiculously long thing even longer by pulling on it," Dale said, pointing a finger at the regulator.

WB ignored him. This guy is snipping my last nerve, he thought. "Jon's probably tired. Anybody know when he had a decent vacation? Not an early Friday, but a whole week off?"

"He could if he wanted," Dale said, turning to Bill.

Take it easy, WB thought. "Sure, and that would work right up until you didn't get paid. If you ask me, he's in an impossible position." He shrugged. "Look, Jon's made himself invaluable, and now we can't do without him."

"And we're going right down the tubes." Dale wiped a sweaty hand on his sweaty brow.

That tore it.

"Hey, Dale," Wild Bill said, standing up from the chair. "He saved the company's ass one time, you remember that? And that was because of a vaccine lot that you screwed up, correct?"

Dale just stared at Bill.

WB walked over to him. "And why did that happen?"

Dale opened his mouth.

"Don't bother answering. We don't care anymore, But remember, nobody tore into you because of that failed batch. That failure was your fault, but Jon didn't criticize you in front of the rest of us, didn't talk behind your back and didn't dock your pay. He was completely supportive of your sorry ass."

"Our only chance," the regulator said, taking a deep breath and returning to his chair near the large work table, "like it or not, is to see his idea through." He turned. "By the way, Dale, when was the last company-saving idea you had?"

"Today. It was to sell the company," Luiz said.

"Brilliant," Wild Bill said, crossing his arms in front of him. "And who would buy us if all we are is a vaccine farm? You tell me."

Dale put his hands up and let them fall, slapping hard against his thighs, "I'm just sayin'—"

"Jon is who Jon is. We all know it. Your 'just sayin'' doesn't educate anybody. We're way ahead of you on that."

"Dale think's it's a woman," Luiz said, scratching his head. "That Jon's in love, or at least in lust."

"So what?" the regulator said, sitting back down. "He's raising money for our group to stay in business a few more months. So what if he has a female interest? And I'm not saying he does. What do you want him to do instead, stay home and study your damn notes? Think you're sick of all of this? Imagine how he feels."

"What I want him to do is straighten up before he ruins this company."

"You don't get that choice, Dale." WB walked over to the table bathed in fluorescent light. "If it weren't for him, this place would have been ruined two years ago, and you would have been thrown out on your ear then. What would you have done? Go work for Pfizer Fucking Pharmaceuticals? I'm sure they'd be happy to have both you and your hygiene."

Wild Bill stuck his face into Dale's. "You pay a price for having Jon as your leader. That price is that he loses his way sometimes. You don't get to pick and choose the parts of a personality you like. You take the whole, the good with the bad."

"Say what you want, Wild Bill," Dale said, arms folded across his chest, lab coat about to pop at the biceps. "He's losing his grip and it will cost us."

"In all his emotional throes and mysteries, Jon came up with a good idea. You didn't. We are working on his idea. As far as I can see," WB said, rubbing his neck, "the only one causing trouble is you. Maybe you should be the one who gets laid."

"Laid?" Dale said. "What . . . you mean with a female?"

"You should try one sometime. I'm sure that there are some species that will have you."

Dale just stared.

"I'm heading out," Wild Bill said, walking over to his chair, putting it back where it was. "Just give his idea a chance. Can you do at least that, Dale?"

WB stared at Dale until he got the virologist to meet his eyes.

"For a few days."

The regulator headed back upstairs. Dale had pissed him off. Dale pissed everybody off, he thought. He also knew that although he'd shut Dale down, it wouldn't keep. Dale was the wrathful Weeble, always bouncing back up with more sarcasm.

And Dale was right.

Shit.

Jon was losing his grip. His head wasn't in the company, and wherever it was, it wasn't doing Jon any good.

He still dressed well, but looked bad. And the boss had no sense of humor anymore. He said he enjoyed his work, but like the guy who says he loves hunting but never hunts, things just weren't fitting.

Maybe it was a woman, maybe not. But it sure as shit was something.

He knocked at Jon's office.

Again, then again.

"Come on in."

Wild Bill opened the door and saw Jon writing something by hand.

"High tech failing you these days, Jon," he said, pointing to the pen Jon had been using.

"Sometimes, only the handwritten word works. Sit?" Jon asked, nodding to a chair.

"I'll stand for this one, but thanks. I'm just here to tell you Jon that people are noticing."

"Noticing? What?"

Wild Bill saw that Jon had put the pen down. "You."

"What about me? Who?"

Wild Bill waved his hand. "Jon, I'm not staying for a third degree. You deserve a warning. You just got one. People know that you're off-kilter."

"What? Not acting right about what? Is not raising more mon—"

Wild Bill put both hands up. "Protest all you want. Things aren't right with you. You know it. They know it. The American people know it. Now, that's all anybody knows, but they do know that."

Bill leaned over the boss's desk, letting both hands support him.

"What the hell is it with you and women? You're like an iron bar just waiting for the woman magnet to pull you in. With them, you are connected, energized. Without, you're—"

Jon slouched in his seat. "I'm tired, Wild Bill."

"Shit on a stick, Jon. I've seen you tired before." Bill stood up straight. "Seen you pull consecutive all-nighters in the lab with the team, then go out and give talks all day. You're not working anywhere near that hard, but you look and act like it."

"OK, OK. I get the point."

"Whatever the hell it is, Jon, fix it."

They looked at each other across the desk.

Finally, Wild Bill turned and walked to the door. Then he whirled. "Jon, you have a big brain, but there are some things even you don't get, such as women, my friend. The only way you can deal with the enigmatic bag they put over your head is to rip it off and walk away. Put your mind elsewhere and make damn sure you and your body follow it."

Jon turned and looked out the window of his office, to the rain-sodden West Lafayette.

They knew now. They all knew.

Heaven had turned into hell.

He turned to his laptop with new fervor, then stopped, turned again, and worked on penning his tenth note in two weeks to her, caught in the emotional black hole's pull.

> Date: March 3, 2016
> Subject:
>
> Cassie,
>
> I attached my latest notes about the current experiment. They are all nervous and excited about its potential results.
>
> Meanwhile, day-to-day operations are disheveled. The virologists and our regulator really had it out yesterday . . . Jon is sleepwalking through his days, and nobody really knows when our project administrator will be back. I am worried about them all, especially Jon. Be good to see you soon. Breanna

# GOOD LUCK TO US ALL

"Everything's in place," Luiz explained two days later, pointing out the nodes on his complex flow diagram.

"Stability?" Jon rubbed his eyes. They were coming to the end soon, and in the next week, he would know, they all would know, whether his idea would work. He choked back a cough from the cold he had had several weeks before.

"The partial antibodies look good," Luiz responded. My baby Bs see them as antibodies. They store them like antibodies and release them like antibodies. The B cells are ready, Jon."

"Only the undifferentiated ones, right?"

"Yep. It would have been much tougher to program a B cell designed to make a specific antibody to stop and make a fragment. Here."

"I saw the toxici—" The S4 buzzed, and Jon reached for it.

"Jon, this is Breanna."

"Breanna, hi. What can I do for you?" Resisting the urge to walk away to take the call alone, he shifted the S4 from his right to left hand, enabling him to sign a requisition for Luiz.

She was talking about tax difficulties, but his heartbeat was hard and rapid as he luxuriated in her voice.

"Yeah. I bet that it's pretty complicated. Sounds like we need some help." He thought for a moment then said, "How about if I call our old tax group? I'm sure this depreciation issue has come up before. Maybe they can get someone over here to help out. How soon do you need them?"

"Early this week, if possible. Would love to get the taxes done by Friday."

"It would be a record if they went out early. How about if I call today?"

"That would be great, Jon."

He hung up.

"Tax issues? More accountant stuff going wrong?"

Dale.

Jon's anger was on him before he knew it. What did Dale care? Always nosing where he didn't belong. Accounting had smoothed out their operation these past two months. Didn't he get paid last week? Damn guy needed to focus on this experiment and not how someone else was doing one's job.

Jon turned from him then, seething. He waited a second, then another, then 3, 4, 5 until he was past his reaction, then said, "Yep. We could use a little help. Don't want to go to debtors' prison."

"No such thing anymore."

Jon snorted. "Ask Wesley Snipes. Let's get back to it. Luiz says we're ready. What do you think, Dale?"

"Will take forty-eight hours to get Bessie ready for her new cells. Twenty-four hours after that."

"Wednesday."

"Yep. We'll inject her with a load of virus. We should know in two days whether the partial antibodies along with the ECF kick off the antiviral attack."

"When should the viral titers be down?"

Luis scratched his chin for a moment. "Thursday afternoon, probably. Friday for sure."

"Think we should do two monkeys?" Jon asked.

Luiz and Dale looked at each other. "Verification is a good idea for sure, but we only have three left: Bessie, Leopold, and Lorraine. If something goes wrong that is correctable, we can always do the correct—"

"In series, not in parallel."

"Yep."

Jon thought for a second. "Whatever you think best. Whatever happens this week, I want you to know that you each have earned your pay."

Then he stuck his hand out and shook each of theirs.

"Good luck to us all." Jon turned and headed back upstairs.

# WARNING BEACON

Next day, Jon was with Breanna, discussing some tax issues, when Robbie called him over to her reception area. He hated to tear himself away from His Accountant. We resonate, he thought, hurrying downstairs. These accounting moments were luxuriant slivers of time for him, perfect moments that slowed his daily roller-coaster ride from excitement to despair then back.

"Dr. DeLeon," Robbie said, with her trademark smile, "this is Mr. David Bryson, from our previous tax office."

Jon shook the hand of the well-dressed man who held a leather briefcase. With every brown hair in place and a disarming smile, he looked to Jon more like the classic salesman than a corporate tax wienie.

"Yes," Jon said, "from T&T Tax Associates. Thanks for agreeing to help with our tax problems, David. Hope it won't tax you too much."

They shook hands. "The pun was unintentional."

"Yeah. Kind of heard that one," David said with an easy smile. "Sounds like a couple of days here is all I need."

"Let me walk you up to accounting." The two turned and headed up the three flights of stairs. In a few moments, they were in Breanna's office.

"Breanna," Jon said on arrival, "this is David. David Bryson from our old accounting firm."

"Oh," David said. "Any way we can change that to 'current'?"

Jon laughed. A taxman with a sense of humor. "Not with Breanna here."

As Breanna and David shook hands, a yellow warning beacon started flashing in Jon's mind.

"I'll leave you two to work out these de—"

S4 went off.

He pulled it from his belt and stared at the number.

His heart all but exploded out of his chest.

He raised his left arm, right arm clutching the phone to his chest like a treasured possession. "Will you both excuse me, please?"

Not waiting for their response, he turned and exited, phone to chest, keeping it there until he walked halfway down the hall.

"Rayiko?"

"Jon." Her voice enveloped him like hot moist sauna steam on a frigid day. He swore he could almost inhale her.

"First, how . . . how are you?"

"Oh, I'm doing OK. My brother is making a slow recovery but can't stay by himself yet."

"How is your family?"

"They are good, but the long time away is wearing on us all."

"Can't believe that you've been on the west coast for six weeks."

"I've been back twice."

"Oh."

"Yeah. I couldn't be from my family for that long, so I've come back for two weekends, including this last one."

"That . . . that was a good call," Jon said. His strength was gone, and he felt weightless, inconsequential on the phone. He closed his eyes and tried to focus on the conversation. "Sounds like your brother really needed you."

*You can't blame her for not contacting you., he thought,* It was the weekend and she needed her family. What was she supposed to do, not see her family for a month, then call him from the airport as soon as she arrived? Man up.

"How are things there?"

Her voice was salve on his angry heart-wound.

"Be nice to have you back. I think it's time for Chris—"

Disconnect.

He closed his eyes, holding tight to the door edge, trying to squeeze it into oblivion. He only wanted a few words with Rayi—

"Dr. DeLeon." Robbie came around the corner, in his face before he knew it.

"Whoa. OK." He took a step back. "Who i—"

"IUPUI on the phone. Did you agree to lecture their postdocs?"

He rubbed his left hand deliberately from his left eye to his right and then back again, letting all the epithets he was tempted to hurl at his impossible schedule pass between them, unspoken. Then he replied, “Sure, Robbie, of course. On the way.”

On Friday, he pulled into CiliCold’s parking lot through air that was thick with rain. It poured off the rim of his hat and out of his shoes when he walked into the office.

“Robbie,” he said, walking through, “we the only ones here today so far?”

“Yep. But, Dr. DeLeon, I just got a call from the day care. My boy is throwing up and now has a fever. I may need to leave early to get him and take him home.”

“Not much choice about that, Robbie.” His eyes were on fire, and his brain felt like clay after a long night studying Luiz’s work on partial antibiotic generation. “What time’s the IU call?”

“Oh!” she said, as she looked at her calendar. “A half hour ago.”

“It was at eight?”

“Sorry, I should have reminded you.”

“Don’t worry.” They’d probably say no anyway, he thought. “By the way, how’s the ringer who’s helping with accounting?”

“OK, I guess, I haven— Oh!” She hurried over to her desk, picking up the phone, dropping her head as she listened. Then she turned around. “It’s my day care.”

“Sure,” he said, nodding and heading back to his office.

He lost himself in his work and thoughts of his Breanna until late that afternoon, when he called the medical school.

He acted surprised that they turned his grant request down flat.

“Isn’t the Clinical Center for Translational Science there to help programs like ours here in West Lafayette, Dr. Sweams?” he said.

“Of course, Dr. DeLeon, but if you are only doing research in primates, then we are not ready for the next step in humans.”

The voice sounded distant, dry, disinterested.

“So what you are saying is that there needs to be some evidence of success in humans before you are willing to fund this?” A hot acid, bile taste coated the back of his throat.

“Yes.”

“What if we have a positive primate study?”

"You think that eventually, you will cure the common cold in humans. Am I hearing you right, Dr. DeLeon?"

"I am telling you that we are in our final phase of animal testing and will be ready to engage with others to plan human trials shortly."

"In what publications can I read about this?"

Jon thought fast. "When we have completed our primate work, we will submit our manuscript for publication."

"Interesting. Any idea where?"

"*Nature*."

Jon winced at the stifled guffaw on the line.

"Well, you're pretty ambitious, I'll give you that. Send me the published manuscript, your CV, and biosketches of your team when the manuscript is out."

"That will take months. We need the financial support now. All—"

"I'm sorry, but that's where this ends for now. Really appreciate the conversation though."

"Thank you." Jon stabbed the End button and dropped the S4 on the leather seat.

It bounced, then rang right back at him.

"Jon, you'd better come on down."

It was Dale.

# FULL VIRAL LOAD

Date: March 4, 2016
Subject:

Cassie,

The experiment was a failure. The virologists are dejected and Jon is saying nothing to anybody. Leadership here is on the verge of collapse. No one is speaking, and for once, the virologists are not filling their notebooks with observations. I have faith that Jon will pull us out of this though. He has not let this grp down yet.

Breanna

He was down the basement steps in twenty seconds.

"Tell me."

"Bessie has a full viral load," Wild Bill said, barely audible.

"What? Say that again?"

"The virus reproduced in the presence of the partial antibodies."

Jon's pulse rocketed at the implication. "The partial antibodies didn't kill them? No neutralization of the virus?"

Silence.

Then Dale said, "'Fraid not."

Jon's strength vanished, and he felt himself collapsing on the basement stairs, banging his back hard against one of the stair lips. He just heard a muffle of voices around him. His left arm was completely numb to the shoulder. Breathing fast. Panting. He caught up with his breath, then forced it to slow down.

A few moments later, when he looked around, Wild Bill, Luiz, and Dale gathered around him.

Wild Bill patted his left shoulder. "Hey, Jon? You all right, man?"

"I . . . I just need a moment. I'll be all right."

"How's that arm?" the regulator asked.

"Better. How's yours?"

The two friends smiled.

"I just can't believe this," Jon said.

After a moment, someone said, "Jon?"

It was Luiz.

"We've checked the titers again and again. We gave a full infectious load on Wednesday, after the antibody testing was complete. Immunofluorescent testing yesterday showed that Bessie's undifferentiated B cells were releasing their partial antibodies."

"So far, so good, right?" Jon asked.

"Yes, but the viral production never stopped. It was like . . ." Luiz paused for a moment. "Like the partial antibodies weren't there."

"Actually . . ." Dale said. Jon sat up, struggling to hear him. "It looks a like, well, like the virus replication rate increased a little."

"But I reviewed it all again last night," Jon said, looking up into his friends' faces. "It all checked. Luiz, you sure you had the right DNA cocktail for the B cells? Did we use the right virus? What about—"

Wild Bill turned around and sat by Jon. "Everything checks, Jon. Just didn't work."

Jon looked down at his watch.

Four thirteen.

On a Friday.

Over.

"Well, let me get your notes and look them over this weekend. Then on Monday, we'll take—" He stopped. How could his idea have failed? "We'll take the next steps."

"Good idea," Dale said. "Let's clear out."

"Luiz, can you leave your note . . . notebook with Robbie? I'll pick it up on my way out. Oh. Guys?"

They turned to look at him.

"Can I have the room for about ten minutes or so?"
"Sure thing, Jon."
"Anything you need."
"OK."

## OFF THE BOOKS

Date: March 5, 2016
Subject:

Thank you for your last note, Breanna. We understand the deteriorating logistical situation there, and are moving at best possible speed to make our overtures to Dr. DeLeon.

The failure of the experiment was a disappointment. Some of our team fully expected it. Yet others are hopeful that they will move on to the next logical experimental step. This is a search that requires diligence to complete.

Things will begin to move very fast now. When the sale is complete, you will be welcome here at SSS. As you will see, your new salary here will make continued financial support from me unnecessary. Triple S takes care of its own. However, I am always here for you. This you know.

In the meantime, my commitment to you remains solid. We will continue to support Jackie in day care, and your apartment is yours for as long as you want it. Please continue to send to me (through the US postal service) your utility bills.

In the meantime, I have learned that after his last loss in court, Ethan has now stopped seeking custody of Jackie and Karen. The agreement is that he will not pay you alimony, will have no visitation rights, and will make no contact with either you or your parents. Your divorce will be final April 30 and you will have your children to yourself.

I have also learned that he and his girlfriend will be going to Oklahoma, his home state. I have emails showing that he has reached out to the state university in Stillwater, expressing an interest in becoming an assistant professor there.

He was vicious to you, and what he did to your daughter was hideous. I have already moved to have his request denied there. I only need to know what else you want me to do. If you like, I can ensure that he finds no position at the university there. I can and will pursue him for years, if that is what it takes to protect you. We have some time to decide, so give it some consideration.

It has been a busy time for you and me. It would be great to see Jackie and have some sweet "off the book" time with you. C

# LEAF OUT

Jon stayed in the CiliCold basement alone, fighting off the pain train, going back over this thought process. It had to inform him, point him to some point he missed: some B-cell issue, some viral change pre-injection.

Nothing.

Five minutes later, he had nothing but an empty mind. With no one around, he opened the door, letting defeat in—its accusations, its smell, its taste, its fury.

Then he got up and walked past Bessie, chock-full of billions of viruses, busily eating her food and chortling away. He noticed that when he passed, she stretched her hand out to him.

He shook his head, then called upstairs. "Shouldn't Bessie be sick?"

"Asymptomatic now. She'll be monkey-shit sick on Monday." Dale called back.

Jon headed up the steps to accounting, knocked on the door that moved on its own, preparing the right end-of-week goodbye for her. He wondered. Should he tell her about the failed experiment?

No, he decided. She probably had a stressful weekend coming already.

Just say goodbye.

He pushed the door open.

"Here it is, Breanna."

"You're my hero," she said to David, hand on his knee.

Jon froze, slammed in the chest by a hammer. Heart filled his ears with its pounding. Chest constricting, breathing quickened, he thought his left arm was gone. He was weightless, pointless, invisible, a wave on a current that had just been thumped into nonexistence.

*What do you want to do now,* he asked himself, *interrupt them? Say goodbye?*

He blinked several times then turned and walked to his office, closing the door, leaning his right side against the wall.

Disconnected.

He rocked to one side then the other, trying to avoid what he now saw had been speeding toward him for weeks, He exhaled in ragged gasps, barely taking in enough air in betw—

The phone rang.

Don't dare answer that.

Again, he waited minutes for the attack to pass, to feel his arm again.

Finally, he opened his office door and walked mindlessly down the steps to the first floor and to Robbie, picking up Luiz's notes.

"You don't look so good, Dr. DeLeon."

"Just . . . just looking forward to the weekend," he said, avoiding eye contact.

What a lie. The last thing he wanted was forty-eight hours to relive the last half hour. What was it that Stephen King said? Oh yeah—

"The thing that gets you about hell is the repetition."

Coatless, he walked to his car.

"I thought that he took it pretty well, considering," Luiz said into his cell, sitting down at home after just getting the evening fire going.

"Not bad. Let's see what happens Monday," Dale answered.

Luiz could barely hear his friend. "Sounds like you're calling from a bar."

"What if I am?"

"Going to take Wild Bill up on his idea?"

"About what?"

"Getting laid."

"Well, there may be a couple of species here that might find me interesting."

Date: March 5, 2016
Subject:

Cassie,

The week was a debacle. All but me have left for the weekend. Luiz, Dale, and Jon are out of ideas. Not a bad time for SSS to step in. I think everyone would climb into their lifeboat.

Breanna

Breanna was aware of much more that that though.

She and Jon had been drawing closer. She knew it, let it happen.

Less of a choice than a compassionate reaction to his running-on-empty lifestyle, his intelligence, and his kind heart.

And she knew that he was clearly falling for her: the unnecessary but kind notes, his ever-present willingness to listen to her. And his tendril reach for her emotions, not her body, had been enthralling.

But now, with the entry of another, the music was slowing, fainter. The Jon sway was coming to an end.

And she knew, hating it, that that last thought of hers just ended the dance.

Good luck, Jon, she wished.

That afternoon, with the first true Virginia rye grass breaking through the softening Indiana soil, the first robins skipping and jumping across the wet driveways, and the earliest tree buds announcing "leaf out" season, Jon threw his head into the brick wall of his house.

# 34

D*e-eep*

Crap.

The bike was turned over, seat down. Cristen, having already removed the anchoring bolt from the rear wheel and gripping the top of the tire to pull the entire assembly out, sighed at the ringtone.

Who was calling on Sunday?

Bad enough to get a flat tire, she thought. The three-mile ride on the slowly leaking rear tire had worn her out, but she'd rather repair it in her lighted garage than in the cold, under the darkening sky with its gusting winds.

Still gripping the wheel, she looked around for her phone.

*De-eep*

Not the garage.

Coming from the house.

First things first.

She bore down, pulling the wheel smoothly out of its lock connected only by the single dangle of the chain on the gear cassette.

*De-eep*

She separated the chain from the cassette.

*De-eep*

The rear wheel came away clean.

*De-eep*

"All right, all right." She carefully put the rear wheel with its flat tire against the wooden garage wall, stood up straight on the warm, worn carpet square. She lifted her hand to run it through her hair, but stopped in mid motion. Her hands were coated in black dirt and grease.

*De-eep*

She walked to the garage sink to wash them. She was going to wash with cold water, but that would never work with Finish Line, so she let the water run hot.

*De-eep*

She soaped and dried, then putting the towel down, she turned to walk into the house.

*De-eep*

She ignored the piles of papers and reams of safety report drafts that comprised the living room.

*De-eep*

And she walked into her study, to the right. The phone was on the cot she used to read and sleep on. She read its display.

Dana

The safety monitor pulled her head back.

The last two texts said it all:

Call.

Please.

She hit the phone icon, plopping herself onto the cot.

The phone rang.

Rang.

Rang.

No pickup.

Concerned now.

Goodness. Maybe Dana was in real trouble. The chemo hadn't bothered her friend much recently. She tried to remember—

"Cristen?"

"Dana, are you all right?'

"No. And neither are you."

Cristen got it at once.

Savages.

She choked back the stinging stomach contents that jammed their way up and into her mouth. "When and how much?"

"We meet with the skin strippers on Wednesday."

"We've already been flitched to the bone."

"I was just on the phone to Devin, Melanie, and Jake. You wouldn't believe h—"

"Yes, I would."

"Nervous they all are. They think they're out of the company."

Cristen gritted her teeth, trying to focus on the words that poured into her ear. SSS didn't give a damn about drug safety. Now, only she and Dana would be there to review the avalanche of safety concerns about SSS products.

And Dana . . . well.

"You know Dana. You and I talked about this possibility. They will hollow our group out, but they won't abolish it."

"Safety is critical."

"You and I think that—"

"We know it."

"And I think we should make that argument—when is it?"

"The 15th. A week from tomorrow."

"Let's make that argument then. But, Dana, I think you can expect extreme pushback."

"You mean they'll argue that what we do is not a priority?"

"No, just take our jobs."

Silence.

"They are amoral, Dana, and they are smart. And their cost cutting saves them money. Think about it." Cristen rolled over, onto her stomach. "You and I have done our jobs too well."

"What do you mean?"

"We pounce on problems right away. And we work well with the reg folks. So safety issues are quickly identified. Labels get changed. Public is informed. No meaningful law suits. No bad headlines for Tanner."

"Of course," Dana said. "I don't see why SSS—"

"Because 'no problems' with SSS translates to 'no need for the department' or 'no need for surveillance.' And—"

"What?"

"They can't be reasoned with."

"What do we do?"

Cristen knew. She knew from the first time those pigs showed up to bastardize their company, their department, weeks ago.

If they wanted a fight, then give them what they wanted.

But not the way they wanted it.

Not now.

Soon.

"You and I will work on our statements in the morning, before we start catching safety events."

"When is the meet again?"

"The 15th."

"K." More than enough time, the monitor thought.

"Can we change their minds?" Dana asked. To her friend, it sounded like the head of safety was almost in tears.

Of course we can't change them, she thought, turning over again, twisting her toes deep into the carpet pile.

"No. But we can make sure they know where we stand." Cristen felt the new steel enter her voice. "See you."

"OK. Sorry about surprising you with this."

The safety monitor's throat caught at the thought of the coming death of her friend. "Listen, it's warming up. Want to go jewelry shopping?"

"Love to, but I can't be out late."

"I'll be by to get you at two."

"Great. Kev would love to see you."

Cristen hung up and walked back to the garage. She returned with the baseball bat—a thirty-four incher.

Wham.

She brought her dad's bat down squarely on the thin-legged table that held the manuscripts she'd been reading.

All the liver enzyme papers went flying.

Wham. She brought it down again.

Wham. Wham. Wham. Wham. Wham. WHAM. WHAM.

In two minutes, the table was matchsticks. Unreadable pages were strewn everywhere.

And she had decided.

Her dad would not approve, but that was OK.

He would understand.

She had eight days, and just one more duty to perform first.

Pulling her Dad's Colt .45 down from the living room shelf, she wondered who should get her bike. She couldn't leave it here by itself. That would never do.

And God knows, they wouldn't let her take it where she would soon be headed.

For now though, she thought, standing up and taking a leisurely stretch, back to removing the split inner tube from the tire before she headed over to Dana's.

# WHAT ABOUT BESSIE?

Monday, March 8, 1:13 a.m.

Jon rolled over. His head still ached, and after little rest Saturday night, he craved the unearned peace of mind that can come with sleep. But turning from the clock, he understood that there would be no rest tonight.

The thoughts came like a waterfall.

What happened last week? What could he have done to prevent the failed experiment? What about Breanna? How could he have gained her affection then lost it? What did he miss in the partial antibody concept? What virus had Dale tested them against? Why point her to a stranger? How long could the company survive? Should he have a big meeting or tell each employee individually about the failure? Why did Breanna desert him? Hadn't he done nothing but be kind? Had he done nothing right? Why was he losing her? What did he do? Robbie trusted him to take care of her job for her. How could he let her down? Where did things go wrong with Breanna? Would Robbie have to work for someone who did not care for her like he did? Why couldn't Breanna see that he cared for her, wanted only good for her, would work to make the good happen?

At 6:17 a.m., five hours later. Two minutes late.

Time to go to work.

Time to ruin people's lives.

This cheese grater of a day was going to work, rubbing his brain raw.

He could only think in extremes. He showered, loathing the process, chose clothes, loathing the choice, pulled his car out, loathing the Cherokee. The sunlight that managed to penetrate the dirty closed window to warm his face could not penetrate his mind.

Jon was focused on the destruction of his friends' careers, friends who had looked to him, counted on him, trusted him, were loyal to him.

And then there was Breanna, the stew in which all his thoughts marinated. She was focused on a non-employee who did not look after her, care for her, want the best for her like he did.

He pulled up, and before he stepped out of the car, a gleaming black car pulled up next to him, stopped, and the driver's door opened.

Bryson.

With flowers.

Jon's left arm went numb, his mind flaming out.

"Hi, Dr. DeLeon."

"Hello, David. How are things going?" The Professional took charge.

"Couldn't be better. I'm glad I ran into you." They stopped just outside the entryway.

"I wanted to drop these off for Breanna. Just to show my appreciation for her devotion to her work. She was right—it was a tough depreciation issue."

"Did you—I know she will be glad to get the flowers—did you get the tax situation resolved?"

*Maybe you should just take them to her yourself, Jon,* Jon's mind hissed at him. *Wouldn't that be a nice touch?*

"All taken care of. We're going to lunch to celebrate."

Of course. After all, Jon thought, all he had for her was to say that she would be losing her job soon. What a contrast.

Jon inhaled a short, sharp gasp of air at the tight grip that his left little and ring finger numbness had on him.

"I know that she has had some tough issues to deal with, Dr. DeLeon. But she keeps her focus on her work. Always gracious, always courteous, always so kind, always positive. And she admits her mistakes. She's quite a catch. Hey, man, what happened to your head?"

Jon was dizzy. "Have a good time. You earned it, and I really appreciate your coming down to help us."

"My pleasure. I know you are making a scientific breakthrough, and I'm glad that I could play a small role in supporting you."

"Thanks, Bryson, we really needed your help."

He walked inside and up to his office but, once inside, turned and left, the idea of being alone yet once more after the weekend repelling him.

The failed experiment.

His failed-idea autopsy was waiting.

His stomach rolled over.

He ran his hands though his hair, turned, and walked down, down, down the steps to the basement.

Luiz and Dale.

They had just arrived, but it seemed like they were waiting for him.

"Any idea what happened?" Jon asked, leaving his coat on.

"Well, it just didn't work, is what happened," Dale said, sitting at the kitchen table. Behind him, a monkey played in its cage, plinking the bars with its fingers.

"What kind of viral loads we looking at, Dale?"

"Pretty big. We've seen larger, but these are significant."

"And your B-cell babes performed well," Jon said, turning to Luiz.

"Uh, yeah, Jon," Luiz said, looking over at him from the spare equipment table. "The partial antibody levels in the plasma were as high as we hoped to produce." Luiz pursed his lips.

"They just didn't kill the virus," Dale added.

"Where's Bessie now?"

Behind me to the right," Dale said, without looking up. He was taking a cigarette out. Jon was going to stop him but caught himself. Why bother? The place would be deserted in two weeks anyway.

Jon's S4 sang out the special ringtone he'd programmed especially for her.

"Breanna?" he said. "Good morning. What can I do for you?"

"Just wanted to tell you that I'm taking an early lunch."

"Jon?" It was Dale. "We have a really serious issue here. Can't you put the phone down for a moment?"

If Jon's phone was a rock, he would have hurled it right at Dale's head. Jon turned away.

"What did you say?" he asked into the phone.

"Offered to take me to lunch. That was very sweet of him."

"Jon, can we—" Dale-monotone kept going.

"Yes, well, you have a good time." He hung up.

Jon's head was bursting, and he rocked a little before he rested both hands on the work table for support.

In a moment, he turned. "Well, Dale, what do you want to talk about that can't seem to wait just a few sec—"

"Jon, we have to get out of this dream world and face the reality—What are you looking at now?"

Jon was staring over Dale's right shoulder into Bessie's cage. Then all walked over to it. He heard the chatter between Breanna and

Bryson as they walked by the stairwell a floor above, his stomach mad-flopping with the reminder that she had a new hero. He gritted his teeth, clenching his neck muscles until they were a painful mass, his head frozen in place.

Just a moment of scientific clarity to see what was going on just inches from my face, he thought. Please, God, please.

"Hey, guys," Jon said in a voice full of pain and wonder. "What happened to Bessie?"

# PNV-154

"Luiz," Jon said, peering into the cage at the young rhesus, who had turned from her food and scampered to the front of cage, reaching her hand out to Jon. "Why isn't she sick?"

"What the—" Dale said, behind him.

"Dale, what virus did you give her again?"

"You only grilled me on it five times." Dale scooted around Jon to his laptop on the table. "Picornavirus PNV-154."

Jon wrinkled his brow, fist-tapping it. "Why a picorna?"

"A logical choice. It's known to cause the sniffles in monkeys."

"Plus," Luiz said, "she had no immunity to it."

"Well," Jon said, stroking the greying hair over his left ear, "she should be sick, right? All that virus on board. Sneezing, febrile, maybe nauseous and vomiting?"

Jon noticed that Luiz and Dale had their heads close to his on either side, looking at Bessie, who looked back at them, then nodding her head, scooted to the far end of her cage, turned, nodded, then rushed back to them, nodding again.

"She's having a good time," Jon said, walking away from the cage to sit on the steps. "If you guys have an explanation, then I'm all ears."

Dale sat down, rubbing his forehead with both thumbs. "Let's just all take this one step at a time." He looked at his notebook, then back at both of them. "Jon, she got the right virus. Here are my assays." Dale brought the laptop over, carrying it by its screen.

"Yeah," Jon said, looking over the Excel sheet, "in vitro tests confirm the bug."

"PNV-154 went in," Dale said, pointing to one collection of cells, "and PNV-154 multiplied in her." He pointed to another collection of cells on the spreadsheet.

"Since she's not sick, she must have had immunity then," Luiz said.

"And we ruined the experiment," Dale said. "Damn."

"But wait," Jon said. "Dale, the virus multiplied. If she had immunity, PNV-154 would have been neutralized well before it had a change to infect thousands of her cells and reproduce itself."

"Well," Dale said, putting the laptop down on a stack of papers, "we can inject the same virus into another monkey and see if they get sick—oh." The laptop slipped off the stack. Jon caught it.

"Thanks."

"That's another rhesus," Luiz said.

Quiet. Then they all nodded

"We have to know."

"Let's also check the original immune tests."

"Goodness, Jon, what for?"

Jon turned, throwing a hard stare at Dale. "To make sure we didn't miss any immunity on Bessie's part, Dale. Something happened. Or didn't happen. We have to figure this out."

"What's all the hubbub?"

"Hey, Wild Bill," Jon said, turning around to look up the stairs.

"Anything going on down here I should know about?" he said, all smiles.

"No," Dale flat-lined, returning to sit at the table in front of the laptop.

"Actually, we're not really sure what we have here, Bill," Jon said, turning to look again at the virologist.

Jon turned and started walking up the stairs, headed to his office. He and Dale were two trains running on the same track, headed for the mother of all collisions. Part of him didn't want to avoid it. He was a foul, unde—

Breanna.

His stomach rolled and squeezed over the thought of her and Bryson at lunch. Would she confide in him now? Get what she need—

"That you on the steps, Dr. DeLeon?"

Robbie.

There she was at the stair top. A blue suit of modest cut, and high heels—stunning.

Only Breanna for you, Jon, he thought.

He rubbed his eyes. "Sure thing. What can I do?"

"There's somebody here to see you," she said, hurrying on in front of him as he climbed the steps.

Following her to her desk in the open foyer, he saw a young man in a black raincoat, pulling a sheaf of papers out of a brown briefcase he opened on Robbie's desk, holding them out to him.

"Dr. DeLeon?" he asked.

"That's right," he said, looking at Robbie as she looked at the man.

Puzzled, Jon leaned down to inspect them.

Quick Claim

The house was finally going to Alora.

Pulling the pen from his pocket, he closed his eyes, shaking his head.

Well, Breanna's out of the picture, he thought. Maybe he could still play a role in Alora's life.

Suddenly, a vision of him, Alora, and Aaron filled his head. With Aaron's baby.

Coughing, he bent over and signed with energetic fury.

*I'm so jacked up*, he thought as he headed back to his office. *Well, at least I was smart enough to get a decent place for myself.*

He stopped in mid step, turned, walked back to Robbie's desk, the server already heading out the door. "Think I'll get a new phone. I've had it a long time, might as well end three relationships."

"You mean two, right, boss?" Robbie said, the smile not hiding the worry in her face at all.

"See you in two days."

"Back on Wednesday?" Robbie approached his face, and he looked up to see her staring right at him, into him. "Dr. DeLeon, I'm really worried about you."

He pursed his lips. He knew her feelings were genuine. "You see so well, Robbie. Yeah. I'm kind of a mess. I need some rest. You take care." Turning from his friend, whose hand was at her mouth, eyes wet, he walked out the door.

# GERSIETY

Jon sprawled over the sofa in his small den, remembering that his new phone lay unopened on the kitchen table for going on half a day now. Zonked, he spent the last eighteen hours after leaving work moving zombielike through a web of empty electronics. Turned the TV on and off, on and off. Same with the computer. Walked from room to room through the night, sitting five minutes here, forty-five minutes there.

Once picked up the phone to call Alora but never dialed.

Picked up to call Wild Bill twice, and then once to Dale to apologize.

Never dialed those either.

Hadn't slept. Hadn't washed. Hadn't eaten. Nothing helped the gersiety, his own mix of anger and anxiety.

He knew he had no right to his anger. *You're not Breanna's husband,* he thought. Right?

*Whatever she chooses to do is not your business. Isn't that right, Professor? If she wants to flirt with somebody else*

*Younger,*

*Closer to her age,*

*That is not your business. You have no standing, Doctor.*

But he also knew that the Brysons of the world were self-absorbed and fleeting. That young go-getter wanted no part of a woman with a marital history. He'd drop her as soon as he got wind of her troubles.

*But not before he got some of that accountant ass, right, Doc? Running his hands through that gorgeous hair that just had to be so soft? Sniffing it. Inhaling her.*

*The two women that you care about, that you love, are being fucked by two different men, while here you sit watching Green Acres on MTV. How would that look on your CV, Professor?*

Jon suffered, strapped into a torment ride that wouldn't end. The punishment pain was biology beyond his reach, physics that he did not rule. He was incapable of assessing, estimating, measuring, fighting.

No more, he thought. No more.

He jumped up and walked to the hidden shelf under the bed.

Reached to the right in the cranny of the frame for a key.

Pulled out the tray.

Put in the key.

Opened it up.

The revolver.

Clean. Silver. Waiting.

Trusty ammunition right by its side.

He pulled the tray all the way out, then tenderly lifted the gun onto the bed. Spinning the cylinder, he watched it twirl with tight purpose on its well-oiled mechanism.

Sitting on the bed, he held a round in his left hand, looking it over like he was inspecting it for defects.

*Don't worry. Where this bullet will wind up in thirty seconds, defects won't matter.*

He popped the cylinder open with his right hand, sighting down the barrel seeing

A notepad.

There on the bedroom table.

Leave a note? Hmmm.

For who?

Alora? She was gone. Toast.

Breanna?

She was with Bryson. Why would she care? His stomach rolled.

But the others might, right? Robbie? How about Luiz and Dale?

To hell with it.

*And with you, Doctor. Nobody cares.*

Jon chambered the round, then turned the revolver in his right hand until the business end pointed straight at the bridge of his nose. Didn't want to miss. No, sir. He'd heard stories. Should be a clean shot, dead on.

Closing his eyes.

Gonna hurt through the bridge of my nose, he thought.

*Just for a moment. And you deserve to hurt.*

Sweating now, heart wildly pumping in his chest as if it knew that these would be its last beats and it wanted to get as many in as possible.

Feeling the curve of the trigger.

Bracing.

*Just do it, Jon. Do i—*

Text message.

Still holding the gun, he leaned over to pick up his phone off the bed.

The sender was only a four-digit number, unrecognizable.

He looked at the message.

# NO CLUE

Date: March 18, 2016
Subject:

Cassie,

We are coming to another financial hurdle. I think buying CiliCold now is a good idea. Put us out of our misery.

I attached some more research design notes. Thx for taking care of me and my babies. Love to see you.
Breanna

P.S. I hear Luiz and Dale going crazy downstairs. No clue.

# BROKEN FEVER

*Your heart must break for it to get stronger.*

He stared at the old S4, took a breath, stared again.

Maybe he deserved to hurt, had to hurt because of who he was.

But did he have to die?

No.

Not today, anyway.

Jon pushed the revolver away from his face, putting it on the tray.

Sat down at his desk and wrote a few words.

Put the pen down and read.

Not satisfied, he snatched the pen and wrote some more.

Then some more.

An hour later, he was still writing, the gun forgotten. The words poured from him like a torrent. Catching them all was like trying to hold the water of an ocean in his fist. But he kept writing, moving to his home office when his pen went dry. Four hours later, with a new sheaf of paper and a half-eaten cold Wendy's hamburger by his side, he wrote,

> I know how I got into this. How the hell do I get out?

Sometime during the exercise, the fever broke, and he recognized the familiar in him.

# THE ONE THAT MULTIPLIED

Back at CiliCold Wednesday, March 16, Jon threw himself into his work. Whatever he had to face, he owed it to his team to give his best to them, for them.

He knew the call had to come.

He both wanted and drea—

The phone rang.

"Hello," he said, surprised at the strength he heard in his voice.

"This is Breanna, Jon."

His heart hammered. The entire weekend burned up in thought about her, yet no words left his mouth.

"Can you come over and sign some checks?"

"Be right there."

As he walked down the stairs to her office, he remembered how many times he had bounded down these steps before.

Before he knew it, he was at the threshold. He knocked and walked in.

"Hi," she said, sitting down.

Cascading hair falling over a perfect face, white blouse, and black skirt just above the knee.

His head pounded.

"Weekend good, Jon?"

He was driven to both stay and get the hell out of there. "Things caught up to me. I needed to get some rest for a few days." His heart trip-hammered.

"You work so hard. And you do it for all of us."

He took the checks from her hand. "How have you been, Breanna?" he said, signing the checks.

"Pretty well, I need to t—"

"Dr. DeLeon?"

Jon turned to the door.

"Robbie, hi. What's up?"

"They're looking for you in the basement."

"Why didn't they just ca—" He reached for his S4, but his hip was bare.

"Here," Breanna said. He knew she was looking at him. "Take mine."

He called.

"Jon? Better come down here." It was Luiz.

"What's up?"

"Easier if you see for yourself."

"I have to go," he said to Robbie, then turned and headed down the four flights of stairs to the basement.

Had to be Bessie, he thought, as he bounded down the steps, skipping the bottom two, turning to Bessie's cage.

Lying on her side against one of the walls, breaths shallow and rapid.

"Well, she's sick, finally," he said. *So,* he thought, *the virus is a disease producer after all, and his partial antibody idea was worthless.*

*OK,* he thought. *That's it. I'm done.*

"Dale, I think I've hit bot—"

"No," Dale said in the key of flat. "You're looking at Leopold. We move the cages to change the view for them."

"What?" Jon said, wiping his forehead as he walked close to where he thought Bessie's cage was. "This is Leopold?" he asked. "You sure?"

"Well, if you want to do a genital inspection, then that's on you, boss," Dale said, shrugging. "But trust me, who you're looking at is Leopold."

"He must be going a forty a minute." Jon watched Leopold's ears twitch. *He knows the voices,* Jon thought. *So ill. We gave him this disease and he still reacts to us, still trusts us.*

"Sick guy," Luiz said, approaching the cage.

"He'll be OK in a few days," Dale said.

"And Bessie?" Jon said, looking at the other cage to his right. "Sick to death too?"

"No," Dale said, scratching the back of his neck. "Should be like Leopold. See for yourself."

"Bessie's new cage location was six feet away. She was bouncing around, playing with Luiz, who was teasing her with a marshmallow. She saw Jon come close and scampered over, paw out for a treat.

"She's not sick," Jon said. "Bessie's not sick." He turned his back and took a few steps. "She's not sick."

He suddenly reversed course. "Dale, talk to me, man. I fully expected Bessie to get sick. Her viral loads were huge. Why is she healthy?"

"Something else," Dale said, walking to the cage of Leopold, who whimpered louder when Dale approached. "Bessie's not immune either."

"Well, that's what we thought, right?" Jon said, pursing his lips over and over. "That's why you infected her with this picornavirus so we could see the impact of the partial antibodies, right?" And looking at Leopold, he added, "The injection should have made her just as sick as he is."

"Not what I meant, Jon," Dale said, scratching Leopold's head. "I mean she's not immune now."

Jon and Luiz turned to look at Dale. "She's not producing new antibodies to the viral load that she's carrying?"

"No immune response at all?" Luiz said, coming over.

"I'm just telling you that she's not generating any reaction to the virus. No IgA, no IgG, no complement."

All three of them turned and quietly stared at Bessie, who, delighted with the attention, chirped happily away at them.

"So," Jon said, rubbing his eyes. "She was not immune to the virus before, had her B cells juiced to make partial antibodies, generated a load of partial antibody makers, made partial antibodies, then got the virus."

Jon scratched his head with both hands.

"The partials didn't kill the virus, the virus reproduced in her, she mounted no immune response, and the reproducing virus has done her no harm. She's perfectly healthy. Yet Leopold who received the same virus is sick."

They peered through the bars and Bessie again who lifted her head, hooted three times, and scooted toward them, hand out for a treat.

"How is this virus reproducing if it's not tearing up tiss—"

"Dr. DeLeon?"

They all looked up the steps to see Robbie kneeling there, showing only legs and face from upstairs.

"You have a meeting with some fundraisers at three."

He shook his head, raising his hands in frustration. "Swell. I'll be there, Robbie."

"I love that woman," Dale said. He sniffed the air. Looking at Jon, he said "You'd better change. You smell like monkey."

"You smell like monkey all the time, Dale," Luiz said.

"Yeah, but I'm not going see strangers to ask for money."

Jon wiped his nose. "Just hope I don't get sick from this—"

He froze. Dale and Luiz just stared at him.

"We have one rhesus left, right?" Jon asked.

Dale nodded.

"OK. Let's see what Bessie's load does to her."

"We already know. It made Leopold sick," Dale said.

"No. No." Jon pointed at Dale's chest. "Let's inject the virus that actually reproduced in Bessie. Not the one that you gave her. The one that multiplied in her."

Luiz stepped back. "No. Can't be."

Dale whistled. "That will be a first. There are bacteriophages, but a virus that—"

"Only way to be sure is to let Lorraine have it." Jon looked at both of them.

"You bet, boss," Luiz said.

"Should know by Monday," Dale added.

# A LITTLE PUSH

"How many employees?" Sheila, the team leader for SSS acquisitions, said. She was incensed.

"Seven," Jeremy said, another member of her acq team. He snorted.

"Seven? SSS is buying a company with seven employees." Sheila stood up, walking around the room. "And they called us in on a weekend for this?"

Hector Seuter, third longest serving member of the team, screwed up his face and put up two fingers. "Dos hombres? Solamente dos?"

"I know that movie. Redford as the Sundance Kid was great," Jeremy said.

"I liked Butch." That was Asher.

"Well, I like golfing," Hector said, mimicking a long drive with his right hand.

"How are you going to golf, Hector?" Sheila asked, slouching in her chair. "It's just mid-March."

"Hey, it will be in the forties today and windy, but no rain. That spells G-O-L-F to me."

They all laughed. The hell with it, Sheila thought. They had been through a lot the past three years. "You know, it's too bad we don't go—"

Cassie walked in.

At once the room was silent.

Cassie walked to the head of the long conference table that made up the second of three rooms comprising her office suite and sat down.

Sheila watched her remove a legal pad and begin writing, saying nothing for five minutes.

Finally, Jeremy asked, "What are we doing here, Ms. Rhodes?"

Sheila watched Cassie as she kept writing. Without looking up, she said, "Waiting for me."

The room was quiet except for the warm air blowing through the ceiling vents.

Then VP-Legal, head still down, continuing to write, said, "This acq was approved by corporate. We are going forward. Understand that clearly."

"Yes, Ms. Rhodes," they all said.

Sheila never heard her group agree across the board on anything. Now they were speaking in unison, for heaven's sake. Herself too.

Cassie, head still down, said, "If I hear you all making fun of another acquisition in a meeting, I'll sack the fucking lot of you. Understood?"

When everyone answered, Cassie looked up. "This is certainly not our usual modus operandi. We are talking about taking over a small private company for a molecule, or in this case a process."

"What does the process do, exactly?"

Sheila watched Cassie. She'd seen it before. It might appear that VP-Legal was formulating her answer, but Sheila knew that she was just deliberating on whether the questioner really needed to know the answer. "It's a process that some think will cure or prevent the common cold."

Sheila knew, without looking, bodies were shifting in their seats. Hers too.

"Where are they with patents?" Asher asked, clicking a ballpoint pen.

"They have no patent application."

No patents? Sheila wondered. What type of group worked on a process without patenting it? Unless—

"Do we know that this works?"

Cassie looked at her, saying only, "Next question."

"Regulatory findings?" Asher again. At least he was in the spirit of this, Sheila thought.

"In good order," Cassie said, putting her pen down and looking up. "CiliCold has a competent regulator. They are in good standing with the FDA."

"Also with the SBA. They registered as a licensed LLC in Indiana and are on the DSBS." That was Jeremy. Now with the program as well, the team leader noted.

Cassie nodded.

"How good is our information?" Sheila asked.

"Impeccable."

Hector cleared his throat. "Says here the accountant is Solana Sherman. Is that my contact person?"

"No, not anymore. It's Breanna Vaughn, and you'll make no contact with her."

"Well then, how do we get their fin—"

"They will be in your inbox before this meeting is over."

More rustling. Sheila felt her blood pumping behind her right eye. Damn it.

"I will tell you," VP-Legal added, "that they are about out of money. They have no funds to try to hide."

Cassie stood up. "This company is a tidbit, but it's the first of its kind acq for us and I want it digested in a month. That means we tender a formal offer to them next Tuesday."

"That's one business day?"

"But it's three days, including this one. I'm looking for round-the-clock effort. You will have the legal and office support that you need."

"Well, with respect, Ms. Rhodes—"

"Yes, Sheila?"

"How do we know they want to be bought? I mean, they're not public, right? Sounds like the employer over there, whoever that is—"

"DeLeon."

"Doesn't have money either. So it's up to the employees. Have they been putting feelers out?"

"Yes. Ajax, but," Cassie said, picking her pen up from the desk, "they withdrew it before Ajax responded."

"That's my point, Ms. Rhodes. Maybe they don't want to sell."

"They just need a little push. I will take care of that."

"Say we get the molecule, then—"

Asher. Still with the program, Sheila thought.

"What happens to them? Do we absorb them? Payout? Something else?"

"Go do your jobs," Cassie said, picking up her pad and walking out.

# TWO DAYS BEFORE

"Damn it, who's at the door at lunchtime?" Jake Haverson threw his spoon down in disgust, almost tipping the bowl heaped with thick chili on its side and all over his fat belly.

"I'll go see, Dad," Danielle said, jumping up and heading to the back door that opened into the eating area from the backyard. Dad seemed to get upset at everything these days. If this was how people were when they got older, she wanted no part of it.

"Jake, there's no law against people coming by at midday," her mom said. "Calm down before you give yourself a stroke."

"Well, we're having lunch. I swear if it's a salesman, I'll— Don't you open that door, girl."

Ignoring her dad, the seventeen-year-old swung the door open wide, astonished at her own dad-defiance.

"It's Crissee. Hi, Crissee," the teenager gushed.

"From across the street?" her dad asked, leaning to the left.

"How many do you know?" Alice Haverson, struggling to reposition her husband's bowl on the round glass table, said.

"I only know the one with the frizzy hair."

"Jake Haverson. Watch your manners. I swea—"

Danielle opened the door wide. "Come in, Crissee," she said, reveling in this rebellious act against her stupid dad. "Haven't seen you since before Christmas."

"Dani, how are you doing?" Cristen said, smiling. "And when are you going to stop growing?"

"Her name is Danielle," Haverson called out.

Dani didn't breathe as she looked at Crissee. Perfectly made-up, dressed to the nines. She didn't look like she worked for a drug company. She looked like a mayor or something.

"I'm eighteen now. I think no more growing for me. And look at these." She smiled ear to ear.

"Wonderful," Cristen said, walking into the kitchen. "When did you get them?"

"Don't share your business, Danielle," came her usual dad-warning.

"New braces, first of this year," Dani said.

"Can I offer you something to eat, Crissee?" Alice said, ignoring the glare from her husband.

Dani watched as Cristen first looked straight at her dad, then said to her mom, "No, Mrs. Haverson. And I want to just take a moment to thank you. You have always been kind to me."

The room was silent. Dani was amazed. Nobody knew how to stop the talking in her house.

Crissee had just done it.

Cristen turned to her. "I have something outside for you, Dani. You have done such a great job mowing my lawn these last four years."

"We were going to ask you to pay her more this year," Dani heard her dad say.

What a moron, Dani thought, putting the side of a finger between her teeth, rubbing it against her new braces.

"I'm not surprised, Mr. Haverson," Cristen said. "But I have no interest in that discussion with you."

"Do not tell me what I won't talk about in my—"

Everyone stopped to hear Dani squeal just outside the house.

"Crissee! Really?"

Dani waited until Cristen moved aside, then wheeled the 9 × 2 into the house, the shiny wheels tick-tick-ticking.

"It's yours now," Cristen said, "if you want it, Dani."

"Crissee, I have always wanted a bike just like yours. Seriously. But I didn't mean yours actually. I mean . . . you love this, Crissee." Dani held her breath. Gears glistened with new oil, the rims gleaming.

"And I still do. But it's in better hands with you now."

"What do you mean?"

"I'm leaving, and it can't come with me."

"What's wrong with the thing?" her dad called from over his food. "People don't give away good things for nothing."

Dani, her teenage heart pounding, watched Crissee take two steps toward her dad.

"I don't like you, Mr. Haverson," Cristen said, standing across the table. Straight. Tall. Challenging. "You are small-minded, insipid, and selfish. Compassion means nothing to you.

"But I, sir, am not like you. I give away things of value to friends. Dani is mine. You should try it sometime. That is, if you have a friend."

Damn. It was in play now, Dani thought. Look at Crissee. Eyes wide open, naked hate flying out at him, yet such a soft voice. Dani had never seen Crissee so focused, so determined, so angry.

She turned to watch her dad open his mouth, then close it.

"Dani," she heard Crissee say, still staring at her dad, "you can find the instruction and maintenance manuals on the Web. If you don't want to take care of it yourself, just take her to Bluegrass on the other side of 465."

"Sure," she said, stroking the seat. "I'm driving now so I can carry it over. I'll take such good care of it."

"OK, then. That's that."

Crissee turned from her dad and walked to the back door. Dani joined her, feeling like her friend was studying her, memorizing her. "It's been good to know you, Dani. Thanks for all your help these years."

"I'll watch over your baby."

The two friends hugged then held hands, Dani's eyes shut tight. She managed to keep them shut when Crissee forced a folded piece of paper into Dani's right hand.

"Take care of her, and she'll bring you home," Crissee said, letting go. Then turning to leave the kitchen and her baby behind, she walked into the bright sun.

"Don't stay out here too long, Dani," her mom said, turning to leave the garage for the house. "You know how Father is."

"I'll be in in five, I promise," Dani said.

As soon as her mom turned to leave, Dani hustled to, and then past, her new bike, wedged up between the wood wall and the green 2008 Camry.

It was already after seven, and the sun had sunk below the high window, calling it quits for the day. After checking that Mom had indeed gone back to the house, and that Dad hadn't entered to "check on her,"

Dani, on her haunches, her back resting against the cold wooden wall planks, opened the note.

A full sheet of white paper with only two lines typed at the top, followed by a short paragraph that contained a URL.

Dani, holding her breath, read the top part:

> A month after you read about me, send the email below.
> You are the best. Your friend, Crissee.

Dani looked at the email, confused. It had a URL, short but unrecognizable. And what did it mean, "after you read about me"? But she knew that whatever it meant, she was not likely see her good friend for a long time.

Suddenly sad, Dani carefully folded the special message, placing it in her jeans' fifth pocket, being sure no part of it showed to raise suspicions. Her heart started pounding, off on a new mission.

In twenty minutes, she had entered the note word for word in her calendar. Not the one her father checked, but her real one. The one between her mattress and box spring, far from long, prying hands.

And for the first time in her life, Dani began reading the newspaper, every day.

# DISTRACTIONS

Jon pulled into the parking lot on Monday, and suddenly braked. Robbie was outside, waving frantically at him against a background of thick gray clouds.

"What are you—"

"Luiz and Dale are looking for you," she said. "They've been calling me every five minutes, wondering where you are."

"Why didn't—" He pulled his cell phone out. "Oh," he said, the "no ring" icon staring back at him from the screen.

"My bad," he said, wrapping his fingers around her arm, soft in the wool sweater. "Little cold out here, isn't it?" He steered her back inside, following close behind.

A minute later, he bounded down the steps and was in the basement. "Heard you were looking for me. What's up?"

Dale and Luiz had their backs to Jon, murmuring as they looked at the three cages that were all on the same table behind them. Jon walked to them and, leaning over their shoulders, peered into each of the cages.

The three rhesus monkeys were scampering around their cages, teasing each other, drinking water, looking for food.

"Which is Lorraine?"

"The healthy infected one on the far left," Dale said.

Jon turned to face Dale. "Healthy? Titers were—"

"High," Dale finished. "Like with Bessie."

"Which cage?"

Dale pointed to the cage to his left, still huddled with Luiz.

"You said 'infected,' right?" Jon said, looking between the bars at the female rhesus, who was now on her back, playing with a toy. She turned her head, looked Jon in the eye, and reached out her hand with the toy toward him.

In a flash, Jon was dizzy. His face was burning up, and the room spun as he staggered back to the table.

"Hey," Dale said, supporting him with an arm while steering him to a chair. "Have a seat."

"This is real?" Jon asked, looking into the faces of both of them. His heart was pounding, and he could barely speak. "What this means is—"

He jumped up and ran halfway up the steps.

"Dios mio," Luis exclaimed.

"Robbie. Robbie! Please close the basement door, Jesus."

"Oh my God."

The three men spoke at once, six arms flailing, controlled by three minds filled with one thought.

# FINISH THE GAME

"It can't be," Dale said, when Jon staggered back down.

"What other explanation is there?"

Jon settled into the chair around the table, struggling to take deep breaths. Luiz sat across from him, Dale on the floor.

"How is this possible?" Luiz asked. "I've never heard of in vivo transformation."

"There aren't any," Dale, said, flipping his laptop open.

"Before we do anything," Jon said, "we need to understand exactly what we think just happened." He pulled on his left ear, then got up and walked to the table. "OK. We know that this picorna—what was the number?"

Dale, getting up and walking over to the table, said, "154."

"Picorna-154 generates the common cold. Leopold showed us that."

"He had no viral load and no symptoms, then received the virus," Dale said, nodding to Luiz. "Thirty-six hours later, Leopold's viral titers went through the roof and he was sick as a dog for another forty-eight."

"Sick as a rhesus, but we forgive you," Luiz said. "Your limited metaphors are a hazard of this work."

"Thanks, South of the Border."

Jon looked over Luiz's right shoulder into the cage of Leopold, who, having heard his name, had his face pressed against the bars, hand out, looking for a meal.

"That's Leopold for you," Dale said. "Sick or not, leading with his stomach."

"OK, OK," Jon said. "So Leopold got the common cold, or at least the rhesus version of it. Next, we treated Bessie with this partial antibody compound, gave her the same virus, and she—" Jon paused. *Did somebody call my name?* he wondered. *What is hap—*

"She developed a viral load, but never got sick like Leopold."

"Right," Jon said. "Right, right, right. So the partial antibody didn't combine with ECF product to make the specific antibody to inactivate the virus, like we thought."

"Like you thought," Dale said.

Jon ignored him. "But the virus didn't make her sick."

"And when we pulled some of that same virus from Bessie and gave it to Lorraine here, the virus reproduced but again, no symptoms. Did Leopold generate his own antibodies?"

"Yes. Like a good monkey should."

"And Lorraine?"

"Like Bes—"

Jon looked up with Dale and Luiz as new light streamed through the opening door at the top of the basement steps.

"Dr. DeLeon."

Robbie.

To Jon, she sounded like she was in tears.

"Robbie? What's happened?"

Still crying, she held some bunched papers down to him.

"What are these?" Jon asked, walking up the steps to her.

He motioned, and Dale and Luiz came up as well.

"Eviction notice," Dale said, peering at one. "I'm used to these."

"Not quite eviction," Luiz said. "But it might as well be."

"They're kicking us out?" Jon asked. Sweat came from nowhere, covering his forehead. "We've been here for four years."

"And never missed a rent payment," Dale added.

"Not eviction," Luiz said, studying the papers. "They are terminating our lease though. That's in their right to do."

"How much notice?" Jon said, tapping his foot.

"End of the month, according to this," Luiz said.

"Which is in t—"

"Three weeks," Dale deadpanned.

"I'll talk with her," John said, "but if the landlord thought this through enough to send the papers, then—"

"We're bread," Luiz finished.

"Toast. God in heaven. Toast, Luiz."

"And she may have a new renter."

"Pretty interesting sense of timing," Dale said, looking at Luiz.

"OK, OK," Jon said. "Let's get back to work."

"That's not all," Robbie said.

"What now?"

"Bills for—" Jon studied the papers she thrust at him. "My goodness. The water bill's tripled. So's the electricity."

"What the—"

"Is our use up?"

"Let me see those," Dale said.

Jon gave the bunch of papers to Dale, who put his horn-rims on to study them.

"Nope," he said, looking over his glasses at them. "Actually water is the same, electricity is up a couple of KHz, s'all."

"Look at the rates, though," Luiz said, pointing to another part of the bill.

"There's a note here. It says that we haven't used water efficiently."

"How do they know?"

"This is an apartment building, right? What's the average water use in other apartment buildings?"

Silence.

"I'm guessing ours is different," Dale said. "They know we're doing more than living here."

"The universe is trying to tell us something."

"I wonder," Jon said. "Maybe not the universe."

"What do we do now, boss?"

Jon looked at both of them. "We finish the game. Let's get back to it." Jon turned back to descend the basement steps.

"Dr. DeLeon," Robbie said, "There's something else."

# GUESS WHAT, DR. DELEON?

"Can we go to your office?" Robbie asked.

"Sure," Jon responded. He turned to Dale and Luiz. "We have some great questions now. You guys are the best ones to get the answers. Be down soon."

"OK," Dale said.

Jon's head was trying and failing to wrap itself around the conversation in the basement with his two scientists. They were all equally puzzled. He feared the research result was the product of yet one more technical mistake, another in a long string of—

Where was Robbie?

That's her perfume, he thought, but she was quiet. Suddenly, he missed her voice. Always so sincere. Maybe right, maybe wrong. But so honest.

He turned around to se—

There she was, behind him, taking those long strides, head down, lost in thought, hair hanging from her forehead to just above her eyes. For moment, he thought he would never see her again. He ached to memorize how she looked in this most ordinary moment.

She's probably concerned about her job. Jon's stomach rolled. But there was only the truth to tell. And truth was, maybe she was right.

But if this new, oversized billing mess was a play for CiliCold, then ther—

They were at his office.

"C'mon in, Robbie," he said, closing the door behind her.

She walked in front of him, but rather than walk to the desk, just turned to face him.

"Guess what, Dr. DeLeon?"

She was holding her hand up to him.

Left hand.

Ring finger.

# GRADUATION DAY

In a flash, time slowed down for Jon.

Even the parts of him that assessed things so quickly, that moved so fast, that sized up situations and dispensed advice dispassionately in rapid-fire cadence, were shocked into silence.

Then he thought, *Alora all over again.*

A writhing sea of hot emotions rose up. *God,* he thought, *that Aaron really gets around.*

No.

He stopped.

This was different.

Robbie had worked so hard to get ahead. And many times, she failed.

*But just look at her now. She's radiant,* he thought.

In her short, thirty-two-year life, so blessed with beauty but filled to the brim with one disappointment after another, the universe had finally alighted on her. She looked fulfilled.

And she would need him no longer.

And with that, it fell on him that she was never his to refresh and restore, to sustain and succor so that he too might heal.

No.

She was part of his life for him to prepare her.

Nothing more.

And now that job was done.

"Robbie," he said, "the look in your eye shouted something spectacular had happened. Come on over here. Tell me everything."

"Dr. DeLeon, I'm so overcome. So full," she said, still standing, hands down and clasping each other. "His name is Dominick. Well, I call him Dom. He's five years older than me and also divorced. He has one child. He proposed three days ago. So that will make three," she finished, cocking her head, looking at him.

Funny thing to miscount about, he thought. "You mean two, right?"

"That's the best news, Dr. DeLeon. I'm pregnant."

His vision blurred. Stay with this, Jon said to himself. Feel her joy.

"Between Shannon, his little Rog, and my new little girl, we will have three."

He smiled. "You tell me now, do you know it's a girl, or are you just wishing yourself into it?"

She smiled back. "Both, b—"

"Tell me all that you can." They walked to the two chairs in front of his desk, each taking a seat.

"Well, Dom is in the oil business," she began, turning to look at him. He comes up here just as a—well, I guess you'd say a stopping or halfway point between Texas and Canada. We met here 'cause a friend of mine had a party and we both went. Anyway, Dr. DeLeon, I . . . I . . ."

He helped her.

"Texas or Canada, Robbie?"

She sighed. "Santa Fe."

Jon smiled and raised his hands from his lap. "But Santa Fe's in New Me—"

"Not this one, Dr. DeLeon. It's in Texas. Not far from Galveston."

He leaned back in the chair, closed his eyes, and laughed. "Well, one thing's for sure, Robbie. No more cold winters for you," he said, turning to her, smiling as he waved a finger her way.

"He has a house that he lives in with his son. Me and Shannon and"—she pointed to her stomach—"will be joining him."

He took a deep breath, then asked, in a whisper, "When, dear?"

She put two fingers up, eyes instantly full of tears.

"Two weeks."

Don't let what's good for her be bad for you, he thought.

"Hey, Robbie, look at me."

She wiped her eyes, which were full of the pain of the innocently sincere, who only want acceptance from life but instead receive punishment.

"Robbie, I am so proud of you."

"What?"

He smiled and gently touched her arm. "Look at you. You're full of the light of the world. And why not? Sweetheart, I don't know everything that you have been through, but I know that it's been rough sledding. You wanted to finish community college but couldn't. Married, but an unplanned baby. And the divorce. You seemed to succeed with all the little things, but despite your effort, you couldn't pull the big things off, Robbie."

She sat still, looking at him. He knew her heart was open, as it always had been to him. He opened up, letting the salve that heals all pour into her.

"You carry an essential truth in your heart."

He reached a hand over the chair to take hers.

"There is no other like you. Relish that feeling."

She wiped her eyes. "I finally got lucky, huh?"

"Fortune favors the prepared, dear. You were ready, and good for you because this demented world hates the blessed."

They let go.

He watched her fidget. "It's going to be a while before I get back up here," she added.

Jon nodded. "Whenever I miss you, I will think of your spirit and relish the feelings that— What on earth is that noise?

Robbie reached into her jacket pocket and, after a little rooting around, pulled out an iPhone.

"Oh," Jon said, placing both hands over his heart. "Your leaving I can live with, but you with a cell? I can't stand it."

They laughed.

"Gotta have it now," she said with a wink. She looked down to read the text.

"Of course."

"Well, Dr. DeLeon," she said, looking up. "I have work, and I know the scientists are waiting to get their hands on you. I just wanted you to know." She pulled out a tissue, dabbing her eyes.

All cleaned up. Ready to go. Job done.

"Good that you did," he said.

"OK."

They stood and embraced. He was going to ask her to write, but he knew that writing wasn't her way. She'd be too busy to call. He would likely never hear from her again. His stomach clenched, and he held her close.

"Robbie, sweet Robbie. Never stop being who you are. You'll win and lose lots of battles, but stay anchored to yourself." He kissed her ear, saying, "You are anointed."

She whispered back, "I know, because you tell me it's so. You always have."

They separated, then walked out of his office, each their own way.

Graduation day, he thought. But whose?

His left arm felt fine.

# BREAKTHROUGH

Jon got back downstairs just in time to hear Dale's conclusion. "So PV-154's been altered," he said, tap, tap, tapping his bald head. "The partial antibodies changed the virus so it infected Bessie but didn't make her sick, and when given to Lorraine, her viruses again produced no illness. That's that."

Jon grappled with this concept. His heart pounded with the implications. "We took an infectious virus and, what, defanged it?"

"Yeah. This one time," Dale said. "I'm not sure what this really means."

"Wait, wait, wait, wait . . . wait," Luiz said. "Bessie had no symptoms, but her viral load went up, right? The only way viral particles reproduce is if they infect a cell, right? And they make more viral particles, which infect more cells, and on and on. Too many cells die, the subject gets symptoms. So how did the viral load go way up without symptoms?"

Jon slapped the table. "You did that, Luis."

"Me? How?"

"A subclinical infection—that's the only way," Dale said.

"No, sir," Jon said. "Luiz's ECF ribosomes."

Dale looked at Luiz, and Luiz at Jon.

"So the virus used these ribosomes to reproduce?" Dale said.

"And it picked up a new protein coat from the ECF as well," added Luiz.

"RNA viruses do it with intracellular ribosomes."

"No way," Dale said. "Ribosomes by themselves in the ECF? That won't cut it. What about tRNA?"

"Well, they must be in the extracellular fluid as well."

"Damn, we're good." Dale and Luiz looked at each other.

"But why would the virus do that?"

They all looked at each other, then said at once, "The partial antibodies."

"We made her cells produce a partial antibody that didn't attach and kill the virus. It stimulated a viral conversion," Jon said.

"With no new RNA?"

"Why can't there be RNA fragments in the surrounding fluid? The antibody opens the door, the RNA squiggles through to the virus's own RNA—"

"And changes the virus."

"So Bessie's OK because the virus did not infect her cells," Luiz said. "It reproduced, apparently harmlessly, in the extracellular fluid."

"And the macrophages can scoop them up with any other ECF debris."

"Or the virus destroys itself. And maybe other viruses like it."

"Whoa," Luiz said, stepping back. "That's moving your queen way too early, ese."

"Yeah well, before we start stroking each other," Dale no-toned, rolling his lab coat sleeve higher up his arm, "we need to reproduce this."

"With the same virus," Luis added.

Dale nodded. "And with different ones too. Maybe an adeno or two. DNA viruses."

"Suppose this is the real deal?" Jon rubbed his nose. "What does it mean?"

"Eh, everybody."

Jon turned to see Wild Bill coming down the steps.

As Luiz brought him up to speed with the results, Jon saw that Bill was slowly turning in a circle as he absorbed the results of the experiments.

"Testing Lorraine was a masterstroke," WB said, turning a chair around to Wild Bill it. "It differentiated the sickness-producing effect of PNV-154 on Leopold from the harmless effect of the transformed virus on Lorraine." After a moment, he asked, "Think you can do it again?"

"We need more of everything for that to happen," Luiz said.

"Got that right. This experiment cost us about fifty K. Needs to be repeated"—Dale thought—"five times."

"Five?"

"Why five?"

Dale shrugged, "Once with this picorna, and then twice with each of two other viruses."

"That's another 250 K."

"That we don't have."

"OK, OK," Jon said. "Say we get it and we reproduce this. What does it mean?"

"Means we have converted an infectious, common cold-causing agent into a harmless bug," Bill offered, pushing his glasses up his nose. "But," he added, "we have to see what the safety implications are."

"Yeah," Dale said, turning to Wild Bill. "What if we learn this new virus eats your sperm?"

"Well, if it's your sperm, Dale, I'd say that's a blessing for humanity," Luiz offered.

They all broke up, Jon laughing until his sides hurt.

"Yeah. Well, not everybody will be so sanguine about side effects. The agency's going to want full safety assessments."

"Gonna need some help."

Jon felt the enormity of the work before them.

"We can't do all this," he said.

"Well, I heard someone is interested in buying us." Wild Bill said, sitting back down, stretching his legs way out on either side of the chair.

"Maybe we don't want to—" Jon started.

"Who?" asked Dale.

"SSS."

"What?" Dale said, twisting in his seat to face Jon and Wild Bill. "Why would they be interested? We're nobody to them. Where did you get this?"

"I know where." The voice came from halfway up the steps.

A familiar one. Jon couldn't beli—

"Rayiko?"

His heart raced as she carefully descended the steps. In a moment, she was down in the basement with them.

"Rayiko."

He took her in his arms, and they embraced.

He had missed her so. His heart trip-hammered. It had been too long, just too long without her here. When they stepped away from each other, his hands were shaking.

"Rayiko. My God. It's so good to see you here."

She met his eyes. "I'm sorry that I couldn't get back sooner." Then, holding him closer, up on her tiptoes, she whispered, "Your heart must first break to get stronger."

He looked at her, his whole body surging with new understanding, new power.

Life.

Then she stepped back.

"But wouldn't you like the answer to your question, Jon?"

Jon licked his lips. "Ah . . . yes. Right. Did you speak to SSS about us, Rayiko? How could you know? Why would—"

She shook her head. "Not me, Jon."

She pointed.

Jon's eyes followed her hand up to the top of the steps. "Who is—"

A brief form, short, with gray and black hair.

Squinting as his pupils dilated, he marveled at how he could see stars that were just up the basement steps.

Then, passing out, he saw nothing.

# TWO SECONDS

"You mean we now have to meet with two safety slobs?" Cassie heard Giles angrily ask the two Triple S executives. "We just spent three hours meeting with the damn Tanner transition team."

"The new departments were supposed to be aligned by now. This is all logistical, not legal. You don't need to pay us to be here for this," Cassie said. This was supposed to be the fire sale day for CiliCold. Everything was in place. She and her team were ready to overture the CiliCold people today.

Now, she had to deal with this Tanner flotsam. Grimacing, Cassie dug at something in the rug with her shoe.

"Does the CiliCold group know you're coming?" Giles asked her.

"One of them does," she replied. "The rest are clueless." *Why does he even care?* she wondered.

"How sure are you?"

Cassie said nothing.

Phone chirped.

She opened her purse, letting it dangle on her arm from the straps as she pulled the cell out.

"Hello," she said.

"Cassie?"

"Who is this, please?"

"The Sister."

Cassie froze. Not only did Doucette know her nickname, she was using it.

She bit her lower lip, then holding her forehead with her free hand, mouthed the word "Meredith" to Jasper, whom she saw was blathering to the support team about his last case. He kept up his yammering.

Cassie dropped her hand and, standing straighter, said, "Yes, Ms. Doucette?"

"Are you talking with Mr. Harto now?" the CEO said.

"I don't really know. Let me check." She put the phone to her chest and asked, "Is there someone here named Harto?"

"Yes. That would be me. David Harto, personnel director."

Cassie turned from him to her phone, ignoring his shit-eating grin. "Yes, he's here."

"He comes from me. Please do as he asks."

Why was the CEO so interested, she wondered. "I understand."

"Cassie? You're neither a safety expert nor a scientist. You're an attorney. Do me a favor and listen at the meeting. Be my eyes and ears. Don't react. Just observe and absorb."

Cassie pulled the phone from her ear and looked at it. Shaking her head, she disconnected the call, then turned to Jasper. "We have to take this meeting."

Jasper turned and faced the wall, looking like he suddenly going to throw a stubby fist through the thin plaster.

"Well, let's get to the damn thing," he said. He turned to the right, and Cassie watched him limp off down the hall.

She walked up to Harto, feeling his eyes wander all over her as she passed by. He didn't appreciate the $2,100 dark-gray skirt and white blouse, she thought.

Only what they covered.

Animals.

"Well, who are these people we are going to see?" she asked, struggling to keep from throwing the Harto pig against the wall.

"We're going to meet with a Dr. Wells, head of Tanner safety, and her assistant, Ms. Sandbridge," Harto said. "They've been resisting the new changes going into place."

Cassie watched the sweat pop out on his head in mini fear bursts. "We've already been all over this. Huge safety departments are a thing of the past. Our other acquisitions made the conversions. There should be no issue here."

"They don't make us safer and are a drain on revenue," Giles said. Cassie watched him try to balance his huge frame on both feet, favoring the left. "I don't know why some people can't get that through their hallowed heads."

Cassie pointed down the corridor. "Well, damn it, get going, Harto," she said. "Let's lay down the law."

Cristen waited with Dana in the small conference room. She watched the two attorneys enter, followed by—Cristen wasn't sure. One was Harto. The other was . . .

Fager.

Jeremy Fager, vice president of Tanner-in-transition or something like that.

A hammer pounded in Cristen's head as Fager made the introductions.

"Glad we could all find the time to meet on such short notice," he said.

"This is kind of cramped," Harto added, squeezing his fat frame into the small space allotted him around the crowded table struggling to seat six people.

"Well, folks," Dana said. "Welcome to safety." She coughed.

Cristen was dead silent, watching Giles pointedly ignore the greeting, instead staring at her and her friend.

The headache was gone.

Eyes narrowed.

"I think," Harto started, clearing his throat, "we are all confused a—"

"The hell with all that," Giles said. Then in a voice that Cristen thought was barely above an icy whisper. "Maybe one of you two," he continued, waving his hand dismissively at her and Dana, "can tell me why the safety department refuses to accept the necessary resource reallocations for the absorption of Tanner into the Triple S family. Our company—" He paused for a moment. "No. Your new company hates to waste money.

"Frankly, I'm embarrassed that we even had to come here to meet with you people," he finished, shaking his head.

Cristen leaned forward.

"Well, Mr. Giles," she said, voice low, emotionless, "maybe you didn't have to come down here at all." Eyes narrowed, she fought the urge to stand. "Maybe you should just head back to wherever they find people like you, so we can get on with our business, which is to try to protect our consumers."

Cassie inhaled, swearing that the room heard her. Who was this person to talk to Giles like this? Sandbridge should be down on her knees, begging for her job.

Cassie ignored the part of her that told her to push back from the table, to find a neutral position. After all, she and Jasper were the power here. Safety was going to contract. That was that. This was just a wasteful courtesy trip.

But these science twerps thought they knew something about the real world, here in this basement.

Well, OK then.

"You mean keep your department fat, lazy, and wasteful," Cassie injected. "Maybe you haven't been keeping up with current events, Sandbridge, but your department's toast. We don't need most of what you do."

So she has a voice after all, Cristen thought. Let's see if she has the belly for the rest.

"You know nothing of what we do, lady," Cristen said, dismissing her comment with a wave of her right hand. "We're here to monitor safety, not be bullied by a pair of corporate Neanderthals who think patient safety stops with their own families."

Cristen was pleased that dead silence ruled the conference room as Cassie and Giles exchanged rock-hard stares with Cristen just across the table. Even Fager sat frozen at the jagged tone of the start of the conversation. He probably wanted us to just put our necks in the guillotine, praising the corporate deities, Cristen surmised, fighting the temptation to spit.

Looking left, she saw that Dana was keeping her head down. Already beaten, Cristen thought. And wrung out. She tried to will her friend to bear down, to finish up strong, but—

"I . . . I think what Ms. Sandbridge here is trying to say—"

That was Harto, she thought, desperately trying to row the rough conversation out of hazardous waters.

"They don't need a translator," Cristen said, holding her hand up, palm toward the SSS personnel director as she continued to return the hard stare of the two lawyers, the rage swelling in her.

"The drastic changes you are recommending to our department," Dana said, "will gut our workforce. We're barely able to keep up now with the daily monitoring and tracking."

"You just have to make your department more efficient," Harto chimed in. To Cristen, he seemed pleased that there was one person besides him at the meeting who would play by the rules. "Surely you've been through cutbacks in the past with Tanner."

"Those were temporary," Dana answered. "And they never crippled safety."

"Might have saved Tanner's corporate life if you had made these money-saving changes years ago," Cassie said, her face not three feet from hers.

Chin jutting out defiantly, Cristen leaned forward, opening her mouth.

She felt Dana's left hand over her right.

Cristen closed her eyes and took a breath, digesting her own bile.

For Dana, she thought, she'd let that one go.

"OK," Dana said. "But don't forget that you are marketing more aggressively. More drug use, more adverse events, yet you've cut our staff by two thirds."

"Which should be no problem at all for you folks," Giles said, waving his hands at Cristen and Dana. "The drugs were all approved by the FDA as safe and effective." Cristen saw that he had fixed his gaze on Dana, like a hawk eyes a sick dove.

"Monitoring their use after the drug's been approved should be"—he shrugged—"custodial."

"That's what we do on the Triple S side of the company," Cassie said, raising both hands from the table, "and if you'd stop crying about your personnel for a moment, you'd see that we put effective safety operations in place."

"SSS safety monitoring is an industry joke," Cristen interjected.

"And yet, Ms. Sandbridge," Cassie said, leaning back in her chair, "it manages to get the job done remarkably well."

"Maybe that's how it looks from the executive floors," Cristen said, leaning over the table, "where efficiency is a sickening synonym for cutting the heart out of an important operation just to save money. But I assure you, Ms. Rhodes, the patient who suffers needlessly because of broken SSS safety monitoring has a different tak—"

"Mr. Giles," Dana interrupted, "I don't think you understand."

*Goodness, Dana,* Cristen thought, *they're here for our scalps.* This was not an argument. It was a hanging. She looked to her right at her friend, who was doing her best to make a fight of it.

Cristen sighed. If this is how Dana wanted to end her career, then so be it.

"Just because a drug is deemed marketable by the FDA," Dana continued, "doesn't mean that we understand all the drug's effects."

"You mean to tell me that the FDA's not doing its job?" Giles asked with sinister silkiness. "That's quite an accusation from a home-grown safety expert."

"Well, no, I mean yes . . . I mean . . ." Dana paused to get a grip on herself, wavering a little in her chair.

"Are you sick, Dana?" Fager asked.

"I'm sick of this argument," Giles added.

Cristen, looking at Giles, leaned over to put an arm on Dana. Dana looked up and smiled, trying to wink.

"Maybe she should be drug tested," Cassie added, waving a hand at Dana.

Cristen ground her teeth, tapped her left foot hard on the cheap linoleum floor.

You have seven, she reminded herself. More than enough to do the job.

She steadied herself.

Dana coughed and sat up straight. "I am fine. What were you saying?"

Enough, Cristen thought. No need for Dana to see the rest.

"Jerry, can we excuse Dana from the rest of this meeting?"

"I think she should stay," Giles said

"Nobody asked you, 'Dr. Giles,'" Cristen said, focused on her friend. "You good to get back by yourself, Dana?"

"I'll head back to my office," Dana said.

"I see," Giles continued, as Cristen watched her friend struggle to stand, then turn and leave the small room. "You would have us monitor the public's use of a drug that has already been deemed safe. Apparently the FDA's approval is not enough for you, Sandbridge."

"We're trying to save lives," Cristen said, "and in the meantime, save your company and your precious jobs."

"You've just lost yours," Cassie retorted, index finger pointed at Cristen's nose.

"Get your hand out of my face, you ignorant skank," Cristen said, smacking it back.

Dead still. Cristen's actions and words stopped the air in the room. Nothing moved.

Turning to Giles, Cassie said, "I think we can cut this staff—"

"You are what is wrong with this system," Cristen said. "You use your knowledge—"

"Yes," Giles said, sighing and looking around the room. "I know, I know. We use it for greed."

"I'm not talking to you. I'm talking to your bitch here." Cristen turned to Cassie. "The one who is so smart, but not smart enough to avoid being used."

Cristen leaned closer to Cassie, whom she saw had her mouth stuck on 'open.' "Whatever stomped on you has you so twisted up inside that you can't see where you should go. You're like a football player who has had his bell rung and is running the wrong way on the field. You don't know direction. You don't feel gravity. You have no sense of up and down."

Cassie yelled, "I know all I need to know about you."

"You don't know this."

Everyone stared as Cristen shoved her chair back and stood, pulling her father's .45-caliber Colt 1911 from her purse with her right hand. The chair tumbled and scraped across the floor behind her.

Ignoring Giles, she pointed it straight at Cassie.

"Your misery ends today," she said, chambering a round.

Cristen quickly pulled the gun back toward herself, while leaning her body from the hips up over the table, her face as far across the tabletop and as close to Cassie as possible.

Chin down.

Cristen positioned her right arm close to her own body, jamming the gun barrel forward and through the bottom of her own chin.

Two seconds.

Just like she rehearsed.

Pulled the trigger.

Cristen's last thought, a fraction of a second before her shattered brain exploded through its obliterated skull, was that it would just be a moment before she was with Dad again.

Suddenly, the room was full of noise. Cristen's exploded head flew across the small table, slamming into Cassie. The lawyer felt her own skin tear open across her forehead. Savage pain ripped first through her left cheek, and then, just a moment later, under her mouth.

Cassie tried to turn her face away, but the flying mush that had just a moment before been Cristen's brains landed across her, like clay that couldn't keep together, the larger chunks of her brain hit Cassie's chin, breaking into pieces as they fell against the neck and chest of VP-Legal. The smaller ones landed higher, forcing their way into her eyes, nose, and mouth, tasting like bloody, salty grits.

Cassie's last thought before she passed out was to wonder who was doing all the screaming. As she lost consciousness, she realized that it was her.

# BIOGRAPHY

Lem Moyé, MD, PhD, is a retired physician, epidemiologist, and biostatistician. After receiving his MD at the Indiana University Medical School, he completed postdoctoral training at Purdue University and the University of Texas. Dr. Moyé has conducted federally sponsored research for over thirty years, including twelve years investigating cell therapy for heart disease. He has published over 220 manuscripts, eleven books including two novels, and has worked with both the US FDA and pharmaceutical companies. Dr. Moyé has taught graduate classes in epidemiology and biostatistics for three decades and has served as an expert witness in both state and federal court. He served as a volunteer physician during the Hurricane Katrina calamity, and his memories of that experience led to his prize-winning book, *Caring for Katrina's Survivors.*

Coming in 2022:

# *Catching Cold: Rivers of Redemption*

Losing it all is winning

9781698705477